Destiny

By Bonnie Hopkins

Brothers, I do not consider myself yet to have taken hold of it. But one thing I do: Forgetting what is behind, and straining toward what is ahead,

I press on toward the goal to win the prize for which God has called me heavenward in Christ Jesus.

Philippians 3:13-14 NIV

DESTINY

ISBN - 13: 978-1477542408
Copyright © 2012 by Bonnie Hopkins

www.bonniehopkins.com

Printed in U.S.A.

Copyright © 2012 Bonnie Hopkins

ISBN-10:147754240X
ISBN-13: 978-1477542408

THIS BOOK IS DEDICATED TO THE MEMORY OF

(JOHN) TAYLOR WILSON
Beloved Grandpa, Great Grandpa, Great, Great Grandpa

Still Remembered

Still Quoted

Still Missed (Cigar and All)

ACKNOWLEDGMENTS

All glory, honor and praise to the Awesome and Mighty God who began and continues to perform this work in and through me. Thank You, Father God!

Family, what would I do without your love, patience and multi-faceted support? Thank you all from the bottom of my heart.

To that special group – you know who you are – who consistently pray, promote and push me through. You are wonderful, and I am grateful.

To Joy and Company Review, for 'getting' the message of my books, and appreciating it in such a wonderful and memorable way. I am eternally grateful to have received the 2011 Christian Literary Award in creative writing for my novel, *'Seasons'*.

To Monica Harris – Your editorial help and expertise are invaluable and so greatly appreciated.

To the prayer intercessors of the Prayers Heard In Heaven (PHIH) Organization, who constantly support and lift me up to our Heavenly Father, thank you.

Thanks to Pastor Will and Lady Shawn Lindsey, and members of Above and Beyond Fellowship for the love and prayers.

I am gigantically appreciative to every church, women's ministry, book club, bookstore, organization, specialty shop, and other groups who graciously welcomed me into your midst.

Readers, readers, readers! So many of you have waited for *'Destiny'*, the follow-up to *'Seasons'*. I am enormously thankful for your patience, continued support, and love. I fervently pray that as you read this story of new beginnings, you will be encouraged and inspired to walk into your own destiny with Jesus. Keep on reading!

Blessings
Bonnie

bonniehopkins.com

P.S. – I love to hear from you. Please drop a line to bonniehopkins08@yahoo.com. A special appreciation to those of you who fuss, poke and prod me for the next book. (Yes, it helps.)

NOTE TO READERS

Finally! The much anticipated sequel to *'Seasons'*, and the second story in the Riverwood series.

In *'Seasons'*, I introduced the Winslow cousins, Jaci, Anita, C.J., and Gina. Their promise to stay in touch with each other fell short after they left Riverwood, Arkansas to go their separate ways. Their lives took traumatic turns into deep troubles and tribulations, where they had to call upon all the spiritual, mental and emotional strength they could muster just to survive.

After twenty years, they are coming out of the trouble to discover and embark on new and exciting lives. God is restoring hopes and dreams they thought long dead, and most importantly, they are finally reconnecting with each other.

Jaci struggled through many difficult seasons before finding her blessings; Now, in *'Destiny'*, you will walk with Anita after she survives a violent marriage and discovers new destinies.

C.J. and Gina also have compelling stories that many will be able to relate to.

The cousins grew up in the small, fictional community of Riverwood, Arkansas. I have therefore dubbed this *The Riverwood Series*. I hope you will journey with these cousins and share their heartwarming stories of deliverance, renewed hopes, new beginnings, and blessings, which faith in God, and their Riverwood experiences prepared them to reach.

Although each story stands alone, you will gain a deeper insight and appreciation for each of the cousins as you read their stories, and are encouraged and inspired to never give up. Enjoy!

CHAPTER ONE

Ron Gilmore brought his silver XJ Jaguar to a stop in the driveway of his parents' fashionable home in the Third Ward area of Houston. As he unfolded over six feet of muscular manhood from behind the wheel of the luxury car, he noticed several women watching him from across the street. He smiled and gave a brief wave of hello as he sauntered toward the door, fully aware of the affect his beige skin, chiseled good looks, and wavy black hair sprinkled with gray around the sides, had on women. After ringing the doorbell, he idly acknowledged the beautiful, unseasonably warm spring day, thinking it was a good day for a round of golf, or better yet, a walk in the park with a special woman.

The door opened and he walked into the house, sniffing appreciably. He headed into the kitchen to hug his mother, noticed she was just pulling a large pan of perfectly browned rolls out of the oven, and rubbed his hands together in anticipation.

A little while later, the family was settled around the table. Ron sliced into the tender, juicy roast beef, speared a piece, dipped his fork into the fluffy mashed potatoes and picked up a dollop of gravy, then pushed the fork full of food into his mouth. His taste buds would have clapped if they could have. It was so good. He broke off a piece of warm roll, buttered it, and tossed it into his mouth. Nothing could match his mother's homemade rolls. He took a drink from his glass of iced tea to wash the food down, and said, "This is so good, Mom." He repeated the process with the goal of finishing his meal before conversation at the table worked its way around to him. Whenever he showed up for Sunday dinner with his family, his parents never failed to carp on him about helping with the family business and his womanizing lifestyle.

The only question in his mind was which one would take the first shot at him today. It didn't take long for the answer to materialize. It was his mother.

"Ronald, are you even trying to find a good woman to settle down with, like your brother is doing? And are you ever going to start helping out with the real estate business?"

He shoved another fork full of food into his mouth and took his time chewing it before answering. "Nope."

She shook her head in disgust. "I know you think you can keep running around with all these wild women without any bad repercussions, but you mark my word, it is going to catch up with you. One of these days you're going to want a wife, and no good woman is going to want an old broken down playboy," she bemoaned. "I just wish I knew where we went wrong with you and your sister. You, wasting your life running after women, and Monique going over there to that God forsaken country and won't even answer my e-mails."

Ron pushed back his irritation, and picked up another fork full of food, determined not to be drawn into the same old tired argument. He often refused to show up for the Sunday meals and subject himself to their criticism, but knew he had to be there frequently enough to avoid adding to their disgruntlement with him.

His dad was busy stuffing his face, but added a regular "Uh, huh" to his wife's comments. Ron knew it was only a matter of time before he would get to a place in the meal to chime in with his own remarks.

Ron couldn't help but wish his parents would say something good about him for a change. Hadn't they noticed he was attending church more often now? Or that his business was flourishing and he was receiving all kinds of awards and recognition for his work as an architect? Couldn't they give him a little credit for that? Yes, he loved woman and enjoyed a variety of them, but what was wrong with that?

He decided he wanted to be gone before his dad could get on his case, and was hurriedly stuffing food into his mouth when the peal of the doorbell caused them all to jump in surprise.

"Now, who could that be?" his mother, Cecelia Gilmore, said, as she headed to the door.

A few minutes later, raised voices from the foyer caused a sinking sensation in the pit of Ron's stomach when he recognized a familiar voice. *Chantal!* His fork clattered to his plate as he muttered, "Darn it, I don't need all this doggone aggravation!" He stood and reluctantly followed everyone as they ran to see what the commotion was about. *What the heck is she doing here?*

A satisfied smirk covered Chantal's face when she saw him, and she stated in a loud voice, "You actually thought you could dump me and I'd just go quietly away, huh? Well, that's not going to happen, and it's not going to make our baby go away either." A look of glee slide over her face when her words brought gasps from the group gathered in the spacious foyer. "So I decided to invite myself to Sunday dinner and give your family the good news. I'm pregnant, y'all, and Ron is the proud daddy," she announced spitefully.

"Ronald Gilmore!" Cecelia exclaimed in a shocked voice.

Ron walked over to the woman and said, "Chantal, this is totally uncalled for. Get out of here or go to jail."

"You can deny it, run from me, and threaten me, but you can't change the facts." The smirk on her face widened. "I'm having your baby, sucker, and you gon' pay me some big bucks." She started through the door to leave, then turned and said in a triumphant voice, "I know how you love to boast about being in control of your own destiny and all, so guess what?" She smiled, spitefully. "You don' lost control of your destiny, Mr. famous architect, because this," she patted her middle, "this is your destiny now. Cha-ching, cha-ching! Now what you got to say about that? Bye, grandma and grandpa. See y'all soon."

When the door closed, all eyes turned to him with accusing stares. "Ronald!" His mother huffed again. "Didn't I just finish telling you something bad was going to happen? That woman's going to drag you through all kinds of trouble trying to get her hands on your bank account, and that successful business you're so proud of is about to go down the drain because reputable people don't want to deal with a person tangled up in all of this kind of mess. Well, don't look to us to help you. We're washing our hands of you."

"We sure are!" Big Pat, Ron's dad, said with a look of disgust. "You are way past old enough to know how to live without all this kind of foolishness."

Ron walked out of the open door without looking back, got into his car, and drove off. The food he had been enjoying so much was now sitting like a stone in the pit of his stomach.

A few days after Chantal's big announcement, Ron finally showed up at his brother Jason's house and was talking to him and his fiancée, Jaci, about the baby situation.

"Ron," Jaci said, "please tell me you are not running around having unprotected sex. I know you're not that irresponsible. Pregnancy is not the worse that could happen."

"It's beyond irresponsible, Ron, and you should know that for a lot of reasons," Jason added. "You know what people are capable of - or you should. Your days of acting like a carefree college stud are over. You are a well known architect. Just last month you were featured in that Architect Magazine – pictures and all. Do you know how many people there are in the world whose main ambition is to get close enough to you to grab some of your bank account? Grow up, man."

Their words were hitting hard simply because they were true. Ron grabbed his head in anguish as he struggled to come to grips with the fact that some things he enjoyed had to go, or his successful life could be lost. "What's wrong with living my life like I want to?" He asked.

Jason gave him an irritated look. "Just ask yourself some questions, Ron. Is it wise? Is it safe? Is it worth it? And speaking of safety, like Jaci said, an unwanted pregnancy could be the least of your worries. There's AIDS and other STDs to think about, and you heard that woman. Her plan is to get as deep as she can into your bank account and to make your life a living hell. You'll never be free of her if she has your child, because she'll be holding that child over your head for the rest of your life. It's just too dangerous to mess around out there now."

"Okay, okay! I don't need to be hearing this right now." Ron had always been confident that nothing could happen to him that he couldn't handle. But lately, his life seemed to be careening out of control. Chantal and her possible pregnancy was just the latest thing.

He always used protection – always! The possibility that it had failed shook him to the core. In addition to her obvious lie that she was on birth control, it also proved that Chantal must have somehow sabotaged his protection. But how had she done it? When had she done it? Had he been so caught up in things that he hadn't been paying enough attention? There was no doubt in his mind that *if* she was pregnant, she had planned it. She had been too smug about it.

"Ron, this is another indication that it's time for a lifestyle change," Jaci chimed back in. "Can't you see that it's causing way too many complications? By the way, how's the situation with Jett?" she asked, trying not to laugh.

Jason didn't try to hold his. He laughed loudly, even as Ron was giving him dirty looks.

"Why are you bringing that up?" He was still upset with Jason for even telling Jaci about it. The mere mention of Jett caused him to shudder as he recalled the traumatic encounter.

A few months ago, while hanging out at a local club, he'd unwittingly picked up a female impersonator who called himself Jett. It still blew Ron's mind that he hadn't been able to tell that what he thought was a beautiful woman, was really a man. What a shock it had been when he took the 'lady' home with him and they got to the crucial moment. The resulting fight had proven just how determined the dude had been. Ron had nursed bruised knuckles for days.

Then, to add insult to injury, Jett started stalking him. He'd be on a date and the guy would suddenly be standing over him, or he'd be leaving his office and Jett would jump out of hiding, full of pleas that Ron give him a chance to prove he could do anything a woman could do. A couple of weeks after the fight, Jett had shown up at his condo, yelling loudly for Ron to open the door, and when he did, Jett pounced, trying to hug him. "I need money for my operation, and when I get that operation you won't be able to tell I was ever a man. Your money will be well spent. We can have a good life together, honey."

Ron's stomach turned sickeningly at the thought that he had actually been attracted to a man. "You'd better get your crazy behind away from me, dude. I'm not giving you any money for an operation," Ron told him, angrily.

Jett's pleas quickly turned to threats. "If you don't give me the money I need, I'm going to the press and tell them about our relationship and how you used me and then tried to dump me. And trust me, when I finish, there won't be a person in this city who won't believe me."

That was the last straw. The guy had embarrassed him, ruined dates, and tried to corrupt his manhood. And now he had the audacity to show up on his doorstep trying to extort money from him? Not hardly! "You don't know who you're messing with. And don't delude yourself, we ain't had no relationship. You're nothing but a lying, deceitful creep, and you're the one who's about to go down." Ron punched Jett in the face and beat him down again, before he threw him off his property.

After thinking of several things he could do that wouldn't exactly be lawful, Ron decided to try the lawful way first. On the advice of his attorney, Ron had a protection order placed against Jett. The attorney said he would handle things from that point.

The following week, an article came out in the community newspapers, advising men to beware of the antics of a certain female impersonator who was prowling the city looking for male victims to blackmail and extort money from. The same week, Jett was arrested on several counts after more men came forward and filed charges against him.

Ron hadn't seen or heard from Jett since then, but learned from his attorney that Jett had jumped bail and left town. He only hoped that was the end of him.

Now, sitting around the table with Jason and Jaci, his memory of the incident with Jett only added to Ron's internal conflicts. How could he have been attracted to a man? Yes, one dressed up to look like a woman, but still a man! That troubled him on several levels.

Jason finally got his laughter under control and said, "It's just hard to believe you got fooled like that. When are you going to get it? It's treacherous out there, Ron."

Ron couldn't deny the joy and peace he saw in Jason since he and Jaci had gotten together. He owned numerous pieces of property around the city, and lived in a fabulous condominium, but lately he was happiest when he was with Jason and Jaci, basking in the warmth of their love for each other. It had gotten so bad, Jason was threatening to make him pay half of the grocery bill, because in addition to his mother, Ron loved Jaci's cooking, and ate with them as frequently as he could.

Was it possible he could want what Jason had with Jaci? He had admitted to his brother that he wished he'd met Jaci first. However, it was quickly pointed out that he wouldn't have had the sense to appreciate her.

But he saw what a jewel she was, how happy she made his brother, and the big question in Ron's mind was…where in the world would he find a woman like Jaci?

Inexplicably, he felt the urge to attend church more often - even Wednesday night Bible study and monthly Man Power meetings. Although it chilled him to hear the explicit warnings that there is a place in hell for all who rejected Jesus, it also made Ron want to know more about God's unconditional love, and do more for Him. Even now, he was designing the church's new educational facility at no charge.

However, giving up his love for women was a whole 'nother' thing. "I love my lifestyle and I'm not giving it up for nothing and nobody. God knows my heart. I go to church just about every Sunday."

Jason shook his head, sadly. "You're trying to straddle the fence, Ron. Just going to church is not enough. In fact, a lukewarm life makes God sick."

"Aw, man, please! What does God care about me having women? It's not like I'm married. I'm not doing anything wrong as long as the women are ready and willing."

Jason gave him a pointed look. "Look at all the problems it's causing, that should tell you something."

"Chantal is all about squeezing me for money, pure and simple. I've already informed her that if that baby happens to be mine – which I doubt - I'll pay child support just to keep her and the law off my back, but that's it. I'm not taking responsibility for a child that I did everything I knew to do to prevent. And I don't feel the least bit guilty about that."

"But what about the child, Ron? It's not his or her fault," Jaci said, softly.

"It's not mine either. I told Chantal how I felt when we started dating, and she agreed, said she was on birth control. Well, she and her baby can get lost, because they ain't forcing me to accept something I don't want."

"But that might change, and you could regret it one of these days, Ron," Jaci pressed.

He waved her words aside and said, "I don't plan to have any future regrets about how I choose to live my life. I have fun meeting women and finding out how many times we're going to dance around the flagpole before we end up in bed together. I don't plan to give it up. I just have to tweak things and learn to be more discreet and careful."

"Leave him alone, Sweetheart," Jason told her with a sigh. "We just have to pray and let God deal with him. But remember this, brother, God is in control, not you."

Aggravation, and the inner battle in his spirit caused him to harshly say, "I'm sick and tired of everybody trying to tell me how to live." Again, he chose to walk out, but unfortunately couldn't escape the conflicts battling within him.

CHAPTER TWO

Two hundred and fifty miles north of Houston in a Dallas suburb, Anita Stanhope was dealing with her husband's sudden death. As the shock lessened, a mantra she couldn't block was tracking through her mind - Relief, freedom! Relief, freedom!

It's wrong to think ill of the dead, she thought, as she sorted through her husband's belongings. Her silent self reproach became a prayer. "Help me, Father. Give me the right thoughts I should have about Frank." But relief was all she was able to muster up.

Nita heard her cousin, C.J., calling her to take a break. She threw the shirts she had just pulled from the closet into a box and walked slowly down the stairs of her large two-story home, but her mind, cluttered with conflicting thoughts and emotions, continued its rambling journey.

"You know," she said to C.J., "even after making the arrangements and going through the funeral service, I keep expecting Frank to walk through the door. Every time the telephone rings, I think it's him. It's still hard to believe he's gone."

"That's normal, honey," C.J. answered. "The way it happened - so sudden and all - it's going to take a while for it all to sink in. Afterall, it's only been a couple of weeks." She led the way into the kitchen where delicious aromas filled the room.

"Yeah, I guess so," Nita answered absently. She sat down at the table, where she stared unseeingly across the room. "Want to hear something funny?" She asked softly. "When Frank didn't come home that night, I just assumed he was with one of his women, which he was. Then, when that cop showed up the next day to tell me Frank was dead, I actually had the crazy thought that Frank was playing a joke on me. He was capable of doing something like that just to throw me off and make me happy to see him eventually walk through the door. And even when I realized the cop was for real, it was still hard to believe, because in my

12

mind, Frank was bigger than human destruction…you know…immortal."

C.J. shook her head in disgust. "He really had your head messed up, didn't he? And Lord, he must have been even more of a rotten human being than I imagined if he was capable of doing something cruel like that. I will never regret that day we came up here and showed him he was merely human. Wow, that felt good! And should have felt extremely good to you."

A hint of a smile showed on Nita's face as she remembered the day her family had taken revenge against Frank for beating and abusing her for years and nearly killing her. "It should have, but when you're in a situation where abuse is constant, it's hard to rejoice in anything. But you know, I truly believe y'all may have saved my life that day. Y'all scared him so bad, he was afraid to touch me again, although he still made my life a living hell with his verbal and emotional abuse. He walked around here for days, ranting and raving about what he was going to do, but everytime one of y'all called, he would almost run. I know he was just a hateful bully – but what bothers me is why I took it for so long." Tears slid down her face. "But one thing I do know is that I'm never…ever… going to be a victim again. Not for anybody!"

Several days after that conversation with C.J., Nita sat at the desk in the study that had once been Frank's domain, her notepad in front of her. She looked over a long 'to do' list, crossed off the last task she had completed and added a few more. Frank had been gone nearly a month and she was still dealing with conflicting emotions. She laid her pen down and began to pray. "Lord, I'm truly grateful that You have delivered me, but is it wrong to rejoice over another person's death?"

Confusion swirled in her mind, and she picked up the phone to call the Counselor she had been talking to since the funeral. The Counselor ran through the same list she had been stressing to her. Release the conflict and confusion to God. Receive His comfort, love and peace. Stay focused on the present, and move on with life. Be thankful.

After hanging up, Nita focused on all she had to be thankful for. A few days after the funeral, she and her three sons had met with Frank's attorney, Tyson McPhearson, who explained the contents of her husband's estate. She discovered Frank had been a good businessman, and had left she and her sons well provided for. Her boys – all college age - had educational annuities, and she had control over a very extensive estate.

Frank, had been a successful dentist, and in addition to his lucrative dental practice, he had been a skilled investor with interests in real estate and any other businesses in which he could make money. There were several bank and investment accounts with large balances, and of course insurance policies that were set-up to pay off all existing debts, including her home and cars. She would be okay financially - the only thing she could thank Frank for - other than her children. But that didn't erase the years of torment she had suffered under his abuse.

She was thankful the school term was almost over and her sons were able to get through the stressful situation without worrying about missing classes.

From the time she had received the news that Frank had been found dead in a hotel room with a hysterical woman with him, her cousins were there to help her through it all – including putting Frank's pushy family in check. She was thankful for her cousins, C.J., Jaci, and Gina.

I will never be a victim again! The litany was making it's journey through her mind again, bringing the conflicting emotions – joy, relief - and guilt - over the other two.

But she was free! Free from living in constant fear that Frank would revert back to the physical assaults he had carried out against her for most of their marriage, and the fear that eventually, he would kill her. Free from living with the relentless stress brought on by knowing that whatever she did, Frank would be displeased and find a way to make her suffer.

Nita walked back to the desk and looked at her list again. At the very top was her cousin, Jaci's wedding in a couple of weeks. This would be the first time in over twenty years that she would go somewhere and not have to worry about Frank's wrath, either before or afterwards.

Now, she could look forward to attending the wedding, and to tackling the next big thing on her list - moving out of this house where bad memories lingered. With her sons all in college, it was simply too big for one person, although her sons didn't agree, and objected – vehemently.

"We would understand if you had to sell it," her oldest son, Frank, Jr., stated angrily. "But this house is paid for, and you don't have to worry about money. We won't have anywhere to call home anymore. If daddy were still alive, we wouldn't even be talking about this," he said, angrily.

Seeing her hurt, Joel, the most sensitive of the three, said, "Mom, I'm sorry. You're right, you should do whatever makes you happy." He tossed an angry look at his brothers. "Get over it," he commanded.

During the same conversation, when she heard similar objections about her plans to return to college, Nita realized something. It was time to take charge of her own life. "Wait a minute, boys. You are misunderstanding something here. I'm not asking, I'm telling you what my plans are. For years, I gave up everything for you kids and your father. Now, I'm going to do some things I want to do for myself. I love you, but that's the way it's going to be. Now if you want to keep this house for yourselves, you can have it, but I won't be here."

"No!" They'd all said. "Mom, you know it wouldn't be the same without you here!" Her youngest son, Mikey said. "If you could wait until things kind of settle down. Please, Mom."

"Baby, I'm sorry. If I'm going to do this, I have to do it now." Their expressions were anything but happy, but that was just too bad.

Now, she snapped back to the present, looked down her list, and noted that travel was highlighted. She had always wanted to travel, but Frank hadn't liked traveling – at least not with her. And of course, if he didn't like it, it was out of the question for her. But now that she had the opportunity to do it, she would – if for no other reason than to find out if this was maybe some pipe dream she'd held on to, just to keep her hope alive.

She had become introverted because she had been forced to hide so much of her life for fear of revealing too much and incurring the wrath of her husband. The bruises he had inflicted not only covered her body, they also scared her emotions. It was time to change that.and start interacting with people again.

The telephone rang, and she noticed it was Dr. Carlton, Frank's partner at the dental practice. She ignored the call. She needed to put everyone associated with Frank behind her.

Before she left for the wedding in Houston, Nita put the house on the market with a sense of relief. Jaci had talked her into being a bridesmaid, along with cousins, C.J. and Gina, and Jaci's friend, Lena. She'd agreed – against her better judgment.

She arrived a few days early so she could be fitted for her dress. Just as she had feared, she looked like an oversized pumpkin in the bridesmaid dress. But it was too late to back out.

She had fun running around with her cousins taking care of last minute errands and talking and laughing about old times in Riverwood. That in itself was therapeutic.

Jaci shared her doubts and fears about her decision to marry Jason Gilmore, the goodlooking Christian man who had worn her down with kindness and persistence. "I keep having these meltdowns about whether I'm doing the right thing," she confessed. "Afterall, I've been single all these years, I've raised my daughter and I'm even a grandmother." She looked around the table in her small breakfast nook. "I've prayed, alone and with Jason, and I can't shake this fear of the unknown. What do y'all think?"

It was quiet around the table while they all thought about Jaci's question. Finally, C.J. said, "Well, with my own marriage in shambles, I'm not the one to be giving any marital advice to anyone, but it's normal to have these concerns, don't let fear rob you of your future."

"But what if I'm making a mistake?" Jaci pushed. "Maxie is back in the picture and he wants us to get back together so he can get to know his daughter and grandchildren."

The others laughed. "That's nobody but the devil," Gina said. "Have you forgotten? Maxie is the man who abandoned you and his child. The man you didn't see hide nor hair of until he heard you were getting married. The man who didn't buy his child a piece of bread or a stitch to go on her back. Girlllll," Gina waved her hands in dismissal, "that should have you kicking Maxie in his behind and running down that aisle to Jason." They all laughed again.

"Jace," Nita said, quietly. "I do understand what you're feeling. Y'all know the kind of marriage God just delivered me from. But, I don't believe I would marry Frank now. I didn't have a clue when I did of who I was. I was young, ignorant and let myself be bullied by Frank into doing what he wanted. By the time I realized I didn't even like him, I was married and expecting my first child.

"After all you've struggled through to become the woman of God that you are, you know that even if there was no Jason in the picture, Maxie couldn't do anything but get out of your face. You're a different person from the young girl he took advantage of. You're strong, mature and know the kind of man you want. Now, if that's Jason, and I think you know it is, then close the door on Maxie and the past and move into your new season."

Jaci jumped up and hugged her. "That's so well said that I can't argue with it, Nita."

Nita smiled. "I have my moments. In fact, I paid dearly for them. The Frank chapter is now closed, and I'm standing at a crossroad wondering which way to go, but I'm going to move on. If I do take the wrong path, I know I'm strong enough to change my direction. I don't have to stay on the wrong road."

"Wow! Listen to our cousin, y'all," C.J. said, with a wide grin. "I think we can all learn from her."

"Yeah, I'm certainly with you, Nita," Gina said. "I'm standing at a crossroad too. But I know I'm going to make it."

"I guess that settles it then," Jaci chuckled. "I've chosen my path. Right or wrong, I'm going to follow it and trust God to go with me."

The wedding was beautiful, and Nita cried from joy she was so happy for her cousin. At the reception, when all single women were asked to gather for Jaci to toss her bouquet, Nita, C.J. and Gina reluctantly joined the large group of women, but took a place in the rear, trying to hide. But Jaci spotted them, and made sure she aimed in their direction. Rather than jumping and pushing to catch it, as most of the other women were doing, the three of them ran to dodge it.

Understandably, they were all disenchanted with married life. C.J. and her husband - a professional basketball player - were in the midst of a divorce; Gina was embroiled in a fight with her step-children over her deceased husband's estate; and of course, Nita's abusive husband had recently died while in bed with another woman. As far as they were concerned, that bouquet could hit the floor where they would gladly stomp on it.

In amusement, Nita noticed the same thing happening with the men. When Jason prepared to toss the garter out to the bachelors, it was obvious he was aiming it in his brother's direction. But Ron Gilmore folded his arms, as did many of the other men, and deliberately stepped out of the path, causing it to land on the head of a short guy standing behind him. The man quickly grabbed it and threw it to the floor. Nita laughed her head off.

Later, when the wedding party gathered at Jason and Jaci's house, Nita happened to overhear Ron Gilmore jokingly tell his friends that they were welcome to that fat woman, since the only thing she could do for him was point the way to a shapely one. Nita wanted to hide in a dark corner as embarrassment flooded her. It was apparent he was talking about her, since she was the fattest person in the wedding party. She vowed right then to do something about her weight as soon as she could. Ron Gilmore's comment would be her motivation.

After she returned to Dallas, life became a whirlwind of activity. The house sold quicker than she had expected. She went house hunting, hired packers and movers, and sent most of the furniture to storage.

She moved into a lovely, spacious three-bedroom condo. All of this, as she went through the ordeal of getting her sons packed up and settled in their schools. Frank, Jr. had decided to transfer from S.M.U. in Dallas, to Morehouse College in Atlanta. A week before the last summer term was to start, she rented a van, and together with her other sons, Joel and Mikey, drove to Atlanta to get Frankie settled into his apartment. Mikey was next. She spent the week after their return from Atlanta, shipping his belongings to Howard University in D.C., where he would be entering his freshman year. She and Mikey then flew to D.C. where they went through the grueling process of getting him enrolled in his classes and settled into his dorm room. Thankfully, Joel, her middle son, had decided to remain at S.M.U. in campus housing because unlike his brothers, he refused to get too far from his mother.

While in D.C., Nita visited her brother's family, who lived in P.G. County, Maryland. As dog tired as she was, she pitched in to help them plan a sizeable dinner party at their spacious home. She wondered what they would have done without her until it dawned on her that they would have been fine, and were just taking advantage of her free labor. She was there nearly two weeks, and was glad to board the plane back to Dallas, after checking on Mikey one last time.

She fell into bed and slept for days, ignoring the items on her famous list and her constantly ringing telephone. Her first thought when she surfaced was that Frank had been gone two months, and she still didn't feel free of him.

When she checked her messages, she couldn't help but wonder . . . why was Frank's attorney and dental partner calling her so persistently? And why was it that each time she noticed they had called, she experienced a terrible nightmare in which Frank was trying to kill her?

After resting up, she decided to visit her family in Riverwood, Arkansas. The visit stirred many memories – both good and bad from her childhood. As a child, Nita had spent many nights listening to her parents' violent arguments and praying fervently that one wouldn't kill the other. Things only worsened after her mother died. Her older siblings left and her father basically ignored her and continued his lifestyle of running after women.

But the worse thing to happen was when her father's sister, Muriel, moved in, supposedly to care for ten year old Nita. Aunt Muriel took great pleasure in generously applying the rod. She didn't like untidiness, idleness, or happiness, which to Aunt Muriel, meant Nita didn't have enough to do. Nita quickly learned what to do to avoid as many beatings as possible, and with her Grandmother's help, became proficient in cooking and cleaning. Aunt Muriel's meanness made her life miserable until her grandparents, and her cousins stepped in.

While in Riverwood, Nita experienced a significant breakthrough. She finally realized who had taught her to tolerate being a victim. Aunt Muriel.

CHAPTER THREE

A few months had passed since Chantal's big announcement. Ron refused to let that situation stop him from his usual lifestyle but was treading more carefully now. His inner conflicts continued. Although he tried to convince himself that his lifestyle was okay, everything else seemed to indicate something different, including Pastor Robinson's sermon on last Sunday, entitled "Are you making God sick?" The Pastor spoke from Revelation 3:13-22, and noted that having one foot in the world and one foot in the Kingdom equated to being lukewarm, and as such, made God sick. He gave several examples of what it meant to be neither hot nor cold, and issued a warning that he who have ears should pay attention to what the Lord was saying in that passage. He ended by asking again, "Are you making God sick?"

It reminded Ron of what Jason had said about being lukewarm. Had his brother and the Pastor been talking? It wasn't a comforting thought that his lifestyle was making God sick.

But Ron ignored the warnings that people and circumstances kept bringing to him, determined to continue enjoying his life. His current woman of interest, Shayla, had just been on the phone trying to convince him to go on a cruise as soon as they could coordinate their schedules. He had put her off. Thoughts of possibly making God sick were too fresh in his mind. Plus, he was concerned that Shayla was getting a little too possessive.

It was Thursday night, and after working late, he had come home hungry. His rumbling stomach forced thoughts of dinner to the forefront of his mind. He could go by Jason and Jaci's, or try to round up one or two of his buddies to go out to dinner. He hated eating out alone. The ringing phone interrupted his thoughts about dinner. From the caller I.D. he saw it was a guy he often worked with in ministries at the church.

After agreeing to work several Sundays, he hung up, and went back to dinner contemplations. "I guess I'll just shoot by and see what Jaci cooked," he said to himself. He found his keys and was on the way out the door when the phone rung again. He started to let it ring when he didn't recognize the number, but shrugged, and grabbed it.

That call erased all thoughts of dinner. It left him trembling in fear, pushed him off that fence he'd been straddling, and changed life as he knew it.

Back from Riverwood, and with life settling down a bit, Nita found a health spa to her liking, and submitted to a grueling routine. She was steamed, starved, and exercised to the point of collapse. She pushed herself, determined to get over sixty excess pounds off of her 5'5 frame.

Her husband had demanded large, fat-saturated meals that had resulted in all of them being overweight. Her boys, who were active in sports, worked their fat into muscle, but she and Frank had kept packing on the pounds. Frank, being a tall man, had carried the weight well, but on Nita, the excess pounds made her look like the proverbial butterball. Under Frank's abusive tyranny, she hadn't been able to maintain the will power to shed and keep the weight off. But now, filled with the motivation to redefine herself, Nita was willing to do whatever it took.

At the end of her six weeks program, she was twenty-five pounds lighter. Continuing her rigorous routine, she existed on little more than carrots, celery sticks, juicing and water, while maintaining her heavy exercise regimen. As the weight fell off, she discarded several sizes of clothes – everything that supported or encouraged the return to her old lifestyle – and weight - had to go. She systematically began rebuilding her wardrobe with the type of clothes she liked – classic, feminine pieces that flattered her now well toned body. She liked how she looked, but Frank was probably rolling over in his grave. He had insisted she wear unbecoming, dark, drab clothes that although very expensive, didn't do a thing for her.

As her weight decreased, Nita started her next phase, which included weekly trips to the salon where she received facials, manicures, pedicures, and massages, while experimenting with different hair styles. Frank never let her cut her hair, but after much deliberation, Nita decided to take the plunge and had it cut into a short, tapered style that complimented her change in appearance. She also enrolled in self-defense and confidence building classes. All a part of her defense against being a victim again. Then came the day! She was down to her desired weight, and looking and feeling great about herself.

Life finally edged its way in. Up to now she had ignored the calls from Frank's dental partner, and his attorney, who had been calling, claiming it was vital to see her. She'd heard that widows were often seen as easy prey, so to protect herself and provide peace of mind, one of the first things she had done was obtain the services of another attorney, as well as an accounting firm, who were now handling legal and financial matters for her. However, Frank's dental partner, Morris Carlton, and attorney Tyson McPhearson, insisted on a meeting with her, and the time had come to deal with them – if for no reason than to tell them to leave her alone.

When Nita was shown into Tyson McPhearson's office, he looked up, took in the woman standing there, and said, "I'm sorry, madam, but I'm afraid you've somehow gotten into the wrong off…" His words trailed off and a surprised expression entered his face.

"Anita?" He stood up, while his jaw fell lower. "Forgive me for staring but you look so different I didn't recognize you. Please, have a seat."

"What's this about, Mr. McPhearson?" Nita didn't really know the man. He had been Frank's attorney and friend, who had supported, and probably shared his unsavory habits. Based on that, she had formed a strong dislike for him over the years.

"Please call me Tyson. No need to stand on formalities."

"Okay. What did you need to talk to me about, Tyson?"

Tyson was almost speechless and could hardly keep his eyes off of her. She was transformed – a beautiful, classy looking woman. "Well, uh . . . I'm afraid the other parties haven't arrived yet. Since they are principles in this meeting, we need to wait for them."

Nita frowned. "Well, I know my attorney and accountant have been in touch with you and Dr. Carlton. And since I specifically requested in writing that all business matters be referred to them, I really don't understand why you both have been so insistent about meeting with me. Perhaps I should have asked my attorney to accompany me. At any rate, please know that I will leave if any legal matters are brought up that should best be handled by my attorney."

"I understand," Tyson replied. Frank had never spoken well of his wife – but perhaps Frank had merely been blowing smoke to hide a jewel. "But Anita, I hope you know that I would never do or permit anything damaging to you. And by the way, I am more than a little put out that you arbitrarily chose to go with another firm without first talking to me. I know more about Frank's affairs than anyone, and believe I'm the best person to advise and oversee them for you." He flashed a smile at her.

Nita didn't smile back, but silently prayed, h*elp Lord!* He was good-looking – with thick, salt and pepper hair, butter smooth brown skin, tall, well built and charismatic . . . *just like Frank,* she thought . . . *and accustomed to getting what he wanted.* "Mr. . . . uh, Tyson, I just felt it was best for me to deal with people I am more comfortable with. After all, you were Frank's friend and attorney, not mine. If this meeting is about trying to get me to change my mind, then forget it. I'm not going to do that. I hope you have everything in order because I will not hesitate to take appropriate actions against questionable issues." She spoke in a firm voice, and this time, she flashed him her newly acquired confident smile.

How could Frank have been so wrong about this woman? Tyson thought. "Well, I realize how difficult it must be adjusting to Frank's sudden death. I wish you had let me help you get through that before making any changes," *and taking all that money away from me,* he thought.

"Actually, I'm doing okay. I . . . " Before she could say anything else, the door to his office opened and Frank's dental partner walked in.

Dr. Morris Carlton had the same reaction to Anita's changed appearance as Tyson McPhearson. "Anita?" He stared at her a long moment. "I have to say, you look wonderful."

Nita smiled. "Thanks."

"You doing alright? I've tried to call and check up on you, but have had no success."

"Yes, Dr. Carlton, I'm doing fine. How about yourself? You and Frank worked together for a long time. I know you must miss him."

"Yes, I do miss him. I'm working with your attorney to buy his half of the partnership, and I expect that to be settled soon. I know you're curious as to why I asked Tyson to arrange this meeting, so I'll get straight to the point." He twisted his considerable bulk around in the chair. "Have you had an opportunity to look over the list of real estate holdings Frank owned?"

"Yes," her suspicion radar went up. "as a matter of fact, I have. But my attorney and accountants are handling those matters for me. Why?"

"Well, you own quite a bit of property that's worth a large sum of money. Do you realize that?"

"Of course I know that," she stated, with acid in her voice. "What is this about?" Her accounting firm was still collecting data and assessing the value of her properties. So far, she only had a ballpark figure, but there was no way she would admit that to him.

Tyson spoke up. "Anita, I want to make it clear that although I'm no longer the attorney of record for Frank's personal estate, I am the attorney of record for the dental practice, and the real estate holdings – mostly commercial - listed as part of Frank's dental practice and co-owned by Dr. Carlton. That is why he asked me to host this meeting."

Anita grew more suspicious. "Okay, gentlemen, let's cut to the chase. Why have you badgered me into this meeting?"

Morris shifted uncomfortably in his chair. "Well . . . Anita, there's a demand or I should say, a request on one of Frank's properties that needs your personal consideration."

"What kind of demand?" Nita asked, curiously.

"There's a woman who . . . uh . . . Frank had dealings with, and she's demanding rights to one of the properties. I know it might seem a bit insensitive of me, but I'm just trying to do what I think Frank would have me to do. She told me that Frank gave her the house she's lived in several years. That house happens to be a part of Frank's personal properties. According to Tyson, if Frank gave it to her, he didn't make it legal. So, she . . . uh . . . asked me to intervene on her behalf. She wants to talk to you about it. She's waiting in the outer office."

Nita scowled. "You mean, one of Frank's women is here, waiting to talk to me?" At his nod, she shook her head. "I don't think so!

I doubt we have anything to say to each other." She looked him directly in the eye, causing him to squirm. "And you're right, Morris, you are being insensitive. I'm the widow here. How dare you come to me with such a callous request?"

His face burned in embarrassment at her bluntness. "Anita, I apologize, but I'm merely trying to tie up loose ends so I can get on with my life. I wish you would reconsider. I promised her that I would arrange for you two to talk. I would appreciate it very much."

"You shouldn't have promised that, Morris." She looked at Tyson. "Is it correct that the property in question is part of my estate?"

"Uh . . . yes, that's correct," Tyson answered.

"Well, that settles it. I don't have any obligation, need, or desire to talk to this woman."

"I know you don't, Anita," Morris said, in a pleading tone. "But this woman is bugging me to death, so just hear her out, if for nothing more than out of respect for Frank's memory."

Nita gave him a disgusted look. "Let me remind you that in that regard, I don't owe any respect to Frank's memory, Morris, so let's not even go there." He squirmed around in his chair again, looking anywhere but at her. "And just what is your interest in this?"

He saw where her mind was going, threw a quick look to Tyson, who looked like he was trying not to laugh, and said, "Believe me, Frank left many unresolved issues that I'm having to deal with. I just need to get back to running my business." His squirming was now accompanied by huge drops of sweat.

Nita was just angry enough to push the issue. "You know what, I'm curious. Call her in here and let's hear what she has to say."

While Tyson hid a smile, suspecting that Anita was about to take a chunk out of the woman's behind, Morris Carlton was realizing that this wouldn't be as easy as he had imagined. He left the office and returned a moment later with a tall, nice looking, woman.

The woman gasped when she saw Nita. "You . . . You're not . . . her . . ."

Nita immediately recognized her. Not surprisingly – since the woman had called and come to her home often enough - looking for Frank as well as the opportunity to flaunt herself in front of Nita and her children.

"Well, well," Nita said, making no effort to hide her dislike for the woman. "It's Ms. Dorothy Gibson. What's this about Ms. Gibson? Didn't you do enough damage when my husband was alive?"

Dorothy kept looking at Nita as though she couldn't believe what she was seeing. She had expected the dowdy, overweight, timid woman she had been able to intimidate for years. Not this woman who was oozing confidence and looking ten years younger than herself.

"Well," Dorothy began slowly. "I've been living in my house for years – with Frank, of course, whenever he felt like it." She shot Nita a smug look. "And uh . . . Frank promised it would always be my home, that he would fix it so I would own it. I don't know what's going on, but Attorney McPhearson and Dr. Carlton are telling me there's a problem. So that's the reason I wanted to meet with you. It's not like you didn't know me and Frank had a relationship. I gave him a lot of my life and he owes me that much. That house belongs to me and my children."

"These children - are they Frank's? And of course you'll have to show proof of it," Nita calmly told her. "And regarding the house, I'll also need to see something in writing."

Although it was apparent that Dorothy had planned to lie and pawn the children off on Frank, she now realized that wouldn't work. "Well, no, but he treated them like they were his . . . they called him daddy and everything. Like I said, Frank made me a promise, and I'll take you to court to make sure you fulfill that promise."

Nita smiled at the empty threat. "Well you go right ahead and take me to court, but that promise was between you and Frank. That house is part of *my* children's estate and they don't owe you anything, and I certainly don't. I lost a child because of you, lady. I'm sure McPhearson here can attest to that, since he's the one who handled the assault charges filed against my husband after he knocked me down a flight of stairs while I was pregnant." She noticed the stunned and embarrassed expression on Tyson's face before continuing. "Yes – I'm not proud of it, but contrary to what he might have led you to believe, Frank demanded his husbandly rights whenever he felt like it," Nita said, when a look of disbelief crossed Dorothy's face.

"He hit me so hard that the baby didn't survive, and it robbed me of the possibility of any future children. This happened after you, Ms. Gibson, told my husband I had been rude to you by asking you not to call or come to my home anymore. I've suffered a tremendous amount of sorrow, abuse and neglect because of your disrespect for my marriage. So, your quarrel is with Frank, and him only. However, I would love to have my day in court with you, Dorothy Gibson."

In the midst of the shocked silence that filled the room, Nita stood and without saying anything else, walked toward the door.

"Anita, wait just a minute, please!" Tyson called to her as she walked away. "Morris, Ms. Gibson, I guess that concludes this business."

"This is not over!" Dorothy yelled to Nita. "You think you're holding all the cards now, but I know what Frank thought of you. He beat the hell out of you anytime he felt like it."

Nita lost the battle with the fragile hold on her temper. She walked over to Dorothy. "Lady, if you had been the least bit respectful of my marriage; the least bit considerate of me and my children, then maybe I would feel inclined to return that to you now, from one victim to another. But you weren't, Ms. Gibson. You were as ugly, cruel and conniving as you could be. You did everything you could to break up my home. But as hateful and mean as Frank was to me, you should have eventually realized that he was never going to leave me and his children."

"Yes, he was!" Dorothy huffed. "He told me he was."

"When? Just how long were you going to wait, Ms. Home wrecker?"

Dorothy frowned nervously and tried to scoot away from her, before saying, "He was going to throw you out of his house – you and those old boys."

"Well, God took care of that, didn't He?" Nita said, silently thanking God. Her anger burned toward the woman, but more so toward Frank for leading the woman on. But she didn't feel sorry for Dorothy. The woman had killed every ounce of compassion she might have been able to scrape up for her. "But I will do this, since you think I owe you something. Because of your diligent effort for so many years to viciously destroy my marriage, and because I know you couldn't have done it without Frank's knowledge - here's what I think it's worth. You have six months, Ms. Gibson. Six months to vacate my house. That should give you sufficient time to find another place, but if you're not out by then, I'll have you forcefully removed from my property. In my opinion, I'm being very generous."

Dorothy's face turned beet red, while her mouth hung open in shock. She jumped up and got in Nita's face. "You can't do that to me. I gave that man years of my life, and you are not going to take what belongs to me." Dorothy looked at Tyson. "She can't do that to me, can she?"

"Yes, she can. She's the owner now," Tyson answered.

Dorothy grabbed her purse and ran to the door. "You just wait, I'll get what belongs to me." She left the office, closely followed by Dr. Carlton.

Tyson took Nita's arm and led her back to a chair. "I am so sorry, Anita." He sat on the edge of his desk in front of her. "I apologize for subjecting you to that. I honestly didn't know about all the circumstances, and I'm really sorry for any part I've played in your pain. I . . . "

Anita stood up again. "Save it, Tyson. You knew exactly what was going on," she said calmly. "Tell me, is she the one who was with him when he died?"

"No, I don't think so," he answered, looking uncomfortable. He stood up from the desk and spread his hands beseechingly. "But Anita, you have me all wrong. Believe me, if I had known about everything she had done to you, I . . ."

"No problem, Mr. McPhearson, it's all good. You see, you've only confirmed that I made the right decision about not retaining your services. If your motives toward me had been right, you would not have set me up to be ambushed like that. So, let me reiterate verbally, what you've already been told in writing, your services are definitely terminated. In the meantime, if anything else occurs that even remotely smells like inappropriate actions on your part, I think suing for malpractice will definitely be in order. Excuse me, Sir." She walked swiftly toward the door. Her litany was singing in her head. *I will not be a victim again.*

After the door closed, Tyson slapped his hand against his forehead, realizing he had blown it. He should have talked to Anita himself before agreeing to this meeting. Now there was no chance to reclaim that lucrative account, and as a bonus, get close to the woman who controlled it. He sat down to think. There had to be a way to make things right with Anita. He just couldn't sit idly by and let all that money – or that woman, slip through his fingers.

CHAPTER FOUR

When the ringing phone interrupted Ron on the way out to get something to eat, his only thought had been to get rid of the caller as quickly as possible. Impatience was apparent in his voice when he answered.

"Ron? Is this Ron?"

Ron tried unsuccessfully to identify the voice on the phone. "Yes, this is Ron."

"This is Jynell, Ron," the weak, shaky voice said.

"Ohhhh! Jynell!" Ron said, a smile covering his face. "How are you, lady?" Jynell was one of the women he had dated before Chantal entered the picture. She was a sharp looking, savvy woman who ran her own insurance agency. He had been disappointed when she had abruptly stopped communicating with him, but it hadn't bothered him too much. He simply moved on to other women. "I've been missing you," he said, in his low, sexy voice.

"Ron, I have some bad news." She paused a minute. "I have AIDS, Ron, and I just wanted to let you know so you can get yourself checked out."

He almost dropped the phone and felt cold sweat pop out all over his body. "Wh-wha-what!" Ron shouted, trying to calculate how long ago he had been involved with her.

As if she read his mind, Jynell said, "I don't know how long I've had it, or who I caught it from – it could have been you for all I know."

On shaky legs, Ron stumbled to a chair and sat down. Stunned, and at a loss for words, he wiped at the beads of perspiration that now covered his face. *AIDS!*

He was silent for so long that Jynell said, "What's wrong, Ron? I can't believe you don't have anything to say."

"I..uh...I'm sorry to hear that, Jynell, and you're right, I don't know what to say. I...uh, uh...I do appreciate you calling and letting me know. How are you doing?"

"If you're asking how long I have to live, I don't know. I'm on medication but only God knows how long I'll be around. Just get yourself checked out. Bye."

Ron sat in a daze for hours – all thoughts of food had vanished. He had never seriously considered his mortality. He knew he would die someday, but in his mind, that had always been far off in the distant future. Now, face to face with a potentially deadly disease that had the power to change life as he knew it, he was rendered immobile.

Troubling questions weaved through his mind. What would this do to his family? What would happen to the business he had worked so hard to build up? What about the child he may have fathered? Would he get the chance to experience the kind of love his brother had, and, yes, he finally admitted, that he himself would like to have someday? Would he go to heaven or hell? Although he had recently started getting serious about attending church and his relationship with the Lord, he had stubbornly refused to change his lifestyle. Did that wipe out his efforts? Where would he have to go to get tested? And if he was infected with the disease, how many women would he have to call and deliver the same crushing news to?

Sitting in the darkness of his fabulous home, he prayed as he had never done before. The next morning he managed to get himself together enough to go to his doctor for the test.

"Oh, God!" Nita had just opened another e-mail from Dorothy Gibson that was filled with crude words and hateful threats. She quickly deleted it. She had been receiving the nasty messages since her meeting with the woman, and she was tired of it. She sighed wearily. Even from the grave, Frank's messy lifestyle was trying to steal her peace. She called her attorney and asked for advice on how to stop the woman's hate rampage, and was told that the firm would handle it. Nita supplied Dorothy's contact information and hung up. "Lord, I pray that's the end of that woman."

Nita spent the next months on self improvement and self-defense classes, and just relaxed. Thanksgiving and Christmas rolled around. After Frankie and Mikey informed her they wouldn't be coming home, the joy of the holidays disappeared. She had hoped that without Frank's daunting presence, she could start a new and joyous holiday tradition with her sons. As it turned out, she and Joel spent the holidays alone and tried to make the best of things.

After the first of the year, she knew it was time to do something else. She knew God had a plan, a place, and a purpose for her, but it was up to her to find it. "Please help me, Lord. Show me the path you would have me take."

She enrolled in a computer class at the community college. When her sons were at home, they provided the help she needed on the computer, but she was on her own now, and was quickly discovering that knowing how to use a computer was a necessary evil.

It was only a six-week course, but well worth it. After she completed it, she had a working knowledge that enabled her to navigate through different programs, as well as the internet. She invested in a laptop and was able to set up a new e-mail account and delete the old one - *take that Dorothy Gibson.*

It occurred to her that e-mail was a good, unobtrusive way to stay in touch with her sons everyday. She could send them a message reminding them of their need for God, and of her love for them. She was soon embroiled in compiling a list of short messages.

The ringing telephone interrupted her. "Always happens when you least want it to," she murmured, as she reached to answer it.

"Hey, Cuz! What are you up to these days?"

"C.J.! It's so good to hear from you. I'm fine, girl. I just finished that computer class I told you about the last time we talked. Whoo-hoo! I'm now a computer expert," she said, chuckling. "Well, at least I'm not afraid it's going to blow up if I push the wrong button. What's going on with you? We haven't talked in a while."

"I'm busy, girl. With this crazy job, and the on-going situations with Randy and the divorce, my brother's baby, and other activities necessary for keeping life and limb together, I'm pretty much going around in circles every day."

Nita laughed. "Yeah, I wondered how things were going with the divorce. And with a baby to take care of most of the time, I know you're super busy."

"Well, Randy is throwing up all kinds of road blocks to keep the divorce from happening, but the baby keeps me from getting bored and actually brings me a lot of joy in spite of the situation with his parents. That's why I called. I want you to pray about something."

"What?"

"Well, Nita, I've been thinking. There's really nothing tying you to Dallas, is there?"

"Mmmm . . . no, I guess not. Joel is here, of course, but I know the only reason he decided to stay in Dallas was so he would be nearby if I needed him. He's such a sweetheart, but I try not to rely on him too much because he does have his own life to live. Anyway, where are your wild thoughts taking you?"

"Nita, remember the conversation we had at Jaci's house, when we talked about all we've experienced in different ways? I was thinking about that, and concluded that God doesn't close one door without opening another. We just have to have the courage to find and walk through it. So, let me ask you, would you consider moving to Houston? The more I think about it, the more convinced I am that it might be a good move for you. Just think, no more fears about running into that witch, Dorothy or any of Frank's other women for that matter. You'll be close to me and Jaci, and all we'll have to do is work on getting Gina here. I like the thought of that."

"I do too, C.J.," Nita said, excitement rising in her.

"Well, I do have an ulterior motive. I have no intention of working on a dead-end job the rest of my life, but I don't plan to sit, soak and sour doing nothing either. So, I'm hoping you feel the same way, and that we can explore some type of business venture."

"Wow! I like the thought of that too," Nita exclaimed.

"Great. But even if the business idea doesn't pan out, I hope you'll seriously pray about moving here to be closer to me and Jaci. Okay, that's it. We'll talk later. Bye."

"Bye, Cij." Nita hung up with her heart beating wildly and her head buzzing. "Now, why hadn't I thought about that?" The ringing phone interrupted her thoughts again.

"Hey, Sis. Surprise, surprise!"

"James! I haven't talked to you in a while. To what do I owe this pleasure?"

They caught up briefly before he got to the point. "Wellllll . . . I was wondering if you'd consider coming back to Maryland for a few weeks to help us out? As you know, we're in the process of expanding our businesses. Two more mortuaries and two more beauty salons and spas will be opening in the near future. We'll be hosting several receptions and dinner parties to announce the expansions and since you're such a great organizer, you could help us with the planning and preparation."

"Hmmm." Nita's mind raced. "Just off the top of my head, it'll give me an opportunity to visit with Mikey and see how he's doing, but I can't promise to stay as long as you're talking about because I'm in the midst of making plans to move on with my own life. Let me think about it and let you know in a couple of days."

"Okay, Nita. We'll be waiting to hear from you. And plan on making several trips."

After praying about it, Nita decided to go to Maryland, even though she knew her brother had plans to work her socks off. But she did want to check on Mikey.

Her brother lived in a beautiful home that sat on a hill in an exclusive P.G. County neighborhood. She had already found out her brother and sister-in-law were avid social climbers. They had selected industries they knew would always be in demand - people were going to die, and people were going to go to the beauty salon and to fitness facilities and spas.

With little opportunity to relax after her arrival, Nita was knee deep in planning the first reception. She'd had plenty of practice planning parties for Frank, so it was nothing new. After two weeks, she was exhausted. Besides, it was time to get on with her own life.

The couple of visits she managed to get in with her son, Mikey, left her worried. Something about him didn't sit right. Mikey was a music lover and a gifted musician, and she could tell he was much more involved in some band he had joined, than his studies. She lectured, then begged him to concentrate on his studies, but it was apparent he wasn't listening. Worry over her baby son took the forefront of her mind, and it was hard to leave him there when she left to go home. "Oh God, please take care of my baby."

Ron couldn't believe that a beautiful, professional woman like Jynell would have AIDS, and the thought that it could have been passed to her from him was devastating. He always used protection, but if it had failed to stop a pregnancy, the same could be true of the disease. He was forced to honestly examine his lifestyle, and what he saw made him cringe.

He had always believed he was smart enough to control his own destiny, but that was clearly being challenged in different ways. He'd had to fight off advances from a man. He didn't want a child, but it seemed he might have one on the way. Now the possibility that he could have AIDS was staring him in the face. The weight of it all drove him to his knees to cry out to God for mercy. Was it too late for him to obtain mercy?

"Oh God, forgive me, and please don't let it be too late for me to be the man you made me to be. I promise to stop acting like I don't know right from wrong, Lord. Please have mercy, and give me another chance, although I know I don't deserve it." He stumbled up from his knees and into his bedroom where he fell across the bed. But sleep eluded him.

Ron hadn't told anybody what he was going through – not even his brother. He just couldn't. Pride, shame and arrogance kept him from being able to share his burden.

While torturous fears about possibly being HIV positive were dominating his thoughts, Chantal called to deliver a vicious jab.

"Hey Ron, just a reminder. Our baby will be here soon so I hope you're getting ready to be a daddy and start shelling out some big money."

He merely hung up the phone . . . not that he didn't want to say something - he couldn't. What if he had passed the disease on to Chantal and the baby?

His telephone was ringing constantly. Calls from women, but mostly from his family and his business. But he was simply not up to dealing with them.

Jason showed up on his doorstep the morning he had an appointment with the doctor to get his test results. His brother's shock at his appearance was obvious.

"Ron! What's going on? You haven't been to work in days, you won't answer your phone, and you look like you're half dead. What's wrong?"

After Ron shakily told him what was going on, Jason immediately cleared his calendar and drove him to the doctor.

They both broke down in tears when the doctor told Ron he had dodged the bullet - the test was negative. Ron profusely thanked God for His mercy.

After giving him time to regroup, both the doctor and Jason lectured him for the next thirty minutes about his lifestyle. "Ron," the doctor advised, "the only full proof prevention against the two issues you're dealing with is abstinence. And if you value life as you know it, you'd better make some changes."

"I've been trying to tell him that for years," Jason said. "I'm grateful that God's mercy has kept you from the worst that could have happened – this time. But you could have gotten a totally different report here today, Ron. One that would have not only affected you, but also those of us who love you. You have to start thinking of someone beside yourself."

"Yes, I realize that. If this experience has done nothing else, it's driven home the fact that I want to live, and to be healthy. So I know drastic changes are necessary."

But he also knew he couldn't do it alone. He had to have God's help.

He went back home to think, thank and pray. As soon as he walked into the house, the phone began to ring. It was his secretary, telling him he needed to call the CEO of a company who had asked him to prepare a proposal for a large housing development. The proposal, which had been due this week, wasn't ready. When Ron called the man, hoping to get an extension, he was informed that the job had gone to another firm. Disappointment filled him. He didn't need the job to survive, but he had been looking forward to the challenge. It was another hit that further weakened that invincible strength he thought he possessed.

He definitely needed to step back and do some serious praying and thinking about his life. He had been thinking about a cruise with Shayla, but now, everything had changed. Although a cruise was still appealing, Shayla's company wasn't. He needed to separate himself from everyone who might interfere with him moving in the right direction.

CHAPTER FIVE

Nita had always wanted to go on a cruise but had never had the opportunity. So when her friend, Ramona and two other friends suggested that she go with them, she immediately agreed.

She went into action, excitedly preparing for the five-day cruise. At the last minute, Ramona's husband decided to go along, so Nita was left without a cabin mate, which was fine with her. She could join the others when she felt like it, or retreat to the solitude of her own cabin to relax when she didn't.

The second day on board, Nita, dressed in a comfortable navy blue capri outfit, was relaxing on a lounge chair reading a book. Such relaxation was still new to her and at regular intervals, she would look up toward the beautiful blue sky, or out at the vast never ending waters, and draw a deep breath of contentment.

It had been a good day. She had gotten up early and joined an aerobics group for an intense workout. After returning to her cabin to shower and change, she'd joined her friends for breakfast. Afterwards, she took a stroll around the deck with Ramona before returning to her cabin to grab her book and sun glasses, then looked for a deck chair in a secluded area. Her traveling companions had decided to visit the ship's casino and play the slot machines, then hit one of the restaurants for lunch. She promised to meet them for lunch, but probably wouldn't . . . she was enjoying herself too much.

Tonight they had plans to go to a show, and she was actually looking forward to that. There was a dance following the show and she'd probably go to that as well. She couldn't remember the last time she experienced this kind of freedom. But as she would find out, trouble was everywhere . . .

Ron did a double take when he first saw the woman. She looked so much like his sister-in-law, Jaci, that he had to stop himself from going over to her. Her hair was short – cut in a Halle Berry style, and she looked as good as Halle, although a little older. Her skin was flawless and looked smooth and soft, and her curvy, well toned body indicated she took good care of it. Who was she? Why did he feel as though he should know her?

Well, he was not the shy type, and after watching her for a while, he decided there was only one way to find out. He walked over to her lounger and when his shadow fell over her, she looked up from her book with a slight frown. She pushed her sunglasses up and a look of surprised recognition appeared briefly on her face.

Ron felt a jolt when her green eyes, so similar to Jaci's, glared up at him. He remembered his brother telling him how Jaci's eyes had mesmerized him. He looked at her intently, puzzlement on his face. "Do we know each other?"

"I don't know, do we, Mr. Gilmore?"

Okay, she was playing games. "Evidently we do, since you know my name. It's just that I can't seem to place you. Do you live in Houston?"

"No, I don't." She stood up and grabbed her belongings. "Excuse me, please."

He watched her walk away, puzzlement about her identity still covering his face. He sat down on the lounger and mentally ran through all the places he could know her from. She had to be related to Jaci, but when had they ever met? He stood and headed to his cabin. Time to pray.

On the way, he saw announcements about a spectacular show and dance. He took note of the locations. Maybe he would see the woman there and solve the mystery.

Later that evening, after spending the afternoon in his cabin, praying and reading the books Pastor Robinson had given him on manhood and honoring God, he decided he had to get out of the cabin or have a bad case of cabin fever. He sat through the show, which was probably pretty good, but his mood made it impossible for him to enjoy it . . . and then he saw her.

Jaci's womanizing brother-in-law! Nita was relieved when she realized Ron Gilmore didn't recognize her. It was understandable, after all, her appearance had undergone a dramatic change. But Nita remembered him, and all Jaci had told her about his playboy lifestyle. A woman just didn't forget a good looking man, even if he was an arrogant, rude, jerk and throwing out ugly comments about her.

Now, she preferred to remain incognito. She was on the cruise to pray, think, relax and revive long lost dreams. She didn't want to be distracted by someone who might feel the need to entertain her - or himself at her expense. Plus, she still burned from the cruel remark he had made about her weight, and truthfully, didn't feel exactly cordial toward him. Darn it! If only she hadn't called him by name! Well, it was a large ship, and hopefully she wouldn't see him again.

She dressed with excitement for the show and dance. The little black dress she had bought just for the cruise was working. It's simplicity was deceiving, but it fit her like it had been made specifically for her newly toned body. She worked on her hair and face until she was satisfied she looked her best. This was her debut of sorts into a world she hadn't been able to enjoy in a very long time. Tonight, on board this luxury liner, she had every intention of enjoying herself.

After a final look of approval, she grabbed her small purse and door key, and left to find her traveling companions.

She found them waiting for her at the entrance to the theater. They were already in a jovial mood, and she joined them. The food was great – the show was great – and Nita was like a bird out of a cage.

They left the show, and headed for the dance. After finding a table, and ordering refreshments, they sat back to enjoy the music and watch the dancing. But it took only a few minutes for her to start getting invitations to dance. At first Nita declined – it had been so long, she doubted she even remembered how. But one particular man was persistent, and she was finally coaxed onto the dance floor by him.

After her first dance, she accepted invitations from several others, but the first guy kept coming back. She was flattered at first, until she realized he had more on his mind than dancing, as with each dance, he held her tighter and then began trying to kiss her and get her to leave with him. She tried to get away from him but he held on – determined to steer her toward the door. She looked around for her friends, but couldn't catch sight of any of them in the crowd. Oh well, she would just have to test her newly acquired self defense training and toss him – which she hated to do but she wasn't going to let him manhandle her. "Look, I don't want to hurt you, so I suggest you let me go," she said, trying to twist out of his grasp.

"Hurt me? How you think you gon' hurt me with your little bitty self?"

"I believe the lady wants to end her dance with you," a voice behind her said coldly.

She turned and found herself gasping in surprise. Ron Gilmore stood there, a tight expression on his face.

"What's it to you, fellow? Maybe you ought to find some business of your own," the guy shot back, still holding onto Nita, and trying to pull her through the crowd.

"Well, maybe I am minding my business," Ron answered, then looked at Nita. "Sweetheart, this is exactly why I wanted you to wait for me. I was afraid something like this would happen. Now, I'ma have to knock this dude's head off." He gave a threatening look to the guy who was shorter, and fifty pounds lighter.

Nita and the stranger both stood there with their mouths open. "I don't want to start any trouble, but if you don't get your hands off of my lady, I won't have a choice. I take strong exception to her being strong-armed like you're doing," Ron said, coldly.

The man snatched his hand back like Nita was a hot stove. He then gave Nita a leering look. "Maybe we'll meet again when you don't have your body guard around to interrupt. We have some unfinished business," he said, before walking away.

"Thanks, I appreciate that," Nita said to Ron, embarrassment covering her face.

"No problem. Are you ready to leave? I'll escort you to your cabin, since I've been dubbed your body guard," Ron replied.

"Yeah, I guess I am since that guy has kind of spoiled my enjoyment for the night. I just need to let my friends know I'm leaving," she said, looking around. She finally spotted Ramona, and with Ron in tow, worked her way over to where Ramona and her husband were dancing. She quickly informed them she was leaving and would see them for breakfast. Seeing their questioning expressions, she knew - she would have some explaining to do in the morning.

Getting into a fight over a woman was definitely not on Ron's agenda. In fact, getting involved with a woman in any way while on the cruise wasn't part of his plan. But the same thing that had drawn him to the woman that afternoon moved him to rescue her from the goon. Simply, she reminded him of his sister-in-law, and there wasn't much he wouldn't do for Jaci, who he loved like a sister.

They left the dance and he realized his solitary existence on the ship had gotten unbearable. It was only the second day, but he felt the overwhelming need for company.

"Thanks, again, Mr. Gilmore. I really appreciate your help," she stated, looking up at him with her jade eyes flashing.

"Call me Ron, and you're welcome, but you have me at a disadvantage. Obviously, you know me, but I am totally in the dark regarding your identity. Who are you?"

"Oh! I'm sorry. I'm Anita Stanhope," she replied.

He gave her a sardonic look. "Okay – a beautiful name, Anita, but it sheds absolutely no light on who you are and how you know me."

"Well, since it's not that important, let's just leave it at that, okay?"

"No, it's not okay, but I'll leave it alone for now. Would you like to get something to drink, or eat? I promise not to manhandle you," he said, smiling.

"Yes, I'd love to," she answered, with her own smile. "If for no other reason than to show my gratitude for coming to my rescue tonight. I don't think that guy had anything good on his mind. I'm grateful God sent you along to help me."

He noticed she was guarded in what she exposed about herself, but had no trouble freely expressing thanksgiving to the Lord.

After locating one of the coffee bars aboard ship, they sat and talked like old friends – surprisingly, mostly about the Lord.

"I gather from your conversation that you are a Christian?" It was a statement that ended with a question mark. Most of the women he usually dealt with seldom, if ever, mentioned anything regarding God or Christianity, or if they did, it was usually just a ploy.

"Absolutely. Me and the Lord have walked together a very long time. I don't know what I would do without Him," she answered, with sincerity written all over her face. "He's the One I must depend on for everything I need."

He tried to keep the intrigue he felt off of his face. "Wow! To be honest, I'm trying to find my way to that place. I'm at a point in my life where I really need Him. Of course I was raised in the church, so I'm not a total stranger to Him, but I left for a very long time, and the road back is difficult. I'm finding that church attendance and knowing God are two different things. It's kind of confusing."

"Not as difficult as you may think. But you do have to give up your own will, accept God's will for your life, and trust Him as the source of everything."

"And that's not hard?" He asked, a cynical expression on his face. "I happen to like my lifestyle, but I'm discovering my lifestyle does not like me."

She gave him a searching look – as though trying to decipher his comments. "Well, I guess you have some decisions to make. But you can't straddle the fence or be lukewarm."

He almost spewed out the sip of coffee he had just taken and felt a shiver at the familiar words. "Yeah, I'm hearing that a lot, lately," he said, with a hint of a smile playing around his mouth. He looked around the almost empty coffee bar, fighting the urge to voice the questions that had been tormenting him, afterall, she was a virtual stranger. He finally gave into the urge, then felt gratitude when she listened intently, nodding her understanding.

"Have you ever felt like you were under attack? Like before you can put one thing behind you, another one hits and knocks you to the ground? And then just when you recover from that, something else comes along and stomps you back down to the ground again?"

"Oh yes," she answered, quietly. "I've been there many times."

"What did you do? How did you handle it?" He cringed inwardly. Was that him, sounding so desperate?

"Well, I know that God is our refuge and strength, and a present help in trouble. Sometimes it seems as if He's taking too long with the help, but really, His timing is perfect. The waiting is hard, but I had to learn to trust Him."

He smiled at her and said, "I sure needed to hear that. I'm glad I rescued you tonight.
Wanna take a walk around the deck before calling it a night?"

"Sounds good. I need to walk off some of the calories I've consumed today."

He grinned. "I have no comment on that. I learned a long time ago not to say anything when a woman mentions anything about her weight or age."

She gave him a cynical look. "Um hmmm! And I'm sure you have many more of those rays of wisdom about women."

He noticed a hard edge to her response, but decided to ignore it. "What do you do when you're not cruising, Anita?" Ron asked, when they came to a stop and stood looking out over the moon lit water.

"Well, right now my life is sort of in transition. So I'm in the process of re-defining who I am, and what I want to do with the rest of my life," she answered.

"I know there's more to your story than you're saying, but I'll let it go for now."

"What about you, Ron? What do you do?"

"I'm an architect. I design all types of structures. You name it, I can design it."

"It sounds like you love your work."

"Yes, I do love it, and I'm pretty good at it."

"That's great. It has to be gratifying to be doing something you love and are good at."

"It is. Ready to move on?" He was enjoying the conversation with her so much that other feelings were stirring in him. Old habits were hard to break.

Oooooh, Lord! This man is lethal. Nita thought – and more than once, questioned the wisdom of leaving the dance and spending time with him. She lost track of time as they sat and talked in the coffee bar, but during their conversation, she discovered something about him that she would have never suspected. It almost caused her to change her bad opinion of him.

His looks she could handle, because she had been around good looking men all her life and knew to look beyond outward appearances or they could be detrimental. But – beyond Ron's good looks, his

inherent charisma, and her gratitude to him for rescuing her –
something about him touched a responsive cord deep within her.

The arrogant playboy she had encountered at the wedding was
nowhere to be found in this man. Now she detected a quiet weariness, an
introspective aura, and a sadness of spirit.

Surprisingly, most of their conversation was about having a
relationship with the Lord. She could see his inner struggle and wished
she had appropriate words to help, but knew that ultimately it was
between him and the Lord.

Things went smoothly until they went on a stroll around the deck
and she felt something totally unfamiliar igniting between them.

"It's beautiful out here, isn't it?" he asked, giving her a long,
searching look.

"Yes, it is," she answered, and wondered why her voice was
shaky. An ocean breeze blew over them, and she shivered. "It's getting a
little chilly," she said, rubbing her bare arms.

He immediately moved closer and put his arm around her.
"Ready to go in?" His eyes and voice held something she couldn't read –
Loneliness? Longing? Need?

"I think that may be a good idea." She shivered again, not from
the chilly air, but from the way he was looking at her. She didn't know
whether to break and run or stand there and see what would happen.
Before she could make herself move, his lips covered hers in a gentle
kiss.

"Ron . . ." she said, in a breathless voice when he lifted his head.
"I don't think . . ." He drew her closer, and this time his lips were on a

mission to totally command. She let herself feel the enjoyment of being held firmly in his arms. *Oh Lord, help me!*

"You don't think what?" He asked. "That we should do this? Well, I don't either. This totally negates my reason for being on this cruise. But I can't seem to stop myself."

He hugged her closer, and this time the kiss was filled with so much passion and . . . it seemed, desperation, that it stole what little breath she had.

Gradually, they came up for air, but continued to embrace each other tightly – as though they both needed the closeness.

"Thank you for tonight," he whispered. "I am so happy we spent this time together. You'll never know how much I needed it."

She was still reeling, and trying to get her errant emotions under control. "We'd better go." She pulled out of his embrace, finally got her feet to cooperate, and began walking. Immediately, she felt his hand, resting against the small of her back in a protective way.

When they got to her door, he said, "I'm right down the hall from you. Will you have breakfast with me in the morning?"

"No, Ron, I already have plans, but thanks again for everything."

"You're welcome. Where are you having breakfast? Maybe I'll see you there. Don't forget, I'm suppose to be your bodyguard." He chuckled as he said it.

"Oh, don't worry about that, I'll be okay." But she told him where her group was having breakfast, certain he wouldn't show up anyway.

He kissed her gently on the forehead. "See you then, I don't trust that dude."

Nita entered her cabin and dropped down on the bed. "What the heck am I doing? Have I lost my mind? I know this man's game, so why would I walk into his trap. And that's what tonight was. That jerk at the dance provided a perfect opportunity for him to make his move."

She undressed, took a shower and crawled into bed. But sleep eluded her. When, if ever, had she been kissed like that? Held like that? She groaned, realizing that for the remainder of the cruise, she would have to watch out for two men. One to run from, and the other to stop herself from running to.

CHAPTER SIX

"What has gotten into me?" Ron asked himself as he entered his own cabin. "I'm not here to get entangled with a woman. I'm supposed to be praying, seeking the Lord, and getting my head together. But even in the brief time I've spent with her, that woman has my mind messed up." *Like its never been before.* He thought.

The nagging thought in the back of his mind that he knew her from somewhere persisted. And the fact that she reminded him of Jaci didn't help much either.

He waited for her the next morning, and was about to give up when the group rounded the corner and headed into the restaurant. Nita made introductions, explaining how Ron had come to her rescue last night.

"Thanks, brother," they said to him, and to Nita's dismay, invited him to join them for breakfast, as well as the on-shore tour and excursion into the city. Ron quickly accepted. He saw the uncertainty and displeasure on Anita's face, and thought, *Too bad, I'm going.*

They left the ship as part of the group, but Ron wasn't satisfied until he had split from them and had her to himself. He had been to the island before, and wanted to re-visit some places he thought she would like. They walked around the township, window shopping and buying souvenirs, then went into a local pub that was off the beaten track, where he knew the food was exceptional. Again, they talked and enjoyed each other's company until they returned to the ship.

She agreed to go to the movies with him that night, although he felt hesitancy in her.

Ron's hope that they wouldn't encounter the obnoxious jerk again went down the drain as they exited the ship's dining room that evening. Anita and the women were walking ahead of him and Ramona's husband, who had stopped to grab some mints from a bowl near the door.

The guy was standing near the door as though waiting for Anita. He grabbed her by the arm none too gently. "Hey, darling! Where have you been hiding?" He gave her a leering look. "I sure want to spend some time with you, with ya' fine self."

Ron watched Anita struggle with the guy, and a look of pure terror briefly covered her face, but was replaced by one of fierce determination. While he tried to push through the crowd to get to her, Anita kicked her shoes off and proceeded to use some kind of move that had the guy lying on the floor before he knew what had happened. Before he could get up, Ramona had her shoe off and was banging the dude all over his head.

"Keep – your – hands - off - of - her - you - slimeball," she said, punctuating each blow with her words.

The Dude managed to crawl away from her. "What is y'all's problem? There was no reason to attack me like that. I wasn't doing nothing." He got up slowly, rubbing his backside.

Ron had finally pushed through the crowd. "I hate to have to fight you, man, but you're either drunk, high on something or just stone crazy. This woman is not interested in you, plus, she's off limits to you. How many times and ways will it take for you to understand that?"

Anita, who was calmly putting her shoes back on, said, "Well, mister, if you feel like trying again, come on. I'm tired of you messing with me. We'll settle this right now."

The guy backed up. "You're crazy!" He continued his retreat, while Anita matched with threatening advances.

"Yes, I am! And I'm not taking nothing off of anybody, so come on!"

A flash of fear covered the guy's face. "Forget it." He turned and limped away.

"Just like a bully! Run when you know you 'bout to get your tail whipped," Ramona called after him.

"And by a woman, too!" Another woman in the group yelled.

The man realized the crowd was laughing at him and the limp became a trot.

Ron had a peculiar look on his face. "Let's go," he said, grabbing Anita's hand. "We have just enough time to catch the beginning of the movie." They walked away, hand in hand.

"I'll call you later, Ramona," Nita called over her shoulder. Then said to Ron, "I'm so embarrassed. I never expected to have to deal with that kind of thing again, especially here."

"What do you mean, 'again'?" Ron asked, remembering the look of terror on her face.

"It's not something I want to get into. Let's go to the movies!"

"Okay, but you have lots of questions to answer," Ron stated, emphatically. "And remind me to never make you mad." A memory stirred at the back of his mind. He recalled how his sister-in-law, Jaci, had taken someone down like that.

But Nita refused to talk to him after the movie, claiming tiredness and her desire to retire. As they walked slowly toward their cabins, he again tried to find out who she was.

"Ron, please don't push that issue. I've said all I'm going to say. Now, it's time to part ways. I've enjoyed spending time with you on the cruise, but I have to tell you that I'm really not interested in a relationship, shipboard or otherwise."

"Why, Anita? You're one of only a few women I've ever met that I wanted to get to know better. Usually, all I'm interested in is a carefree romp with a woman, and then on to the next one," he was stunned to hear himself admit.

"I know that, Ron, and thank God I do, or I might be tempted to do something stupid."

Her remark just further confused and frustrated him. He kissed her when they arrived at her cabin door. "Call me," he said, softly, then handed her a business card with his cabin number scribbled on the back. "I'm going to be very disappointed if I don't hear from you."

"No, you won't," she said flippantly. "You'll just move on to the next woman."

She didn't show for breakfast the next morning, or the trip ashore they had planned at the next port. When he questioned Ramona about her, she would only say Anita had decided not to go. He was disappointed. He looked for her the next day, knowing it would be their last full day aboard before the ship reached the final port, but she was nowhere to be seen.

The following morning, as he was waiting with the crowd to disembark, he spotted her and made his way to her and gave her a long look. "I've missed you. Where have you been?"

"I thought it best for us to part on a positive note," she answered.

Frustration filled him. "Anita, who are you? Why won't you tell me anything about yourself? I'd like to stay in touch with you, will you give me your contact information?"

"No. Look, we've had fun on the cruise, so let's just leave it at that."

"Are you married? Is that it?"

She hesitated before answering. "No."

"Then, why won't you give me your contact information?"

"Because I don't want to."

He sighed. "Well, do you still have the card I gave you?" Without waiting for an answer, he pressed another card into her hand. "You can call me at any of these numbers, night or day. Will you do that?"

"I don't think so. Maybe you need to know how women feel when you say cruel things to them, or treat them like they're nothing but a piece of meat. But I do appreciate everything you've done for me, and I've enjoyed the time we spent together. I wish you well, playboy, and hope you get things straight between you and the Lord." She handed his card back to him and walked away without another word.

Her words stung and anger and frustration filled him. He didn't like the feeling. She was the first woman in a very long time that he'd genuinely wanted on a level beyond the physical.

Two weeks later, Nita had pushed the cruise – and Ron Gilmore - to the back of her mind, and boarded a plane to Maryland. She would help her brother while there, but her main reason for going was to check on her son.

Mikey's attitude could only be described as insolent. She'd seen it before, but then it had been directed toward his father – never her. Before leaving, she made a last trip into D.C. to visit Mikey. It wasn't good. First, she had to wait around on him, although he knew she was coming. When he finally showed up, he delivered the news that he was on academic probation and planned to drop out of school.

"Mikey, you haven't even made a year of school. You're a very intelligent young man, and being on academic probation is unacceptable. Instead of dropping out of school, you need to drop whatever is interfering with your studies and make them a priority."

Mikey frowned at her. "Don't you get it, Mom? This college thing isn't my scene."

"But Mikey, baby, what are you going to do? If you're not in school, you know your financial assistance will end."

He rolled his eyes at her. "You're just saying that to make me do what you want me to, but you can forget it because I'm grown and I'ma do what I wanna do."

She gasped. "Mikey! What in the world has gotten into you?"

"I just need for you to give me my money and get off my back."

"Your money? You mean the money from your education fund?"

"Yeah! I told my homies we could use it to front the tour we're getting ready to do."

"Oh no! Mikey, you told them about your education fund?"

"So what's wrong with that? It's mine."

"Oh honey, you shouldn't have done that. That money is only for educational purposes. That's how your dad set it up. If you don't use it for that, then it stays where it is. The attorney explained that to all of you, remember?"

"I'm a member of the band, and we need that money now. I know you can get it for me."

"I'm sorry, Son, but that's not possible. I suggest you work on getting your grades back up to par so you can stay in school. I'm not saying you have to abandon your music altogether. You can always participate in the school's musical programs, but Mikey, now is not the time for you to be running around with some rock band. You need to finish school first."

He looked at her like she was stupid. "It's a jazz band," he snidely stated, "and the guys who recruited me said they already have gigs lined up for us in several cities. But I have to pay my part of the expenses. At any rate, school is not in the picture anymore, Mom."

Tears slid down her face. "Please, baby, think about this. The places where these bands play are not always the right kind of environments for a kid like you. All kinds of unsavory things go on, including heavy drug use. I'm begging you, Mikey, if you don't want to go to school, then come home. I'm sure you can find a band to play with there, and you'll be close so I can keep an eye on you. Please do that for me."

"Are you gon' shell out my bucks or not?"

"No, baby, I'm not," she replied, wiping at the tears that rolled down her face.

"Then you can get outta my face. I'm tired of being hassled about what I want to do. I got it from dad, and now here I am getting it from you. Well, I got better things to do." He walked away from her without looking back.

Mikey's obsession with music had always been a bone of contention between him and Frank. Mikey preferred music to sports, but Frank had insisted he play sports, making it hard for Mikey to fit music into his schedule. But he never put the music down. He was good at it, and played several instruments.

"You have to help me with this, Lord. Basically, he's grown, and I can't make him do anything. Please God, keep him in Your care."

When she returned home, she found several messages from Tyson McPhearson. "Oh Lord, what does he want?" She groaned, and called him back to get it over with.

"This is Anita Stanhope. I'm returning your calls. Is something wrong?"

"No, no, nothing's wrong. I just wanted to apologize again, and let you know your attorney and I have just about got things squared away."

"Yes, I know. She keeps me very well informed."

"I was wondering, Anita…uh…would you consider letting me take you to dinner sometime soon? I feel so bad about everything that's happened. I'd like to at least try to compensate for all we put you through."

"Thanks, but there's no need for that. I've moved on, and everything is going well."

"Are you enjoying your new place?"

"Yes, very much. But how did you know about that?"

"I make it my business to know. You'd be surprised what I know about you."

"That sounds a little creepy to me. I'm not sure I like that."

"It's because I care, and I want to make up for failing you in the past. I owe you that."

"You don't owe me anything, Tyson."

"Well, we won't argue about it. So, how about that dinner?"

"I don't think so, Tyson. Listen, I need to go. Thanks for calling."

"Wait, Anita. Before you hang up, let me say something. I'm intrigued by you and I confess I'm attracted to you. Can we start over and get to know each other? I would like that very much. Will you at least promise to think about it?"

She hung up wondering what that was all about.

As she was telling Jaci and C.J. about her conversation with Tyson the following weekend, they both looked a little dubious.

"Wonder what his game is? I'd tread carefully, Nita" Jaci advised.

"Huh, I don't have to wonder what his game is," C.J. stated. "He's after this good-looking, wealthy widow. He lost you as a client, but if he can marry you, that's all the better. And he's not going to let some other man beat him to the punch. Yeah, Nita, be careful."

"I wasn't married to crafty Frank all those years without learning something about people. I don't trust him as far as I can pick him up and throw him."

"So, have you thought anymore about moving down here?" C.J. asked.

"Yes, I have, and I'm going to do it," Nita said, with a smile. "I want to start taking some college courses, and I figure I may as well get settled down before I start. Jaci, do you think Jason has time to help me find a place soon?"

"Of course. You just need to let him know the kind of house you want, the area you want to live in, and your price range. He'll take it from there."

"Good. I'd better start packing when I get home, because I know I'll be moving soon."

Jaci shifted her weight around uncomfortably. "Oh Lord, these babies are so heavy," she said, with a groan. "So, Nita, tell us about your cruise. You know, Ron was on a cruise at the same time and mentioned he spent some time with a woman who reminded him of me. He said he actually hoped something would develop between them. Now for Ron, that's a biggie. I've never known of him having that kind of attraction to any woman," Jaci said, rubbing her middle.

Nita looked down, wondering how much to admit. "Okay, listen, but this is strictly between us. Ron and I were on the same cruise, and I am the woman he told you about. I recognized him, but he never did figure out who I was. Drove him crazy! So don't say a word to him about this, Jaci. I know we're certain to run into each other eventually, but just leave him in the dark for now."

"But why didn't you tell him who you were?" Jaci asked, with a puzzled expression.

"I suppose I got some kind of perverse pleasure out of it. I've been miffed at him every since your wedding when he hurt my feelings."

"Oh Lord, we have a monster evolving!" C.J. chuckled.

"I did have fun with him though," Nita said, omitting certain details. Ron was different somehow. He seemed to be troubled or burdened about something."

Jaci gave her an amazed look and said, "You're very perceptive. Ron has been going through a lot lately. God is working on him big time!"

"Yes, he did kind of allude to the fact that something was going on in his life." Nita recalled.

"Yes, well, he's had some terrible trials recently. Even if you had told him who you are, I doubt if he even remembers what he said at the wedding."

"Okay, moving right along," Nita said with a smile. "Cij, what was that business idea you wanted to discuss with me? Maybe we can begin working on it."

"Wow! You're certainly not letting any grass grown under your feet these days, are you?" C.J. answered. "That's a good thing though. I'm really glad to see it. Anyway, you know I owned a bookstore and gift shop when Randy and I lived in Detroit. I was planning a similar business here, but my marriage went south before I could move on it. But I don't think book stores are doing well now, so that may not be the way to go. What do you think?"

"I like the idea, but I agree, it may not be the one. I know of several bookstores that went under," Nita answered. "Let's keep praying and thinking."

"Okay, we'll let the Lord guide us. I'm not ready to do anything now anyway."

"How is the divorce going? Is Randy still fighting it?"

"Yes. He knows it's going to happen, but he's stalling things just to be mean."

A couple of weeks after the cruise, Ron had almost pushed the mystery woman to the back of his mind. He was still miffed with the way they had parted, and was trying to convince himself it was for the best. Obviously, she had issues with him, but her refusal to talk about it made it impossible to resolve.

Before he was ready, Chantal had the baby, and unfortunately for him, the DNA test confirmed he was the father. His distrust of her . . . he didn't put it past her to have someone rig the test . . . prompted him to get a second opinion from a different laboratory. Much to his chagrin, it came back with the same results. He started paying a generous amount of child support through the D.A.'s office, and ignored her constant threats and demands for more. He was already paying more than the law required.

A man from Maryland had called him last year about designing some facilities for him, but at the time his schedule was full. He noticed the same man had called again, and after giving it serious consideration, Ron called him.

The guy had his fingers in all kinds of ventures. "I need you to design a mortuary, and I don't mean the standard, run of the mill funeral home. I want ultra modern, state of the art,…the whole works. And then, I'd like to see what you can come up with for a health spa and salon facility. I have new places opening soon around D.C. and Maryland but to be honest, I'm not exactly pleased with my architect."

They scheduled a date for Ron to come to Maryland to discuss future projects. Ron had also been talking to his Pastor, Gerald Robinson, quite a bit. The man was a nice guy who didn't beat around the bush, but was straight and to the point. Ron told him a little about what had been happening in his life recently, including what happened on the cruise. He'd had to fight off disillusionment when Pastor Robinson told him frankly . . . "You reap what you sow, and Ron, it sounds like you've sown a lot of bad seed, and your harvest is plentiful and bitter. Although God forgives the sin, He won't deal with the consequences. My advice to you is to start planting the right seed for the kind of harvest you want to see in the future. Like any crop, it'll take some time before you see it, but it will come."

For the next few weeks, Nita was back and forth between Dallas and Houston. She loved one of the places Jason found for her and after closing on the purchase, she was working to get it ready to move into.

Before long, she was going through another exhausting relocation, determined this would be the last one for a long time. It wasn't long before all the rooms of her new spacious two-story condo had been set up and decorated to her satisfaction.

She spent time driving around the city, just to learn her way around. Thanks to her GPS and the maps she printed out from Mapquest, she never got lost, however, she did have some close calls when she mistakenly turned the wrong way on one-way streets. But one finger salutes and angry shouts from other drivers had been the worse that had come of it. She kept venturing out until she felt somewhat comfortable navigating.

But eventually, she was fighting boredom. It was too late to enroll in current semester classes so time hung heavily on her hands. She rearranged furniture, repainted one of the bedrooms and brought new accessories for the downstairs bathroom before she reprimanded herself and left the house alone.

She decided to catch up on her reading one morning, but that didn't work either. She finally tossed the book that wasn't holding her attention to the table next to her recliner, and turned her attention to what lay beyond the floor to ceiling wall of windows beside the chair. The seller called it a natural preserve but to Nita's way of thinking, it was what her grandmother called a thicket. Whatever it was called, it reminded her of Riverwood, and filled her with nostalgic yearning for the life she had known growing up there, at least when she edited out the painful memories – heartbreak, loneliness, and fears that only a ten year old can know after her mother goes to heaven and she is left with an apathetic father, older siblings lost in their own pain and issues, and a caretaker aunt who hated children.

Nita forcefully pushed away that particular set of memories, gazed out at the 'thicket' and tried to draw solace from more pleasant things the reminiscent scene brought to her mind, namely, all the crazy things she and her cousins had gotten into. Memories of their outrageous shenanigans brought smiles and chuckles. Then, there had been her grandparents - her refuge. She conceded that despite some bad times, Riverwood represented the best time of her life, other than the months since Frank had died. Sad.

Frank. She tried not to dwell on thoughts of him. But even after months, he often reached out from the grave through reoccurring nightmares to torment her. She tried to push away the boredom, but unfortunately, there wasn't much to distract her. She soon jumped up from the chair and walked slowly from the family room through the dining room and into the kitchen.

Although she wasn't really hungry, she opened the refrigerator and pulled out fruit and cheese, then went into the pantry to get a box of crackers. "Emotional eating! I know better!"

She ignored the voice of wisdom and bit into a cracker. Comfort eating was a strong pacifier. She hadn't heard from Mikey since that last conversation in D.C., and had no idea where he was since the school had notified her of his withdrawal. He hadn't answered any of her calls and that alone was enough to drive her crazy. Her only glimmer of hope was that her e-mails to him hadn't been returned.

"Dear God, help me remember that You are my source of peace and everything else I need. You have never left me or forsaken me, and I know You won't do it now. Please send my son home to me, or at least let me know where he is."

She peeled an apple and cut it into slices, while she searched her mind for something to do, or someone to talk to. C.J. was at work, and Jaci was so close to delivering her twins that she was miserable and didn't feel up to doing anything.

Nita took a bunch of grapes to the sink and washed them before popping one into her mouth. Her thoughts trudged on. Her cousins had made sure she was settled into her new home, and knew how to navigate the freeways, and get everywhere she needed or wanted to go. She had joined their church, had a local doctor, therapist, gym and hair saloon, as well as other essential services in place. Now, it was up to her to build and fill her life from this point, and there was no Frank to dictate what she could or couldn't do.

"So why am I sitting here on a beautiful Thursday, with no hope or expectation of seeing anyone except the people in the gym until the weekend?" She bit into the cheese and crackers, followed by a slice of apple. "This is totally unacceptable. I've worked too hard to get that extra weight off to sit here and munch it back on." Another mouth full of cheese and crackers, followed by a handful of grapes this time, found the way into her mouth. "Now Lord, You know You have to help me, because if you don't, I'll end up in a place I don't want to be."

She had never forgiven herself for dropping out of college and marrying Frank Stanhope, and considered it the worst mistake she'd ever made, although he had given her three beautiful boys which she wouldn't take all the money in world for, and a baby girl, which he also took.

As she continued eating, her conversation with the Lord rolled on. "I know it's no accident that I'm still alive because any number of Frank's beatings could have killed me. So, Father, You must have something for me to do to make a difference in this world. I certainly don't intend to become a bitter, lonely, old lady. Nope, the devil is a lie if he thinks he's going to steal this new season of life from me. So, here I am, Lord, use me to do Your will, and do it soon, because I'm about to lose it up in here."

Nita dumped the rest of her food into the trash. "Okay, it's time to do something constructive." She went to the computer, pulled up the church's website and studied the various ministries. She read about the ministry for domestic violence victims, and knew she definitely had something to offer that ministry. "Thank You, Father," she said as she hit the print button to print the ministry information.

She left the church's website and started exploring the curriculums of different colleges, searching for courses that might be of interest to her. After printing out information from several area universities, she decided to see if she could catch up with her cousin, Gina. She was glad she had called when she heard the joy-filled welcome in Gina's voice.

"Nita! I'm so happy to hear from you. I've been meaning to call you but you know how it is, just never got around to it. Tell me about everything, girl. Are you settled in yet?"

"Yeah, I am. I think I'm going to like it here, and of course the best thing is that I'm close to Jaci and C.J. How are things going with you?"

They spent the next half hour catching up. Nita's heart was singing as she hung up. "Thank you, Lord! No more desire for comfort munching!" The telephone interrupted her praise, and she noticed it was her CPA calling from Dallas. They discussed her finances as well as some strategies she needed to put in place for tax purposes. The CPA suggested some kind of non-profit Foundation that could be used as a tax shelter. An idea popped into Nita's mind. Why not something to help women in the same predicament that had held her prisoner for so long?

The CPA thought it was a great idea and said she would begin working with Nita's attorney to set up a Foundation. Nita called her friend, Ramona, who worked in public relations and marketing, and her former Pastor and ran the idea by them. By the time she got off the phone with them, a plan was in the works.

When Nita looked at the clock, she saw it was barely eleven thirty. All week, she had sat each day and watched early morning slide into mid-morning, then early afternoon, and gradually, late afternoon, which gave way to nightfall and bedtime – only to repeat the pattern the following day. But no more. "I refuse to let my days go down like that."

She sat down at the computer and quickly drafted a list of things she wanted to accomplish through the Foundation. After typing two pages of thoughts and ideas – she had plenty to pull from her own life -

she saved it, printed it out and decided she would go over it again after giving it more thought and doing some research.

Feeling energized from her activities over the last hour and a half, she decided to visit Jaci and maybe cook dinner for her. Two hours later, she was busy at work in Jaci's kitchen, after stopping at the grocery store on her way there. She was making baked salmon, fried sweet potatoes, fresh green beans, and cornbread - all of which Jaci declared she was craving when Nita had called to see what she wanted.

She peeled and cut sweet potatoes into strips and gathered brown sugar, cinnamon, butter and some allspice to add to them, planning to fry them like Grammy used to do. She said to Jaci, who was sprawled on the couch in the adjoining family room, "Girl, it's been years since I fried sweet potatoes. Frank didn't like them, so that meant I didn't cook them. I'm trying to remember, but I think maybe we're forgetting some vital ingredients. They used to be so good when Grammy cooked them. But I guess they won't be too bad. It's hard to mess up a sweet potato."

"Girl, how ever they turn out, I'm going to eat them. I've had a taste for them for weeks, but I just haven't felt like tackling it, and the housekeeper just gets a blank look on her face when I ask her to cook something she's not familiar with. You just hurry up and get them cooked."

Nita laughed. "Okay, I'm hurrying as much as I can. Once I get these going, it's not going to take long to finish the rest. The salmon is already seasoned and ready to go in the oven, and everything else is in progress. You want something to drink?"

"Yes, I do," Jaci answered, trying to find a comfortable position. "I don't know what I'm praying for most - for these rascals to get here, or for them to hold off as long as possible. I know it's going to be a circus around here after they come."

"There'll be enough of us around to help you," Nita told her. "Is your mother still planning to come?"

"Yep, and the last I heard, daddy is too! Can you believe that?" Jaci asked, a disgusted look on her face as she reached for the glass of juice Nita had brought her. "I will never understand people. Especially my own. I was basically alone when I had Randi, and Lord, did I need somebody. But daddy was angry at me, and raising so much hell that mama wouldn't help me either. Now, they are both raring to get here, and this time, I really don't need them. I have Jason, his parents, Randi, Patrick, you and C.J., Sister Sadie, even Ron, to name a few."

"Well, don't complain, because you're going to need everyone of us, when both of those babies start yelling in the middle of the night. And Jaci, about your parents, just forget what's in the past. You know they're trying to make up for when they failed you before, so let them do that, and be thankful. I'd give anything if my mother were still alive, and my daddy showed any interest in doing something for me. But girl, he's hobbling around on his old arthritic knees and hips, still trying to run after women half his age."

They both laughed at Nita's description of her daddy. "My goodness, Nita, when is he going to realize his days for that are over?" Jaci asked. "That's why we're working on Ron, trying to keep that from being him in twenty or thirty years. Speaking of Ron, when he knows Jason is tied up, he stops in to check on me during the day. And today is one of those days."

"Oh geez, I wish you had told me that sooner!" Nita said, with panic in her voice. "I don't want to be anywhere near Ron."

"Well, you can't leave until you finish cooking. And anyway, y'all are going to run into each other sooner or later, so it might as well be today."

As though conjured up by their conversation, the back door opened and Ron walked in. This was the moment Nita had dreaded since moving to Houston.

CHAPTER SEVEN

Ron's eyes immediately fell on the woman who was busy in Jaci's kitchen. Their eyes met and her green eyes sparkled defiantly before she turned away. He took in everything about her, noticing how the capri pants she was wearing hugged her hips and displayed her beautiful legs. Her hair was longer and now covered her head in loose curls.

"Who is this woman, Jaci?" He inclined his head in Nita's direction as he spoke.

Jaci smiled, mischievously. "Ron, don't you remember my cousin, Anita? She was in the wedding. I thought you never forgot a beautiful face."

He sorted through his memories of the wedding. Nothing. And he would have definitely remembered her if she had been there. His gaze returned to Anita. "For some reason, I don't remember you." He could see Anita was getting a kick out of his confusion – just as she had on the cruise.

"Hmmm, wonder why?"

Anger rushed through him. "I don't get it. Why the games, Anita? Why didn't you just tell me who you were?" He walked across the room to the large framed picture of the wedding party that sat on the shelf of the entertainment center. He studied the picture intently, going from face to face. He placed every person, except the plump woman with long hair. He looked back to Anita, then back to the picture. "Oh! You were the fat one," he said, snapping his fingers. "No wonder I didn't recognize you. You've made quite a transformation."

"But you're still a rude, arrogant, condescending jerk," Nita shot back.

Ron continued to stare at her. "I don't understand. Why all the subterfuge, Anita?"

Nita turned her attention to something on the stove. "There was no subterfuge intended, Ron. As I tried to tell you then, I was on a personal quest. I wanted . . . needed . . . some relaxing space, and really didn't want to go into long explanations. Also, I didn't want you to feel obligated to entertain me, even though, that sort of happened anyway."

Memories from the cruise assailed him. Their talks. Her in his arms. The kisses he couldn't get out of his mind. "Did it look like I minded?"

"Well, I was also a little miffed at you. . . remember after the wedding when we all came back here? You made it a point of telling your buddies the only thing I could do for you was to show you the way to a slender woman."

Something clicked in his mind. "Oh! You were the one whose husband had just died. I remember. But that was then. Things have changed in a lot of ways," he said in irritation. "If you had mentioned being a recent widow, I might have made the connection to Jaci, because I heard about her cousin's husband dying. As it was, your uncanny resemblance to Jaci – especially the green eyes – kept drawing me to you, but I couldn't put it all together because you carefully avoided providing all the pieces. Why did you do that? It nearly drove me crazy." *And still is.*

He was suddenly walking toward her, and was hugging her tightly without even thinking about it. "I've missed you," he said, then he kissed her like he'd dreamt of doing for months. "I've missed you so much," he groaned again. "Why did you leave me hanging like that?" The next kiss went on and on.

Jaci was clearing her throat to get their attention, and when that didn't work, she said, "Uh . . . excuse me! Hel..lo! guys? remember me? I'm still here."

Ron reluctantly pulled away from her and stepped back. "You owed me that," he told her in a shaky voice that he hardly recognized as his. "You still owe me."

Jaci's eyes were open wide in shock, and she said, "Okay, guys, now that you've come up for air, want to tell me what's going on?"

Neither one answered. Ron took a seat on one of the bar stools, and Nita returned to her cooking duties.

"Okay, then," Jaci said. "Ron, since Nita is here, you don't have to baby sit me because she'll be here for a while. As you can see, she's fixing some food for me. So no more distractions. I'm ready to chow down."

"Me too," Ron stated. "Something smells good, and I'm not leaving until I eat." He settled himself on the bar stool and watched as Nita finished the meal.

He stayed until Jason got home. He needed to talk to his brother. It bothered him that just in their short time together on the cruise, Anita had affected him so deeply. Far more than the women he casually slept with. Just talking to her and spending time with her had touched places deep within his heart, so much so, that he hadn't been able to get her out of his mind.

Ironically, that had helped with the decision to do things God's way so he wouldn't have to deal with any more bad harvests. He had cut things between him and Shayla – or tried to – but he was finding that she was aggressive and had come to expect certain things from him – things he had never promised. She wouldn't accept that things were over between them and continued to push every possible button trying to make it difficult for him to stick to his decision of celibacy. His vivid memories of Anita helped.

Jason sat back to listen as Ron tried to explain all this, then said, "Maybe you haven't settled in your own mind exactly what you want and you're sending the wrong signals out."

"What! I didn't get that reaction from Anita when we were on that cruise. We spent a lot of time together, talking, sightseeing, shopping, and just having fun. She wasn't pushing all up on me like that. I was the one making all the moves."

Jason leaned forward. "Really? Anything else you want to tell me about that cruise?"

"Yep," Jaci hollered from across the room where they thought she was watching television. "Ron has plenty to explain. And I'm just waiting for Nita to bring her little behind back over here so she can answer some questions too. Honey, they almost devoured each other – and right in front of me and my babies."

Jason's eyes shot back to Ron. "Well?"

"We just had some unfinished business . . . and that's none of your business."

Jason's laugh filled the room. "Okay, but getting back to your situation, you need a wife, man. Now I know that hasn't been on your agenda, but in light of this change you've decided to make, maybe you'd better start thinking and praying about it. You definitely don't want to marry just any woman, and the kind of woman you want can't be picked up off the streets."

Ron gave him a cynical look. "Tell me about it. When I first met Shayla and she told me she was a Christian and wanted to live for God, I actually thought I had found the right kind of woman. Boy, was I wrong."

Jason started laughing. "What happened?"

This time a disgusted look came from Ron. "I've been to church with her and seen her acting all sanctimonious, but it's a different story out of church. Man, I'm having to literally run from her. It's enough to make me want to stop going to church. Thank goodness I know that's not my reason for being there."

"Yeah." Jason said, still laughing. "Been there, done that. But you can't give up. Keep praying and getting yourself together. God will send the right woman across your path. But if you're not ready, you'll miss out on her."

"I've already had a taste of that," Ron said, shaking his head. "Anita." He had a bleak look on his face. *Doggonit, she had felt so good in his arms.* "She won't even talk to me because of how I acted when we met at the wedding. I don't even know where to start in trying to convince her I'm not the horrible person she thinks I am. But I could really…you know."

Jason was laughing at him again. "Well, brother, as you well know, I went through all that with Jaci. And as a matter of fact, you didn't help by trying to run her off. So, you're just getting payback. But, you still have some things to work on. That's what you need to be doing."

"Like what?" Ron asked, belligerently. "I'm a hard-working, church going, reasonably decent looking man. I don't drink, chew or smoke. What's wrong with me?"

"That's for you and the Lord to work out. But one place that comes to my mind where you might start is with your child. Bone of your bone and flesh of your flesh. It's not right to ignore that child's existence, Ron. Here you are waiting for my kids to be born so you can be the doting uncle, and you have a child of your own that you won't even acknowledge. Something is wrong with that picture, Ron."

"I can't go there, Jason. That child shouldn't be here as far as I'm concerned. And the only reason it's here is because of a conniving, greedy woman. Now that's what I call wrong."

"Maybe so, but the fact is, the child is here. Two wrongs don't make a right."

"And a right on my part won't erase her wrong," Ron argued stubbornly.

Nita left Jaci's house as soon as she finished cooking. Ron's presence unsettled her in ways she didn't know how to deal with. She wanted to hold onto her grudge against him, but she'd seen sides to him that surprised her, and discovered she could actually like him if she let herself. Plus, the attraction between them was hard to deny.

Over the next few days, for fear of running into Ron again, she avoided Jaci's house. She worked on the Foundation, which she had named, 'Help and Hope', and was holding phone meetings with some people Ramona had recommended for the board.

Joel came home for the weekend, and they spent a lot of time talking about Mikey. Nita confessed that she spent many sleepless nights worrying about him, and was plagued with fears of him lying dead somewhere. "I'm thinking about hiring a private investigator."

While Joel went out that evening with Patrick, she started cooking up some food for him to take back with him. As she cooked, she prayed, asking God to guide her regarding Mikey. She decided to wait a while before getting an investigator to look for him.

The telephone interrupted her cooking. She looked at the caller I.D. and didn't recognize the number, although she could tell from the area code that the call was from the Dallas area. She assumed it was a call for Joel, who was constantly pursued by a variety of girls.

"Hello," she answered, a tinge of impatience in her voice.

"Anita?"

82

She didn't recognize the voice. "Yes, this is Anita."

"Well, hello there. This is Tyson. How are you?"

"Oh. I'm fine, and yourself?"

"Great, now that I'm talking to you. You left town without telling me. I had to get the information from your attorney after convincing her we had unfinished business. And here I am, still waiting to hear back from you on our dinner date."

"Yes, but I did tell you that's totally unnecessary."

"You're missing the point, Anita. Frank, rest his soul, was my client and I respect that, but Frank's gone now. He left a very attractive and intriguing woman behind, and I would like to get to know that woman in a more personal way. Am I making myself clear?"

She was so dumbfounded that it rendered her speechless. She had hoped he would forget about her after she showed no interest in him. Evidently she had been out of circulation for so long that the men she was encountering were able to catch her off guard – the goon on the cruise, Ron, and now, Tyson. She didn't know how to deal with any of them.

"I . . . uh . . . honestly don't believe I would feel comfortable with that, considering your relationship with Frank."

"Like I said, Frank is gone. I know he was your husband, but I also know the kind of husband he was to you. I hope you won't let any unwarranted loyalty toward him ruin your life now. You're a young, beautiful woman with hopefully a lot of years of life ahead of you."

"Believe me, that's not happening. I'm getting on with my life, Tyson."

"Then how about dinner? I can be there in three or four hours. I promise you a wonderful evening, because I'm hoping this will be the first of many."

"No, thanks. Like I said, I'm not particularly interested in going out with you, Tyson."

"Anita, don't say no, please. I've gone to all the trouble of finding your number, then getting my nerve up to call you. I'm going to be really disappointed if you say no."

"Tyson, let me remind you that you're not on my list of favorite people."

"I know that. Which is exactly why I'm trying so hard to change that. Please, Anita, give me a chance to redeem myself."

She remembered her recent loneliness and boredom. If nothing else, it would give her something to do and an opportunity to get in some much needed practice in dealing with men. She wasn't attracted to him at all despite his good looks, but maybe it would take her mind off of Ron Gilmore. "Hmmm, let me think about it."

"Are you sure I can't convince you to let me come this weekend? Like I said, I can be there in just a few hours."

"No, I'll stick to my plan, and I won't be pushed into doing something I don't want to do. Unless you want to move further up to the top of that unfavorable list."

He laughed uproariously. "You are something else. I can't wait to get to know you better, and spend some time with you. So, will you call me next week? If you don't, I'll be calling you, uh, if that's okay. I'm finding out I have to tread carefully with you."

She smiled. "Like I said, I'll think about it, Tyson." She hung up the phone before he could say anything else.

"Umph, umph, umph!" Nita shook her head. "Imagine that. Frank would be doing summersaults in his grave if he knew his buddy was making a move on me."

She threw another load of Joel's dirty laundry into the washer and went back to preparing containers of food for him. Afterwards, she decided to call Frank, Jr., hoping to catch him before he went out for the evening.

"Hi Son, how are you? I haven't talked to you in a while. You doing okay?"

"Yeah, Mom, I'm fine. Just trying to keep the grades up to par. I'm loving it here, and I'm really glad I went ahead and transferred. I'm thinking about changing my major too."

"Yes, you told me all that in your last e-mail. I'm glad things are going well, but take your time before you make any major decisions. Sometimes, your first choice is the one closest to your heart. Others tend to come for other reasons."

"I appreciate that, Mom, and I miss you. How are you liking it in Houston?"

"Like you, I'm loving it. It's so good to be near my cousins, and have new things to do and look forward to." She told him about the Foundation and other things she was planning.

"Do you like your house?"

She wondered about his question, knowing he didn't agree with her moving out of their home in Dallas, and had found one excuse after the other not to visit her. "Frankie, I love my condo. It's spacious, but not too big. There's enough room for you boys to spread out and relax when you're here, but small enough to have a cozy feel to it."

"Well, I know JoJo is eating you out of house and home."

She laughed. "As a matter of fact, I'm cooking food for him to take back tomorrow."

"Mom, I'm going to come see you soon, I promise. I just, uh, haven't been able to do it yet. I understand why you felt you had to sell the house, but that was home for me, and I have to work through that."

Saddened, she understood. "Okay, Son. By the way, Joel and I have spent some time this weekend trying to locate Mikey. Not knowing where he is, and how he's doing is really weighing heavily on me. I'm considering hiring an Investigator to look for him."

"Mom, don't worry, Squeak can take care of himself."

Nita smiled at the nickname Frankie and Joel started calling Mikey when his adolescent voice started changing and his words often came out squeaky.

"He might act crazy, but he has the same survival instincts you taught all of us. I've been trying to reach him too. Maybe it'll finally penetrate his thick skull that he has a family who cares about him. I know I'ma kick his behind when he does show up."

Nita laughed again. "That's the same thing Joel keeps saying. But as far as I'm concerned, I just want to hug him and tell him how much I love him."

"You do that all the time with your e-mails, Mom – if he's reading them. I know they always come at the right time for me."

"I'm glad to hear that, Son." She was choked up because Frankie hadn't ever been good at expressing his feelings. "Well, listen, you can always call me if you need to. You know that."

"Yeah, I know. I'll try to do that more often, okay?"

"Okay, Son. I'm so glad I caught you before you left for your hot date – I know you have one, so I'll let you go get ready. Have fun, and re…"

"I know. 'Remember who I belong to." He finished her routine statement.

C.J. and the baby came by Sunday evening after Joel left. C.J. had been so tied up with her job and the baby situation that they hadn't talked in a while. After catching up on everything, the conversation worked it's way around to Jaci.

C.J. said, "Girl, I feel so sorry for Jaci. She is so miserable these days. I'll be glad when she has those babies so she can get comfortable again."

"Yeah, she's pretty miserable, but that's something you can't rush. The other day, Jaci had me stretched out trying to fix fried sweet potatoes the way Grammy used to cook them. She said she had been craving them for days. I tried, but they just didn't taste like Grammy's."

C.J. laughed. "Well, Jaci loved them, so you're going to have to do some more for her. She said Jason and Ron ate them all before she got her fill of them."

"Oh, Lord, I should have known that. Ron was sitting there waiting for me to get them ready, and I thought Jason was going to throw him out of the house when he got there."

"Yeah . . . that's an on-going thing for those brothers. Ron hangs out there more than he does at his own place, but I understand. Have you ever noticed the atmosphere in their home?" C.J. asked. "You don't have to wonder why everyone likes to be there."

"You are so right. You can just feel the warmth and love there that seems to emanates off of Jaci and Jason. There's just something special about their love for each other."

"Umm Hmm! There's love, but there's also a tenderness between them. You can tell they cherish each other and what they have together, and they don't take it for granted."

Nita sighed. "Thank God they were both mature enough to know what they wanted, to recognize it when they found it, and to know they both have to depend on God to keep it."

"Now that's where the blessing is – keeping the Lord at the center of the relationship," C.J. said. "The rest of us sure did blow it, didn't we?"

"Yeah, girl. Big time!" Nita agreed.

"Speaking of Ron. I hear y'all were going after it so hot and heavy you almost set fire to Jaci's kitchen. What's up with that?"

"Nothing, girl. Just Ron, the playboy in action," Nita answered.

C.J. gave her a searching look. "You sure about that? Jaci didn't get that impression."

"Yep. I'm sure."

The following week Tyson called and convinced her to go out with him that weekend. "But this is only on a trial basis because I'm not sure I should be doing this," she told him.

"I promise you won't regret it," Tyson answered.

Things went surprisingly well on her date with Tyson, and in fact, he returned for the next several weekends. It was one thing to go out with him, but in reality, she still didn't know if she liked him all that much. He brought too many memories of Frank to her mind, and his aggressiveness didn't help. He was constantly trying to give her advice about what she should or shouldn't do, and still trying to convince her that her move to Houston had been a mistake. But low and behold, she had a social life! At least that was Joel's amused take on it.

CHAPTER EIGHT

Ron was running late. He turned onto the 610 Loop and was thankful to see that traffic seemed to be moving, but he was still ten minutes away from the restaurant. He pushed a button on his cell, and a few seconds later Pastor Robinson's deep voice filled the interior of the SUV.

"Ron? Where are you, dude? I hope you're not going to tell me you have to cancel. I'm already at the restaurant and ready to order."

"Hi, Pastor Robinson, just letting you know I'm on my way. I was late leaving my building site, but I'm just a few minutes away."

"Alright then. See you in a little bit."

It wasn't long before Ron wheeled into the parking lot, found an empty space and walked briskly into the restaurant where Pastor Robinson was waiting. It was their regular meeting place to talk about the building project Ron was handling for the church, but Ron knew to expect the Pastor to do a little mentoring.

After they ordered, Ron presented a schedule that showed the status of the project and answered numerous questions the Pastor had. By the time their food arrived, they were ready to move on to other things.

The pastor didn't beat around the bush. "So, Ron, how are things going with you?"

Ron sighed. "Well, I hate to admit it, but not too good." He produced a weak smile. "And I have to tell you, that sermon about making God sick is still haunting me."

The Pastor laughed hilariously, then said, "So you think you're making God sick, huh?"

"I have a question," Ron said. "Is there a reason a man attracts a certain kind of woman? Is it because of some weakness in him?"

The Pastor chuckled. "God is working on you, Man. He's been working on you for a while now. So what kind of women are we talking about?"

"I hate to say it, but it's as if every woman I get involved with now is dishonest, deceitful, and out for what she can get."

"Do you think you sub-consciously attract these women because they fit into the kind of lifestyle you enjoy?"

Ron was thoughtful, then said, "A few months ago I would have agreed with that, but as you know I've been going through some things over the last months. That lifestyle is just not working for me anymore. I'm ready to explore life with different, more Christian-minded women. But either the woman's phony, or if she's for real, she doesn't believe I am."

"Uh, huh. So, tell me, are you thinking about possibly finding a wife?"

The question made Ron squirm. It was something that he couldn't bring himself to admit yet. After a long pause, he replied, "Maybe. I guess it's about time."

Pastor Robinson grinned and gave him a pointed look. "Hard to come to grips with that, huh? Well, you know you can't change the women, so that leaves you. You have to submit yourself to God, work toward becoming the man He wants you to be, and trust Him to send the wife He wants you to have. Now, it's not going to be easy. You've been going in the same direction as the devil a long time. So if you think that rascal is going to be happy about you trying to turn around, you're wrong. He's going to fight you with everything he can."

"So what do I do? Are you saying I won't be able to do it?"

"No, not at all." Pastor Robinson grabbed his iPad and punched some keys, then handed it to Ron. On the screen was a passage of scripture from First Corinthians 10:13.

Ron read the scripture, then looked up with a frown on his face. "I don't understand."

"God wouldn't tell you to do something and then not give you the strength you need to do it. You're going to have to walk this out with the Lord, Ron, and it's not going to be easy. I'll e-mail more scriptures to you when I get back to the office. I want you to confess them several times a day, because they are weapons that will help you conquer weaknesses. Be as serious about it as you would if you were taking a life-saving medicine. You think you can do that?"

"Yeah, I guess I'll have to."

"But the first thing you'll have to do is go before God, ask for forgiveness for the kind of lifestyle you've led, repent, and commit to turning around."

Ron groaned. "I have to do that? I don't know, Pastor Robinson."

"Now you know you do. If you know to do better and don't, it's a sin. Follow King David's example. You can find his prayer of repentance in Psalm fifty-one."

"Okay. Put that one on the list you're going to send," Ron said, with a frown.

Jason and Jaci hadn't convinced Ron to accept his role as 'daddy' to Chantal's baby. He knew they were right - it wasn't the child's fault - but as far as he was concerned, that was beside the point. He didn't know if the child was male or female, and didn't care. He had no plans to ever see Chantal again, or her child either. But his plans were about to change.

A couple of days after his lunch with Pastor Robinson, he got a phone call from Samuel Morris, a corporate executive for an oil company. He told Ron he was the father of one of Chantal's children, and that he had been seeking full custody of his four year old son for a long time without any success. He knew his child didn't live with her, but whenever he called to insist on his visitation rights, she evaded him until she could get the child to the apartment that he helped pay for. He finally hired a private investigator to keep her under surveillance.

One night the Investigator called Samuel and told him to meet him at a housing project that he had followed Chantal to a couple of times. He wasn't sure, but suspected that was where she kept the children. When Samuel got there, the Investigator led him to an apartment where he was sickened by what he found.

When he and the Investigator pushed the door open and walked in, an intoxicated man appeared to be engaged in inappropriate behavior with a girl of about eight, who was swiftly flung away from him when he noticed the men had entered the apartment. Samuel immediately called the police, while the Investigator took pictures. Several other children, including his son, were crowded around a large screen television, while a tiny baby on a battered sofa was crying and sucking hard on an empty bottle that had been propped up under her mouth. The intoxicated man was the only adult there, and Samuel kept him there without much effort. After the police arrived, he told them of his suspicions that the man had been sexually abusing the little girl. The children were turned over to CPS, and eventually, several other adults were arrested.

Ron had been unaware that Chantal even had other children, but Samuel had forced her to give him the names of all of the fathers of her children, then made it his business to locate them.   He informed them of the conditions the children were living in, and strongly encouraged them to step up and take responsibility for their children, and help him send Chantal to jail.

As he listened, Ron was filled with anger and self-depreciation at his own lack of judgment. Everything he was learning about Chantal showed she was rotten through and through. Too late, he was finding out what happens when you pick up women in clubs and have no interest in learning anything about them.

Samuel informed him of all the Investigator had discovered. Chantal survived by using her looks and an expertly erected façade of sophisticated intelligence to attract wealthy men. Her objective was to have babies by these men, then extort and squeeze them for money to support her exorbitant lifestyle, while the children were left in the care of others and neglected.

"Man, I admit I'm ashamed of myself," Samuel moaned. "If I hadn't been out chasing women irresponsibly, she wouldn't have been able to use me to bring an innocent child into the world. It pains me that my son has suffered because of my stupidity."

Sickened and distressed by what he heard, the following morning Ron found his way to the county home for neglected and abused children. After producing a copy of the birth records and DNA report that Chantal had proudly thrown in his face – indicating that he was the father of a female infant, he was led to a room filled with babies.

When Ron looked down at the tiny scrap of humanity the CPS authorities said was his, he broke down in tears. The poor little baby was so frail, it was easy to see she hadn't been getting enough to eat. The clothes she wore were old and stained, and way too big for her little body. The little face he looked into was somehow familiar, and he realized with shock, that it was because she looked like him. He cried harder. How could he have deserted his own child and left her in the hands of the terrible woman who had birthed her? It was a good thing she was already in jail, otherwise he'd be tempted to find her and do her some harm. He had paid big bucks to that woman to take care of this child.

But what really disturbed him was having to admit his own failure toward the child. During the baby's few months of life, both of her parents had failed her. Now, here she was, with two able bodied, intelligent parents, in a county home for abandoned and neglected children, half starved, and the most pitiful thing Ron had ever seen.

Tears ran down Ron's face. He walked over to a wall, leaned his face against it, and gave into the sobs that racked his body. He finally walked back to the crib and clumsily picked the tiny baby up and hugged her. "I'm sorry! I'm so sorry for failing you. You didn't deserve how you've been treated. He hugged the squirming baby tight against him. "I'm going to do better, I promise." He gently laid the baby back down and walked out of the building to his car. He sat there a long time. He didn't know what to do, but knew he couldn't leave the baby there.

He was finally able to get himself together enough to go back in and ask the people in charge what he needed to do to be able to take the baby home with him. He left to purchase an infant car seat, then returned to the home to get the baby whose name they informed him, was Destiny. Immediately, he knew Chantal had chosen that name out of some perverted need to show him she was in control. As soon as he was in the car with the yelling baby, he had no idea what to do. He hadn't thought beyond the point of getting her out of that place.

"Lord, what have I done?" Ron moaned, as he sat behind the wheel of his car listening to the screaming baby. To say his life was a gigantic mess was putting it mildly. He examined the emotions running through his mind...anger, hurt, frustration, fear. But it all came down to the basic question: What in the world was he going to do with a baby?

Chantal had been arrested for neglect and child endangerment, welfare fraud, and a list of other crimes. He hoped she would be in jail a long time.

But thankfully, she had been convinced by someone - probably Samuel - to relinquish her parental rights so her children would have the opportunity for possible caring, loving and permanent homes. Now as he sat there in agony, Ron was tempted to take Destiny back inside the home and beg them to do whatever they felt was best. But something...he didn't understand what...made it impossible for him to follow that urge.

His desperation led him to his parents' house, hoping they would help him. He should have known better. His mother grudgingly took the time to go shopping with him to purchase a few necessities he would need for the baby, but his pleas that she help him take care of Destiny fell on deaf ears. And of course, his dad was full of I told you so's.

"You've made your bed, now sleep in it. It's about time something happened to make you grow up and act like a man. I'd say this is it. Now you better handle your business."

He didn't need to hear that right now. He needed help. He left his parents filled with more anger and more desperation. He knew Jason and Jaci were tied up in their own baby issues so any help from them was out of the question. No way would Jason let him dump the baby on them. He headed home, still without a clue as to what to do with this baby, and no one to help. He thought about his aunt and uncle, but since uncle Stanley's health wasn't the best, he knew he couldn't go there. He searched through the file of his mind…surely there was someone he could call on for help, but not one person came to mind.

He thought about going through his contact list of women. "Surely I can get one of the women I've dated to come over and help me." The baby finally fell asleep, giving him the opportunity to explore who he could call from his list. But when Shayla's name popped up, he realized that would only open a different can of worms.

But he had to do something! He had picked the baby up around eleven this morning. It was almost three now. His mother had fed and changed her, but it would only be a matter of time before she would wake up and need something he didn't know how to provide.

Right on cue, the baby's screams kicked in. Ron picked her up and tried to comfort her. "Oh Lord, what a mess!" He knew he was in trouble when he started praying without even thinking about it. "Father, help me, please. And if You can't see Your way to help me, then help this baby because I don't know what to do with her. I don't even know how to change her diaper, and she smells like she needs some help right now."

Hearing his voice, the baby stopped crying and looked up at him expectantly. Ron gave a sigh of relief, but it was only a short reprieve and it wasn't long before she started screaming again. He'd thought a while ago that his life was a mess, but he hadn't known the half of it. A baby! It didn't take a whack upside his head to know he was in deep trouble, and so was this little baby who was dependent on him.

The baby - his baby - continued to yell her head off. "How can so much noise come from something so tiny?" He questioned. But he had no idea what to do to stop it. He felt the pressure of tears behind his eyeballs, and knew he had to do something. He grabbed the hastily bought bag of items his mother had insisted he needed and headed out the door.

CHAPTER NINE

Almost two weeks had passed since Nita had run into Ron Gilmore. On the days when Jaci assured her that Ron wouldn't be coming around, she would go over and cook dinner.

Today Nita was cooking the steak and gravy, mashed potatoes and biscuits Jaci had asked for, and was almost finished when the doorbell at the back door began ringing incessantly.

"Now who is ringing that doorbell like that?" Jaci asked, with a frown. "Can you see who it is, Nita, because it doesn't look like they're going to stop."

Nita went to the door and stumbled back in surprise when Ron pushed past her with a baby in his arms. "Ron?" She followed him into the family room with a puzzled look.

"Ron!" Jaci said, trying to stand up. "What . . . whose . . . baby is that?"

"Y'all got to help me," Ron said, in a voice filled with desperation. "I don't know what to do with her, and she won't stop screaming."

"Ron, what are you doing with this baby?" Nita asked. "Where's her mother?"

Without answering, he pushed the baby into Nita's arms, collapsed into a chair, and dropped his head into his hands. "She's mine," he finally said. "Her mother is in jail where I hope she stays for a long time." He waved his hand toward where Nita stood with the baby. "Look at this pitiful little child - nearly starved, and smelling and looking like something dogs wouldn't touch."

Nita looked down at the baby and noted he was right…the child did look pitiful. Her heart broke, and tears came to her eyes. "But, what are you going to do with her?"

"Nita, I don't know!" He drew a frustrated breath. "I can't take care of her, and I can't find anybody who will help me."

"What about your mother?" Jaci asked. "Won't she help you?"

"All she would do was go with me to a store to buy diapers and milk and a couple of things for her to wear. Both of my parents are of the opinion that she's my problem, not theirs."

"When did you get her?" Nita asked, as she gently shook the baby, then searched in the bag Ron had tossed to the floor and pulled out a half-empty bottle. She stuck the bottle in the baby's mouth and walked over to a chair to sit down.

"This morning." He told them the whole story with a look of shame. "When I saw her at that place, I just couldn't leave her there. But now I don't know what to do with her."

Jaci looked as though she was about to cry. "Oh Lord, Ron. You know I would help you if I could, but look at me – I'm already about to burst at the seams with babies. Can't you ask one of your lady friends to help until you can make some other arrangements?"

"Naw. That would only open the door to complications that I don't need right now."

"Do you have anymore milk?" Nita asked. "She's hungry. When did you last feed her?"

"There's a couple more bottles in there. But the way she's going through it, that's not going to last long. And it must be going straight through her because she smells awful."

"Yes, she does smell kind of bad," Nita said, as she got another bottle then pulled the diaper back to take a peek. "Whoo! She's way past due for a new diaper, because this one is full. Ron, you need to change her."

"Aww-Naw! Uh, uh! I ain't hardly gon' be dealing with what's off in there. Mom put a new diaper on her and tried to show me how to do it, but I'm not doing that."

Nita and Jaci looked at each other and collapsed laughing. "Brother, you have a lot to learn and a short time to do it," Jaci told him. "It's going to take some time for you to get her into a nursery, and you can't throw her off on just anybody. In the meantime, that leaves you, daddy." She held her stomach, still laughing. "I can't wait for Jason to get here and see this," she gasped.

"Oh, God," Ron groaned. "I'll never hear the end of this." He covered his face with his hands, groaning even louder. "I have an important business trip scheduled tomorrow. I've put it off because of all I've been dealing with, but finally thought it was okay to go ahead and schedule it. Now, what am I going to do?"

Nita was smiling at the smelly little baby, who was looking up at her with a smile, now that she had appeased her hunger a little. "What's her name, Ron? And how old is she?"

"Her name is Destiny. She's about three months old."

"She's hardly larger than a newborn, so it's apparent she hasn't been getting enough nourishment. You need to hurry up and make an appointment with a pediatrician and get her checked out so you'll be able to get her into a nursery. I bet that woman didn't even take this baby in to get the shots she needs. I don't know the whole story, but there's no excuse for this." Nita had a look of dislike for Destiny's mother on her face.

"Yeah, I'd like to give her a good kick in the rump, if I could get my leg up high enough to do it." Jaci said, with a look of disgust. "What about her other children?"

"Well, the dude who called me has his son, but I don't know about the others," Ron said, scowling.

Jaci ripped into him. "Now see, Ron, this is what we've been trying to tell you. Why in the world did you get mixed up with this woman? You should have known better. It's been one thing after the other because you refused to listen. I just…"

He held his hand up. "Jaci." He sighed, heavily. "I've already heard it from Mom and Pops. And nobody is telling me anything that I don't already know myself. Honestly, she's a beautiful woman, very articulate, always dressed to the nines and liked to have fun…all the things I pay attention to. Our only mention of children was that we would do whatever it takes to prevent them. When I knew anything, she was in my face, telling me I was going to be a daddy."

Nita stood with the baby in her arms and gave Ron a piercing look. "Well, you did it this time, didn't you, playboy?" She turned to Jaci. "If you don't mind, I'd like to give her a bath."

Jaci groaned, gratefully. "Oh, thank you, Nita. Just go upstairs and look into the first bedroom on the right. There's all kinds of baby stuff in there, and you're welcome to use any of it. And Ron, you need to go with her and try to learn everything you can, because brother, you might as well face the facts…you are in deep stuff."

Ron reluctantly followed Nita up the stairs and watched as she selected what she needed. They went into an adjoining bathroom where Nita ran warm water into the face bowl and gently slid the baby into it. Destiny gurgled in enjoyment and gave Nita a gummy smile. "This baby is way too small for her age, Ron," Nita said, as she bathed her. "What was that woman thinking…starving this child like that. Makes me so angry."

Ron looked on sadly. "Yeah, me too, but at least that's all behind her now. She'll never be hungry again if I have anything to do with it."

Nita patted the baby dry, then found some cream for diaper rash among Jaci's baby supplies and smoothed some of it on Destiny's irritated bottom. Then she rubbed in lotion and powdered her all over before putting on a diaper and slipping her scrawny little body into one of the sleepers Ron's mother had thought to get. She gently brushed Destiny's now fresh spikes of hair and wished she had a ribbon to put on it. She tried to hand the baby to Ron, who backed up and refused to take her.

"Uh, Uh! I might drop her," he said, shaking his head.

"Nope, daddy-o, you're going to have to learn, and now is as good a time as any to start." She pushed Destiny into his arms, and right away, the baby began to scream, and Ron looked like he was about to join her.

Nita cleaned up and told Ron she was going to throw the clothes the baby had been wearing in the trash, then led the way back downstairs.

"Wow! She looks so much better," Jaci exclaimed. "I can hug her and give her a kiss now," she said, reaching to take the baby from a grateful Ron.

"Yes, she's precious, and she really enjoyed that bath. She didn't start crying until I gave her to Ron. I don't think she trusts him not to drop her," Nita stated with a chuckle.

Destiny was still screaming, and Jaci shook her head and said, "Here, Nita. I think she's only going to be happy with you."

Nita took her and sat down. "Hey, sweetheart, what's up with all that noise?" Destiny looked up at her, smiled and settled contentedly in her arms like she belonged there.

"Would you look at that? Destiny thinks she's found her mommy," Jaci said, smiling.

"Oh, no," Nita responded. "Destiny has a mother, and I ain't her. So let's discontinue that thought immediately."

But Ron, who had been sitting quietly, looked at Nita with excitement. "Nita, I know it's a lot to ask, but…" he hesitated, as though unsure how to continue. "I need your help, and Destiny needs your help. I don't have anyone else I can ask at this point, and like I said, I have a business trip tomorrow, and will have to be away for at least a couple of days – maybe more. Will you help us? I'll pay you well, and will also pay for anything else you think she might need. I know she needs more clothes, food, diapers, and all that stuff that Jaci has upstairs for her babies." His hands were spread out beseechingly toward Nita as he pleaded. "Well?"

"Gosh, I don't know, Ron. It's been a long time since I had full care of a baby. That's a big responsibility, and we don't even know if she has any health issues. What if she gets sick? I couldn't even get medical attention for her."

"That's easily solved," Jaci said. "All Ron has to do is give you a medical power of attorney, giving you the right to obtain any medical care she might need. But really, I'm thinking all this child needs is lots of TLC and food, and she'll be fine. And Nita, you would be helping me as well, because I would do it if I was able. You've raised three children of your own, and I dare say, you didn't know the first thing about taking care of them either - at least the first one - and they all turned out okay with their big old selves."

Ron knew the right and responsible thing to do was cancel his trip, but his haywire, overloaded emotions were telling him he needed some space to think and pray about a solution. If Nita could give him that time, he would take it. "Please, Nita," he begged. "I wouldn't ask if this wasn't an emergency, but even if I didn't have my business trip, I wouldn't know how to take care of her. If you don't want to do it for me, will you do it for Destiny?"

Somehow – Nita wasn't quite sure how – she left Jaci's house with a baby that day. She and Ron stopped on the way to her condo, and bought everything she could think of that the baby would need. Ron helped her unload, then left, leaving Nita and Destiny looking at each other. One of them wore a big gummy smile, and the other a 'what was I thinking' look.

Over the next few days, Nita and Destiny went on a few shopping excursions, which Nita thoroughly enjoyed. She continued her visits with Jaci, with Destiny in tow. Jaci couldn't believe the change in the baby, who grinned most of the time now – as long as she had Nita in her sight.

When Nita took the baby by to meet C.J., she was expecting to get an ear full from her outspoken cousin. But C.J. only advised Nita not to become too attached to the baby.

"Believe me, I'm speaking from experience," C.J. said, with sadness. "I know if Geordie's parents ever get their acts together and take him, I'm going to be one messed up woman," she said, shaking her head in disgust as thoughts of her brother and sister-in-law's irresponsible behavior filled her mind. "Of course, I tell myself I don't have a choice in keeping him, but I know I'm only deceiving myself, not to mention, I'm enabling them to be lousy parents. So where is this baby's mama?"

"In jail," Nita answered. "According to Ron, she'll be there a long time for child abuse, neglect, abandonment, fraud, and other crimes I can't even think of."

"Girl, that woman will be out of there before you know it. The prisons are so crowded, they look for excuses to let people out. If she didn't kill someone, she won't be in there long. And you know she's going to come looking for this baby when she gets out."

"Well, Ron did say she relinquished parental rights to all her children, including Destiny. And I don't think Ron or the County will let her renege. The conditions those children were living in were deplorable and disgusting, and there was child molestation going on. She won't get Destiny back."

"I hope you're right. But Nita…that doesn't mean Ron won't marry someone to provide a mommy for Destiny. Ron won't hardly be trying to raise this baby by himself. So, I'm just saying, be careful and don't get too attached." She gave Nita a hard look. "Or is my warning coming too late and you already love her?"

Nita sighed. "I think I fell in love with her the moment Ron pushed her into my arms."

"So, how long are you going to be playing mommy to her? What about your plans for working in a ministry, going to school and getting your Foundation off the ground?"

"I really don't know. Ron and I didn't work out any details because he was in a hurry to go on a business trip. He's called a couple of times, but we only talked about Destiny."

"Well, I hope he knows he's got to come with some money. He can't be expecting you to take care of her financial needs too. Babies are expensive."

"No, he understands that," Nita answered. "In fact, he gave me a credit card and told me to use it for whatever she needs, and that's what I'm doing. Although, when the bills come in, he might have a conniption fit, because Destiny has a full wardrobe, cases of milk, juice, cereal, bottles and diapers, blankets, and all the stuff that goes with a baby, plus, a portable baby bed. I love shopping for babies, and I never had the opportunity to shop for a baby girl."

C.J. laughed. "You've been having fun. But I'm sure she needed everything you bought, and will continue to, because there's always something else where babies are concerned." She laughed again. "I would love to see Ron's face when he sees those bills!"

Nita laughed with her, as she picked up Destiny, who was waking up. "It's going to be interesting to see his reaction. He also gave me several hundred dollars, and promised more when he returns."

C.J. sobered. "Looks like he's taking care of business. You have to appreciate that."

"Yeah, I guess so," Nita said, with a thoughtful look on her face. "There's still a lot to consider if I continue to keep her though. My boys' reactions for example."

"What if they don't like it? Will that change anything?"

"Nope," she said with certainty. This baby needs me and you know what? I need her. I know she's not mine, and that she can't replace the baby girl I lost, but her presence has filled up the empty places in my heart and home these last few days. Ron is a jerk in a lot of ways, but I've seen glimpses of a good person too. Considering the attraction between us, I admit I'm walking on a double-edged sword with the playboy and his baby, but I'm going to do it. And as far as my other plans go, I'll just play it by ear."

"Will she continue to live with you?"

"C.J., I don't know all that right now," Nita said, in exasperation."

"Well, like I said, be careful, Nita. I'd just hate to see you get hurt, and this situation is ripe with all kinds of ways for that to happen," C.J. said, sadly.

"I know. I'll just have to deal with it."

CHAPTER TEN

Ron dreaded what he knew was waiting for him when he returned from his business trip. He had been in his element the last few days, because he enjoyed the challenges his job gave him. It was a productive trip, and he was returning home with contracts for four different structures. It more than made up for the lucrative job he had lost. Although he wasn't hurting financially, he had the added responsibility of a baby now, and he meant to see that she received everything she needed. He would never forget the condition she had been in when he first saw her. "Lord, help me not to let that happen again," was his constant petition to God. But filed away in the back of his mind was the thought that perhaps there was a good family somewhere who might be looking for a baby to adopt.

Even though he was trying to take care of his responsibility to the baby, nothing had changed. He still didn't want a baby. Thank God Nita had agreed to take care of her while he went out of town, but now that he was back, the problem of what to do with her was starring him squarely in the face. He only hoped Nita would agree to keep Destiny if he paid her enough. But he didn't know enough about Nita or her circumstances to know if that was a viable arrangement. He was tempted to go to Nita's house as soon as he got off the plane to discuss it, but he was tired and weary from the trip, and in no state of mind to carry on a rational conversation. But he knew some decision regarding Destiny's future had to happen soon. He pulled his phone from his pocket and called Nita.

"Nita, hey. This is Ron. How is everything?"

"Fine. Destiny is eating and trying to grin at me at the same time. Are you back?"

"Yes, I am, and I know we need to talk, but honestly, I'm bushed right now. Do you mind if we do it tomorrow?"

"Sure, that's fine, Ron."

"Okay, I'll come by your place first thing tomorrow. Do you need anything?"

"No, not a thing, but let me warn you, you're probably going to have a stroke when you see your credit card bills."

Ron laughed. "I doubt it. I know she needs a lot of stuff, and Jaci has already told me that she'll continue to need things. So don't worry about that. I'm just thankful you're taking care of her for me."

"Actually, I'm glad to do it. I kinda love this little dumpling."

He was quiet for a moment, then after clearing his throat, said, "Glad to hear that. It's more than I can say about her, or her abrupt entrance into my life. I'm motivated by guilt more than anything else."

"That'll change when you start spending time with her. You'll see."

"Maybe." He answered in an unsure tone. "I'll see you tomorrow."

He started the arduous task of dealing with the heavy traffic to get to the freeway. He finally made it to Interstate 45, then headed north toward Highway Two Eighty-Eight where he found traffic at a standstill.

"Darn it!" he yelled. "I'd like to come this way just once and not encounter this mess!"

His ringing phone interrupted his tirade. He looked, and groaned – his mother. "Mom, hi. I can't talk now, I'm stuck in traffic. I'll call you later."

He drove the rest of the way home and tiredly pulled his briefcase and luggage from the black Navigator. He headed straight for his bedroom and shower, then fell into bed. He was in a deep sleep when the sound of the doorbell finally penetrated. He groaned and turned over, hoping whoever it was would leave. That didn't happen. The person laid on the buzzer, demanding a response. He threw on a robe, trotted down the stairs and snatched the door open with an aggravated look on his face. There stood a woman, hands on hips, and a stare as irritated as his. He looked at her closely, his sleep clouded eyes trying to place who she could be. "Yes?"

"Boy, move and let me in," she said, pushing past him. "And bring my bags in."

Ron's mouth fell open and he tried to rub the sleep out of his eyes. It sounded like…no, couldn't be. She was out of the country, following after some professor. But when he looked again, he saw it was indeed Monique – his long lost sister.

"Monique? What strange wind blew you in?" he asked, giving her a bear hug, then dragging several large pieces of luggage in.

"I've been traveling over twenty hours, give me a break with the questions." She looked around the two-story condominium. "Nice digs. How long have you been here?"

"About four years. How did you know where I live?"

"Your secretary told me. Thankfully, I was able to make her remember me. She told me Jason is expecting twins any day, so his house was out, and that left you, because truthfully, I'm not ready to deal with Mom and Pops yet."

"And where is the world renown professor?"

"I don't know. I left him in Dubai getting it on with one of his students."

"What? So, are you here for a visit, or are you back to stay?"

"I'm here to stay. I'm tired of that arrogant, pig-headed jerk. I've been dragged all over the world, waiting for him to marry me. Now, here I am, about to be over the hill and without a husband or children - and he decides he wants a younger woman so he can have lots of children."

Ron looked at her in amazement. "You mean he dumped you?"

"That's a rude way of putting it, but yes, that sums it up. I could have stayed and continued working at the university, but that was too restricting. It was time to come home."

"So what are you going to do?"

"If it's okay, I'd like to stay here until I can find a job and get my own place. I'm sure I can get a position at one of the local colleges, or one of the school districts. I'll try not to cramp your style too long."

Ron didn't feel like getting into what was going on in his life right now. Instead he said, "Look, I'm just getting back from a business trip and I'm bone tired. Just make yourself at home in one of the other bedrooms. I have some things to take care of first thing in the morning, and you'll probably still be knocked out when I leave, so I'll see you when I get back. Oh! and welcome home, Sis."

"Thanks, little brother. I knew I could count on you."

"You might revise that when you find out what's happening in my life."

The next morning, Ron talked to Jaci to get the name of the pediatrician she and Jason had selected to care for their babies. He then headed to Nita's house. He couldn't believe how nervous he was. Many issues about his future rested on the conversation he was about to have with Nita regarding the baby who had invaded his life.

When Nita opened the door, she was holding a very different looking Destiny. "Hi Ron. Come on in," she invited. And when he did, she immediately thrust the baby into his arms.

"How you doing, Nita? Hey, Destiny!" he said, looking at Destiny with an unsure smile. Destiny returned his look a few seconds before her face crumbled and she started screaming. "Oh, Lord, what's wrong with her?" He asked Nita with a concerned look.

"Nothing," she answered. "She just has to get to know you."

"How long is that going to take? I can't take this screaming."

Nita laughed. "Well, it depends on you, and how much time you spend with her. Come on in and make yourself comfortable. Want something to drink or eat?"

He looked up from the baby in his arms, and said, "Yes, to both. I didn't take the time to eat anything before I left home."

"I'll make you some toast and eggs. How's that?"

"Wonderful!" He answered with a huge smile. "Then, I guess we need to talk."

Nita played with Destiny while he ate, then put her down for a nap. "Okay, what are your plans for Destiny? She asked from across the table."

"That depends, Nita. Jaci told me you had been looking for something to keep you busy." He paused, looking uncomfortable. "So, I would like to offer you a job taking care of her until I can make some decisions. Is that possible?"

"Yes, I'll do it, but with some stipulations. I know she needs to spend time with you. So, you can't just leave her here and forget her. I'd expect you to keep her on the weekends, or whenever you're free. That'll give me a breather, and give you time to bond with each other."

"I don't know . . . " A doubtful expression covered Ron's face as he shook his head.

"And another thing," Nita continued. "When she's ready, and she won't be until she's checked out by a doctor, and she's been cleared, I would suggest you put her in day care at the church. I do have a life, and other things to do during the day. I'll drop her off in the mornings, and we'll coordinate who will pick her up. That way, she'll get to see you during the week."

He gave her a hard look. "I can see you've given this some thought. And I have a feeling you've also discussed this with Jaci and Jason."

She smiled. "Yes, and they've asked me to do two things. First, to help you by providing a stable home for Destiny, and two, to make sure you do more for her than throw money at her. In other words, they want you to be a daddy to her, Ron. Maybe it's time to put your playboy days behind you."

Anger swept through him at her words, but there was too much at stake for him to blow it. He stood and walked to the window overlooking a nice patio. After calming down at bit, he turned and spoke. "This is a nice place. Do you like it?"

"Yes, as a matter of fact, I love it. I love the layout and the spaciousness of it. And I also like the location. It's off the beaten track – surrounded by quiet residential streets and . . ." She noticed his tight expression. "Something bothering you?"

He walked back and sat down at the table, and gave her an angry look. "Yes, it bothers me that my family is putting their two-bit interference in this. I'm very capable of making my own decisions. And I certainly don't appreciate your playboy remark."

"Well, of course you're capable, Ron, but your family only wants what's best for you and Destiny. And I guess the truth hurts, huh?"

"How I live my life and handle my business is no concern of yours, or theirs either. Anyway, as I was saying, I need help because I don't know the first thing about taking care of a baby. And I'm just going to be honest about this, okay? I didn't ask for this baby, and I'm only doing what I can for her out of a sense of responsibility and guilt. I'm ashamed of myself for what she's had to go through but this business about her staying with me on the weekend is not acceptable. I'm not ready for that and I still plan to have a social life."

"Um hmmm." Nita said, in a way that let him know she had guessed at the social life concern. "Well, whether you like it or not, you're a parent with responsibilities that have to take priority over other things. I've also thought about a way to remedy your lack of knowledge about babies. My son will be here this weekend, and that will be a good time for you to come over so I can start teaching you how to care for her."

He ran her suggestion through his mind, recalling that his sister was at his place, and unless she had changed, she wreaked havoc wherever she was. "Why does your son have to be here? Is it that you don't trust me, or yourself?" He asked, recalling their hot embraces.

"My son was going to be here anyway, which is good, you can meet him, and to your other question, the answer is yes, to both of us."

He chuckled. "I appreciate your honesty because I was getting ready to slam you if you had lied," he said, giving her a knowing look. "Okay, I guess I'll have to give it a try since you're willing to help me. Anyway, I have a houseguest, so it may be good timing."

"Well, we'll see how it goes this weekend, then see if you feel comfortable enough to take her next weekend. Will you still have your houseguest then?"

"I don't know." He saw a question looming in her eyes about who his houseguest was, and knew exactly where her mind had gone. And because he was ticked off with her, he decided to let it go unanswered. *Let her stew!* "If it's okay I'd like to bring her by later today so she can meet you and Destiny."

"We'll be here, so I suppose it'll be okay," Nita replied in a clipped voice.

Her obvious annoyance had Ron struggling to keep from laughing. She wasn't as immune to him as she pretended. "Okay, I'll be going. I need to pick my guest up so we can run a couple of errands before coming back here."

Houseguest! "Is that what they're called these days?" Nita mumbled. She went back over her conversation with Ron and all she had agreed to, and decided - it was definitely one of those 'what was I thinking' days.

Fretting sounds from Destiny let Nita know nap time was over, and it was time for a diaper change and some food. She felt a flicker of hope when the phone started ringing as she was going to the crib to get the baby. With every phone call, she could never stifle the hope that it would be Mikey calling to let her know he was alive and well, and would be coming home. The disappointment she always felt when it wasn't him chipped away another piece of her heart.

"Mom!"

"Hey, Baby!" Nita answered with a smile. "Are you still coming home?" It wasn't Mikey, but Joel. Holding the phone in the crook of her neck, she prepared to feed Destiny, who was already smacking her lips in anticipation.

"I'm just calling to let you know I'm getting ready to get on the highway. I have some friends with me, and I'll have to drop them off, so I'll be a little later than usual getting home."

"Who are these friends, Joel? Do you know them well enough to travel with them?"

"Yeah, Mom, they're okay. In fact, they're young ladies, and one of them, I sorta like. The other one is from Houston and they're planning to hang out together this weekend."

"Oooh! It's like that, huh? Well I want to hear all about her."

"Okay, Mom. Now, I have to go pick them up, so we can get on the road. I just wanted to let you know what's going on, so you won't be looking for me too early."

"Alright. And I have a houseguest who's waiting to meet you."

"A houseguest? Who is it?"

"You'll just have to wait and see. You be careful, and I'll see you when you get here."

"Okay, Mom. Don't worry, I will."

Nita hung up the phone with a smile. "Lord, thank you for Joel, and I'm trusting that one day soon, I'll pick up the phone and it will be Mikey."

She finished feeding Destiny, played with her a while, then put her on a blanket on the floor to play. "And Father, I also thank you for this little one that You've sent into my life. Bless this child, Father." Destiny grinned as though she understood every word of Nita's prayer.

"I've got to prepare some refreshments for your daddy and his houseguest. Are you going to be a good girl for me?" She groaned when the phone rung again.

"Hey, Nita." It was Jaci. "Did you and Ron talk? How did it…Ohhh!…go? Ohhh!"

"Jaci? What's wrong? Are you having pains?" Nita asked in alarm.

"No, I'm alright. One of those rascals is just kicking hard. What about things with Ron?"

"Jace, are you sure it wasn't a labor pain?"

"Geez, every time I feel the least little twinge, y'all start thinking I'm in labor. I know a labor pain when I feel it."

Nita laughed. "Every labor experience is different, Jaci, and it has been a while since you felt a labor pain, so I wouldn't be so snippy about it, Missy. Anyway, things went okay with Ron, I guess. He agreed to everything, and offered me the job before I said anything."

"That's great, Nita. I truly believe that when he starts spending time with the baby, things will change. At least we're praying that will happen."

"Me too, Jace. He admits he doesn't want her, and is only acting out of guilt. You have to give him credit for being honest about it I suppose. And at least he's trying."

"Yeah, Ron's for real. He'll tell it like it is, and he's really not a bad person. I hate he got himself into this, but that can't be changed at this point. He mentioned something about putting her up for adoption, but I sure do pray he'll change his mind about that."

Nita's stomach sunk to her toes. "Oh no! Jaci, we can't let him do something like that!"

"We'll just pray about it. Hopefully the plan will work, and he'll grow to love her."

"Something just occurred to me," Nita said, thoughtfully. "He told me he has a houseguest. He wouldn't say who it is, but I know it's a woman. Do you think it could be someone interested in adopting the baby? Or, " her heart cracked a little, "someone he's considering marrying? He wants to bring her by to meet Destiny later this afternoon."

"A houseguest? Usually, he refers to his women as friends, and when one is staying with him, he doesn't mention it at all."

"Well, it's going to be interesting to find out who she is. I'd better get off, so I can get some kind of refreshments together for them. I'll come by tomorrow – if you're still there."

"Okay," Jaci answered. "Me and my load will probably still be around. Mama and daddy should be arriving sometime soon. Mama is frustrated. If it had been left up to her, she would have been here days ago, but daddy couldn't decide when he wanted to leave. I don't know why he finds it so hard to leave little old Riverwood for a few days."

They laughed. "Talk to you later, girl." Nita said, before hanging up.

Thankfully, she had gone shopping and stocked up on food for Joel to take back with him. She made sandwiches filled with chicken salad, smoked turkey and brisket, fruit and green salads, then mixed a lemon pound cake and put it in the oven. The phone rung again. "Am I ready to deal with him?" She questioned, when she saw Tyson's name on the caller I.D. She picked up the phone, not feeling the least little regret about what she was about to say to him."

"Hi, Anita. How are you?"

"I'm fine, Tyson, and yourself?"

"I'll be fine as soon as I see you this weekend. I'm going to fly in, so can you can pick me up at the airport?"

"Uh…look, Tyson, I have to change our plans for this weekend. I've taken a j.." A loud yell from Destiny interrupted her. The baby was playing with a toy and rolling around on the blanket. When she was full, dry, and happy, she loved to scream her enjoyment.

"What was that?" Tyson asked.

"That was Destiny. And I was saying I've taken on a job. I'm taking care of a baby."

"And why would you do something like that?" he asked, in a demanding voice. "You don't need the money, and even if you did, you could do something besides babysitting. I don't know why you agreed to do something like that. And why do you have to cancel our plans? Anita, this is totally unacceptable. I really don't like being pushed aside like this."

"Maybe we can plan something for another weekend."

"I'm very disappointed, Anita. I was really looking forward to seeing you this weekend." He sighed. "But I'm telling you now, keep next weekend open for me."

"I can't commit to that right now, Tyson. And I don't particularly care for your attitude. I lived with Frank over twenty years and had to endure his tyranny and abuse. I told you upfront that since the Lord has delivered me from that, I'm not going to be stupid and walk into that same type of relationship again. So let's get something straight right now. I do as I please, when I please. Don't ever think you can tell me what I can or cannot do. I have to go now. Goodbye."

Fuming, she hurriedly hung up the phone. "Geez! That dude is tripping. I don't know why I ever agreed to go out with him in the first place."

Two hours later, she was still waiting on Ron. When the doorbell rung, she was sure it was them. But when she opened the door, she found a delivery man standing there with a huge floral arrangement. She eagerly tore open the card, curious to see who it was from.

"Anita, please accept my deepest apology. Although my intent was to express my desire to spend time with you so we can get to know each other better and become friends, and hopefully, more, I realize that I overstepped some important boundaries because of my eagerness. I am not Frank, and anything I said that reminded you of him is not representative of who I am. Please forgive me, and give me another chance." Tyson

She grimaced. "Well, he is persistent."

Ron was disgruntled when he left Nita's house that morning. He wished for the luxury of going home to an empty house so he could sulk, but his sister's presence there nixed that. The next best thing was to make good use of the day, and he knew, even if Monique didn't, that it was time to let the rest of the family know she was back. Monique, who dreaded the explanations she knew would be demanded, wanted to hide out at his place until Sunday, when she would show up at their parents' house and surprise them.

But Ron knew if he went along with that, his family would come down on him, and he was in enough trouble. He talked her into going to see them today and getting it over with.

They first went to Jason's house, where Monique reunited with Jason and his son, Patrick, who had been barely a teenager the last time she saw him and was now in college. She hugged Jaci, welcomed her to the family, as well as the expected new arrivals.

Afterwards, they headed to Big Pat and Cecelia's home - and neither of them were anxious to see their parents. But Jason went with them to act as a buffer. When they all walked in, their parents lost it. There was much hugging and crying, and then, hugging Monique again, as they admitted they had almost lost hope of ever seeing her again.

Monique begged off on making long explanations, only stating that she was home for good, and she would tell them everything later. Surprisingly, they were so happy to see her that they agreed. Soon after that, Ron explained that he wanted to take her by Nita's house, then back to his house where she could get some more rest.

When Nita opened the door, she gave Monique a curious look before inviting them in. "Hey, Nita," Ron said. "I'd like to introduce my sister, Monique. Monique, this is Anita." The ladies shook hands, and Nita told them to have a seat, then offered them some refreshments.

Monique glanced around and stated, "I love your place."

Ron said, "Refreshments? I'm hungry! Don't you have any real food?"

"Didn't I just feed you this morning?" Nita asked Ron. "Y'all come on to the kitchen. I'm sure there's enough to fill you up, so help yourselves."

"Thank you, Nita," Monique said, as she grabbed a plate and filled it with sandwiches, salad and fruit. "I'm so hungry! I haven't had a good meal in days."

"It's been days since you had a good meal?" Nita asked curiously.

"Yes. I've been trying to relocate me and all my affairs from the mid-east to here. That's no easy task. Just the travel along is enough to nearly kill you. And when I finally got to Ron's house yesterday, my exhaustion was greater than my hunger. Then today, Ron insisted I visit my parents before coming here, and there was too much tension there for me to eat anything. So, I'm just getting settled and relaxed enough to enjoy some food. What do you have to drink?"

Nita went to refrigerator and pulled out pitchers of tea and lemonade.

"Thank you," Monique said, with a big smile, as she took a bite out of a sandwich.

While Ron piled food onto his plate, he speculated about the flowers he saw sitting on the dinning table. They hadn't been there this morning. Were they from a man? He looked at Nita. "Yeah, I appreciate this. I'll square things with you later. Is Destiny sleeping?"

"No, I don't think so, even though she's unusually quiet." Nita went into the family room and looked into the crib where she found Destiny fascinated by a mobile Nita had just put up over the crib that morning. Destiny let out a squeal of joy when she saw Nita, and mobile forgotten, she reached for her. Nita picked her up, and carried her into the kitchen. "Look, Destiny, we have company." Destiny grinned and bounced in her arms.

Ron reached for Destiny and gave her a hug. "Monique, this is my daughter. Destiny, this is your Aunt Monique. She's been away from the family seven or eight years."

Monique gasped, causing the food in her mouth to go down the wrong way. She started coughing and struggling for breath, while tears filled her eyes. "Daughter?!" She looked from Ron and Destiny to Nita, then back to Ron. "You jerk! Why didn't you tell me about this? I have this beautiful little niece, and nobody bothered to tell me?" She looked at

Destiny again. "I'm going to give you a hug, honey, but Auntie needs to finish eating and digest this news. Okay?"

Sighing heavily at Monique's scolding, Ron handed Destiny back to Nita and said, "Well, it's a long story, but the bottom line is, I'm not sure what I'm going to do with her."

Monique's eyebrows raised in question. "What do you mean you don't know what you're going to do with her? She's yours, isn't she?"

"Yeah, she's mine."

With her mouth full again, Monique started berating Ron. "You need your butt kicked from here to kingdom come, wherever that is. How're you going to sit here, in the presence of this baby and her mother and say that? That's low, Ron – even for you. What? You don't want to give up your womanizing ways? Is that it?"

Ron and Nita started laughing. "Nita's not Destiny's mother. Her mother's in jail. Nita's a friend who agreed to take care of her for me while I decide what I'm going to do." His eyes were on Nita as he spoke. "I don't know what I, or Destiny, would do without her."

Monique's eyes widened. "You mean you're not this child's mother?" She said to Nita around a mouth full of food. "Ron, at least your choice in women has improved. Those cows you were dealing with years ago would never do this."

"Well, I'm not one of his women," Nita quickly stated. "I'm recently widowed and just relocated to the city, so I'm kind of at loose ends right now. When Ron asked if I would do it, I agreed. Who wouldn't love to take care of this little sweetheart?" She said, hugging Destiny.

"So how long have you been a widow?" Monique asked.

"Not quite a year. I have three sons – all grown, or at least they think they are."

Monique looked incredulous. "What? You don't look old enough to have grown sons."

Nita laughed. "Well, they're college age. And I guess you can chalk the way I look up to genetics, because if my face reflected the kind of life I've had, it would tell a completely different story."

"Well, whatever the case, you're beautiful, and those green eyes are gorgeous – just like Jaci's. She looked at Nita closer. "As a matter of fact, you look a lot like Jaci."

"Understandable, since we're first cousins. And the green eyes are a family trait from our maternal grandfather's side of the family. Almost every child born into the family has them."

Monique sent a speculative look toward Ron. "What's wrong with you, brother? Have you gotten so jaded that a good woman doesn't appeal to you? You better recognize!"

"I don't need you to tell me how to recognize a good woman," Ron huffed. "But I do have a suggestion for you. Mind your own business."

"Now you know me better than that," Monique answered, as she picked up another sandwich and started eating again.

After they finished eating, they moved into the family room where Monique took Destiny from Nita and sat down to hug and kiss her.

Destiny sat quietly for a minute, looking at Monique with curiosity before she let loose with a scream, prompting Monique to hurriedly give her back to Nita. "Okay, I guess we have to get used to each other." She looked around the room. "This place is just beautiful, and so spacious. I hope I'll be able to find something like this."

"Well, talk to Jason. He's the one who found it for me."

"I'll do that," Monique answered. "By the way, would you happen to have a computer available? Now that I've rested a little, and my stomach is full, I need to check my e-mails."

"Sure," Nita said. "It's right in here." She showed her into the office that adjoined the family room. "Just over look all that junk scattered on the desk."

"I love this!" Monique exclaimed as she walked into the office with bookshelves lining two walls and a floor to ceiling wall of windows on another wall. "And it's right here next to the family room. This is just too perfect. How many rooms upstairs?"

"A master suite, two other bedrooms, a bathroom and a large linen closet."

"It's exactly what I would like to have." Monique said, still looking around.

Nita walked back into the family room where Ron had made himself comfortable on the sofa and was flipping through television channels in search of sports.

"I saw the flowers on the table. Are they from anyone significant?" He questioned. "And if so, are you certain that won't affect our arrangement?"

"I wouldn't have agreed otherwise. Have you seen Jaci today? I talked to her earlier and she was feeling some discomfort, but she denied it was labor pains."

"Yeah, Monique and I went by there a while ago. She seemed fine, but what do I know?"

He pulled his cell phone from his pocket and dialed a number. "Hey, Patrick, what's up, nephew?" After listening a minute, he yelled, "What? How long ago? What hospital?"

Nita, who was listening, was immediately standing over him asking "What's going on?"

Ron ended the call and told her that Jason had taken Jaci to the hospital. "They don't know, but they think she's in labor. Right before they left, Jaci's parents called and said they were almost here. Patrick will take them to the hospital when they arrive."

"I want to go," Nita said, excitedly.

"I do too," Ron answered.

But before they could make a move, Ron's phone rang. It was Jason, who told him that their parents, aunt and uncle, Jaci's daughter, Randi, Sister Sadie, and soon, Patrick with Jaci's parents would be crowded into the waiting room.

Nita shook her head. "Well, I think that's enough people. And I don't know if it's a good idea to take Destiny into that environment since we don't know if she's had her shots."

Ron stood. "I guess I'll head up there after I drop Monique off. She probably won't want to go since we have no idea how long this is going to take. Jason said it could be hours."

"You got that right," Monique called from the office. "I'm ready to crash again."

As they were getting ready to leave, the door leading from the garage opened and Joel came in, dragging two large laundry bags. He stopped when he saw the strangers standing in the family room with his mother. "Hi," he said, a questioning look on his face.

"Uh, Joel, this is Ron Gilmore and his sister, Monique. They're Jaci's brother and sister-in-law. Ron, Monique, this is my son, Joel."

"Hi, Joel, how are you?" Ron said, with an outreached hand.

"I'm fine," Joel answered, reaching to shake their hands, his face still full of questions. "Uh, What's going on, Mom? Who is that?" He asked, pointing to the baby.

Nita walked over to hug him. "This is Destiny Gilmore. Ron's baby girl," Nita said. "She's the houseguest I was telling you about over the phone."

Joel's eyes went from Nita to Ron, then back to Nita. "Oh." A troubling expression covered his face. "Why is she staying here?"

"I'll explain it all later. There's plenty to eat in the kitchen, and don't leave those bags in the middle of the floor."

"Okay, I'm . . . " His words trailed off as he searched Ron's face. "Hey, wait a minute. Did you say you're Ron Gilmore?"

"Yes, I'm Ron Gilmore. Why?"

"The famous architect?"

Ron smiled. "Yes, I am an architect."

"Wow! I don't believe this. My roommate and I were just reading about your designs in a magazine. He's an architect major, and I'm in engineering. Hey, do you think you could give us some pointers about what we can expect? That sure would be gre...."

Nita interrupted. "Don't bother Mr. Gilmore, Baby. He was just on his way out."

"Oh, okay. So you're going to be around, huh?" Joel asked Ron.

"Yep," Ron answered. "We'll get to talk."

"Cool. I can't wait to tell my buddy. But first, I eat."

"Nice kid," Ron said. "Are all your sons that friendly and protective? I can tell he's not comfortable with strangers here with you." A shadow crossed her face. She never answered.

After a few seconds, Ron said, "Are you sure you don't want to go?"

"Yes, I'm sure, but if you like, I can drop Monique off so you can go directly to the hospital," Nita offered. "I need someone up there who's going to keep me informed."

"Not necessary, but, if you're sure you don't mind, I'll take you up on it. That'll keep me from having to double back, because that hospital is in the opposite direction from my house."

"Okay, let's do that." She went toward the kitchen. "Joel, do you need anything? I'm going to drop Ms. Gilmore off."

"No, Mom. I'm going to eat, then make some calls. I'm in for the night."

"Okay, I'll see you in a little bit." She picked up the bag she kept filled with Destiny's stuff, grabbed a bottle from the refrigerator, her purse and cell phone, and led Monique out.

CHAPTER ELEVEN

As soon as the door closed behind them, the phone started ringing. Joel answered it, and responded to the man's greeting.

"No sir, she's not here right now. This is her son. Is there a message?" After listening for a minute, he said, "Oh yeah, Attorney

McPhearson, I remember you from when we met in your office after my dad died. Well, I'll tell her you called. Yes, I do see some flowers, so that must be them." He paused to listen again. "Oh, you know about the baby my mom's keeping? Yeah, Mr. Gilmore's baby. Ron Gilmore, the architect. Okay, I'll be sure and let Mom know you called to see if she got the flowers. You're welcome. Bye."

When Nita returned, and Joel told her about Tyson's call, she groaned. "Good grief! That guy is about to get on my nerves. Well, at least I don't have to call him, since you already told him I got his stinking flowers," she huffed.

Joel was chuckling. "Oh, man! I bet dad's turning over in his grave." His chuckle turned into laughter. "Nope. Dad ain't liking this at all. Well, what's up with you and Mr. Gilmore? Mr. McPhearson was asking questions about him and Destiny."

"Hmmm. I hope you told him it's none of his business. And I'm just taking care of Destiny for Ron until he can make other arrangements."

"You can shoot me that line, but I saw the way he was looking at you. The dude's interested, and so is that McPheason dude. I'ma keep my eye on those dudes."

"All in your imagination. Did Ron call yet? I really would like to know what's happening with Jaci." She placed Destiny on the blanket spread on the floor, and settled on the couch to look through the sales papers she'd been meaning to look through all week. Joel got down on the floor and began playing with the baby, and soon had her giggling in delight.

Somewhere around two in the morning, Ron called to let her know Jaci had delivered, and she and the babies were doing fine. Nita immediately called C.J., then Gina.

The next morning she was dragging because of all the late night excitement, and was glad Ron wasn't ringing the doorbell at the crack of dawn. When he did get there around nine, Destiny was already dressed and fed.

"Ron, I was thinking. Maybe Monique can take care of Destiny for you."

Ron laughed. "Please. I wouldn't trust my dog, if I had one, with Monique. She may be good for a couple of hours of babysitting, but after that, she'll be ready to throw the baby out the window. She's a high strung nerd, and the only thing that holds her attention for any length of time is mathematical equations. That's what she does – she's a math consultant."

"I guess that's why she likes this place so much – the previous owner was a college professor. Anyway, I want to change our plan for today a little bit. I was looking at this baby bed in the paper and I'd like to get it for my bedroom. That way, I won't have to cart this portable crib up and down the stairs twice a day. Do you think you and Joel can go pick one up and put it together for me?"

"Sure, but what about Destiny? I'm supposed to be learning how to take care of her, remember?"

"Oh, don't worry, you have the rest of today, and tomorrow. And I'm sure you're a quick study," she said, smiling. "Let me get Joel up, or he'll be in bed all day."

An hour later, after Nita fixed breakfast, and they had eaten, Ron and Joel left to go pick the bed up. But instead of the hour she had thought it would take them, they were gone over three. They came back with a bed, high chair, play pen, bouncer and other contraptions she was unable to identify. Instead of the store she had sent them to, they had gone to a high end store.

Nita's mouth fell open when they unloaded everything that was stuffed into the back of Ron's SUV. "What in the world have you done? I didn't ask for all this stuff."

"I know, Mom," Joel answered. "But the woman at the store told us we needed all this stuff. And anyway, that bed you wanted was out of stock at the first place."

"I like the selections at this place better anyway," Ron added. "Destiny might not need some of these things yet, but she will eventually. This'll keep you from having to haul it in by yourself. Joel and I can put everything together today."

Nita laughed. "They recognized two chumps when y'all walked through the door, didn't they? But what can I say except thank you?"

While she cooked, did Joel's mountain of laundry and looked after Destiny, Ron and Joel were upstairs in her bedroom, putting the bed together, and then downstairs with stuff spread out all over her family and dining rooms, trying to figure out how to put the other things together.

"It seems to me that an architect and aspiring engineer could put this stuff together in a snap," Nita told them in amusement. "What's wrong, guys? Need some help?"

"These doggone instructions are confusing," Ron answered, frustratingly.

"And some of the screws are missing," Joel added.

She walked back into the utility room laughing. "Well, don't have Destiny getting hurt because y'all didn't put that stuff together right," she called back to them.

Later, as they were eating the honey roasted chicken wings, potato salad, and baked beans she had fixed, Joel said, "Mom, did you know that Ron is not only an architect, but also a structural engineer? He can do the design as well as the structural. That's what I want to do," he said, enthusiastically.

"No, I didn't know that," Nita replied, looking at Ron. "So, you're a nerd too. I guess all of you are, because Jason is deep into the technology and software development stuff."

Ron grinned. "I wouldn't say that, but our parents wouldn't accept anything from us but our best. I hated it then, but I'm thankful now. After getting my architectural degree, I decided I needed to get one in engineering as well, because I want to be on the cutting edge of planning and design, as well as structural," he explained. My buildings are well planned, esthetically pleasing and structurally designed to withstand hurricane strength winds. I really don't understand why that hasn't been happening long before now, since we're in a hurricane prone area. That's one of the reasons my firm is in demand. People love my designs, and the structural integrity gives them added value."

"And don't forget…big, big bank!" Joel stood and took his plate to the sink. "Mom, I'm going to shove off and hang out with my friends for a while."

"What friends? The ones who rode home with you?"

"Yeah, those," he said, with a big grin. "I won't be out too late though, because I want to go to church with you in the morning."

"I don't know if I'm going to church, Son. It may not be a good idea to take Destiny into a crowd without knowing if her immune system can handle the germs. What do you think, Ron?"

Ron shrugged. "I don't know, I'll leave that up to you. But if she does catch something, we're already planning to take her to the doctor next week. It should be okay."

"Well, I'll pray over her, and ask the Lord to protect her because I really hate to miss church, and I'd like her first Sunday with us to be in church." She looked back at Joel who was preparing to leave. "Son, just remember who…"

"I know, I know…who I am, and who I belong to. Geez, like I could forget."

While Nita called and talked to Jaci and her parents, and got a report on twins, Jared and Jarea, Ron had charge of Destiny until she was put to bed in her new bed. "I can tell, you're going to be a good daddy," Nita told him. "You even handled the diaper changes well."

He blushed and smiled. "I guess. You're a good teacher, but I'm nowhere near ready to tackle her on my own, though. We still have to get past her screaming when I pick her up, and the diaper changes when she poops. But I feel much better about it than I did a few days ago."

"You're going to be fine…both of you."

Ron looked at her uncomfortably. "Nita…Joel and I had a chance to talk about a lot of things today, and I don't know if you'll appreciate it, but he told me a little about your husband, and your life before he died. Now, I understand why Joel's so protective of you, and I don't think he's wanted to expose the extent of his anger toward his dad to you. I really think telling me about it, kind of helped him vent. I'm sorry you had to go through that for so long. You're a strong woman. I don't know how you did it."

Nita sighed. "It was only by God's grace, and my cousins and brother, who came to Dallas and beat the living daylights out of him and threatened worse if he ever raised his hand against me again. And of course, my sons, especially Joel, soon became my protectors."

"Why did you stay with him? Surely you could have found someone to help you."

Nita contemplated the question she had asked herself so many times. "I can't answer that – and I've tried to. It's the reason I have regular sessions with a counselor. Not as often as I did right after Frank died, but enough to help me through difficult periods."

"Joel also told me about Michael. I take it you still haven't heard from him?"

Nita rolled her eyes. "I'm going to have a talk with Joel about spreading our family business. He knows better than that."

"I'm glad he did. First of all, you probably wouldn't have told me, and secondly, I think he needed to talk to another man about it. I'm glad he felt comfortable enough with me to do so."

"If that's the case, I am too. It would probably help Frankie and Mikey to vent to someone too. But Frankie won't even come home because he can't deal with the changes I've made in my life, and Mikey just ran away from me." The tears that were never far away when she thought about her other sons, were suddenly rolling down her face. "I don't even know if Mikey is still alive."

Ron moved to engulf her in a comforting hug. "Go on and cry, honey. You have every right," he said, holding her close. "I wish I could say something to take your pain away, but I'm not that smart. I do want you to know that I think you're a great mother, and I'm glad you're taking care of my child for me. I also want you to know that I'm ready, willing and able to give you a strong shoulder to cry on, and to be a friend whenever you may need one. Okay?"

She nodded, yes. "Thanks, I apologize for dumping on you like this." She got up to grab a kleenex from a box on a corner table. "You're just full of surprises today, aren't you?"

"Nobody can accuse me of being insensitive. Why do you think women love me?" he asked, in an arrogant tone.

"Oh Lord, the jerk is back. But I really appreciate all you've done today, for Destiny, Joel, and myself."

"You're welcome. But can I have something else?"

"What?" She asked, her tone and body language loaded with suspicion.

"See where your mind went? Straight to the south! Shows how well you know me, or don't know me. No, what I want is for you to fix some food for me to take home. And I need to take enough for Monique too, because I know she didn't cook anything for herself."

Nita laughed. "That's all you want? Well, sweetie, you have more than earned it with all you've done today. Joel may not be too happy when he finds out you took the food he's planning to take back with him, but I'll fix something else for him before he leaves tomorrow."

They went into the kitchen, where she loaded up containers of food for him, then walked him to the door.

Before he opened the door, he leaned down and placed a soft, lingering kiss on her lips. "I didn't want to disappoint you since this is kind of what you thought I was talking about wanting," he said, then at her look of outrage, he pulled her close with his free arm, and kissed her again more thoroughly. "Okay, let me confess," he said in a husky voice. "I want to do that every time I see you, and let me warn you, I plan to keep doing it. Destiny's arrival in my life and some other things have distracted me, but I have every intention of pursuing what we started on the cruise." He released her and opened the door. "I'll see you tomorrow after church."

Nita's lips burned from his hot kisses, and her knees trembled. Just like they did each time he kissed her. "Not good!" she scolded herself. "Not good at all." Before she went to bed, she ignored still another call from Tyson.

Ron and Nita took Destiny to her first doctor's appointment on Monday. Destiny got two shots, with more scheduled for the future, and a complete exam that revealed problems with her ears.

The doctor told them, "Looks as though this problem with her ears has been there a while, but I don't think it's ever been treated. We'll treat it with antibiotics for now, and see if that works. If not, she'll have to have some drainage tubes in both ears. You need to bring her back next week – so be sure to stop at the front desk and make an appointment. She's beneath where she should be on the growth and development chart, so I'm prescribing vitamins along with the antibiotics."

Ron explained a little of Destiny's history. "We've only had her a little over a week now. Believe me, you would have been appalled at her condition when we got her."

"Well, basically, she's pretty healthy. Keep feeding her as much as she wants to eat, and add a little cereal to her milk. We really need to get her weight up."

"Okay, I'm glad you said that," Nita stated, "because I've already been doing that. Maybe I'll add just a little more now that you've said it's okay. And Doctor, what about day care?"

"Well, not yet. Why don't we see where she is next week. Maybe I can be more specific when we see how she's coming along then."

When they left the doctor's office, Ron was filled with anger. "Chantal has a lot to answer for," he said in a furious voice.

On Wednesday, around mid-morning, Tyson McPhearson walked into Ron's stylish office, and strode toward the reception desk.

"May I help you?" The gray haired woman behind the desk asked as her gaze took in the tall, well dressed man.

"Yes, I'm Tyson McPhearson and I'd like to see Ronald Gilmore please."

"Do you have an appointment, Mr. McPhearson?" The receptionist, Anne Cowling, knew that Ron often made appointments without telling her about them.

"No, I don't have an appointment," Tyson said, with a slight edge to his voice. "Is he in?" Tyson glanced at the door that obviously led to a hallway and more offices. It stood slightly ajar. He walked rapidly around Anne's desk and went through the door.

Ron sat at a drafting table which held a large computer monitor. His head jerked around and a frown immediately marred his face as the strange man entered his office abruptly.

"I'm sorry, Mr. Gilmore, he just rushed right by me before I could stop him," the distraught receptionist, who was trailing behind Tyson, stated.

Noting the guy's angry expression, Ron's first thought was that he must be the husband or boyfriend of one of his former female associates. Although he didn't make a habit of dating married women, one slipped through every now and then.

"Who are you? What do you want?"

"I'm Tyson McPhearson." The man with a full head of salt and pepper hair pulled a business card out of a gold case and laid it on Ron's desk.

Ron read the card aloud, "Tyson McPhearson, Attorney At Law, Dallas? I know you're not a client, and you're not my attorney. So, like I said, what do you want?"

"I'm here to talk to you about Anita Stanhope." Tyson's voice was courtroom aggressive.

Ron's eyes narrowed, but never wavered from the man's hard stare. "What about her?"

"I'm here to tell you to take your little snotty nosed brat and get out of Anita's life."

"What!" Ron's voice went up an octave as adrenalin sent his brain and body into overdrive. "Look! I don't know what stupid bug bit you and caused you to come crashing into my office making ridiculous demands, but you better watch your mouth or my daughter won't be the only one with a runny nose, but yours will be running red. If I were you, I'd hightail it out of here right now." Ron rose to his feet and the two men stood head to head with each other.

"I've done my research on you. You're nothing but an immature womanizer without enough sense, even at your age, not to impregnate a woman, and who doesn't have enough character to step up to the plate like a man and marry the child's mother. Then you have the unmitigated gall to dump your child on a good hearted woman like Anita. That's just not acceptable! So like I said before, stay away from Anita or you won't like the consequences."

"And if you don't get your old, gray haired behind out of my office, you're definitely not going to like the consequences."

Tyson's nose flared at the reference to his hair and age. "Don't let the gray hair fool you. Anyway, Anita will no longer be your babysitter, understand?"

"What I understand is that you'd better stay out of my and Anita's business."

Not moving an inch, Tyson stated, "I came to you man to man to ask you to stop taking advantage of a woman who is very special to me. If you want to take this to another level, fine with me."

"You can go - now! You stay on your end of Texas, and I'll stay on mine." Ron walked around the desk and across the room and opened the door. "Anne!" His loud yell had the receptionist running into his office in seconds, a questioning look on her face. "If this dude is not out of here in ten seconds, call 911 and tell them there's a murder in progress." Anne looked from one man to the other, saw the anger on both of their faces, and ran back to her desk where she reached for the phone.

"I'm going because I've said what I came to say," Tyson stated in a cold voice. He walked slowly to the door, then turned and gave Ron a challenging look before leaving.

Ron walked back behind his desk and picked up the phone. "Nita? Who in the devil is Tyson McPhearson? and what exactly is he to you? I thought you told me you didn't have anyone who would object to you taking care of Destiny."

CHAPTER TWELVE

When Nita hung up after Ron's tirade over Tyson, she was angry at two people – Joel, for running his mouth to Tyson, and Tyson, who had interfered in her life after she had just told him where to get off.

She had been fighting with her schedule. If Destiny couldn't go to daycare soon, it could complicate her plans to go to Maryland to help her brother, as well as her work on the Foundation. She had already cancelled a trip to Dallas, but thanks to technology, a lot of the paper work for the Foundation could be accomplished over the phone, e-mail and fax machine.

"Oh, God! Was it just days ago that I was complaining of being bored? Grammy used to always say, be careful what you ask for, because you just might get it, and when you do, you might find out you don't want it, or don't know what to do with it. Well, I'm at that point. So guide me, Lord, and show me what to do. I can talk to Ron about it, but I already know he's not going to be very happy to hear I'm bailing out of my agreement. I'd better learn to think things through before making anymore commitments, or I'll have jerks like Tyson running around like a loose cannon." Without giving herself time to think about it, she composed an e-mail to Tyson.

Tyson. I chose to document this message in writing for obvious reasons. What part of what I told you about interfering in my life did you not understand? How dare you go behind my back today and attack a friend I told you I had agreed to help. You were way out of line, and I hope you realize what a serious offense that was. Any further actions like this will be considered harassment, and appropriate steps will be taken to bring it to an end. Do not call or come near me or anyone I know, and that includes pumping my sons for information.
P/S – You lied. Your actions are very much like something Frank would do. That's distasteful, unacceptable and yes, scary." Anita Stanhope.

She hit the send button, and waited to see if it went through.

A few minutes later, the phone started ringing, and hoping to answer it before it woke the baby, she picked it up without checking the caller I.D.

"Anita? Tyson. I don't know what to say, except . . . you're right and I'm sorry. There's no excuse for my actions, and I will call Gilmore and apologize. I care about you, and I know I let you down in the past. I'm trying to make up for that by not letting anyone else take advantage of you or hurt you."

"Well, you're filling that role pretty well yourself, Tyson. I told you, I'm well able to take care of myself, and to make my own decisions. Even if someone is taking advantage, I reserve the right to let them, and to handle it in my own way. Now you need to cease and desist. Don't call or come to my home anymore. And flowers aren't welcome either – so don't waste your time or money. I am going to keep this e-mail for evidence that I've asked you to stay away."

There was a long pause. "Okay, Anita, take care of yourself."

Later than night she called Joel, and told him what had happened.

"I'm sorry, Mom. It didn't occur to me that guy would go off like that."

"I know you didn't mean any harm, Baby. You were just being your innocent, cordial self, and I wouldn't change that for anything. But you need to learn that everyone you talk to might not have innocent motives."

"I will, Mom. This is a good lesson."

She drew a frustrated breath after hanging up. "Men! I'm tired of them for today."

She got Destiny down for the night, then worked on some ideas for the Foundation a couple of hours.

Right on schedule, Destiny started fretting, and Nita knew she needed to be changed, and wanted to eat. But after she was full, she would go back to sleep.

While the baby slept, she prepared a draft of a brochure, which she e-mailed to Ramona.

At that point, she was tired and ready to relax. She decided to read in bed for a while, and as she was really getting into the book, she was interrupted once again by the phone. She looked and didn't recognize the number but could tell it was an Arkansas area code. "Who could that be?" she wondered aloud, and thinking it might be a family member, decided to answer it.

"May I speak to Anita, please?" A male voice requested.

"This is Anita. Who's calling?"

"Hi, Nita. This is Tony. Tony Caston from your hometown, Riverwood, Arkansas. It's been a while, but I hope you still remember me. How are you doing?"

"Yes, I remember you, Tony. I'm fine, how are you?"

"I'm just great. I've thought about you many times over the years, and always with regret that we didn't get together. I'm so happy to finally be in touch with you again. And I would really like to see you."

"Uh . . . Tony, how did you get my number?"

"Oh, your dad told me about your husband dying, and how you're all alone now. Sure did hate to hear that, but you know things happen for a reason."

She ignored the obvious direction of his mind, and said, "Sooo, where do you live now, Tony? Didn't you leave Riverwood years ago?"

"Me and my wife called it quits, so I'm back."

"That's too bad, Tony. Ending a marriage is never easy."

"Well, we had only been married a few years, and really, we shouldn't have gotten married in the first place. Splitting up was the best thing we could have done, especially since you're back in the picture now."

"Was that your first marriage?"

"Not hardly. I've been married four times, but I haven't given up yet. That's why I was so glad that I ran into your daddy, and he told me about you being a lonely widow woman. I just think that's God working things out for us to give it another try."

"That's not true, Tony. And I'm not interested in a relationship. I have a full life and I'm very happy with things as they are."

"You just think you are, but every woman needs a man around to look after her needs, if you know what I mean."

Oh Lord, another pushy man! She thought. "No, I really don't know what you mean, Tony. I'm sorry that my daddy misled you, but like I said, I have everything and everyone I need in my life right now."

"Well, I would sure like to come see you, Anita. Is that possible?"

"No, my schedule is really tight, Tony, but you know what? I'll probably be coming to Riverwood in a few months, so why don't we plan to visit with each other while I'm there?"

"Now see, it sounds to me like you may need someone to get you away from all that stress. Why don't I drive down to Houston this weekend. Surely you have time for a homeboy."

"No, Tony. My weekend is full. Like I said, in a few months I'll be coming to Riverwood, and I'll be sure to have Daddy tell you when I'm coming."

"I really hate to wait that long to see you, Anita. Why don't you think about how you can fit me into your schedule. I'm not comfortable knowing you're all alone in that big city."

"Believe me, I'm not alone, Tony. Look I have to go. You take care now. Bye."

She quickly hung the phone up. "What was Daddy thinking to give that man my phone number? Oh Lord, I hope he didn't give him my address too."

The next day she called Ron and told him about the possible dilemma with her schedule. "I had already promised my brother I would come and help out with his events before I agreed to take care of Destiny. Then, I was hoping it would work out, and that Destiny would be in daycare by then, but if that's not soon, it looks like things may overlap."

"And what were you going to do with her when you took off?" Ron asked in a hard voice. "I know you don't think I'm ready to take care of her every day. And plus, I'm scheduled to be out of town around that same time. So what are we going to do?"

Do you think Monique would agree to help you a few days?"

"No, I don't think so. Do you just have to go?"

"No, I don't have to go, but I did promise to do it several months ago."

"But that doesn't mean you have to go. Can't you cancel?"

"Ron, look, we have three weeks or so. Surely we can come up with a plan that works for both of us."

"Well right now, I don't see the possibility and frankly, don't want one."

Anger rose up within her. "Let me lay this on you, sweetie. I love Destiny, but she is not my child. It's not fair of you to expect me, a mere stranger, to take on all the responsibility for her. Yes, I did promise to take care of her, and I'm willing to do that, but I have no control over how things can change."

"When you agreed to do it, you didn't mention anything about having to go out of town. Now, here you are trying to renege on your promise when you know I'm depending on you."

"Ron, why are you being so difficult about this? I'll only be gone for a few days, and you would only have her at night for goodness sake. You could make arrangements for someone to come in and take care of her if you're not willing to try."

"All I'm saying is that I shouldn't have to, or if I had known up front, then maybe I could have been ready to deal with it. And I told you, I'm due to be out of town myself around the same time."

"Well, I don't know what we're going to do, but I know this…you better have your behind at my house this weekend, because the following weekend, I have plans and she's going to be with you."

"Nita, I…"

She hung up on him.

Ron was so frustrated when Nita hung up on him that he wished for a drink of something stronger that the tea and soda he had in the house. Just the thought that she could be planning to leave Destiny . . . and him, to go out of town was bad enough, but what really troubled him was that she obviously had plans with another man next weekend – probably that Tyson dude.

Just the thought of that made jealousy rear it's ugly head, and pushed him to do what he had been working so hard to overcome. He called Vickie, a woman he hadn't talked to in a while and made a date. It bothered him that Nita could disconnect from him and Destiny and go on

with her life when he and Destiny were emotionally attached to her.
Maybe Nita wasn't Destiny's biological mother, but she sure as heck was
the closest thing to it. If she loved Destiny as she said she did, she would
see that the child was taken care of – at any cost. Was he being fair to
Nita? Definitely not.

It was time to do some serious thinking about a permanent
solution. He'd kept the option to put her up for adoption in the back of
his mind, but since Nita had so conveniently taken over the care for her,
he hadn't bothered to look into it. He should have known...nothing is
ever settled...not the way his life had been going lately. He had to make
a decision about it soon because Nita and Destiny were already attached
to each other – had been from the start – and he had to admit, he liked
having a reason to stay close to Nita.

When he arrived at Nita's Saturday, she was true to her word.
She left Destiny with him, went into her office and closed the door. He
struggled with the yelling, the dirty diapers, and trying to feed her all
day, while Nita only came out of the office to grab something to eat and
run upstairs. When he asked her how to mix the cereal into the formula,
she quietly showed him, then went back into hiding.

He was so worn out when he left that he almost cancelled his
date – the date he had hastily made out of anger. His desire for the
company of a woman was the only thing that kept him from doing that.
He realized later that canceling would have been the wise thing to do.

Vickie was a beautiful, poised lady, with a great smile, curvy
body, and a look in her eyes that invited him to go as far as he wanted to
go. He considered it. It had been so long. But when he kissed her,

something was missing. He chalked it up to being tired and tried to forget Nita, but her face kept floating before his eyes.

Darn it! What was wrong with him? He had a desirable woman in his arms who was ready and willing, and he couldn't get with it. He pushed her back against the cushions, concentrating hard, and kissed her again, and this time, it seemed as if things might improve. But in the midst of the hard to generate passion, he groaned, "Nita."

The next thing he knew, Vickie was shouting all kinds of expletives and telling him to leave. That had never happened to him before, and he was badly shaken. He couldn't bear to go home and face the moping Monique, who had taken over his home. As a last resort, he went to his brother's house. But it was chaotic there, with the babies yelling, and too many people trying to take care of them. Both Jason and Jaci looked stressed. Jason confided that they were anxious for everyone to leave so they could try to establish some order and routine for their household.

"I think what I truly miss is my wife," Jason confessed. "I can't even have a decent conversation with her, and can't even sleep with her because if one of the babies is not needing to be fed, then the other one needs to be changed, or someone is in the bedroom checking to see if Jaci needs something. Man, I hate it. I know all the confusion will pass eventually, and I'll have at least a part of my wife back. My only consolation is I know she feels the same way."

Ron started laughing. "I thought I was the only one frustrated tonight." He told Jason about what had happened with Vickie, and what had been going on with Nita and Destiny. "Nita frustrates the heck out of me, but right now, even if I thought Vickie would open the door for me,

I'd rather be at Nita's than there or at my own place with Monique. I guess I've been through so much that I'm just totally messed up."

It was Jason's turn to laugh at him. "Brother, I don't believe I've ever seen you in better shape. I think you're finally trying to grow up, but something in you is fighting it. Let it happen, Ron. That's your heart speaking and it's telling you where you're supposed to be. And I don't care how frustrating it can be, you're not going to be happy anywhere else."

Ron exercised his customary action when something was said that he didn't want to hear – he left without saying a word, and drove to a jazz club, where he settled in and listened to the music until his body told him it was time to go home.

He recalled all the scriptures he had been confessing, and knew he needed to repent. If he had been successful with Vickie tonight, it would have put him right back where he'd started out. He fell on his knees, seeking God's forgiveness and asking for strength to walk in God's will.

The next day, he went to Nita's after church, and took over the care of Destiny. Today, he had a different attitude, and surprisingly, Destiny seemed more comfortable with him. She smiled at him more, was more patient with his clumsy attempts to change and feed her, and didn't yell nearly as much. Nita cooked a great dinner, fixed a container for him to take home, and disappeared into her office again. They still didn't talk, but he was comfortable, and when it was time to leave, he felt a reluctance rise up in him. He wanted to stay. But he resisted, and left in a hurry, telling himself he was happy to finally have the weekend behind him.

When he got home, Monique grabbed the food Nita had given him and ate nearly all of it. Then, she proceeded to tell him she didn't know how long she would be staying because in spite of having a healthy bank account, she didn't have a job, and couldn't get the kind of place she wanted until she had a stable income.

"I'll check around and see if there's a vacancy in one of my buildings you can move into, and if not, I'll sign the lease for you. I know between me, Jason and Pops, we can find you something you'll be pleased with. How's the job search going?"

"Well, I'm getting good feedback, but no one is hiring right now. Things are so messed up that you almost have to know someone to get a foot in the door now."

"By the way, Nita is insisting that Destiny spends next weekend over here. I'm not looking forward to that, but at least you'll be here to help me."

Monique shook her head. "Naw, brother, I'm not ready for that."

The urge to slap her was strong. He was housing, feeding and doing everything he could to help her, and she couldn't help him out? "Well how are you going to learn if you won't even spend some time around her?"

"I'm waiting until she's old enough to use the bathroom and eat by herself...then I'll be able to deal with her. Not now, though, brother."

Ron exhaled wearily. "Nita says she needs some time to do some other things. She does much more than I should expect as it is, but unless I can find someone I can trust to relieve her, I don't know what I'll do. Mom and Pops are so negative toward me that they've extended it to Destiny, and ignore her existence.

"Ironically, they're so excited over Jason's twins that they've almost moved into Jason's house, and are squabbling with others over the babies. I know they don't like how Destiny got here, but does that justify withholding their love and support?" He sighed and bowed his head in defeat. "I don't know. It may be best for Destiny if I put her up for adoption so she can start over with a family where she doesn't have to fight the negativity stacked against her by people who know too much about her history."

Monique dropped her head. "I'm so sorry, Ron. No doubt, your family is really letting you down. Why don't you and Nita get together? That way, at least Destiny will have the parents she deserves."

Ron gave her a crazy look. "Your brains must have gotten fried in that Dubai desert. I'm trying to see that the baby is taken care of, but that doesn't change the fact that I don't want to be a daddy."

"Well fried brains or not," Monique said, with a stubborn look, "I like my idea. Anybody who is around you and Nita very long can see that you're attracted to each other."

"Funny." Ron said. "How do you get off trying to advise me about my life? Maybe you need to take a closer look at your own."

"Believe me, I have, and I don't like it. It was never my intention to be alone and homeless at my age. It just happened that way because I made some bad decisions. I hate my life, because although I love my career, it can't keep me warm at night. It can't give me a hug when I need it. It can't comfort me when I'm sad, and it can't love me back." Monique looked as if she was about to boo-hoo. "Don't make the wrong choice on this, Ron. Whether you realize it or not, you need Destiny, and you need Nita."

He sat quietly, in deep thought for a long time before he said, "well…until recently, I would have argued that you are wrong. But to be honest, right now, I just don't know."

"Maybe you're just stuck in a habit and too stubborn to change."

Ron got up and left the room without saying another word. He had a lot to think about and pray about. He laid back on his bed and thought about the scenario with Vickie. Just how far would he have gone with her? The probable answer didn't reassure him. What the heck had he been thinking? Did he really want to sow more negative seed by sleeping with another woman he didn't even want? He cringed as he had a sudden visual of making God sick.

He was already dealing with consequences. Was it wisdom to walk back into the same lifestyle and put himself in danger of even more consequences? How many times had he secretly coveted the peace, joy and contentment he saw in his brother? And how long would he deny the feelings that were growing in him for Nita, and yes, baby Destiny too? When would he face the truth? Nita and Destiny had made a home in his heart, but did he have a home in theirs? " Everything is way too complicated. Help me, Father," he prayed earnestly.

CHAPTER THIRTEEN

Nita was still upset with Ron, and spoke to him only when necessary. Thankfully, when they took Destiny for her follow-up exam, she was doing so well, the doctor cleared her to start day care in a week. But she was still undecided about what to do about going to Maryland. She would have to make a decision soon, because the dates for her brother's events were quickly approaching, and nothing had been settled regarding Destiny.

Another heavy burden settled in her heart about going to Maryland . . . Mikey. The thought that while there, she could be within miles of where he was and not know it, opened a hole in her heart that couldn't be filled. But the same could also be true for Houston, or Dallas. He could be anywhere and she not know it. And not knowing was killing her softly. Also, although she did know where Frank, Jr. was, having to accept that he didn't want to see her, bore another hole in her heart.

An ironic thought passed through her mind. When Frank was alive, she'd been convinced he was her only problem. Now that he was gone, problems seemed to be coming at her from every direction. Another one of Grammy's sayings came to mind. "Don't expect life to be easy. Heartache and trouble will dog your heels from birth to death. But God gives rest in between battles, and when He does, don't forget to be grateful."

She shook off the distress that was trying to pull her down, and began working on the Foundation. Gratefulness rose up within her. Something good was coming out of the years of abuse she had suffered.

Although Tyson hadn't called again, floral arrangements arrived every few days. The first one had been accompanied by a note that said, *"I know you said not to send you flowers, but please let me reserve the right to send flowers to who I want...and I really want to send them to you. I beg you, accept them in the spirit in which they are offered."* Ty

She pushed annoyance out of her mind. She was tired of being stressed out over men. Ron, Tyson, Tony, her daddy, her sons...she wanted to throw them all into the river of no return.

154

While she was plotting that river scene in her mind, the phone rang, interrupting her. She ran to answer and was delighted to hear her son, Frank, Jr. on the line. "Hey Baby! It's so good to hear from you. How are you?"

"Mom, I'm fine, and I was calling to tell you I want to come see you...not this coming weekend, but next weekend. Is that okay?"

"Oh yes, Sweetheart. I would love that."

"Can you make reservations for me?"

She smiled. "Sure, give me the times you want to travel, and I'll take it from there." She scribbled down the times he gave her. "Joel is planning to come this weekend, but I think I'll call him and tell him to wait until next weekend so you guys can see each other."

"Yeah, that would be great. Just shoot me an e-mail with the flight information when you have it. I'm looking forward to seeing you, Mom. I miss you."

"Me too, Frankie." She hung up with tears of joy in her eyes, and hugged Destiny who was chewing on a toy.

Tony had become a nuisance, and was calling her almost every day. She decided to make some calls to Riverwood. The first call was to her daddy.

"Hey, Daddy, how are you? This is Nita."

"I'm doing pretty good, you doing alright? How you liking Houston? Tell the truth, one big city is just like the other to me. Way too big, with too many cars going every which way."

Nita laughed. "I suppose you're right, but at least I have my cousins here."

"Oh, yeah, that's right. How them girls doing?"

"Well, Jaci just had twins. And C.J. is taking care of her brother's baby, and working."

"Well, what about you? What you doing with yourself these days?"

"I'm busy too. I'm taking care of a baby for a friend, working on a project I'm starting, and looking at getting into school sometime in the near future. And that's why I called you. Why did you tell Tony that I'm a rich, lonely widow woman who's all alone in the big city? That's not true, and that man is worrying the socks off of me."

"Hee, hee! I guess I wasn't thinking and kind of went overboard. He keeps asking questions about you and I know y'all used to be friends, so I figured it was okay to give him your number. I didn't know he was gon' make a nuisance of himself."

"Well, he is. He's calling everyday, trying to come see me. Remember, I haven't seen or heard anything about this man in years, so I have no idea what kind of person he is now. Do you? Do you know where he's been, or what he's been doing? He could be a criminal, a murderer, or a drug dealer for all we know. Did you even think about that, Daddy?"

"Umph, umph, umph! Naw, I didn't. You don't think about all those kinds of things in a little place like Riverwood. He seems okay, but I admit I don't know about all that stuff you mentioned. And I surely don't want him bringing no more trouble on you. I sho' do hate I put you in this situation, Baby. I ain't never been much of a daddy to you."

"It's okay, Daddy. You're just being you. I just have to figure out how to deal with him. I'll talk to you later."

She called a distant cousin who was a beautician and heard all the gossip from the women who came to her shop. After hearing her ramblings about Tony, she knew she had to find a way to make things clear to him the next time he called.

Saturday morning, Nita and Destiny went to visit Jaci and the twins. While she was there, C.J. also showed up with Geordie, and they had a chance to have a 'cousin' visit, which they hadn't been able to do in a while. Jaci was stressed out trying to deal with the babies, and keep peace between her mother, Jason's mother and Sister Sadie.

"Truthfully," she whispered, "I'll be happy when they all go home. They're driving us crazy and are constantly placing me in the position of referee. I don't need that."

"What its going to come down to is, you and Jason are going to have to tell them in a nice way of course, to go home," C.J. stated.

Nita pondered the situation before saying, "What's really sad is that Ron is really struggling and needing help with Destiny, and his parents refuse to do anything to help him, but they're over here fighting over your babies. Now don't get me wrong, Jaci, but your babies have so many people who love them and want to do for them, while Destiny has almost no one."

She told them about the disagreement she and Ron were having because she was thinking about going to Maryland. "He objects to me going because there's no one to help with Destiny. I had to remind him that Destiny is his child, not mine."

"Monique is staying with him, why can't she help him with Destiny?" Jaci asked.

"She says she's not any good with babies." Nita saw their looks of disgust, said, "I know, don't even go there. I'm taking Destiny to Ron this evening and Monique has left for the weekend. In all fairness, I think she does love Destiny though."

"Hmmm," C.J. said. "I wonder if Ron's parents realize how wrong they are?"

"I don't know. I think they're being unfair to both Ron and Destiny, but maybe I'm a little prejudiced," Nita answered, then said, "Well, I do have some other interesting news."

"What!" C.J. and Jaci said simultaneously.

Nita giggled. "Tony Caston – remember him? He's trying his best to hook up with me."

"What?" Jaci said, again. "How did this come about?"

She told them all that had transpired up until now. "I still want to kick my daddy's behind, even though he just wasn't thinking. Anyway, this guy's bugging the heck out of me. I've put him off a couple of weeks, but he's very persistent."

"Oh my goodness," C.J. said. "So, what's his story?"

"Well, he's been married several times, and I don't know how many children he has, but from his comments, and the scuttlebutt around Riverwood, he's looking for the next wife to take care of him, and thinks he's found her in me."

"Oh, Lord, Nita," Jaci said, worriedly. "We have to find a way to run him off...I mean once and for all. You don't need that kind of mess around you, just when you're getting your life back together. It may be time to pull off a cousin caper."

They laughed uproariously. "Now, what can we come up with? Surely, we didn't leave our bag of tricks in Riverwood, C.J. said."

"Let's think and pray on it," Jaci said. "It's a crying shame how people come crawling out from under rocks when they think there's some easy money they can grab."

"And I thought the attorney was the one I needed to watch," C.J. grumbled. "Maybe I should take another look – he might be the person you need. After all, he's an attorney, so he's probably pretty well fixed for money, but then again, you never can tell. He tried to stake his claim on you mighty quick. That's not a good sign since he knows how much Frank was worth."

"All I know is Tony is spreading it around that he's going to marry me. Now that's pretty ridiculous when we haven't even seen each other in decades. And the sad thing is, I don't think he's going to give up anytime soon."

"I think there's a solution we haven't talked about yet," Jaci said, with a sly look. "Ron. Now, Nita I know how you feel, but remember I saw y'all in action. That kiss between you two looked pretty serious to me. Think about it."

After giving her a dirty look, Nita ignored Jaci's comments. "Well, y'all keep thinking and praying. I'm going to leave now so I can get ready to drop Destiny off to Ron. Cij, are you free tonight? Want to take in a movie and go somewhere for dinner? I feel like a bird out of a cage and want to get out and do something."

"Sounds great if I can get a babysitter. So I'd best get to moving now too."

Nita dressed in casual beige slacks, a dressy blouse and a brown blazer before she loaded Destiny into her SUV and headed to Ron's house. She arrived to find not one, but two women there – and from the amount of tension in the room two very angry women. She spoke pleasantly to the women sitting on opposite ends of the long, curved sofa, and walked into the kitchen to put the food she has prepared for Destiny into the refrigerator. Ron, holding Destiny above his head and talking to her as he followed Nita into the kitchen, was acting as though it was no big deal to have two angry women sitting in his living room. He followed, as Nita walked back into the living room where she grabbed Destiny's bag from beside the door.

"Uh...ladies, this is Anita," he said, waving a hand in her direction. "And this is my daughter, Destiny. Nita, this is Shayla, and this is Velma." Both women looked at the baby, frowned, and cast angry, suspicious looks in Nita's direction.

"You have a baby?" Shayla asked in a shocked voice. "You have some explaining to do."

"Yeah, I'd like to hear about that too," Velma stated.

"The only thing I have to say to both of you is that you need to leave," Ron replied with a pointed look.

"Uh, uh," Shayla said, with a angry look. "You gon' tell me why you were misleading me while you were having a baby with another woman." Her look transferred to Nita.

Nita headed up the stairs with Destiny's bag, and Ron, seemingly unmoved by the emotionally charged atmosphere in the room, ignored Shayla's comment and followed her.

Unsettled by the situation with Destiny and Nita, Ron went to the Men's Fellowship Meeting Saturday morning, hoping to hear something that would help him or maybe provide a little encouragement. He heard more than he bargained for. Pastor Robinson had a powerful, but troubling message, which had Ron squirming as he listened . . .

"Men, it's time to grow up! Many of us are married on paper, but foot loose and fancy free in our actions. Others are single but running around indulging in things that God only ordained for those who are married. We're sowing wild oats that are detrimental to us and to those who love us, and planting seeds – literally – that are bringing forth a harvest of children who are neglected or abandoned by us, while we go on to repeat that process over and over.

Let me tell you, if you don't want the harvest, if you're not prepared to take care of the harvest, then be careful about spreading your seed all over town. God is not pleased with that!"

Ron quickly looked around to see if all eyes were on him, because he knew the Pastor was directing his message to him. But all he saw were others who, like him, looked like they had just been slammed. The only reason he didn't act on his desire to leave was because that would have been an open admission of his guilt.

"If you think I'm talking about you, then I must be, because the Holy Spirit knows whose heart to pierce. I'm having to do way too much counseling with men who are living raggedy, ungodly lives. But it's not my goal to condemn you, but to tell you what the Word of God says, and what God expects from us.

"It's disturbing to see so many of our women struggling alone to raise children who need the love and guidance of both parents. Too many women who desire to be in Godly marriages are unable to because no Godly men are available. So, out of desperation, they resort to piece meal relationships, accepting what they can get from a man. And a BMW – black man working - especially if he's supposedly a Christian, is a premium because there are so few of them. This makes our women vulnerable to pretenders prowling around our churches to prey on them. Sad.

"Every time we fail to stand up as true men of God, we're failing ourselves, our women, our children, our churches, schools and communities.

"We're faced with all kinds of choices everyday, but men it's time to choose who you will serve. I encourage you, choose God. Be accountable and responsible in living for Him and bringing glory and honor to Him. By doing this, you sow, and ultimately reap a fruitful harvest. By continuing to choose yourself and a destructive, ungodly lifestyle, you are sowing, and will ultimately reap a harvest of discord, destruction and death. Believe me, nobody but satan will be laughing. I'm not saying this is easy – it's not. But men, we've got to do it. Too many of our lives and our families are being destroyed. Think on these things, brothers."

Ron walked out of the fellowship hall in an almost shell-shocked state. Pastor Robinson's words, on top of his already conflicting emotions weighed heavily on his mind. It rubbed him the wrong way to have a baby forced on him, although he had finally accepted that it wasn't Destiny's fault. But the fact remained – he didn't know what to do with her.

He drove home with his mind going around in circles. Dread filled him when he remembered Nita was bringing Destiny to him, and he would have her for the rest of the day and night. He definitely wasn't ready for that.

He sank into a chair when he got home and stared into space. What was he going to do? He thought about calling Nita and begging her not to bring Destiny, but as she had so forcefully pointed out, Destiny was his child, not hers. He was still sitting there, submerged in despair when the doorbell rang. He looked at his watch, and noted unhappily that Nita was early. But when he opened the door, he stepped back in surprise. "What the heck! Velma?"

The woman at the door was an old acquaintance who had moved out of town when she wanted more from him than he was willing to give. He hadn't heard from her since.

"Hey, lover! Look who's back," Velma said, happily. "I didn't call because I wanted to surprise you. How're you doing? Aren't you going to invite me in?"

Ron stuttered. "Oh, uh, sure, uh…come on in. Have you moved back to town?"

"Yes. My company transferred me back here to head up a new division. I'm glad for the promotion, but I'm especially happy to get back to you. I never should have left, and hopefully, some other woman hasn't snapped you up. So tell me, what's happening with you?"

Still a motor mouth. Who can get a word in? Ron thought. "Well, I'm not married, but I am involved."

"Oh really? Well, we need to talk about that."

"Yes, really, Velma. And there's nothing to talk about. In fact, I'm expecting someone shortly, so I'm sorry you'll have to leave."

"Cancel, honey! After all, we use to have a good thing going. Surely I can pull rank."

"No, I don't think so, Velma. We had our time and moved on. Let's leave it at that. But it's good to see you, and I wish you well in your new position." He was leading her back to the door when the doorbell sounded.

Darn it! He'd hoped to get Velma out before Nita arrived. He reached around Velma to open the door, and his mouth dropped. *Could this day get any worse?* It wasn't Nita, but Shayla who strolled in. A strong expletive jumped into his mouth and struggled for release.

Shayla. He'd been trying to end things with her, but she was hanging on like a leech. She had permanence on her mind, and was showing up unannounced at his home more and more.

"Who. Is. This?" Shayla asked, with attitude coming off in waves.

"Uh, Shayla, this is Velma. Velma, Shayla. I'm sorry you guys didn't call me before coming over here. I was just explaining to Velma before you arrived, Shayla, that I already have plans for the rest of the day, and you guys need to leave."

"You mean this is not who you're waiting for?" Velma asked. "Geez, Ron. At least you didn't use to have women showing up at the same time. It's good I'm back so I can get you back in line." She had an amused, but vicious look on her face.

"Huh! I don't know who you are, but you ain't running nothing here," Shayla stated firmly and sat down on the other end of the sofa.

Ron stood with a look of total amazement as they tossed snide remarks back and forth. Didn't he just tell both of them to leave?

That was the mess Nita and Destiny walked into. He couldn't help but notice how great Nita looked. He only wished he could have prevented her from walking into this situation.

Ron took Destiny from her and led the way into the open layout of his condo. He introduced everyone, and followed a cool and calm Nita upstairs. He hoped the other two women would leave like he asked them to.

"You look beautiful. Where are you headed?" Ron asked, when they entered his bedroom where Destiny's crib was set up in a corner of the room.

"Now that's not any of your business," she answered, as she quickly unpacked Destiny's bag, then reached to take her from Ron.

"Desi, you be a good girl for Daddy now," she said to Destiny, and then looked to Ron, "Are your lady friends here to help you with her?"

"Nope, not hardly. They're not here at my invitation."

Nita looked at him pointedly and said, "Do I need to take Destiny back home? I'm not liking the atmosphere in this place. Are you sure she's going to be okay?"

"You're welcome to stay here with us."

"And join this party? No thanks! Destiny ate a little while ago, and if you give her a bottle I think she'll take a nap. But don't let her sleep too long, or she'll be up tonight."

He barely acknowledged what she said. "Who are you going out with? Not that Tyson dude I hope."

"No, why?"

"Who then? I promised Joel I would look after you, so I need to know who you're going out with?"

Nita grunted disgustedly. "I think your hands are full enough. I'm not trying to tell you what to do with your friends downstairs, am I?"

"I just want you to be careful. Some of those guys out there are rapists or worse. Have you thought about that?"

"Yes, of course I have, and you can keep your scare tactics to yourself. Now I have to go, and you need to get back to your own…uh…dates." She stood up and handed Destiny to him and walked out of the room.

He followed her down the stairs and walked with her to the door. Before she could get the door open, he pulled her close and kissed her lightly on the lips. "Remember what I said, and be careful, okay? I'll call you later." Destiny let out a scream when she realized she was being left. He closed the door with a frown of worry on his face and turned to face the angry stares from the women in his living room.

CHAPTER FOURTEEN

Nita pushed down her disappointment about what she'd encountered at Ron's house. After all, he was just living up to his playboy reputation.

When C.J. arrived, they searched the internet for a movie, then decided where they wanted to go for dinner.

"It'll be so nice to have a relaxing night out with someone I don't have to be on P's and Q's with the whole time," Nita told her cousin. "That's how I always feel with Tyson."

"And that's why you see so many women sitting home alone on the weekend, or just getting together with some girlfriends to do something. Trust me, it's better than dealing with some of the men out there."

"True. But wouldn't you like to have a nice man – one you feel comfortable with – to go out with sometimes? I would. I'd be satisfied with nothing more than just a friendship thing –without dealing with hidden motives."

"Good luck finding him. They usually have something more in mind, which is why you have to watch and listen to them closely. I know I sound kind of cynical, but I'm just trying to warn you about what single woman have to deal with," C.J. explained. "You know I'm a realist."

"Yeah, everyone who knows you realize that," Nita said, laughing. "Are you driving?"

"Yes, I might as well, or I'll have to be giving you directions all evening."

"We'll go out the front door then, instead of through the garage."

Nita set the security alarm, then opened the door and let out a shrill scream when she came face to face with a strange man standing on her door step. "Oh my God! Who are you? What do you want?"

C.J. yelled, "I'm calling the police, mister, so you better get away from here."

"Ladies, ladies! I'm just looking for Anita."

They looked at the guy closely. "Why?" Nita asked.

"I'm Tony Caston, Anita. Don't you recognize me?"

Nita's eyes narrowed. "What are you doing here, Tony? Obviously, I didn't recognize you, and I certainly wasn't expecting you to show up unannounced at my door."

The years hadn't been kind. His face showed numerous scars and imperfections that looked like the result of some terrible fights, and the little hair he had left was slicked down by some kind of greasy concoction. He was dressed in stiffly pressed jeans and a sports coat, with shoes that could have stood some polish. His grin revealed ill kept teeth, and he had a large fake diamond earring in his left ear.

"Well, I'm here, so are you going to invite me in?" Tony asked, with a wide grin.

"Tony, didn't I tell you I was busy this weekend? Why are you here?"

"Anita, if I hadda waited on you to tell me when I could come, I wouldna never got here. We home people, and I don' drove all the way to Houston to see you, and you don't want to invite me in? Now that's a crying shame."

C.J. huffed impatiently, "Well, what did you expect? It's rude to show up unannounced."

"Tony, this is very inconsiderate and nobody would blame me if I didn't invite you in. But since you're here, come on in for a few minutes, but let me tell you, you've been on camera from the moment you drove into this address, so don't think about trying anything. But if you do act crazy and try something, we will deck you so fast you will regret you ever left Arkansas."

Tony looked a little shocked. "I can tell y'all the same girls who used to run around Riverwood terrorizing everybody."

Nita resignedly stepped back so he could enter, and while he was busy checking the place out, C.J. was digging in her purse for what Nita knew was the can of mace she kept there.

She showed Tony into the family room, while C.J. escaped to the kitchen. She searched the man for something – anything – that would nudge a memory, but unfortunately, there was nothing left of the Tony she remembered.

"You have a swanky place here, Nita. Your husband obviously left you in good shape. Yes, yes, very nice," Tony stated, as his eyes continued to scrutinize the place.

"Not really, Tony. I have children to take care of and put through college."

"His eyes darted around the room as though trying to calculate the value of everything. "You buying this place, or you just renting it?"

Nita didn't answer. "C.J.!" she yelled. "Come on in and say hello to Tony."

"Okay, in a minute," C.J. called back.

A few minutes later, C.J. came out of her hiding place and walked slowly into the room. "Tony, how are you? It's been a long time, huh?"

Tony's eyes slid over C.J. in an assessing way. "Oh, yeah, You're the one they call 'Red', right?"

He had made an enemy. C.J. hated the nickname. "Right." She said, barely hiding her distaste.

Nita stood and said, "Well, Tony, C.J. and I were just leaving to go to dinner. You're welcome to go with us, but we do have other plans for later and I know you must have other plans for this evening too."

He failed to hide his disappointment. "Oh. Naw, I thought we could spend some time reminiscing about old times and all. My only plan for the evening is to be where ever you happen to be. Just show me where I can freshen up, and I'll be ready to ride."

Nita and C.J. exchanged outraged looks. "What my cousin is trying to tactfully tell you, is that we're being hospitable by inviting you to dinner, but after that, we have plans that don't include you," C.J. explained.

Her words flew right over his head. "Well, you know what I say about plans…they are made to be changed," he said, as he headed toward the powder room Nita pointed to. "Ain't you got nothing cooked?" He asked over his shoulder. "Don't make sense to spend money when you can eat at home just as well."

Again, Nita and C.J. exchanged looks filled with amazement. "We have to find a way to get this dude out of here, C.J.," Nita whispered.

"I don't think that's going to be easy," C.J. answered. "It's like talking to a brick wall."

"I thought your children were grown and gone," Tony said, with a frown, as he came out of the powder room. "You got grandchildren? I see all this baby stuff you have."

"No, I don't have any grandchildren."

"Oh." He shot another questioning look to the baby stuff, and made himself comfortable in a chair, as though he planned to be there for a while.

Nita could tell - the baby stuff worried him.

C.J. disappeared into the kitchen again as Tony started making his move on Nita.

"You look great, Nita. I'm glad we've found each other again."

"Tony, let me make this clear. Anything, other than friendship is out of the question. Now, that's the way it is and nothing is going to change that." Nita said.

"I know that's what you keep saying, but I been married enough times to know how women are. Their minds can change with the wind."

"My mind won't be changing," Nita said, forcefully, wondering if he had mental issues.

He smiled at her. "We'll see, Sweetheart. I can be pretty convincing."

"I'm not your Sweetheart! And basically, we're just strangers."

"Strangers? Anita, we've known each other all our lives."

"No, Tony. We knew each other when we were basically just kids – over twenty years ago. We're different people now. I don't know you, and you certainly don't know me."

"Your daddy said you're alone, so I figure you need a good husband, someone to make sure nobody takes advantage of you."

"Tony, my daddy has no idea what's going on in my life. And I think you've read way too much into what he said."

He laughed nervously. "That might be true, but I can tell from this place that you ain't nowhere near broke."

"And I can tell by your conversation that you are, so what in the world would my cousin want with you?" C.J. said, hotly.

"This is me and Anita talking. You ain't got nothing to do with it."

Nita's cell phone rang, and she pulled it out of her purse and saw it was Ron calling.

"Nita, is that dude still there?"

"Yes."

"Do I need to come over there?"

"Yes."

"Okay, I'll be there shortly."

She looked at C.J. and said, "Ron's on the way."

C.J. smiled her relief. "That's good."

Tony was looking confused, but didn't say anything. Fifteen minutes later, Ron and Destiny were at the door.

When Ron entered, he handed the sleeping baby to Nita, then went back to his truck to get the baby's bag, and what looked to be a laptop bag. She introduced him and Tony, and sat down holding Destiny.

Ron gave Tony a searching look and said, "So you're Nita and C.J.'s homeboy, huh?"

"Yeah, that's right," Tony answered, with a question in his eyes about Ron's identity.

"How did it go today, Ron?" C.J. asked. "Did you and Destiny enjoy your day?"

"I wouldn't say enjoy is an accurate description," he answered. "Destiny's not real happy with anyone except Nita. She starts screaming for her, and won't shut up. She just went to sleep when we started driving."

"Funny! Well, you're just going to have to spend more time with her, daddy."

"Yeah, that's what Nita keeps telling me." He picked up his laptop bag. "I need to check my e-mail and catch up on some things since I haven't had a chance to do it all day. I'll be in here if you need me, " he said, pointing to the office. "Hope you have a good trip back to Arkansas, Tony." He went in the office and closed the door.

A few minutes later, C.J. said, "I guess I'll be going since our plans are shot. Tony, nice to see you again. You be careful now."

Nita followed her to the door to let her out. "Good night, Cij. See you tomorrow."

The movement woke Destiny, and she let out a scream. When she looked up and saw Nita's face, she quickly changed it to a smile. "Hey sweetie," Nita said to the baby. "Did you have a good time today?"

Destiny grinned and jumped happily in Nita's arms. Noises from her bottom let Nita know a diaper change was needed. She went to the office and stuck her head in. "Ron, sorry to disturb you, but Destiny needs to be changed."

"Okay, no problem," he answered. He took Destiny and headed upstairs.

Tony's whole body was screaming questions. "I didn't know you were involved with somebody. And I sure as heck didn't know you had a baby."

"That's why I kept telling you my daddy is not the right person to be getting information about me from. Daddy has no idea what's going on in my life."

"I can see that," Tony said in disgust. "But you should have told me, Nita. All those times we talked on the phone, you didn't say nothing about that guy and having that baby."

"But I did tell you repeatedly that I was only interested in friendship with you, Tony. Anything beyond that was not your business. You had absolutely no business showing up here unannounced, Tony, especially after I told you not to come."

Ron came back and dumped Destiny in Nita's lap. "She's probably hungry too," he said, and went into the office. This time he left the door open.

Nita stood. "Well, Tony, I'm going to have to call it a night. I hope you'll have a safe trip back home. Are you planning to leave tonight, or tomorrow?"

"Well, actually, I was thinking that I could stay here with you and we could get reacquainted. I didn't bother about a hotel room."

Before an outraged Nita could get a word out of her mouth, Ron was standing in the office door. "I don't know how you could have thought that dude, but let me make this clear…you won't be staying here tonight or any night. Now do we need to have a discussion or anything else about that?" Ron's aggressive tone and stance spoke volumes. Tony got the message and hurriedly stood.

"Oh, uh, naw, my man, that's cool. I guess I'll probably just go ahead and hit the highway back to Arkansas tonight."

"That's a good plan. You can be at home by morning if you leave now," Ron advised.

Tony walked briskly to the door and headed to his car. Ron followed him out and watched him get into the late model car. "I'd be careful on the way out of town if I were you. Houston cops are very suspicious when they see out of state license tags driving around the city at night. They'll pull you over just to harass you."

Tony looked around as though expecting cops to jump out from everywhere. "I'll be sure to do that," he said, before driving off.

Ron watched him turn the corner before he came back into the house.

Nita put Destiny down and ran and hugged him. "Thank you! I've never been so happy to see anyone." She hugged him again. "How did you know?"

"C.J. sent me a text."

"Oh." Nita said.

He looked down at her a long time before stating, "I don't know what rock that fellow crawled out from under, but he's a hoodlum if I ever saw one. Why the heck did you let him in here, Nita? That was just stupid. All you needed to do was look at him. That dude is looking for an

easy score – in a lot of different ways. Don't ever do anything like
that again."

Nita bristled. "Wait a minute! Just where do you get off calling
me stupid? And who do think you are, telling me what I can't do? You'd
better check yourself, mister."

Ron sighed in frustration. "I didn't say you were stupid. I said
what you did was stupid. All I'm trying to do is keep you out of
dangerous situations."

Nita drew a calming breath. "I know you're right. I just hate to
be yelled at."

"I was worried to death about you when I got C.J.'s text.
Anyway, since I'm here, we need to talk. And I'm hungry, got anything
to eat?"

"Now you know I always have something around here to eat.
Let's see what we can find," she said, picking Destiny up and leading the
way to the kitchen.

They had a lot to talk about. He needed to know if Nita was still
planning to go out of town, and if so, they had to decide what to do about
Destiny. And since he now realized how shaky their arrangement was, he
had to make some major decisions. He was a little put out with Nita, but
had to admit she was right…she did have a life that didn't include
Destiny – or him.

He hadn't been able to get Pastor Robinson's words out of his
mind since this morning. He had heard it all before, but because of his
present circumstances, it had really hit home. But the thing that most

disturbed him was the question Pastor Robinson had asked: What could he do about this situation that would honor God?

How could anything he did at this point honor God, since God wasn't responsible for the mess he had made? He needed a permanent solution for Destiny. Would God guide him to one?

As they sat eating sandwiches and homemade soup, Ron decided to get right to what was on his mind. "Nita, I need you to help me make some decisions about Destiny. I'm in a very unstable position right now, and to be honest, I truly don't know what to do. I realize you have a life that doesn't include Destiny, and I can't expect you to give up anything for her."

Nita nodded. "What you're describing is what every parent has to deal with at one time or the other. And you're going to have to do some things that you don't necessarily want to do."

"But how, Nita? My job keeps me on the go. In fact, this trip next week is only the first of many just on this particular project."

"Well you don't have to worry about her this time. I've already called my brother and told him I won't be coming. So Destiny will be right here with me."

Relief spread over his face. "I'm glad to hear that. It really takes a lot of pressure off."

She smiled. "Well, the truth is, my son, Frankie, wants to come home next weekend. The thought of seeing him kind of tipped the scales in favor of him and Destiny, and gave me more reason not to go than to go."

"Whatever played into your decision not to go, it means I don't have to worry about what to do with her. But I still need a more permanent solution. This is certain to come up again."

Her heart sank. "What kind of things are you considering?"

"Well, the only other thing I can think to do is put her up for adoption. There has to be someone who would like to have her."

Anger shot through Nita. "I can't believe your old irresponsible behind is sitting here talking about giving your own child away because you don't want to deal with parenting issues. What if every parent felt that way? No, sweetie, all parents struggle through them the best they can."

"Maybe that is the best thing. Not just for me, but for Destiny too."

"Huh! Right now, the only thing I'm hearing is your own selfishness. You're not thinking of Destiny."

"That's easy enough for you to say. You've never been faced with this kind of decision."

She gave him a hard look. "And how do you figure that? I had three children under four years old, and a husband who knocked me around when he felt like it, and threatened to take my children and destroy me if I ever tried to leave him." She pulled the hair off of her forehead and pointed to a scar a little larger than the size of a quarter. It was raised, puckered and ugly looking. "This is what I got for even thinking about leaving. And you're telling me I've never been faced with a hard decision?"

Ron's mouth fell open in shock. "Oh God, Nita, I'm so sorry." He reached to touch the scar gently. "I don't know what to say."

"There's nothing to say. I didn't tell you this to make you feel guilty. I was merely trying to show you that sometime you have to dig deep inside yourself to do what you have to do."

He shook his head. "Maybe I just don't have what it takes to make that kind of sacrifice for a child I didn't want in the first place."

"And you think staying in that abusive situation was easy? No, I stayed because I knew I couldn't leave my children. Was that the right decision? I don't know."

He sat there with his head down a long time, then said, "Everybody – you, Jason and Jaci, and even Monique - is telling me to step up to the plate and be a daddy to her. But with the exception of you, nobody is offering any help. I can't do it alone."

"Ron, you're not alone. Yes, I might have to leave her sometime, but that doesn't mean I'm abandoning her. I love that baby, Ron. And I believe you do too, or you would if you let yourself."

A tiny smile played around his mouth. "I guess I do love her. And that's why…I know it doesn't sound like it, but I do want what's best for her. I just don't know if that's me."

Nita prayed for God's guidance before speaking. "Okay, Ron, consider this. I don't want her left with someone who may not love her and care for her or keep her safe. So, if you do decide to give her up for adoption, please don't do it without letting me know."

"See, that's the thing. I don't know if I can accept never seeing her again or knowing if she's loved or cared for."

Lord, do I want to take on raising another child at this point in my life? "I would have to pray about it, but I would consider adopting her. I made lots of mistakes raising my boys, but hopefully I learned enough to be a good mother to her."

"But what if I wanted to be a part of her life? Am I supposed to just sign and walk away and never see her again?"

"I would be very disappointed if you did. But do you think you would be able to handle her calling another man daddy?"

His head snapped up and he stared at her. "You mean you're going to get married? To who? I hope it's not to one of those jokers I've seen. I couldn't tolerate the idea of either one of those jerks around my child."

"I wouldn't rule marriage out if God sent the right man along. But think about this - if someone you don't know adopted her, you would have to tolerate her calling them mommy and daddy, and they may not agree to you being in the picture."

He groaned and rubbed his hands over his face. "Uh, uh. Right now, I suppose I need to keep things as they are until I can sort through it all. Is that okay with you? Will you help me until I can make a decision?"

"Yes, I'll help you. But Ron, you need to pray about this. I don't believe it's God's will for you to give your baby away."

He was reminded again of Pastor Robinson's message on manhood that morning. "I have been praying about it, and will continue to do so. Do you need anything?"

"No, Ron, I still have the credit card you gave me, and some of the money as well. You're good."

"Well, I need to pay you anyway," he said, and laid several hundred dollars on the table. "Just keep using the card for whatever you need."

Nita smiled. "Thanks, Ron."

"Okay, well, I'm going to leave. I'll drop Destiny off sometime tomorrow." He grabbed Destiny and her bag and walked to the door, then turned, pushed her hair back, and kissed her gently on the scar, and said, "Don't open this door for anyone tonight."

Ron left feeling as though a ton of weight had been lifted from his shoulders. Things were okay again – at least for now.

CHAPTER FIFTEEN

Nita could hardly contain her excitement. Frankie was coming home today. It had been too long, and that, added to Mikey's disappearance, had been a heavy burden on her heart. But thankfully, Frankie had decided to push through whatever had kept him away.

Joel, along with Jason's son, Patrick, had already left for the airport to pick him up, while Nita put the finishing touches on the meal that included all of Frankie's favorites.

But when the door opened, Frankie was accompanied by a tall, slender young lady who clung to him like she was afraid he was going to get away.

Nita hugged Frankie, and was introduced to the girl, whose name was Blanca. She welcomed her and looked at her son, who refused to return her look. "Frankie, I wish you had told me you were bringing company. Maybe I could have fixed something special for dinner."

"Oh that's alright Mrs. Stanhope," Blanca said. "We won't be staying for dinner anyway. I've made reservations at a hotel downtown. We'll have dinner there, and then we have plans to attend an event with some friends."

"Oh. I see." Nita knew she didn't do well in hiding her disappointment. "Frankie, I was looking forward to us spending some time together as a family. Nothing against you, of course, Blanca, but we haven't seen him in such a long time." She held the tears demanding release. Apparently Blanca was the one calling the shots in Frankie's life now.

"Mom, don't worry, we'll get together. Wow, you look fantastic," Frankie said, hugging her again. "How did you lose all that weight?"

"Thanks, Baby. I've just been exercising and watching what I eat. It's as simple as that, and it's easier since I don't have you boys around to cook for everyday."

"Well, you better watch out, or some old dude will be trying to capture you, and I know you don't want that."

"And why wouldn't I, Frankie? There's still a lot of life left in me."

A surprised look briefly crossed his face as though the thought of another man in her life was out of the realm of possibility. "Well, you know…"

Blanca interrupted. "We really need to be going, Sweetheart. We have a busy evening ahead of us. And I agree with him, Mrs. Stanhope. You really do look wonderful."

"Thank you, Blanca. I sure do hate you won't be staying for dinner. Frankie, do you think you'll be able to come by tomorrow and spend some time with me?"

"I'm going to try, Mom, but Blanca has planned a pretty full schedule." He leaned over and kissed her. "We have to go. See ya."

Joel said, "We'll be back as soon as we drop them off, Mom. And don't worry, me and Pat will take care of all that food you cooked." He hugged her and hurried out.

The tears she had been holding escaped and ran down her face as she watched them leave. Frankie and his friend hadn't bothered to get beyond the foyer. The tears turned to sobs. "Lord, where did I go wrong with Frankie?"

Despair weighed heavily in her heart as she went into the family room, picked Destiny up and hugged her, then went into the kitchen to feed her. Afterwards, she went to her bedroom, where she put Destiny down for a nap, and changed into a comfortable lounger and turned on the television. An hour later, she heard Joel and Patrick come in and knew they would be in the kitchen for a while. Joel was sensitive enough to realize how she was feeling and wouldn't bother her, and he knew to put any leftovers away before going to bed.

The phone rang, and her heart jumped. *Frankie?* But it was Ron calling to tell her he had arrived in D.C.

"So did your son get in?" He asked.

"Yes, he did, but he brought his girlfriend with him, which he omitted telling me he was doing…and she had made hotel reservations for them downtown. I don't even know if I'll see him again while he's here. They weren't here long enough to sit down and visit, because his

girlfriend was anxious to get on with their plans." Tears were
streaming again, and she sniffed.

"Are you crying?" He asked, softly.

"Yes. I'm so disappointed, Ron. I wanted so much to spend some
time with my son, and I'm hurt that he didn't feel the same way."

"I wish I was there with you to offer a shoulder to cry on. You
have every right to be upset. He should have told you about his plans, at
least that way you could have been prepared."

"Never said a word," she choked out, as fresh tears escaped.
"Not even when he asked me to make reservations for him."

After a long pause, Ron said, "well, you know Frankie loves
you, but he's probably still working through some issues."

"I know, but it doesn't make it any easier. I have to go." She
hung up and boo-hooed.

The next morning, Frankie called around ten, and said he wanted
to come over.

"Is Blanca coming with you?" Nita asked.

"No, she has plans with her friends. She wanted me to go with
her, but I begged off."

Nita had to stop herself from expressing heartfelt relief. "Okay,
I'm happy I'll get to see you before you leave. Do you want Joel to pick
you up?"

"No, Patrick is on his way and we should be there shortly."

"Okay, Baby. I'll see you when you get here." Her spirits soared
as she hung up and hurriedly dressed herself and Destiny.

She had intended to introduce Frankie to Destiny last night, but the way things happened, she hadn't had a chance. She had no idea what his reaction to Destiny would be.

When Frankie arrived, he came in looking around the condo. "It's nice, Mom - much smaller than our house in Dallas, but I guess it's okay."

"It's plenty large enough for me, Frankie. So, tell me about your girlfriend. Why didn't you tell me she was coming?"

"I didn't know it when I talked to you. Don't you like her?"

And you couldn't call me back with that little tid-bit of information, she thought. "Well, honestly, I can't say that I like her right now because she didn't stay around long enough for me to find out. How did you two meet?"

"She's a senior at Spellman, and we met at a social function. But she grew up in Atlanta, and her parents are prominent citizens there."

"Oh really? Sooo, why is she hanging out with a sophomore?" Ordinarily, Frankie should have been a junior, but his transfer had caused him to lose some credits.

He smiled. "What's not to like about me?" He answered, while looking around and finally spotting Destiny sleeping in her playpen in the corner of the living room. "Who is that?"

"That's Destiny. She lives here with me most of the time."

"Who does she belong to?" He asked, with a frown. "And why does she live here?"

"She belongs to a friend, Ron Gilmore, and she's here with me because he's a single parent and needs help right now."

Frankie looked at her with disgust. "You've let some dude dump his baby off on you? Are you that stupid?"

Hot anger shot through her. "Caring for an innocent baby no matter who she belongs to doesn't make me stupid, Son. You know, I just saw something that I've prayed I would never see in any of my children. I saw cruelty coming out of you that reminded me of your father, and that hurts my heart." Tears streamed down her face as she turned and walked into the kitchen.

Frankie slumped down on the sofa, with a disgruntled look on his face.

Joel, who had walked into the room in time to hear most of their encounter, said, "Man, what's wrong with you? Have you forgotten how many beatings mom took to keep dad off of us? Well I haven't! If I ever see her crying again over something you said, I'm going to kick your behind!"

Although Frank was the oldest, Joel was taller and more muscular. Frankie stood up. "I'm just being honest. Mom is just stupid, letting some guy use her, and after the way dad treated her, she ought to know better. I just don't want to see her getting hurt again."

Joel scowled. "Did I hear you call our mother stupid?" When Frank just looked at him, Joel grabbed him by the shirt and was getting ready to hit him.

Nita ran into the room. "Joel, stop it! He has a right to his own opinion." She wiped at the tears on her face. "The last thing I want is my children fighting each other."

Joel gave him a dirty look. "You ever talk to my mother like that again, you'll wish to God you had never been born. Mom's just being

herself by loving that little baby. You need to get your head out of
your butt and start recognizing." He stormed out of the room and up the
stairs, then came back.

"You know what? It steams me that both my brothers are so
insensitive to our Mom. You don't know how often she cries over both
of y'all. You talking about Ron using her, but look at the way you're
hurting her. If you came around more, you would know that Ron's
actually a good guy, and he's probably one of the best people Mom could
have around because he's not going to let anybody hurt her."

Frankie grunted, then said, "If that's what she wants then fine.
I'm out of here! I'll call Patrick and see if he can take me back to the
hotel."

Nita heard his comment as she came back into the room. "Well,
maybe that's for the best, Son. But you don't have to call Patrick. I'll
drive you back. But let me say this. I love you, Son. You're my first
baby. I've loved you since I knew you were on the way. But my days of
taking abuse from anyone are over. If or when you decide to come back,
I'll welcome you, but you must come back ready to show me respect and
to accept the decisions I make about how I live my life. My victim days
died with your dad. Understand?"

A frown marred Frankie's face, but he answered, "Yes, m'am."

"I'll go with you, Mom," Joel said. "Is Destiny's car seat in the
truck?"

"Yes it is. Just give me a few minutes to get her ready." She
picked up the baby and headed upstairs to change her.

It was difficult for Nita to get through the remainder of the day,
as she tried to fight off the despair her argument with Frankie had

caused. In her wildest dreams, she wouldn't have thought that could have happened.

Joel ate leftovers from the refrigerator, then decided to visit some friends. Nita retreated to her bedroom with Destiny, and while the baby napped, she decided to read to take her mind off of her troubles.

Before she knew it, she was napping too, and woke up when the phone rang. It was Ron.

"Hey, Nita! How are things? Any better?"

"No, not really." She told him about Frankie's return visit. "I ended up taking him back to hotel."

"That's too bad," Ron said. "I know how badly you wanted to see him. So do you think the girlfriend is the problem?"

Nita sighed. "She's the one I would like to blame, but really, the blame rests squarely on Frankie. He never should have sprung her on me with no warning, and he's acting like a real jerk."

"Why would he do that?"

"I really don't know. I'm baffled over his actions and attitude." She decided not to mention Frankie's remarks about him and Destiny.

"Well, it's probably going to be Sunday night before I can leave here. These people have a full day of events planned tomorrow, and the ones I'm scheduled to attend are spread out until late in the day. I sure hate that because I'm ready to come home."

"Hmmm, that's crazy. Wonder why they did it like that?"

"I wish I knew. He mentioned something about his sister, who was supposed to come and coordinate things, but since she couldn't make it, his wife just kind of messed everything up."

A tiny light flickered in the back of her mind. "Ron, where are you?"

"I'm in D.C. and Maryland. Why?"

"Who is this guy you're working for? Would it be James Sullivan?"

"Yeah, but how did you know that?"

"I'm the sister who was supposed to be there. Ron, is James anywhere near you? Would you put him on the phone?"

A few minutes passed before she heard her brother's voice. "Hello?"

"James?"

"Yes, this is James. Who is this?"

"James, this is your little sister. Your architect is a friend of mine. Small world, huh? How are things going?"

"Nita! Girl, why aren't you here? I need you bad. Anna has things so messed up, but we're making it through. I like Gilmore. He's designed some beautiful facilities for me. Can't wait to see them up."

She chuckled. "Where is Ron? Put him back on."

"Nita? You mean James is the brother you were supposed to come and help out?"

"Yep, you got it."

"Amazing."

Ron did a lot of praying and thinking while in D.C. He woke up each morning thanking God that his life seemed to be on the right track...or was getting there. But his mind quickly went to Nita, where it stayed. He wondered how she was doing, and if she had gotten over her disappointment with her son. He wanted to hold her and comfort her, just be there for her. She had endured so much pain during her life, and he was sure he didn't even know the half of it.

Nita's brother told him a little more about the abuse her husband had inflicted on her, but even he said there was a lot he didn't know. Ron wanted to grab her oldest and youngest sons, and strangle both of them for hurting their mother like they were doing. But he doubted Nita would let that happen. He admired her strength, the love she extended to everyone, and even her kindness toward those she knew were seeking to use her – like the shyster lawyer and the Arkansas hoodlum. He saw dollar signs in both their eyes, and knew they regarded her as a soft target. But not if he could help it. In fact, he planned to run both of them off for good.

A thought struck like lightening, sending him into shock. Was he also guilty of taking advantage of Nita by pushing his child off on her? "Oh, God help me!"

He had fallen for Nita on the cruise, and she had been dogging his thoughts like no other woman ever had before. But Destiny's arrival had confused the issue.

But now he knew beyond a shadow of doubt. He loved her. And by Sunday, when he was on his way home, he was, for the first time in his life, seriously contemplating marriage. He knew he was ready to forsake the lifestyle he had loved for so long. But was he really ready to be a husband and father? Would Nita ever believe that his feelings for her had everything to do with their destiny together, and not just Destiny's well-being?

He didn't dread getting back home this time. In fact, he could hardly wait for the plane to land. He wanted to talk to his brother, then get to Nita.

He alternated between praying and ranting and raving against the traffic. The closer he got to his brother's house, the more nervous he felt. This was a step toward changing his whole life, and that was pretty scary.

After he got to his brother's house, he lost no time in asking Jason if they could talk privately. He saw the curious look on Jason's face as he led him into his office.

Ron began, nervously. "Uh…Jason, how do you know if you're ready to be a good husband or not? How do you know if one woman will be enough when you're…you know…used to playing around with lots of women?"

Amusement settled on Jason's face. "So you're thinking about getting married, huh? To who?"

"Nita."

"Are you sure?"

"Yes, I think so."

"You think! You mean you don't know for sure?" Jason shook his head. "Not good, brother. Not good. Several possible candidates came into my mind. Chantal, since she's your baby's mama. Then there's Velma, Shayla, Vickie. The list could on and on, so I didn't know who you could be talking about, but you most definitely should."

"It's Nita. But what if I'm wrong, and only caught up in the situation with Destiny."

"Well, is it because of Destiny? Do you love Nita? Is there another woman you think you might want other than Nita?"

"No! I mean, yes! I do love Nita. When I'm with another woman, the only one on my mind is Nita. Remember when Vickie cussed me out for calling her Nita?"

Jason burst into laughter. "This could be it for you brother."

"No other woman has been able to move me lately. I can't be around her without wanting to hold her and kiss her. That's pretty disconcerting. I just never thought something like this would happen to me."

"This is the place in your life that's probably going to determine your destiny. You have to pray that God will guide you, because where He guides you to is where your peace will be."

"I'm just worried that I don't have it in me to be the husband Nita needs? The last thing I want to do is bring more pain into her life."

"That's your starting place and your guiding star," Jason said, smiling. "If you keep that mind set, you'll do everything in your power not to do that. You know what? I think you've already chosen your path," he teased. "You're just scared to travel it."

"Huh!" Ron looked uneasy. "Remember, I have a lifetime of yielding to temptation to overcome."

"Ron, I'm not trying to say that once you make a commitment to a woman that you won't ever be tempted. Nope, temptation is everywhere. Sometimes I feel like I'm walking through a mine field. It seems like every step I take could be the wrong one. I know I'm going to be tempted, but the victory comes in not yielding."

"I don't know if I'm strong enough not to yield. It would be a constant fight."

"And you think I don't have to fight?" Jason asked, a cynical look on his face. "If I'm making this sound easy or simple, believe me, I don't mean to. It gets mighty hard out there because some of those women look awfully good and they know how to come on strong. I have all kinds of opportunities everyday."

"So what do you do? How do you handle it?"

"It just wouldn't be worth it. Surely you know that by now."

"Yeah, but come on, I know you must seriously think about giving in sometimes."

"Even if I did think about it, Jaci told me that if I ever cheated on her, she would know and would return tit for tat. I don't know if she meant that, but I do know the Word of God says that whatever you sow, that shall you also reap. You already know what the thought of my wife with another man does to me. I still can't believe how crazy I went that time."

"Yeah, you really lost it," Ron said, laughing hard. "But you know Jaci would just leave your behind before she would do something like that."

"And that's better? Either way, I wouldn't have my wife and I'm not taking that chance. Plus, as her husband, I'm answerable to God, and responsible for protecting my family in everyway."

"Darn! That some heavy responsibility."

"Yep, it is. So what it comes down to is, am I willing to risk everything – my wife, children, a home I love to come to at the end of the day - for a few minutes with a stranger? Someone who could bring any number of complications along to destroy my life? No way! I'm happier than I've ever been in my life, have everything I've ever wanted in a woman right at home. If I have to pray for strength twenty-four/seven I will, and trust that God's strength is made perfect in my weakness."

Ron looked more nervous than when he'd arrived. "I just don't want to commit to something I'll be sorry about, but I don't want to lose something I'll wish for later on."

"Well, you can't keep messing around just because you're afraid to commit to one woman. You should know that by now."

Ron sat there in deep thought. Nita was years ahead of him in her relationship with the Lord. She was beautiful, kind and generous, and she loved Destiny as though she were hers. He liked and respected her, and enjoyed being in her presence. But was what he felt enduring love, lust or gratitude?

Jason observed the battle going on in his brother, but knew it was Ron's to fight. He finally said, "Well, count up the costs on both sides of the issue, weigh it out and see what wins."

When Ron recalled all the troubles his lifestyle had caused him over the last months, he knew he didn't want to play anymore. He was tired of the consequences, although just one would be a lasting reminder, but that was enough. "I already know what wins," Ron said. "Nita and Destiny." He walked to the door. "See ya, brother. Thanks."

Admittedly, giving up other women was like throwing out a pair of favorite shoes that were falling apart. They were no more good, but it still hurt to part with them. However, the *right* woman had been presented to him in a couple of unconventional ways, and destiny was calling. He headed to Nita's house.

Twenty minutes later he was pulling into her drive way. "Hello!" He said, groaning with pleasure as he engulfed her in a tight embrace.

"Hey, Ron. It sounds like you're really happy to get back."

"Yeah, I am because I have lots of things on my mind."

"Well, come have dinner first. I made spaghetti and meatballs, tossed salad and garlic bread. If Joel had been here, you would be out of luck because this is his favorite meal."

"Well, I'm happy he wasn't because this is so good," Ron said, as he attacked the food she placed in front of him, and ate as much as he could hold before sighing contentedly. "I'm stuffed. That's eight or ten extra hours in the gym."

"Well don't blame me. I didn't force it down your thr..." She stopped, a puzzled look on her face. "Why in the world are you starring at me like that?" She questioned.

Ron's eyes never left her face. He finally spoke – his voice shaky and lacking its usual ring of confidence and arrogance. "What kind of man would you consider marrying?" He asked, curiously

"Well first of all, he would have to be a Christian. He would have to be strong, secure enough in himself to be able to love God, love and cherish me, and honor our marriage vows. He would have to be a man that I loved enough to give up the freedom I'm enjoying now, because I don't want to ever get trapped in another marriage of misery. We would have to be compatible in all the ways that count - ways I've observed in some marriages – like Jaci and Jason's. Why?"

"I just need to know," he said quietly. *Was he that man?*

"What about you? Will you ever forsake your playboy ways and settle down?"

"Well, until recently, I've liked being free and responsible for no one but myself, but now, it's time to leave that behind me. So…yes, I would consider it. He paused a few seconds, then asked, "Would you consider marriage to me?"

She was quiet a long time before answering. "No, because frankly, I don't think I see the characteristics in you that I would seek in a husband."

Ron's heart cracked in pain. "Well, maybe that's because you haven't had the chance to get to know the real me," he said mockingly, knowing it was a tired, flippant line.

The look Nita leveled on him told him she knew it too. "Please! Can't you be real for once in your life. I know there's a good man in there somewhere. You just need to grow up, become the man God intended you to be, and let him out of there."

He struggled to fight back anger, even though he knew she was right. "What gives you the right to come down on me like that? You haven't done so well yourself."

"You opened the door when you asked if I would consider marrying you. I was just trying to answer as honestly as I can. And you're right, I haven't done well. I tried to do it right, but my husband didn't know how to appreciate it, and he actually tried to beat it out of me."

Ron felt lower than a snake. "I'm sorry, Nita, that was a cheap shot."

"Yes it was," she agreed, quietly.

"So how would you handle it if you had it to do over?"

"I wouldn't do it again – not like that. I am here today because God kept me from being killed. He kept me sane, helped me to raise my children and protect them from the violence as much as possible, and He's giving me another chance to live in peace and contentment, and fulfill my purpose by contributing something good to this world. That's why it irks me to see you wasting your life."

"Excuse me! I am not wasting my life. In fact, I am contributing something good by designing structures that are beautiful, practical, safe and enjoyable. I'd say that's a gigantic contribution to the world."

"Yes, in that area of your life you are. But what about in other areas? What about when you go home? Is there peace and contentment there? Or do you look for reasons not to go home? And what about your child? Do you have peace about raising her?"

He gave her a disconcerted look. "You shoot from the hip, don't you, lady? You know Destiny was nothing but an accident as far as I'm concerned."

"Ron, no child is an accident. Every child is a gift from God. And however she got here, she's here! She didn't ask to be born and shouldn't have to suffer simply because her parents are selfish, immature, and irresponsible."

Another jolt of anger made him level a hard look at her. "I'm about tired of you dumping on me. Should my life be turned upside down because of some silly, money grubbing woman's decision to have a child so she can gouge me for money?"

"Well, have you considered marrying the woman and providing a home for your child? I mean you must have enjoyed spending time with her at some point. Destiny wouldn't be here if you hadn't."

The look he gave her could have propelled her into the next county. "There is no way I would marry that woman."

"Why not? She was good enough for you to sleep with. Be fair about it. She didn't do any more wrong than you did."

"Now that's where you're way off track. That woman deliberately set a trap for me. I was just having a good time."

"See! That's what I hate about your lifestyle. You're just having a good time, but it's hurting innocent people – especially children. Destiny didn't ask to be conceived while you were having a good time, so why did she have to suffer?"

"That may be, but two wrongs don't make it right. You know as well as I do that Chantal is not wife material. She's dishonest, conniving, deceitful…and a criminal! What rational man would marry a woman like that?"

"So what kind of woman would you marry?"

He drew an impatient breath. "One like my mother, like Jaci, or like you tried to be."

"There's that old double standard. You want to live like the devil, but marry a Godly woman. Don't you know that Godly women want Godly men - not ungodly heathens? They know it's better to remain single than be yoked to an ungodly man and live in hell."

Ron laughed. "Are you kidding? There are just as many women like Chantal as there are men like me. You don't even know what's going on in the world."

"Yes, I do, and it saddens me. That's why I'm content with my life as it is right now. But I have children who will probably be looking to marry someone in the future, and I shiver when I think about the women they could end up with."

He gave her a hard look. He was flustered, but refused to leave it alone. "Okay. Would you marry me if I became the kind of man you want?"

"Not unless I saw evidence of it," she answered, calmly.

"But what if you did see the evidence. Haven't you even noticed that I'm trying?"

"Yes, I've seen some changes, but frankly, you're not there yet."

CHAPTER SIXTEEN

What. Was. That?

Nita lay in bed in the semi darkened room listening to the rain pounding on the roof and spattering against the windows. It was one of her favorite sounds, but one seldom enjoyed since her childhood days in Grammy's warm bed in the room they called the backroom.

She snuggled down into the warmth and comfort of her bed, savoring the pleasant clatter. "Lord, I'm not going to try and figure out what that conversation with Ron was about. I'm just going to lay it on Your altar and trust that You'll give me the wisdom to understand."

She lay there, enjoying the sound of the rain, and continued to pray, "Father, please let my children be somewhere warm, dry and safe. And yes, Destiny and Ron, too."

She was still trying to get over the fact that Ron had insisted on taking Destiny home with him since he didn't plan to go to work the next day. She smiled, turned over and snuggled deeper. She drew a contented breath, found a comfortable spot and let the music of the rain lull her into peaceful sleep.

She woke up Monday morning feeling rested and relaxed to find it was still raining. There was no Destiny to drop off at daycare, so she decided not to go to the gym. After checking her e-mail, and sending out her usual message to her sons, she settled in her favorite chair by the window, and sipped on a hot cup of coffee, while she tried to unravel the conversation with Ron.

Had he been speaking hypothetically, or was he actually contemplating marriage to her? He had looked rather disturbed when he left, but what had he really expected her answer to be? In light of his recent thoughts about finding a permanent solution for Destiny, what was his true motive for marriage? Could it be he saw her as a convenient answer...a mother for Destiny, while keeping the baby under his wings, and a wife when he needed one to use as cover from a determined woman? And would she consider marrying him just to hold on to the baby?

Her mind took a flying leap to the other men who had invaded her life. She could only hope they would leave as easily as they had come, but she doubted it.

Tyson. She hadn't started out with any great expectations from him anyway. In fact, she still didn't know why she'd even agreed to go out with him…maybe the desire to find out what was really on his mind? Anyway, he was a big disappointment. She looked across the room at the latest floral arrangement he had sent. The dude hadn't given up.

Tony. She shook her head in disgust. What a pitiful excuse for a man! He didn't even try to hide his desire to marry a woman to take care of him. She hadn't heard from him since Ron had thrown him out, and hoped she never would.

"Lord, have mercy! If these are the kind of men I have to look forward to, then maybe I need to come to peace about remaining single the rest of my life. Or You need to send me a decent man – and quick."

Ron. Her thoughts led her back to Ron. In spite of his womanizing reputation, and Destiny aside, he had shown her kindness and concern. He was hardworking, generous, thoughtful, and hadn't hesitated to protect her in some touchy situations. And although he was honest about not wanting Destiny, he hadn't let that stop him from trying to do what was best for her. Additionally, he was obviously trying to make some lifestyle changes.

She groaned. "Lord, I don't know why my mind is taking me around in these circles this morning. But when I consider these three men and weigh out my ideal against reality, Ron would be the winner – even though he's no prize. But at least I'd get the bonus of a baby girl. I know this might be an unconventional way of thinking, but I'd rather have a man I know is at least making an effort to live for You, than have to continue to fight off the Tysons and Tonys, whose motives are questionable, for the rest of my life. Anyway, it's time to find something to put into my rumbling stomach."

She picked up her now cold cup of coffee and headed to the kitchen. She was standing in the open refrigerator door, trying to decide whether she wanted turkey bacon, eggs and toast, or if she could settle for a bowl of oatmeal, when the unexpected sound of the doorbell caused her to jump. "Wonder who that could be?" Thinking of Tony, she made use of the peephole, and saw it was a delivery man with a huge floral arrangement. "Tyson's up to his usual tricks."

She opened the door, offered the guy a tip, which he told her had already been taken care of, and walked slowly back into the kitchen with the flowers. The card was larger than he normally sent…greeting card size. Her mouth fell open when she saw the signature.

The pre-printed card read, *"I know I blew it. Will you give me another chance?"* Her mouth fell further open when she read his handwritten note.

"I know you like flowers, and forgive me for not sending them before, and for treating you like you're only my babysitter. You are much, much more, and from now on, I plan to demonstrate it. Please keep an open mind about me, and about my question, which wasn't hypothetical." Love, Ron.

She stumbled to a chair and sat down in amazement. She re-read his note a few times before she smiled, then started laughing. "This is a weird turn of events. So what should my response be?"

She ate a bowl of whole grain cereal, and decided to do some work on the Foundation. She had no idea when Ron would bring Destiny back, but she refused to call him. She had been hard at work for almost three hours when the ringing phone interrupted her. *Lord, please let it be Mikey*, she uttered her usual prayer. But the caller I.D. showed Tyson's name. "Oh, Lord!"

"Hi Anita. How are you?"

"I'm fine, Tyson. What do you want?"

"Well, I was sure hoping for a warmer reception. I'm still on your unfavorable list, huh?"

"As a matter of fact, yes. I don't take kindly to being told what to do, or who I can see."

"Anita, can we please start over? I promise not to try to tell you what to do. I miss you, our time together, our talks about life and everything. I understand if you're not ready for a relationship, but I sure would like to continue our friendship. Is that possible?"

"No, Tyson, and I have to go now."

"Okay," he said disappointedly. "You take care, Anita."

The next call a few minutes later was C.J. "Hey, Cij, what's up?"

"Just calling to see how things are going."

"Oh, Lord! I have a lot to tell you about, girl. Too much to tell on the phone. When can we get together?"

"Oh darn! I have a full schedule at work this week, and Friday, I'm leaving to take Geordie to South Carolina to see his parents. Is that crazy jerk back again?"

"No, no, it's not about him. Thank God. But I did just get a call from Tyson."

"Okay. You think Ron can send him packing, like he did Tony?"

"Well, uh, there's some new developments with Ron. Big ones!"

She squealed. "What, girl? Tell me!"

"Nope. It'll wait until you get back, and there might be more by then."

She squealed again. "You're wrong for making me wait like this. You must know it's something I'm not going to like, huh?"

"Well...maybe."

"That's okay then. I ain't hardly wanting to hear something that's going to run my blood pressure up before I leave town. There's enough to do that already."

"So have you had any ideas about the business?"

"Well, I've been praying about it, and know you have too. Anyway, just out of the blue, someone I met through the job said he likes the way I do things, and asked me to plan and coordinate an event for him. So that got me to thinking, maybe we need to look into event planning or something like that. We can expand it in several ways. What do you think?"

"I don't know. Is there a big enough demand for that kind of business?"

"That's what we have to find out. At any rate, this just kind of fell into my lap, and I'll really need your help with it. Please?"

"Sure, I'll help you. And I'll also start doing a little online research on event planning."

"Great! I'll call you when I get back."

"Okay, C.J. Have a good trip."

"I'll try, but you know to be praying, right? Bye."

Shortly after C.J.'s call, Nita got a surprising call from Frankie.

"Hi, Mom. You doing alright?"

"Frankie! I'm fine, Baby. What about you?"

"I'm fine. I just want to apologize. I'm so sorry for acting like such a jerk. I shouldn't have brought Blanca with me when I knew you were wanting to spend time with me. And I'm also sorry for all that other stuff I said. I just want to let you know that I love you and I'm sorry for hurting you like that. I guess you should have let Jo go ahead and beat me down for doing that. You have enough to worry about with Mikey missing, and I don't need to add to that. I'm so sorry, Mom."

Tears were streaming down her face. "Baby, I'm sorry too. I suppose I should have explained about the baby being here rather than springing her on you like that."

"Well, I want to come back and see you soon. Is that okay?"

"Yes, Baby, you know it is. Just let me know when. And I hope it'll work out so Joel can be here. I want you two back on good terms."

"Okay, mom. I guess you haven't heard from Squeak, huh?"

"No, but you know I'm still praying."

"Yeah, I know you are, Mom. I'll be back in touch after I see when I can come."

Thank God! "Okay, Son. I love you, and remember who you are, and whose you are."

"I know, Mom." He was laughing when he hung up the phone.

Nita was boo-hooing. "Thank you, Father for answering my prayers about Frankie."

When the phone rung again a few minutes later, she knew it was time to give up trying to work anymore. This time it was Ron.

"Hey, Nita, you okay? Did you get some rest last night?"

"Yes – to both questions. Thank you for the flowers. They're beautiful. I'm still trying to digest the card, though. How's Destiny?"

"She's fine. In fact, I'm getting ready to bring her home if you're ready for her. We had a rowdy night, but I think she's understanding that she's going to be here some of the time. I took her to see her grandparents this morning. That was interesting."

Nita gasped. "You did? And how did that go?"

"Jason and Monique went with me, and we all confronted them about Destiny."

"And what did they say?"

"Believe it or not, Pops was the first one to admit they were wrong, but Mom agreed. They promised things were going to change. Listen, can we talk when I get there? Our conversation last night didn't go as planned."

"If that's what you want, yes, we'll talk."

"It's what I want. And oh, have you cooked anything for lunch?"

She laughed. "No, but I can fix something."

"No, don't do that. I'll bring something, or I'll take you somewhere if you prefer."

"No, uh…bring something…surprise me."

"Alright, we'll see you shortly." They arrived a little while later, with Ron juggling Destiny and a large bag filled with something that smelled wonderful.

Destiny screamed with joy when she saw Nita and fell into her arms. She turned and looked back at her daddy with a triumphant smile, and hugged Nita again.

"I think she's glad to see me," Nita said, with a smile.

"Well, she almost saw you at two o'clock this morning. Her screaming had me and Monique both pulling our hair out. But I realize she needs to spend more time with me, and I want her to know her grandparents, even if they don't want to know her."

"Well, let's eat while the food is hot. It smells great."

They ate the delicious food from a popular Italian restaurant, then she gave Destiny, who was more than ready for a nap, a bottle and put her in her crib. Afterwards, she waited for Ron to say what was on his mind.

"Nita, I love you and want to marry you. You've known since the cruise that I'm attracted to you physically, but the way you've opened your heart and home to Destiny has been like blinders being removed from my eyes and my mind. Truthfully, until recently, I didn't care about a woman's character or anything beyond her outward characteristics, but my experiences over the last several months have taught me a lot. I not only need more, I want more. And beside God, you are the person I need and want most."

Nita sat quietly, not sure how to take in what he was saying, but praying for wisdom.

"You have become such an essential part of my life that I want to be close to you all the time. Because of you, I'm drawing closer to God, I'm learning to love and care for my child, and I'm more at peace with myself. You bring out the best in me and motivate me to try and be a better man. I'm praying more, and asking God to help me become a man who honors Him in all my ways."

He moved closer, and his hands went to her face, where they caressed every part of it from her lips to her forehead. He ran his thumb over the raised scar that remained from one of Frank's beatings, lowered his head and tenderly kissed it. "I hate what Frank did to you. If he were still alive, I'd probably be looking for him right now," he stated, softly. "I'm just now coming to understand that a man can love a woman more for what she is on the inside than for how she looks on the outside. You are so beautiful both inside and outside that I don't see how he could fail to appreciate what he had, so much so that he could hurt you like that. I know we're not supposed to speak ill of the dead, but I hope the jerk is burning in hell." He kissed her lips softly, then said, "Nita, will you marry me? I know I'm not all I should be, but I am trying hard to get there. Will you be my wife and Destiny's mother? Will you let me take care of you, and protect you from jerks and hoodlums? We both need you so much, Nita."

Her heart pounded as she pondered his proposal. She prayed silently, *Lord, give me wisdom and a sound mind.* She felt him watching her, waiting for her response.

"Tell me something, Ron." She met the eyes that were probing hers. "Why now? Why me? And be honest, if Destiny wasn't in the picture, would you be asking me to marry you? You keep saying you're not the same man – and I do detect changes – but what is driving these changes? And are they changes for the duration, or just something to get you through a rough patch and then it's back to business as usual?"

"I'm not crazy, Sweetheart."

"Huh?" She looked at him in puzzlement.

"It's insanity to keep doing the same thing expecting a different result, and I'm ready for a change."

"Oh."

"You stir things in me that I've never felt before. I can imagine life without Destiny, but I can't imagine life without you. I've agonized over whether I'm good enough for you, and I should be ashamed to admit it but I take a little comfort in the fact that if you put up with a jerk like Frank all those years, then surely you'll have a little mercy for me too."

"So, are you trying to convince me, or yourself that you're done with your playboy lifestyle? Have you prayed and asked God to show you who your wife should be?"

"You. I don't have to convince myself. I've already tried to talk myself out of doing this. But I can't, because I need you. I've never known the peace or contentment with other women that I have with you. I know I have a lot of growing to do, but please believe me, if you marry me, I'll do everything in my power to make sure you'll never regret it. I promise I'll never dishonor you or our marriage in any way."

"But what about Destiny?" she asked, quietly. "You can't leave her out of this."

"No, but because of you I'm learning to accept my responsibility as her father. And because of that little baby girl, God has brought us together. I truly believe God wants us to love each other and be a family. Chantal had no idea when she named her Destiny, how true it would be. I'm learning that God has a sense of humor, and what a person means for evil, He'll get in it and work it out for good in wonderful ways."

"Amazing. Who would have ever thought it. Ron Gilmore quoting scripture."

"Yeah, I'm surprised about that myself, but I enjoy reading the Word and listening to it. I can't believe how much power there is in it."

"I don't know, Ron. You have to admit it's a long stretch to believe you."

Ron hung his head. "You know some of what's happened to me. Destiny is evidence that speaks for itself – but there's a lot you don't know."

"Well...are you going to tell me everything or not?"

He twitched in his chair, scratched his head, rubbed his hand across his face and took a long breath. "I'm not proud of some of the things I've done in life, in fact, some of it makes me ashamed. But here it is..."

He started talking, and told all. "Things actually started unraveling before I hooked up with Chantal, but it just snowballed after that ...one thing after the other. Maybe I'm just getting old, but I just don't want to deal with all that anymore."

Nita nodded. "Obviously, we're both at turning points in our lives, Ron, but it would be unwise to rush into anything. Why don't we give ourselves time to discover what God would have us do."

"I know what I want, but I can understand if you need some time. I had to tell you how I feel though."

"Ron, I do need some time. You can see my visible scars, but you can't see the emotional scars I carry. I can't commit to a relationship until I'm sure I'm whole again. And I think you would benefit from a long cooling off period as well. Afterall, you still have women, hot and heavy, after you. But beyond that, we don't really know enough about each other. God commands that a husband and wife be equally yoked, but are we? For instance, what is the depth of your relationship with the Lord? Who are you and what do you really love - other than women and architecture? What's your favorite sport and sports team? Color? Food? Have you ever been arrested? How old are you? When is your birthday?

Are you the jealous type? How do you handle anger and disappointment? Do you hit women? Or do you verbally and emotionally abuse them? Do you have any emotional disturbances? Can you cook anything? What are your plans for the future? I plan to start a business and go back to school, so how do you feel about that? Are you a neat freak or a slob? Do we have anything in common, other than Destiny? Do we even like each other and spending time together? I love your daughter, but can you accept my children, and my responsibilities to them? The list could go on…those are just things that are coming to mind now. So…well?"

Ron looked overwhelmed. "I see what you mean, but we can learn all that stuff about each other."

"That's exactly what I'm suggesting, Ron. Let's be friends for now, and see what happens, okay?"

"And just what would being 'friends' entail?" He asked with a skeptical look.

"Basically, spending more time together, doing some fun things together to see how we get along, and praying about this. It's a starting point."

"Would we be seeing other people while we're just being 'friends?"

"Yes, if we want to. We'll just be friends, remember. And who knows, we may meet other people along the way – people that God has for us."

"Well…can I ask you out for dates…without Destiny? And send you flowers and be a shoulder for you to lean on like I promised Joel?"

"Of course," she said, laughing.

"Can I still kiss you?"

"I don't know if that's a good idea. That might muddy the water too much."

"And how long are we going to do this?"

"I don't know," she said, agitatedly. "We just play it by ear, see how things go."

He sighed. "To be honest, I don't particularly like the idea, but I admit it does make sense. Jaci put Jason through this kind of stuff when he wanted to marry her, and I guess it's worked out okay."

"This will also put to rest questions that may be hanging around in the back of our minds. On my part, I may wonder if you only want to marry me to get a mother for Destiny, and on your part, you may wonder if I'm only marrying you to get Destiny? And another big issue for me is your womanizing. I won't go that route again, Ron."

"And I wouldn't ask you to," he answered solemnly.

CHAPTER SEVENTEEN

Frank had been gone a year, and a lot had happened during that year. Nita had moved to another city, started a Foundation to help domestic violence victims, traveled a little, and had plans to take some college courses and start a business. Destiny, who was seven months old, had been with her four months. She was now a busy, roly-poly baby who was crawling all over the place and even trying to take steps. Three men had been in serious pursuit of her, with one proposing marriage. And Mikey had disappeared.

Joel, who hadn't been home in almost a month due to school activities, came home for the weekend, and she decided to tell him about Ron's proposal. Joel was the son who stuck with her no matter what. He didn't care about being called a mama's boy or worse by others. He was the son who had stood between her and Frank and said, "I love you, dad, but I love my mom too, and what you do to her – hitting on her and treating her like you do is not right. You need to stop it, get some help or something. When you hurt her, you hurt all of us, and I hate I have to say this, but I'm not going to let you do that anymore. You hurt my mother, I hurt you."

Surprisingly, Frank had backed down. And strangely, after that, Joel was the son that Frank seemed to favor.

Now, after hearing about Ron's proposal, Joel slid close to her on the sofa and laid his head on her shoulder. "Mom, you know what I think? He asked.

"What, Baby?"

"I think you should go ahead and say yes to Ron. I mean the guy's got his own bank – and plus, he's got Destiny, and you know you don't wanna lose her. But I really think he'll treat you right too."

"Oh come on! You know you're the one who wants to hold onto Destiny!"

He grinned. "Yeah, I do kinda like the little stink bomb."

Nita gave him a look out of the corner of her eye. "Why do I feel like I'm being sugared up for something? Come on, what is it?"

"Well, since you moved down here to Houston, I miss you, and want to be closer so I can keep an eye out. I've been thinking about transferring to Prairie View University. I'd really like to experience a predominantly Black campus, and I hear they have a pretty good engineering program too."

"Joel, don't think you have to keep an eye out for me. I don't want you under that kind of pressure, honey. I'm perfectly capable of taking care of myself."

"Well, there's more to it, I confess. Remember the girl I told you about? Well, she's decided to transfer too, so I can kill two birds with one stone. I can be close to both of you. And I really would like to work with Ron a little, too. I can learn a lot from him."

"Well, you've always known your own mind, and it sounds like you've already decided what you want to do. So what do we need to do?"

"I've already filled out my application, and I know there won't be a problem with me being accepted. This is a good time to do it since this term is almost over. We just need to get the finances transferred, and take care of the housing and all that stuff. So, it's a go?"

"Yes, Baby, it's a go."

"And what about Ron? Are you going to marry him? I really think you should, Mom."

"And just why do you think that? Did he pay you off?"

"Naw, naw! He couldn't do that…not that he would try, but I wouldn't say it if I didn't think he'd be good for you."

"Well, I'm thinking and praying about it. There's a lot to consider. Oh, by the way, Frankie wants to come back. He's going to call and let me know exactly when." It pained her to see the dark look that covered Joel's face.

"Well, don't let him spoil things for you and Ron, and you know he might try. That dude hates for things to change. I don't know why he thinks everything should stay the same. I'm surprised he was able to make the decision to transfer to Morehouse."

"Joel!" she scolded. "That's just his personality, Son. Everyone can't have the happy go lucky disposition that you have. Anyway, that's where he'd always wanted to go, and even though he hasn't expressed it, I know that like you, he didn't go at first because he didn't want to leave me at your dad's mercy."

"Yeah, yeah." He snapped his fingers. "Hey, maybe we can ride up to PV and scope out the campus while he's here."

"That's a great idea," she said, giving him a grateful hug.

"Jaci, I want to marry Nita, but she's put me off, saying we need to pray and get to know each other better. She won't even talk to me about my proposal. She obviously loves Destiny but when it comes to me, well, I just don't know."

"How do you really feel about Nita, Ron?" Jaci asked. "Do you want to marry her just because she loves your child, or because you have real feelings for her?"

"I'd be lying if I said her love for Destiny doesn't play into it, but I was attracted to Nita before Destiny even came on the scene. I think I fell in love with her on the cruise, before I even knew who she was. She drew me like no other woman ever had before. Yeah, I love her and would want her even if there was no Destiny in the picture."

"You know what, Ron? Your reputation is working against you. Under the best of circumstances, Nita would have a right to be leery, but with you she has even more reason for concern. She lived in a hellish domestic violence situation for a long time. The man was a womanizer who flaunted his affairs in her face and beat her if she objected. So any man with a known reputation as a womanizer is an immediate turn off for her. I don't blame her."

"But Jaci, you know how hard I'm working to change. I have changed! Doesn't that count for anything?"

"Yes, it does, to those of us who know you and have seen the changes take place. But we don't even know if they're going to last. I mean you were out there for a very long time. And you know what they say about a leopard changing its spots."

"What about your husband? He hadn't changed too long before you all got together, and you took his word that he had changed for good. Has he disappointed you?"

"No, and he'd better not!" Jaci said, laughing. "But it wasn't all that smooth for us either, and our situation was a little different. Jason had already committed his life to the Lord and had made a change before we met. But the first time Nita met you, you made sure she knew you were a player. Then there's the little matter of Destiny, a story that explains itself. Nita has every reason to be cautious. In fact, I don't know if she'll ever trust another man again."

"I would never, ever do anything to dishonor her, or hurt her. You know that."

"I'm not the one to convince."

"Just like Jason knew you were the right one when he met you, I know Nita is the right one for me. I love her, and I want to take care of her and cherish her. What can I do to prove I mean it? I'm sending her flowers and love notes everyday, and doing what I can to protect her from money grubbing jerks. I want to take her out to nice places, buy her things…you know …the works. I've asked Jason and my parents to be on the lookout for a good piece of property for me. I'm getting ready to build a house for us. I know she likes that condo, so I'm designing the house to be as much like the condo as I can."

"That's all well and good, Ron," Jaci said, "but don't you think you may be jumping the gun a little?"

"No, I'm ready for a house, even if things don't work out with Nita."

"Good! I can't wait to see what you come up with. You really outdid yourself with this one. I truly love my house." She said, looking around.

"Thanks."

"But Ron, you need to keep something in mind, brother. Not only do you have to work to get her, but you'll have to keep working hard to keep her…the love, the caring and cherishing…all of that has to be for keeps. Nita's had a really rough life since childhood. It's time for her to be nurtured. My concern is, do you have it in you to do that?"

"Yes. But if I ever have any doubts about being the man who can do that, I'll back off because I certainly don't want to add any more hurt to her. What did you mean about her having a rough life?"

"Well, I don't know if I should…"

"Come on, tell me. I want to know everything that will help me understand her, and know what to do to become the man she needs."

"Okay. But if you ever let Nita know I told you, you're going to be in big trouble." Jaci told him in a serious tone, then continued. "Nita grew up in a house where her parents didn't get along, and were constantly fighting. So, Nita was afraid and miserable most of the time. Then her mother died and her father's sister moved in with them. That old hag was as hateful as she could be. If it hadn't been for our grandparents, Nita's life would have been a lot worse, but they intervened and insisted on Nita spending a lot of time with them. I believe Nita's childhood played a big part in her being vulnerable to Frank. I think she was hoping to find the love and security she didn't get as a child when she married him. But Lord! She stepped right out of the fire and into the furnace."

"It was that bad, huh?"

"Yes! But in spite of everything, Nita was always the most loving and giving one of us cousins. I was the planner, C.J. the fighter, Gina, the encourager, and Nita, the nurturer. Of course, our male cousins were all hellions. One time…" Jaci stopped, thinking back to the time when Nita's aunt had knocked her to the floor. That was the only time they had seen their grandparents angry enough to fight.

"One day, we all went to Nita's house to see if she wanted to play ball. When Nita started out the door, her aunt told her to come back, she couldn't go. "Why?" Nita asked. "I've finished all my work."

Her aunt grabbed a water pitcher and hit Nita over the head with it. Nita fell to the floor with blood gushing from her head. Her aunt said, "I've told you about sassing me!"

We didn't stop running the entire mile to our grandparents' house. We thought Nita was dead. Grandpa climbed into his old truck, and drove to Nita's house and went in. He told her aunt, "Tell my son-in-law I came to get Nita, and I'm going to keep her. I'm not going to let you mistreat her anymore. We'll be back to get her clothes, but if I stay here now, I'll be tempted to hit you the same way you hit her." When the woman didn't say anything, grandpa yelled, "come on, Nita, let's go!" Jaci had tears in her eyes, just remembering what Nita had gone through. "Nita lived with our grandparents after that. She has an older brother and sister, but they seldom came around."

"Yeah, I met James," Ron answered, absently. "So, what happened? I know y'all didn't let that hag get away with that did you?"

Jaci started laughing. "Now, you know! Nobody was going to get away with doing that to one of the cousins! Nope, Aunt Muriel had to go down!"

"So, tell me! What did y'all do?" Ron asked, excitedly.

"We planned one of our famous cousin capers. People feared our capers!"

"Aw, man!" Ron exclaimed, with a smile. "I want to hear this."

"We started watching for the perfect opportunity to get Aunt Muriel back, and we finally got it. For some reason, Aunt Muriel still used the old outhouse that was barely still standing, despite the fact that they had indoor plumbing. Of course, we came to the conclusion that she went there to meet with her brother, Satan, because we truly believed that our grandmother was right, and she was the devil's sister.

One day we watched for her to make a trip to the outhouse, and followed her. Once she was inside with the door closed, we went into action. Our cousins, Buddy, Dusty and Big Ben threw ropes around the leaning building and then they put all their weight into pulling the structure to the ground. Aunt Muriel whooped and hollered, but no one heard her except the ones causing her trouble. We laughed until our stomachs hurt watching her trying to crawl out of the overturned outhouse. Aunt Muriel left the next day, stating she couldn't stay in a place where people allowed their children to act like heathens. Grammy made it a point to tell her that it takes a heathen to know one."

"So, what happened to her?" Ron asked. "Did she ever come back?"

"Heck, no. No telling what we would have done. We were pretty terrible."

"I believe that. I saw Nita bring a dude down on the cruise," he said, laughing. "And I remember how you brought down that woman who was stalking you. Remind me to tread lightly around you cousins."

"Well, you had to be there to understand how people took advantage of others when they thought they could get away with it. We righted a lot of wrongs in that community."

"Well, I'm going to keep trying to let Nita know how I feel, and show her that I'm the one she can depend on to love her and take care of her."

"Good. Now, I've got babies to feed."

CHAPTER EIGHTEEN

Nita prayed hard over the next week, as she prepared for Frankie's visit. And to say that Ron was taking up a lot of space in her

220

head was putting it mildly. He was sending flowers every day, with love notes, no less.

Surprisingly, Ron's mother called, and thanked her for helping Ron and taking such good care of Destiny. "I know we haven't been as supportive as we should have, but we were just so disgusted that he got himself into this mess, but as my children reminded us, it's not the baby's fault. They made me feel so bad I cried, because they were right. I have to start doing better by that baby, even though I'm running back and forth to Lufkin to check on my mother. I have two sisters and two brothers up there, but you know I have to do my part too."

"Well, I'm so glad you had a chance to visit with Desi. I love her, and Ron is really trying, but she needs to know others in her family . . . especially her grandparents."

"Oh, she's going to. Me and her grandpa fell in love with her. In fact, anytime you need a break, don't forget we're willing to baby sit. I can't take her on full time, but I can keep her some of the time."

Nita hung up the phone praising the Lord. "Lord, thank you! All we have to do is give You time and You'll work it out. Thank You so much, Father, because I know that had to be hurtful to Ron for his parents to ignore his child like that."

Frankie arrived mid-day on Friday, and after Nita picked him up from the airport, they went back home and had a nice visit. "I apologize again for acting like such a jerk on the last visit, Mom. When I told Blanca I was coming to Houston, the next thing I know, she had made reservations to come with me, and planned all that other stuff. I went along with her because…well, I didn't know how to get out of it. But I did realize that weekend that she wasn't the one. I don't think she's realized it though. She's still trying to get me to change my major."

"Son, you can't blame everything on Blanca. You could have told her you were coming to visit with your family and that anything else was out of the question. Instead, you chose to dump me and Joel. That was your choice, not hers."

"Okay, you're right. I should have manned up and told her to stay in Atlanta. But I felt so bad about the way I treated you that I'll do it right the next time, Mom. I'm so sorry."

"Just remember what I told you about respecting my decisions." She went over to him and kissed him. "Joel should be here in a little while, and I want you two to get along, alright? He's in the process of transferring to Prairie View, and plans to drive up there tomorrow to look around. He's hoping you'll go with him."

"Why's he doing that? I thought he was happy at SMU."

"I'll let him tell you why himself. I'm going to a get together tonight at Jaci's house, so you guys have the whole evening to hang out."

"What kind of get together?"

"Just a bunch of people getting together to eat and wind down. It's the first time I've been able to go, so I'm really looking forward to it."

"Will Destiny's dad be there?"

"Well, yes, I'm sure he will, but that's not why I'm going. There'll be lots of other people there as well. Why?"

"Just curious, that's all."

"Hmmm. Well, we'll talk more tomorrow. But now, I have to finish cooking and get ready for tonight."

That night, Jason, Ron and several of their friends had taken over kitchen duty and were serving up heaps of fried fish, fries, hush puppies, cold slaw and pickled tomatoes.

"Hey, Nita," Jaci greeted her happily. "I don't know how to act tonight. This is my first social event since the twins were born, and although I'm so tired I can hardly see straight, I'm more than ready for a little socializing, and plus I'm celebrating having my house back. Girl, I don't mean to sound ungrateful, but I'm so happy my parents, Jason's parents, and Sister Sadie have finally decided to go home."

"No, that's understandable."

"I hope so because I do appreciate having the help and support, but it was just time for them to go."

Nita laughed, then said, "I'm happy to be here too because I haven't had the chance to attend casual gatherings like this in a very long time. I can't tell you how much I've been looking forward to it." Nita was happy to see Monique and C.J. already there, and to meet a few other people. "Now, show me to the food," she said, handing Destiny to Lena, one of Jaci's friends, who was eagerly reaching for her.

Ron slid up to her and placed a kiss on her forehead and whispered, "Hey, Sweetheart. Sit down while I fix your plate, what do you want?"

"Everything." she answered enthusiastically, then sat down to talk to the other ladies. A few minutes later, he handed her a plate piled high with food, and she eagerly dug in. She was enjoying the food when she heard the doorbell ring. A few minutes later, a woman strode into the family room. The bottom fell out of Nita's stomach – along with her appetite – when she recognized one of the women she had seen at Ron's house.

The woman searched faces until she spotted Ron in the kitchen. She worked her way around groups of people, shot a spiteful look at Nita, and continued until she reached Ron. She threw her arms around him and planted a possessive kiss on his lips. "Hey, lover! Surprised to see me?"

Ron did look surprised, then agitated. He looked across the room and locked eyes with Nita, then leaned over and said, "Velma, what are you doing here?"

"Well, I went by your place hoping to spend some time with you, and when I didn't get an answer, I remembered how you use to hang out here on Friday nights, so I decided to take a chance. Why didn't you invite me? You know how much I love fish," Velma chided.

Nita watched as Ron spoke softly to the woman, then led her out of the room. She tried to hide the fact that the woman's presence bothered her. She picked at the food she had been enjoying only moments ago, and wondered what Ron and the woman were doing. Monique, Jaci and C.J. all realized what was going on and exchanged irritated looks.

"Now don't jump to conclusions, Nita," Jaci said to her. "Just wait and see how this shakes out. Ron looks as upset as you. She's been here with him before, but that was a long time ago. I thought she had moved out of town."

"I've seen her before." Nita answered, quietly. "At Ron's house. And apparently, she's back."

"I thought I recognized her." Monique said, snapping her fingers. "Yeah, she just moved back to town and I get the impression that she's back to stake a claim on my brother. I thought he had sent her on her way though. Shame on him."

Nita's enjoyment in the evening was gone. She was unsettled. Yes, they had agreed to see other people – at her suggestion, no less – but seeing Ron being kissed by the other woman was like sticking needles through her heart. She felt a doozy of a headache starting, and decided to leave. She hurriedly gathered up Destiny, said goodnight and walked out the door.

Velma's presence only complicated matters for Ron and Nita. Although he had told her he was in a serious relationship, she refused to accept that. Unfortunately, Velma saw an opportunity to take advantage of the situation.

"Really, Ron," Velma stated in a harsh tone. "I know you have a child together but that's no reason for you to tie yourself to that woman. People have babies together all the time and then go their separate ways."

That grated on Ron's already frayed nerves. The courtesy he'd been trying to show her for old times sake was out the window. She caught the blunt of his anger, before he showed her to the door and told her in no uncertain terms to stay away from him. He had every intention of leaving to go to Nita's house, but Jason and Jaci talked him out of it.

Ron decided to go home, even though he really wanted to go to Nita's. For once, he was glad Monique decided to follow him home shortly. He was actually happy to have her company.

"So, what's up between you and Velma?" Monique asked.

"Nothing. Not anymore," Ron answered with a sigh.

"Haven't you told her that? And if so, why is she so determined to pursue you?"

Ron shrugged. "I have no idea. I've told her in no uncertain terms that it's over."

"Did you tell her Nita's not Destiny's birth mother?"

"Of course not. It's not her business."

"Do you love Nita, Ron?"

"Yes." He got up from where he was sitting and walked restlessly around the room. "Do you think Nita will talk to me if I call her?" The tense look on his face spoke volumes.

"No, I don't," Monique said, laughing at her brother's pained look. "I'm not an expert in the area of relationships, obviously, but I think you handled it all wrong tonight, brother."

He sighed. "I know. I have to convince Nita to marry me soon. I don't think these other people are going to leave us alone until she's my wife."

"True, but if you want that to happen, you'd better start making these other women understand beyond a shadow of doubt that they don't fit anywhere in your life. Nita's not going to marry you until you do."

Ron stood, and headed slowly toward his studio. "Yeah, I know you're right. I need to do something to get my mind off of this mess, so I think I'll work on my house plans. Pops found a piece of property that I think is going to work. Of course, I'll have to do some re-development in the area, but I need to be able to start work on the house as soon as I can."

"I would think Nita's input would be included in the plans for the house," Monique said.

"She'll like it. I'm making it as similar to her condo floor plan as I can, although it'll be larger." He turned to the computer and became engrossed in the plans on the screen. "Goodnight, Sis."

"Goodnight," Monique answered, thoughtfully, then said loudly, "I'll be doggone. My womanizing brother is in love."

He heard her laughing all the way upstairs to her bedroom.

CHAPTER NINETEEN

Dang! She was having too many headaches these days – brought on by these scoundrel men. She gave the baby a bath and put her into bed, thankful she was so worn out she didn't fuss.   Her throbbing head kept her from following the show she was trying to watch on television. She stomped into the bathroom and swallowed two aspirin, then stepped into a hot shower, hoping that by the time she finished her headache would have relented. It didn't. She rubbed her favorite body lotion into her skin, slipped into her nightgown, climbed into bed and turned off the lights and television. Normally, she didn't like sleeping in a totally dark room, but with her sons in the house she felt secure enough to do it.

"I know I need to pray, Father," she whispered into the darkness, "but right now it probably wouldn't get beyond the ceiling anyway." She sighed and turned over, seeking a more comfortable position. "Am I overreacting, Lord? Should I be this angry? And why am I?" She turned over again, the comfortable position still eluding her. She was contemplating turning the television back on when the phone rang. It was Ron. "I'm not talking to him." She hit talk, then off, as hard as she could, hoping to convey her frustration somehow.

The next day, although she knew she would run into Ron, she attended church with her children. Sure enough, he came up to them as they were leaving.

"Well, at least you can't hang up on me," he said, jokingly. "Can we talk?"

"Are you taking Destiny for the rest of the day?"

He hesitated. "Well, I was hoping we could spend the afternoon together."

"Huh! No, that won't be happening, Ron." She gestured to the baby, who was in Joel's arms. "You can drop her off tonight." She handed Destiny's baby bag to him and walked off, as the transfer of the baby was made between Ron and Joel.

She took her sons to a popular restaurant and enjoyed a good meal with them, before heading to the airport to drop Frankie off. Joel didn't stick around very long after they got back home. He left after packing his car and promising to call her when he arrived.

Nita settled down in the quiet house and relaxed. She managed to get a nap in before the doorbell woke her. She opened the door to let Ron in, carrying an untidy Destiny. "I see she's eaten, since most of it's on her face and clothes. Ron, why didn't you change her? I know she has some clothes at your house, and if not, she always has a change in her bag," Nita grumbled, as she headed upstairs with the baby to bathe and get her ready for bed.

"I didn't think about it," Ron admitted, as he followed her up the stairs. "Look, Nita, we are going to talk before I leave here tonight. Will you please accept my apology?"

She sighed and headed into the bathroom, where she ran water into the face bowl to give Destiny a quick bath. "Lord forbid I end up with another Frank on my hands." She gave him a pointed look.

Ron looked offended. "I know I've done a lot of things that I'm not proud of, but abusing and beating women have never been among them. I know you don't believe I'm capable of that."

She wrapped a towel around the baby and went into the bedroom – Ron right on her heels – to lotion, powder and dress the baby in pajamas. "I don't want to believe it, but who knows what a person will do? I will tell you though, that if you ever try something like that on me, you'll be dealing with some severely wounded body parts. The woman that let herself be a victim all those years is gone."

"I know. I've seen you in action remember. That guy on the cruise ship is probably still trying to recover." He chuckled and took Destiny and put her in the baby bed. "Besides, I have much better ways of taming my women."

"What? You, Tarzan?" She hit her chest in imitation of the jungle man, "Me, Jane?"

"Naw, Babe," he said, grinning. "My ways of persuasion are more gentle and subtle."

"Uh hmmm, but the message is still the same - I'm the man, hear me roar!"

"Naw, Babe, I have better ways."

She gave him a outrageous look. "Maybe Jane prefers Tarzan."

Now his gaze was filled with outrage and he walked over to her. "That's not going to happen because this is how I take care of my woman," he said. "Softly, sweetly," actions followed his words as he planted soft kisses all over her face, "lovingly, tenderly, caressingly."

Nita felt herself sinking under the spell he was weaving and stopped it before he could go any further. "You get out of here, Ron Gilmore. Or you won't like the consequences."

His victorious chuckle filled the room. "You better be glad I'm a changed man because both of us would like the consequences very much, but I can wait. Come on, Sweetheart, walk me to the door." He grabbed her hand and led her out of the room and down the stairs. He kissed her lightly before opening the door. "I'm starting on our house tomorrow," he tossed over his shoulder. "Goodnight, Babe. I'll call you."

"If you think sweet talk and kisses will get you out of the doghouse, you're wrong. I'm still very angry with you." She heard him chuckling as she slammed the door.

Nita stood there a long time with a bemused expression covering her face. That man had worked her like she was a puppet and he was the puppet master. She really had to get a grip.

The following day Ron was juggling a busy schedule. Another big job for an exclusive hotel and spa had been offered to him from a corporation he had designed several structures for in the past. It was too good a deal to pass up. He also needed to take another trip to Maryland to move the projects along for Nita's brother, and he was considering taking on a multi-million dollar mansion for a couple in Austin. The church expansion project was also underway. It was a bad time to start on his own house, which he wanted to be spectacular, but he had to do it. He would be a very busy man for a while.

He picked up the phone to order flowers for Nita before moving on with his day. He had tried to call her last night and this morning and she was not answering.

He took comfort in the fact that he'd gotten her usual morning e-mail. He went back to it and re-read the message. "Trust in the Lord with all your heart and don't lean to your own understanding. Acknowledge God in all you do today and let Him direct your path. Remember who you are and whose you are. Love ya!"

Ron smiled. "That is certainly right on time." *I hope she's taking this one in herself*, he thought. He was so glad that during one of their talks, Joel had mentioned the daily messages Nita sent to her sons. He had wasted no time in begging her to add him to that distribution list. It was amazing how each message seemed to be right on time just like this one was. He quickly hit reply and sent a response to her, telling her what a blessing it was, and ending with 'I love you too.'

CHAPTER TWENTY

A month later, Nita was up to her neck in projects. When she remembered how she'd thought she would be lonely and bored after moving to Houston, she could only chuckle. She and C.J. were making tentative steps toward their event planning business, and working on the event C.J. already had lined up, which was a fiftieth wedding anniversary celebration. Thank God the people had given them a six-month window.

The Foundation was consuming more of her time than she had envisioned, requiring her to spend hours on the computer, telephone, and take regular trips to Dallas. She had enrolled in an online event planning course that taxed brain cells that had been dormant for years and rebelled when she tried to study or comprehend all the reading she had to do for the class and the Foundation. Add Destiny into the mix, and her participation in the church's Survivors of Domestic Violence ministry, and she was fighting to keep from becoming overwhelmed. Her days of relaxation, cooking and eating healthy meals were now spent in a frenzy of activities. Her diet suffered. She was grabbing fast food, or something quick, easy and full of calories as a way to balance her overbooked calendar and To-Do-List. Working out became crucial or a return to her former weight problem was imminent.

So it was on this Monday morning, that she was opening the door to the tall, muscled, good looking guy standing there with a variety of equipment scattered around his feet. Women swooned over him everywhere he went, and although he quietly endured the unsolicited interest, the only attention he craved was that of other men. "Hey Doug," Nita greeted. "Am I glad to see you! I need you to help me work off some stress and calories."

"Hey, Anita," he answered in his deep, James Earl Jones voice. He came in and started setting up his equipment, while his eyes ran over her body in an assessing way. "Let me remind you again, an hour workout two days a week is not going to be enough. You're going to have to get in some cardio, as well as some weights just to maintain, since obviously, your diet has gone haywire. You gained three pounds last month, lady."

"Oh Lord," Nita groaned, as she started on her warm up stretches. "I can't let that happen, Doug. I definitely have to make some changes."

"Well, think about coming into the gym three days a week for a cardio work-out, and we'll use these sessions for the weight training. That should do it, but you'll also have to lay off the high fat foods. When you first started at the gym you were doing fine with your diet. You have to get back to that."

She was breathing harder as they got into the work-out. "I. Don't. Think. I. Have. A. Choice."

"No, you don't," he answered. "You might also consider coming into the gym first thing in the morning, when you drop the baby off at the nursery. If you get on a daily regiment, we can incorporate everything into those sessions and eventually let these private sessions go. Come on! Put your back into it! That's it! You think you might want to try that?"

Unable to get words out, she could only nod her agreement. Later, as she struggled up the stairs on legs as shaky as Jell-o, Nita mentally tried to fit still another activity into her schedule. She headed to the shower and stood under the hot water for a long time as she tried to work things out. The only conclusion she could reach was that Ron was going to have to help out more with Destiny. And doggonit, that meant she was going to have to talk to him.

He called her everyday and left a message that he loved her. He sent flowers - or something - everyday, and he was always sending text or e-mail messages to ensure, he told her, that he was always on her mind. It was working, but she had a point to make. She was determined he wouldn't force her to change their agreed plan. She spent as little time as possible in his presence, knowing his particular talents of persuasion only spelled trouble for her.

A routine doctor's visit reminded her that Destiny would be a year old in a few months. She could hardly believe it. "Lord, where did the time go?" There was nothing left of the mal-nourished, pitiful, smelly baby Ron had pushed into her arms and begged for help months ago. Destiny was now a plump toddler, taking clumsy steps, and getting into everything that grabbed her attention. So, in spite of her already full schedule, Nita added a reminder on her calendar to plan a simple birthday party.

But a month before Destiny's birthday, when Nita told Monique and Ron's parents about the party she was planning, it suddenly mushroomed into a major affair that included Ron, whose birthday was coincidentally on the same day. The guest list was expanded to include other family members and some of Ron's friends, and the simple menu of ice-cream and cake she had planned now boasted Cecelia's gumbo, and T.C's famous ribs and potato salad, among other things. They decided to make it a surprise for Ron.

Okay, she realized a lot of guilt was behind the elaborate plans – Ron's family trying to make up for their failures with both father and child - but good gracious! They wanted to move the party to Ron's parents' much larger home, further shattering Nita's vision of a small affair in familiar surroundings for Destiny.

After talking to Ron – she'd finally had to break down and start talking to him – they reluctantly agreed to move the party. But Ron wasn't happy about it.

"Why couldn't they just leave things alone, come by, drop off a gift for Destiny and be on their way?" He grumbled. "I would have been happy to spend the day with just you and Destiny, but I went along with the kiddie party because of what you said about making memories for her. But it's no telling what they'll come up with."

Knowing his frustration and disappointment with his family, Nita tried to put a positive spin on things. "Just be grateful, Ron. Afterall, a few months ago they wouldn't even acknowledge Destiny's presence in the family. You have to accept their effort to make up for that." She gave him a pleading look. "So you are going to cooperate, right?"

"Yeah, I guess so. I suppose this is one of those times you're always talking about when I have to put my child first, huh? And guess what? So much was going on when Destiny landed in my life that I didn't pay attention to the actual date she was born. I guess Chantal would be happy to know just how well her plan has worked out. Destiny and I have the same birthday. Ain't that one for the books?"

"Yes, it sure is," Nita answered, without letting him know she was already aware of that fact. "Well, you have time, but don't forget to get a present for Desi."

CHAPTER TWENTY-ONE

Time passed quickly, and Ron was so busy, he procrastinated in getting a birthday gift for Destiny. Before he knew it, it was the day before the party. He had planned to run by the Galleria to pick up a present right after work, but decided to go home and change since he had been wading around in mud all day on one of his construction sites. He was just getting out of the shower when the phone rang. He impatiently threw on a robe and ran to answer, hoping it wasn't a long winded person. It was his buddy, Walt.

"Hey, Man, what's going on?" Ron picked up the phone and said.

"Hey, Ron, I've got some bad news. I mean some really bad news. I don't know how to tell you, Man. I, uh – just don't know how to tell you."

"Walt, what is it? Is it about my family? Come on, you're scaring the heck out of me." Walt, a criminal courts judge, wasn't the kind to get shaken up like this.

"It's Charlie. Did you watch the evening news?"

"Naw, I've been on a site all day and just got home. What about Charlie?"

"Somebody shot him, Ron. Guy went home for lunch and found Charlie there in a compromising position with his wife. He grabbed his gun and blew both of them away."

"Oh God, oh God, no. No!"

"I'm shocked, but admittedly, not too surprised. We've been telling Charlie for years to leave those married women alone. His brother called me a little while ago to make sure we knew. They don't have any plans for the services yet but he said he would let us know."

"I don't know what to say, Man. Did you call Jason?"

"Yeah. He's all broken up. He asked me to call you and T.C."

Tears were rolling down Ron's face. Charlie was one of his closest friends since high school days. "Well, thanks for letting me know. I'll check in with you later. Take care."

"Yeah, you too, Ron."

Ron stumbled to the bed and fell across it and didn't move for a long time. He wanted to call Jason, but knew he was in the same shape as himself. His next thought was to call Nita. He pushed the speed dial and waited, praying she would answer. She didn't, and he left a message.

"Babe, I need you to call me back. I just got some really bad news about one of my best friends." He hung up after leaving the message and got up from the bed. He wondered around the room aimlessly, all thought of the shopping spree for Destiny forgotten. "Doggonit, Charlie, why did you have to go and do something stupid like that?" He yelled at the top of his voice in an effort to relieve the hurt. It didn't help. He picked up the phone and called his brother.

"Hey, Jaci. Where's Jason? How's he holding up?"

"He's right here, Ron. He's not doing too well." After a pause, Jason was on the phone.

"Can you believe this?" Jason asked. "I am totally blown away. I couldn't even talk for a while after Walt told me. I'm still sitting here in a daze. I guess we should probably go by and see his mother at some point, but I'm in no shape to do it tonight."

"Naw, me neither," Ron said. "I was just checking on you, Man. I'll talk to you later."

He started wondering around the condo again. He needed someone - some kind of human comfort – but he had no one. Not even Monique. Where was she anyway? He was getting ready to call her when the phone rang. "Nita!" He almost dropped the phone in his haste to answer. "Nita, I'm so glad you called me back. Thank you."

"What's going on, Ron?"

"Charlie, one of my best friends, you met him at Jason's house. Anyway, he got killed today, and I'm, uh, I'm not doing too well."

There was a slight pause. "Oh. I'm so sorry to hear that. Are you okay?"

"No. Uh, Nita, can I come over? I really need to be with you and Destiny tonight."

"Sure, Ron, come on over," she answered without hesitation. "Are you hungry?"

"Believe it or not, I don't have an appetite. Maybe later. I'll see you in a little bit."

"Okay. And be careful, Ron."

"Yeah, Babe, I will." For the first time since he'd gotten the news about Charlie, he felt a lightness in his heart. He hurriedly dressed and headed for Nita's house.

He grabbed her in a close hug as soon as she opened the door. "Thanks for letting me come over, Babe. I just didn't feel like being by myself tonight."

Nita hugged him back and told him she was sorry again. "I know no words can help how you're feeling right now. This is one of those times when nobody but the Lord can bring comfort and strength." She led him into the family room – strange, since their usual path was to the kitchen. "Tell me about your friend. How long had you known him? How did he die?"

He spent the next hours holding onto to her hand and talking about all the things he and Charlie, along with the rest of his buddies, had gotten into over the years. They had all agreed to remain confirmed bachelors – until Jason met Jaci and broke the circle. Talking about Charlie seemed to get him to a place of acceptance, which he realized had been Nita's plan. Before he left she fixed him a gigantic triple-deck ham, egg and cheese sandwich to take home.

The next morning he went with the guys to visit Charlie's mother to offer comfort and any other help she might need – and the needs were great. Charlie made good money as a sales representative for a major pharmaceutical company, but he spent it faster than he made it. Charlie's mother, siblings and friends had to take care of his burial expenses.

Ron left Charlie's mother's home and drove as fast as possible along the 610 freeway towards the Galleria, trying not to let the heavy traffic and the events of the last two days get to him. It was his birthday, but he couldn't shake the depression hanging over his head.

Nita had sent text messages reminding him to get a present for Destiny. It was his birthday, but everyone, including Nita, seemed to have forgotten. It was all about Destiny.

Shame hit. Was he actually jealous of his child? And how could he possibly be so frustrated that he couldn't celebrate his own life? Just this week, he'd heard that Jynell, who had told him she had AIDS, had passed away, and then news had come about Charlie. *I need to get a grip!* "Lord, help me fix this ungrateful attitude and fill me with Your peace." He found a parking place in the underground Galleria garage and headed into the mall to get something for Destiny.

Nita had told him to get an outfit and a toy. But guilt caused him to over compensate, and two hours later he came out of the mall loaded down with several outfits and too many toys.

"Hey, daddy, you're late!" Nita said, when she opened the door for him, carrying Destiny in her arms.

"Not that late," he answered, grumpily. "I got a little carried away at the mall." As he walked further into the house, his mouth fell open, and he dropped the bags. The first thing he noticed was a big sign that said, 'HAPPY BIRTHDAY, RON AND DESTINY!' Before he could digest that, he was hearing, "SURPRISE, SURPRISE!" from the crowd of people in the room. Anyone who meant anything to him was there, including his buddies, Walt, T.C., and Blake. It hit home again that Charlie would have been there too, if it were possible. Shame over his moments of ungratefulness, along with sadness over Charlie overtook him and what did he do? Wrapped his arms around Nita and Destiny and cried like a blubbering idiot. He had some serious repenting to do later. Before he could feel ashamed at being overcome by emotion, Jason, Blake, Walt and T.C. had joined the circle and were crying along with him – remembering Charlie.

Nita wiped at the tears in her own eyes and announced, "Okay, everyone, now that both our honored guests are here, let's eat!" Ron's dad ushered everyone into the spacious kitchen where a huge pot of gumbo, platters of ribs and wings, bowls of salads, along with fruit and cheese trays waited.

Two hours later, most of the food had disappeared and Cecelia and Monique brought out the large cake and gallons of ice cream. After they sung happy birthday to Ron and Destiny, Nita started bringing out the gifts – mostly Ron's. Destiny was so full and tired she was delirious.

The thoughtful gifts he received brought more tears to Ron's eyes. He didn't doubt Nita had something to do with the selections. Matching tee-shirts for him and Destiny, books on being a great dad, a large family Bible, golf shirts, and CD's of his favorite artists. But it was Nita's gifts that sent him over the edge and had the tears gushing again. First she handed him a large wrapped picture frame. His mouth dropped in surprise when he ripped the paper away and saw it. She had taken Destiny to a professional studio and had a beautiful portrait taken to commemorate her first birthday. He rubbed his fingers over the glass, cherishing it. "Thank you, Nita," he choked out. "I hadn't thought of getting a picture taken of her."

"Well, here's a little something else I thought you might like." She handed him a large photo album. She and Joel, who was a photography buff, had taken countless pictures of Destiny from the time she had arrived. There was page after page of Destiny in every possible setting and pose. Ron didn't get past the first few pages before he was boo-hooing.

"Thank you again. I owe you so much more than I can ever repay."

His mother jumped up and grabbed the book. "Let me see that," she demanded. But when she started looking at the pictures Nita had carefully laid out in the album, she too started crying. "These are precious memories of my grandchild that we wouldn't have if you hadn't done this. How can we ever thank you, Nita?"

"You're quite welcome and I enjoyed doing it. It gave me a chance to practice on that scrapbook software program I was suckered into buying."

"You did this on the computer?" Cecelia asked.

"Yep, sure did. It's amazing what you can do on a computer."

"Oh my!" Cecelia said, as she continued to flip through the book. "You know, I'm getting my family's history together and I would love to do something like this. Do you think you could help me? I need to get started on it soon, so my mother can see it before…she's been real sick you know."

"Do you have everything together?" Nita asked. "If so, it won't take long."

"Now see that's the thing. I don't. I'll have to collect stuff from other family members."

"Well, let me know when you're ready. That's a wonderful thing to do for your family."

"And the way mine is expanding I'd better hurry up and get started," Cecelia chuckled.

Cecelia looked back down at the album and shook her head sadly. I should have been doing this for my son and grandbaby. I'm sorry, Son. I let you and this baby down."

"It's okay, Mom," Ron said, wiping his face with a napkin.

When the party started breaking up, Nita gathered up Destiny's large assortment of gifts (the grandparents had gone crazy) and Ron packed everything into Nita's SUV, and she took off with a sleeping Destiny.

"Hey buddy, let's go do some real partying, catch a little jazz and run some women," T.C. suggested on the way out.

But Ron had other thoughts about what he wanted to do. "Thanks, but I'm planning to spend the rest of my birthday at home with my family. And after what's happened to Charlie – well, I'm just not in the mood."

"What family?" T.C. asked."

"Nita and Destiny."

"Aw, man!" T.C. yelled loudly. "Another one done bit the dust. When did all this happen? Is that the reason you've been missing in action lately?"

"Yep, and that's the reason I'm going to be missing from now on. My days of running women are over."

"I'm with you, Ron," Walt said, slapping him on the back. "It's time for all of us to be settling down. Way past time, really."

"Yeah, way past time," Ron said, sadly, thinking of all the years he had wasted.

He hurriedly thanked his family for everything and rushed to his car with his gifts. He couldn't wait to get to Nita and Destiny. He grabbed his phone and called her. "Hey, Babe, I know you need help getting all that stuff unloaded. I'm on the way there."

"That's okay, I'll get it later. I'm going to get her ready and put her to bed. You go on and enjoy the rest of your day."

"You don't get it, do you?" He asked in a solemn tone. "The only thing that will make this day even better is being with you. I've missed you since you won't let me spend much time with you."

"That's because of your Tarzan moves."

He chuckled. "But how much longer are we supposed to be praying and thinking? Nita, we love each other. I know I want to be with you and Destiny every day. I want to take care of you and be the husband and father you both deserve. This has been the best day of my life. I don't want it to end. Please . . .?"

A long pause, a sigh, then, "Okay, Ron, come on by for a little while, but don't even think about bringing any of your Tarzan moves. I'd hate to have to bust you on your behind."

He cracked up laughing, then said, "Thanks, Sweetheart. I'll see you in a few minutes." He pushed the end button on the phone and exhaled a relieved breath.

CHAPTER TWENTY-TWO

As soon as Nita opened the door, Ron shot across the threshold and engulfed her in a hug so tight she could hardly breathe.

"Thank you again for everything, Babe. You are such a blessing to me and Destiny."

She extradited herself from his arms and said, "You're welcome, but your family did most of the work, and it was great, wasn't it?"

"Yes!" He gave her a reprimanding stare. "Why didn't you tell me about the surprise? I spent all day walking around depressed because I thought everyone had forgotten my birthday. I was actually jealous of Destiny, and mad at my family and friends." He grabbed her hand. "Come on, let's sit down."

After they got comfortable on the sofa, he started talking. "Nita, today I experienced God's mercy in a lot of ways. My family's love, the child I didn't want but have grown to love, the woman I love and want to spend the rest of my life with, friends who cared enough to share my birthday. I felt God's love flowing to me like I never imagined. And when I remember how Charlie died . . . well, it just hit me hard. That's why the tears were flowing so strong."

"Ron . . . the important thing is that you're realizing how good and merciful God is. And it's wonderful that you have it within you to be thankful for that mercy. Also, you have to understand that everything happens in God's timing. A year ago, you wouldn't have been ready to feel this gratitude or receive this mercy. You wouldn't have even wanted it. But it's because of everything that's happened that you've opened your heart to God."

"You're right, I wouldn't have been ready a year ago." He squeezed her hand. "So what's going on with you? I have to catch up since you hardly talk to me anymore."

She told him about all she was doing and sighed. "It's good your parents are going to spend more time with Destiny, because I'll have to do more traveling for the Foundation soon."

"So, tell me about this Foundation that has you running up and down the road."

She gave him a brief description of the Foundation's mission. "Can you see the irony?"

He smiled. "Yeah, I can. Sounds like a great project. Is it just for Dallas? I'm sure there's a need for it here too."

"I'm open to the possibility of expanding it to Houston if I can get the funding for it."

"I'm sure that's possible," Ron said, thoughtfully.

After worship the next day, Nita headed to the church nursery to get Destiny. Normally, Ron would get her and take her with him to his parents' house, but today she was going with them so she told him she would get the baby while he finished his duties. She stopped along the way to speak to people, taking her time because there was always a line. She got there in time to avoid a long wait, retrieved a happy Destiny and her bag, and groaned when she noticed Destiny was wearing different clothes. That meant a mess of some kind was in the bag. Just as she came out of the nursery, a woman suddenly jumped out of a corner and blocked her way.

"I need to talk to you," the woman announced in a loud, hostile voice. "You're interfering in my and Ron's lives, you and this baby, and that's just not going to work."

"What?" Nita frowned and looked at the woman questioningly. She looked vaguely familiar and Nita struggled to place her. "Who are you? What are you talking about?"

"Don't act crazy. My name is Shayla and you know exactly who I am. You think you have it made just because you have this baby. Things were going fine with me and Ron until you showed up with this baby."

Nita looked at the woman like she was crazy. "Look. I don't have anything to do with what's going on between you and Ron. So get out of my way. Your problem is not with me."

"Yes, it is you! And I want you out of Ron's life, or I'm going to cause you more trouble than you can handle."

"Nita?" A voice behind her called. "You want me to call security?" It was one of the nursery workers.

"No, that's okay," Nita answered. "I can handle it." She turned back to the woman. "I don't know what your problem is, but this is God's house and I'm not going to dishonor it with this kind of mess. Get out of my way."

"Oh. You think you running things? Uh, uh, Sister. You ain't running nothing and we're going to get this straight today." She crossed her arms and spread her legs.

"Look!" Nita said more forcefully, looking the woman in the eye. "Whatever is going on with you and Ron has nothing to do with me. I'm not going to say it again. Get out of my way!"

"Nita, I've called security and Ron!" The nursery worked yelled behind her.

Something in Nita's demeanor, along with the threat of security registered with Shayla. "You can tell Ron that Shayla Matthews said this is not over." She turned and walked briskly toward the exit when a security guard rounded the corner with Ron right behind him.

"Nita, you okay?" Ron yelled, as he ran up to them. "What did that crazy woman do?"

Nita walked away from him, her head swirling. The scene had resurrected memories of similar ones with Frank's women. "Just leave me alone."

Ron ran to catch up with her. "Nita? what is it? Talk to me."

"I dealt with crazy women like that for years. Women who had no respect for marriage or God. I will not subject myself to that again. Now you'd better get your business straight and keep that crazy woman away from me. I'm going home." She pushed Destiny into his arms. "I know your parents are expecting me, but please express my apologies."

"Let me explain, Sweetheart," Ron begged. "That woman means nothing to me."

Nita lifted her hand. "I don't want to hear it." She turned and walked away.

Ron watched Nita walk away with a heavy heart. He shifted Destiny in his arms and walked slowly out of the church and to his car. He drove to his parents' home where he told his family about the scene at the church and why Nita had changed her mind about coming.

"Boy, you mean to tell me you've got a woman good enough to be raising your child, and you're still out there messing around with these trifling women?" Ron's dad asked, disgustedly.

"No, Pops. Give me credit for having more sense than that. That woman was someone I dated before Nita's time. And it was just a fling. The women out there now are just crazy. They don't understand casual dating. You go out with them a few times and treat them nice, and they think you're ready to get married. I told her it was nothing, but she refuses to understand that. She wants to get married, and thinks I'm the one."

Ron hung his head sadly. "Nita's history with her deceased husband is a big part of the issue. I don't know if she'll ever be able to differentiate her relationship with him and with me. Things may never work out between us." He sat down with a miserable look on his face.

Ron's mother put Destiny down so she could roam around the room with Jaci's twins, then said, "You can't give up, Son. You've planted some bad seeds that are going to produce some bad harvests. That's what's going on. I hope you didn't think that just because you decided to straighten up, things would miraculously turn all sunny side up for you. No, life is not like that, Son. You reap what you sow. Now what you need to be doing is praying that God will be merciful enough to give you the woman you want. And the rest of us will be praying with you on that. But you're going to have to deal with some consequences, Ron."

Later that evening he dropped Destiny off at Nita's but didn't stick around. He had a lot of thinking to do. Perhaps it was time to face the fact that realistically, he and Nita couldn't expect to have a successful relationship, considering their conflicting histories. How could Nita, who carried the physical and emotional scars from more than twenty years married to an abusive womanizer, ever believe he could leave his womanizing life and settle down with one woman? And how could he expect that she could, after all she'd endured with Frank?

He sat in his darkened bedroom thinking. His love for her made it difficult to accept these realistic conclusions. Then, there was the matter of Destiny - hanging between them like a pendulum. It was when his thoughts reached that point that he turned to God and begin to pray.

CHAPTER TWENTY-THREE

In her own quiet bedroom with Destiny asleep and the telephone quiet, Nita was struggling with similar thoughts. "What could I have been thinking to even consider marriage to another man with a history of womanizing?" She asked herself. No answer came and she shook her head and began to pray. "Father, Your Word tells me that with You all things are possible and that nothing is too hard for You. But my own emotions tell me that what happened today with Ron and that woman, will always be happening – just like with Frank. And Father, I just can't do that again. I love him, Lord. But I must accept that he is who he is – a womanizer. Tears escaped and slid down her face. "But Father, Destiny ties us together. She couldn't be more mine if I had given birth to her. How can I give them up?"

She had lunch with C.J. and Jaci on Tuesday, during which the situation with Ron was discussed. C.J. confessed, "I could say I told you not to get involved with him and his baby, but really, if God is in the mix, who am I to say it can't work. And surprisingly, I've discovered Ron is an okay dude, which is probably why these women find it so hard to let go when he's ready to end things with them. But the important thing is, where is his head? What are his intentions. You can't hold his past against him if he's repented and is trying to live right."

Jaci listened quietly before saying, "Nita, I know both sides better than anyone, other than you and God, of course. I've seen Ron struggling to change, and I've seen you struggling to overcome your own issues after life with Frank. Nobody can change the past, Nita. Ron can't change what he's done, and you can't change anything about your life with Frank. I don't know the answer – nobody but the Lord knows. But I do know this. That man is so in love with you that he can't think straight – and it has nothing to do with Destiny."

"Yeah. So he keeps telling me," Nita answered.

"Well, don't forget that, when you're weighing things and praying. I'd be the first to tell you if I thought he'd be no good for you. But I've seen how he's grown and matured. I believe he's going to make someone a great husband because that's what he wants to be now. So, my thinking is, why can't that be you? And what about Destiny? What we need to do is pray that God's will be done in this situation for each of you."

Ron hadn't called, sent texts, e-mails or flowers over the last few days. She tried to ignore the bereft feeling in her heart caused by his absence, but frankly, it was hard. She missed him. Is this the way he felt when she refused to talk to him?

As communication remained in limbo between Ron and herself, that often quoted saying of her Grammy's came to mind – 'Be careful *what you ask for, you just might get it'.* - Although she had demanded that they spend time apart, praying and thinking about a possible future together, and she had gotten what she asked for, somehow, she hadn't envisioned it happening with this kind of communication rift between them. Yes, she had been upset over the Shayla Matthews confrontation, and yes, maybe she should have let him explain, but she never expected him to shut down like this on her. But perhaps this was the answer.

He was picking up Destiny every day and dropping her off, but didn't linger to talk. Tonight he stayed long enough to say, "I'll be out of town a few days next week, but Monique will pick-up Destiny and bring her home everyday. Just let her know if you need anything else."

"Okay, I will," she answered. He quickly turned and went out the door. She wanted to ask where he was going but his demeanor was like a wall erected around him.

Joel was completing his transfer requirements for Prairie View University. The regular school year was almost over and he was planning to attend summer school at Prairie View to make up some lost credits.

The following Saturday, she and Joel drove to Prairie View to look at apartments. They found one they could lease for the summer, with the option of renewing it for the next semester. Nita made a list of everything he would need for the apartment with the intention of going shopping. Joel didn't care about décor but she did. There was also the matter of housekeeping supplies that he would need. She lectured him all the way back to Houston on being a responsible tenant, along with maintaining a good academic standing.

"I got this, Mom," he groaned impatiently, with glazed over eyes that meant he had tuned her out. "I know what I have to do. It's not like this is the first time I'll be on my own."

"I know that, Son, but I just have to be Mom from time to time. I don't ever want you to forget who you are and whose you are."

He repeated the last sentence with her. "Like I could forget," he said, with a smile. Then with a serious look on his face, he said, "Mom, I have some questions for you too. What's going on with you and Ron? How's the house coming? I would really like to see it. Also, when are you going to make a decision about marrying him?"

Hard questions, which she had no answers for. "I hate to tell you, Son, but I don't know."

"Mom! You mean you haven't seen the house? I don't understand. Aren't you curious about where you'll be living? And what about Ron? That dude really cares about you."

"There's a lot of uncertainty about that right now, but as soon as I know something I'll let you know, okay?"

"I'm disappointed, but I know you know what you're doing," he answered in a sad voice, then perked up quickly. "I think I'll go hang out with Patrick for a while."

She laughed, glad he had moved on from her sad state of affairs. "That's fine, even though I thought we'd treat ourselves to a nice restaurant for dinner tonight."

"That sounds good, but can we do it after church tomorrow? And you're going to cook some food for me to take back, huh?"

She groaned. "That means I have to make a trip to the grocery store because I haven't shopped in a while. I might as well get it over with since I don't have Destiny to contend with."

The remainder of the day was spent shopping, cooking and cleaning her house. It occurred to her that if her life continued as it was, she would definitely have to get someone to come in a couple of days a week to help her.

As planned, when they left church the next day, they went to a restaurant someone had recommended to Joel. While they ate, they talked about the transfer, and how serious he was about the girlfriend. "I'm so proud of you, Son. Of my three sons, you're the one I worry the least about." She was quiet for a minute. "I worry about Mikey so much it would drive me crazy if I let it. That's why I try to keep myself busy. It terrifies me to think about all the possibilities."

"We just have to hope he's okay, Mom," Joel replied in a comforting tone. "I'm planning to beat his behind when he does show up. Have you thought anymore about getting a private investigator to look for him?"

"Yes. He's put out some missing person feelers, asking for information. If that doesn't work he'll do something a little more aggressive. And of course I'm praying continuously that one day I'll answer the phone, or open the door and it'll be him."

"Me too, Mom. I keep expecting to get an e-mail or a text from him. He's got to know how worried we must be about him."

"Well, let's not let it spoil our meal," she stated, trying to interject some cheer into her voice, and digging into her grilled seafood plate."

Joel packed his car and headed back to Dallas shortly after they got home. Feeling a little out of sorts, and chalking it up to being tired and needing some rest, Nita laid down. But rest didn't come and she felt worse as the day wore on. When the doorbell rang, she opened it to find Ron standing there with Destiny.

"Hey, Ron. When did you get back?"

"Friday. You know Monique would have brought her home if I hadn't been back."

"Oh. Okay." She was thinking there was a time when he would have called to let her know he was back. But that scene with Shayla had halted that kind of communication.

"Well, I hope it was a good trip." She walked to the family room to sit down. Her stomach was upset and her head felt like it was going to burst.

Destiny made her way to her and began to crawl into her lap. Nita picked her up and hugged and kissed her, but was so nauseated she thought she would throw up.

"You feeling okay? You don't look too good," Ron observed.

"I'm okay. I think I've just been overdoing it. Joel was home this weekend and we drove up to PV yesterday to look for an apartment for him. I hope this little lady is tired because it's going to be an early night for us."

"You sure?" he asked, and when she nodded, said, "I'll see you later then," and headed to the door.

True to her word, Nita prepared for bed early. Normally she would have emptied Destiny's bag, which was usually full of dirty clothes, and washed them, and re-packed the bag for the day care the next day. But she felt so bad all she could think about was taking something for her stomach and downing some pain medicine for her head. She fed Destiny and put her to bed with a bottle, then laid down.

She slept fitfully for a few hours, and woke up to an urgent need to empty her stomach. That was just the start. For the next few hours, it seemed as though her stomach was trying to turn inside out. A raging storm outside matched the one going on in her body. "Maybe I can tough it out until morning. Help me, Lord, "she whispered weakly. But the stomach cramps kept getting worse, causing more frequent trips to the bathroom. When Destiny woke up and started screaming, Nita feared that whatever was wrong with her might have infected the baby as well. She needed to call Ron - at least he could take care of Destiny.

The ringing telephone jolted Ron out of a deep sleep. He looked at the clock and saw it was one o'clock in the morning. Dread filled him before he reached for the phone. It couldn't be anything good at this time of night. When he saw it was Nita, his heart accelerated. There was no way she would be calling unless something was wrong. He grabbed the phone. "Nita?"

Her weak voice, telling him she was sick, was enough to propel him out of bed and to the closet to throw on some clothes. "Why didn't you call me before now?" He demanded before reminding himself she didn't need to hear that right now. "I'll be there as soon as I can." He was in the SUV before thinking he should have let Monique know what was going on. Oh well, he would call her later, he decided. He managed to get there quickly and ran through the storm to the door. It took so long for Nita to answer that he panicked and was trying to figure out how he would get in when the door finally opened. He ran in to find her bent over nearly to the floor of the foyer, clutching her stomach.

He picked her up and took the stairs as fast as he could. He could hear Destiny screaming and wondered if she was sick too. He laid Nita down and ran to check on Destiny. She didn't seem to be in need of anything except a new diaper and a bottle. He ran back to Nita. "Sweetheart, what's wrong? What can I do? Do you need to go to the hospital?"

"No, I don't think so. It's my stomach and head," she said, weakly. She struggled to get up to go to the bathroom, but almost fell. He lifted her and carried her into the bathroom, where she tried to throw up but nothing came up. Her face and nightgown were drenched with sweat.

He carried her back to the bed and tried to think, but Destiny's screaming wasn't helping at all. "Help me, Lord. Show me what to do!" He prayed.

"I need to take you to the hospital, Babe. You're very sick."

"No! the baby...it's too bad to carry her out. I'll be okay when it's all out of my system. Just let me rest a little bit."

Ron didn't agree, but didn't want to argue with her.   He prayed as he scrolled through his phone contacts. "Lord, there has to be someone I can call." A name jumped out at him. Without a second thought he hit the call button. When the groggy voice answered, he was so stressed he could only blurt out, "I need you, Doc. I know it's late and it's storming but can you get here as soon as you can?"

"Ron Gilmore? Get where?"

He rattled off Nita's address. "You know where I'm talking about?"

"Yes, I know the place." A slight pause. "Okay, I'll be there soon."

"Please hurry, Doc," he pleaded, and noticed that Nita was struggling to get up again. He hung up and got her to the bathroom where she slid to the floor and said, "Go take care of Desi. She may be sick too."

He ran back to Destiny and picked her up. She stopped crying immediately and twitched, letting him know she needed to be changed. He quickly changed her and ran downstairs to get a bottle. When he got back to the bedroom, Nita had somehow managed to close the bathroom door, and he could hear her groaning. He ran to the baby, gave her the bottle, and was wondering what to do next when his phone rang.

"Okay, Ron, I'm on the way, but what's going on?" the voice demanded.

"Thanks, Doc, I know I owe you big. My family is sick. How far away are you?"

"Almost there. Give me about ten minutes."

"Right." He disconnected and went to the closed bathroom door, trying to decide if he should go in. "Nita?" No answer. "What the heck! I'm going in there." He pushed the door open and found her still on the floor, hugging the commode and straining to purge an already empty stomach. "Come on, Babe, see if you can lay down. I have a doctor on the way, and hopefully the worst will be over soon." He picked her up and carried her to the bed where she rolled into a ball and started to shiver as though she was cold. "Help her, Father. Please let the doctor know what to do for her, and if Nita needs to go to the hospital, let her understand that."

"Yes, Father," Nita whispered. "Help us all."

Thankfully, Destiny was now busy sucking the contents of her bottle while she quietly watched them. He looked at his watch – where was the doctor? Hadn't it been ten minutes? He was just about to call again when the doorbell pealed. He sprinted down the stairs and opened the door. "Hi, Doc, come on in."

The tall, attractive woman with long braids hanging around her face, was dressed in pajamas with a raincoat thrown over them. She came through the door and said, "Okay, lead me to the patients."

Ron led her up the stairway and into the bedroom, where Nita was still rolled into a ball of agony on the bed. The doctor looked at him, at Nita, and then at the baby standing in the crib across the room. "You've got a lot of nerve, dude. Calling me in the middle of a stormy night to come take care of one of your women."

"Come on, Doc. We had our day and that water's been under the bridge a long time. Can you do something for her? Do you think she should go to the hospital?"

The doctor sat down on the bed and started examining Nita. "Tell me what's going on with her."

"Terrible vomiting, and she mentioned her head hurting. She's hot and sweating, then she cold and shivering. She's really sick, Doc."

"How long has this been going on? And what about the baby? Is she showing the same symptoms?"

"Well earlier in the evening, I noticed Nita didn't look well but when I asked if she was okay she said she was just tired and needed some rest. Then she called me an hour or so ago and told me she was sick. The baby was crying, but after I changed her and gave her a bottle she was okay."

"I'll check her out in a minute." She turned back to Nita and started asking questions. "Okay, Sweetie, can you answer some questions for me? I'm going to examine you, so can you sit up a minute?"

When the doctor fired questions to Nita, and started removing her drenched night gown, Nita looked up to find Ron standing there watching, and said weakly, "Get out, Ron."

He chuckled. "Well, she's not too sick to know what's going on." He grabbed Destiny from her bed and left the room.

Ten minutes later, the doctor came out of the room and found Ron and Destiny in a bedroom across from Nita's. "Based on what she's telling me, I believe she has food poisoning. She's just about purged the contents of her stomach, but I'm going to call in a couple of prescriptions to an all night pharmacy and you need to go pick it up. I've given her a mild sedative that should make her rest a little, but we need to kill the effects of that bad bacteria."

"Okay, where am I going?" Ron asked.

She told him the name of the pharmacy. "It should be ready by the time you get there."

He went to put Destiny back into her bed, and the doctor walked over and started examining her. Destiny screamed loudly. Ron looked apologetically to the doctor. "Sorry, she acts like that around people she doesn't know."

"That's okay, we'll get used to each other. She's alright I think. In the meantime, can you point me to the kitchen? I need a cup of hot tea."

He led her to the kitchen, showed her where she might find some tea bags, grabbed another bottle, ran back upstairs to quiet Destiny, then ran out the door to the pharmacy.

On the way to the pharmacy, he called Monique, who fussed because he hadn't told her what was going on. He told her he would get back to her when he could. He was gone about thirty minutes, and when he returned, Destiny was asleep, and the doctor was relaxing in the other bedroom, sipping on a cup of tea. "Here you go, Doc," he said, handing her the bag. "Is there anything else I need to do?"

The doctor took the bag and looked at him with a smirk. "Somebody finally got to that jaded heart of yours, huh, Playboy? Well, I'm glad to see it, although I admit I'm surprised because I truly didn't think it could happen." She went into the bedroom where Nita was dressed in another nightgown, and seemed to be sleeping. "The baby's fine. She must not have eaten any of what Mommy had."

"That's good," Ron said, as he went to the opposite side of the bed and grabbed Nita's hand and squeezed it. "I can't remember ever being so scared. So you think she'll be alright after you give her this medicine?"

"Well, I can't be certain it's what I think it is until I run some tests, but if it is, hopefully it'll do the job." She administered a shot and said. "Honey, I need you to drink this, okay? We need to get some good bacteria in your system."

Nita shook her head, protesting.

"No, Babe, you have to take this," Ron said, and lifted her into a sitting position so the doctor could get the concoction down her throat.

"All right then," the doctor said. "She'll be out of it for a while, so I'm going to lay down across the hall and try to get a little sleep. Call me if she needs anything."

Ron covered Nita with the sheet, and stretched out on the other side of the bed, and started praying. "Lord, please touch her and make her well. I need her Lord, and Destiny needs her. I don't know what we would do without her, Lord. And Father, while You're at it, help us to know what Your will is for us. Nobody but You knows, and we can't move forward in any direction until You show us the way to go."

He thought Nita was sleeping but she whispered quietly, "Yes, Lord, show us Your way and help us to walk in it. Amen."

He found the television remote, hit the mute button and settled down to watch a sports channel. "Get some rest Babe. I'm right here."

He didn't realize he had nodded off until Nita's moving around on the bed woke him. She wasn't fully awake yet, but it wouldn't be long. He went across the hall and woke the doctor. "She's waking up."

CHAPTER TWENTY-FOUR

The woman coming through Nita's bedroom door was smiling and talking to Ron, who was close behind her. *Oh, so I wasn't dreaming. This man brought one of his women into my house!* That thought was followed by the realization that she felt better. *Thank you, Lord!*

Hey, Lady! How are you feeling?" The woman asked, as she grabbed Nita's wrist and started checking her pulse. "You had us pretty worried a little while ago."

"A little better, thank you," Nita answered. "Who are you?" *and what are you doing in my house?*

"I'm Dr. Walters, an old friend of Ron's, but call me Natalie. He called me in a panic and asked me to come over and see if I could do anything for you. Looks like you're over the worst of the little gremlins that were attacking your digestive system. I think that seafood you ate yesterday was tainted. I wouldn't go back to that place if I were you, and I'd like to know the name of the place."

Nita mumbled the name of the restaurant. "I sure do appreciate everything, Natalie, although I'm sorry we had to get you out in the middle of the night in this bad weather."

"No, don't even think about that. It's been good to see Ron so freaked out over somebody. I use to wish that would've been me, but like Ron said, that's water under the bridge and wasn't meant to be. But I think he's hit the jackpot with you. I heard you guys praying together, and you have that beautiful child together. Anybody who can tame this one," she pointed to Ron, "has to be pretty special."

"Thank you," Nita said, softly. "Am I going to be okay now?"

"I believe so. But I want you to come into the office later on today and let me run some tests just to be sure. Drink a little broth with some crackers if you feel hungry but nothing heavier than that."

"Okay."

"I'm going to give you another shot and some of this other nasty stuff, and then I want you to sleep a little more. I'll be gone when you wake up, but I'll see you later on this afternoon." She followed her words with action, and looked at Ron. "Just bring her into the office, I'll work her in."

Ron came back into the room a few minutes later. "She's gone, Sweetheart. I'm taking Destiny downstairs to feed her. You get some sleep, and expect to have some company when you wake up because I called Monique and let her know what was going on. I know she's called the rest of the family and they'll be showing up before long."

"Okay." She was already drifting off to sleep, but with a nagging thought at the back of her mind. She woke up around eleven, and struggled into a sitting position. She sat there a few minutes until the room stopped spinning and gradually pulled herself to her feet. Her knees were weak and she felt as though she had been run over by a train, but at least the terrible stomach cramps and headache were gone. She walked slowly into the bathroom and turned on the shower, stripped, and stood under the cleansing water, scrubbing her body and hair with a fragrant body wash. She combed some moisturizing conditioner through her hair and went into the closet and slipped on some dark blue trousers and a white top.

She was just walking into the bedroom when Jaci burst through the door. "Girl, you had us so worried. How're you feeling? Better?"

"Yes! But I gotta say, I've never been so sick."

"Hopefully, it's over now. Ron said you could have some broth and crackers. You want me to bring it up here or do you feel up to going downstairs? You have a house full. Ron's parents, Monique and my family are all here. And I called Joel, because I wanted to find out if he was okay. He is."

264

"That's what's been nagging at the back of my mind!" Nita said, snapping her fingers. "Thank you, Jaci. I was afraid he might have been sick too, but thank God we ate different things at that restaurant. I'm coming down, but hold on to me while we go down these stairs because my legs feel like rubber."

Jaci laughed. "No, I'm going to call Ron. If I let you fall I'll have to whip his behind."

When Ron came through the door, Nita walked to him and threw her arms around his neck. "Thank you so much for coming to my rescue last night. I don't know what I would have done without you."

He hugged her close. "Just don't scare me like that again, okay?" He pulled away and looked down at her. "And you don't have to thank me. I love you, Nita, and there's nothing I wouldn't do for you."

She looked down. "I know, but in light of how things stand between us, I'm especially appreciative, Ron."

He smiled. "I think after last night we can handle anything. Come on, let's go face this crowd downstairs."

A couple of hours later, she was sitting in the doctor's waiting room with Ron. They hadn't been there long before the nurse was calling her into the doctor's private office. The woman looked different with her braids pulled back, in her white coat, and a stethoscope hanging around her neck.

"How are you feeling?" She asked without preamble.

"Pretty good, considering I almost turned inside out last night. I have never felt so sick in my life, and believe me I've been through some bad times."

The doctor hesitated, as though not sure how to proceed. "Anita...I have to ask you something. When I examined you last night, I noticed some suspicious looking marks on your body that appears to indicate you've been beaten. Now, I don't think that's Ron's style but it has been a lot of years since . . ." she stopped, looking a little embarrassed. "But if by chance he is doing that, I want you to tell me."

Nita smiled, and decided she liked this lady. "Yes, I was beaten by the man I was married to more than two decades. The places you noticed were made where he punched me with his fist wearing a large ring, which left deep cuts and scars. But there are also internal damages that can't be seen."

"I figured as much. Where is he now?"

"Dead."

"Good. How did he die? How long ago?"

Nita gave the doctor a brief explanation of how and when Frank died. "I met Ron right after Frank died, but our lives didn't get all mixed up until several months ago."

The doctor looked puzzled and did a quick calculation. "And the baby?"

"Ron's, not mine, at least not by birth. I've had her for most of her life."

"Wow! This gets more intriguing. I can't tell you how impressed I am to learn Ron's taken on the daddy role. And you're a remarkable lady as well." She stuck her hand across the desk. "I'm really happy to meet you, Anita." They shook hands, and the doctor led her into an exam room. While the exam took place, Nita told her about the Hope and Help Foundation and all she wanted to accomplish through it.

The doctor got excited. "That is so wonderful! It's like giving the devil a major karate chop every time a woman is helped. If you don't mind, I'm going to talk to my medical group about this and see how we can get involved. Each year we provide financial support to selected non-profits. At any rate, you can count on me in whatever way you need – doing medical exams and treatment pro bono - anything. And do you think we can refer our patients to the Foundation for help?"

"Thanks, Natalie." Tears filled Nita's eyes. "I'm starting in Dallas, but if I can get enough funding, I'll expand to Houston. But I'm sure we can work something out, even if we have to send them to Dallas."

After completing the exam and tests work-ups, Natalie hugged Nita. "I'll let you know what we come up with, but I think you'll be fine. Now just eat very lightly for a few days and take it easy until your strength returns. And take care of Ron. He's special and he's crazy about you, but you're special too."

"Thanks," Nita said, smiling. "Although I'm not happy I got sick, I believe God is in the plan and will use it to do something good. I really appreciate everything you've done."

"Ohhh, don't speak too soon. Just wait until Ron gets my bill. But he can certainly afford it." She looked at Nita questioningly, "So are wedding bells going to be ringing soon? Just tell me to mind my business if I'm getting too personal."

"No, it's okay. We have talked about it but can't seem to reconcile our conflicting pasts."

"Ooooh!" The doctor looked thougtful. "I think I see the problem." She paused for a moment. "Anita, let me tell you something about Ron. He knows himself very well, and he has the kind of integrity that you don't find in a lot of people. He'll tell you like it is. If he's not ready to settle down, he will tell you up front, and nothing is going to make him do it. He told me up front that he was only interested in a casual relationship. He didn't change his mind, even when I tried to put pressure on him because I really wanted to marry the guy. He quickly broke it off and turned it into a friends only relationship. He still remembered to send me flowers for my birthday and other special days – until I told him I was in another relationship. Yes, he's been out there a long time, and he's run into some women who think that just because he's kind and considerate and treats them well that he loves and wants to marry them. But take it from someone who knows, when he tells a woman he doesn't want to marry her, she can forget it, because he's not going to do it. On the reverse side of that equation, if he's asked you to marry him, you can believe he's ready because he didn't come to that conclusion lightly, baby or no baby. Now you might want to consider that when you're making your decision."

"Thanks, Natalie," Nita said, thinking about Shayla and Velma. They certainly didn't understand the man.

They left the doctor's office and were headed to pick up Destiny when Ron had an idea. "Hey, we're not too far from the house. Do you feel up to driving by?"

When they drove up to the structure that only had the frame up, Ron tried to describe the lay out of it to her. I know you can't tell much about it in it's present state, but a week from now it'll be totally different.

You'll be able to see how the rooms are laid out. I'll bring you back if you want to see it."

"Of course I want to see it, Ron."

"Know what? You're the first woman I've ever asked to marry me, and the first one I've wanted to build a house for. Did you realize that?"

"No, no I didn't," she answered, slowly. "Why is that, Ron? I know there has to have been other women that you wanted to spend your life with."

"Nope. In fact, I didn't even think about it until Jason married Jaci and I saw how things were between them. I just never cared deeply enough for someone to want to harness myself to them. I didn't realize it's not a harness. It's about wanting to be in that person's presence, wanting to care for that person, love that person, protect that person. I just didn't know, Nita. But now, I do know I want that with you."

She slumped down in the seat. "Look, I'm kind of wiped out now, and you have to be too. Can we talk about this some other time?"

He gave her an irritated look. "Well, when? We've been in a communication embargo, and I need some kind of resolution. What about those other dudes hanging around?"

She laid her head against the headrest. "I really don't feel up to this now, but you're determined, I see. You have to understand, Ron. I was very young when I married Frank. He beat my self-esteem, confidence and self-worth into the ground, and made me question my judgment about men. The only other man I had been somewhat serious about before Frank was Tony – remember Tony?" She smiled at the expression on his face. "So you see, my only relationships didn't provide a lot of opportunities to learn how to make good judgments about men. So I decided not to jump into another relationship without giving myself time to study men – different ones – in order to know exactly the kind of man I may like to have as a husband."

He gave her a look she couldn't decipher. "I'm going to pick Destiny up now if you're okay with that." He made a turn that would take them onto the 288 Freeway. "And what have you discovered about the men you've come across so far?"

"Well, let's see. The guy on the cruise ship was the first encounter, after my negative one with you at Jaci's wedding that is. There's been Tyson, Tony, and you. I should count you twice since I've encountered you twice and seen two different sides to you." She smiled weakly.

"And Tyson? Has he asked you to marry him?"

"No, but I think he would have if I had given him an opening, which won't happen. However, Tony did."

"And . . ."

"You threw him out," she said, with a chuckle. "And wait just a minute. Why are you questioning me about the men in my life? What about you and your groupies?"

"I don't have any groupies," he snapped. "You're the only woman I'm interested in."

"What about Shayla and Velma? And only God knows who else? Don't sit here questioning me like you're so innocent. I'm ready to go home, hurry up and pick Destiny up."

He made a left turn onto his parents' street and was pulling into their driveway a minute later. "Yeah, well, like I said, we're going to have to reach some type of resolution. About everything."

"Fine. That suits me fine." She slide lower in the seat when he threw the door open angrily. "I'm not getting out, so please hurry up, I'm ready to get home."

"I'll be right back," he replied, and walked briskly to the door. After a conversation with his parents, he came out with Destiny knowing he probably had a new argument in front of him. While he was buckling the baby into the car seat, he said, "I don't want you to have to contend with Destiny alone while you're not feeling well. So, either I stay and help you the rest of the week, or she goes home with me."

Before Nita acknowledged his words, she turned in the seat and smiled at Destiny. "Hey, Sweetie Pie. You ready to go home?" Destiny smiled, kicked her legs and gurgled happily. Then Nita said to Ron, "That's not necessary. I've taken care of children when I was in a lot worse shape than I am now."

He gave her a long look. "Not this time, Nita."

"Well, I don't want you to take her, and it's totally unnecessary for you to stay because I'll be okay."

"Okay, Destiny is going home with me. You only had two choices and since you don't want me to stay with you that's how it's going to be." His jaw set stubbornly.

Tears sprung from her eyes and rolled down her face. "Please don't take her. If that means you're staying then so be it."

He almost lost it when he saw her tears, and he felt lower than a snake. "Don't cry," he pleaded. "Babe, you know that medicine makes you drowsy and sleepy, so what are you going to do when Destiny is yelling for attention? You're barely able to sit up now, so I know all you want to do is crash."

"Whatever." She said in a quiet voice, then after a pause, said, "Okay, so you stay, but you're going to be sorry because I'm going to do my darnedest to make your life a living hell." She turned her head and looked out the window.

Relief filled him. He had gotten what he wanted. "Alright, I'll drop you off and go home to get my stuff."

"You may be in my house the next few days, but you better stay out of my way."

He gave her an aggravated look. "Doggonit, woman! My only concern is that you re-gain your strength. You're about to collapse and you're as mean as a hornet and acting like the wicked witch of the west. But we'll call a truce – for now, but we are going to resolve things soon, one way or the other."

CHAPTER TWENTY-FIVE

On the way home, Nita's head dropped against the window because she could barely keep her eyes open. She would never admit it, even though she was sure he could see it, but he was right. She was so exhausted she could barely get out of the truck at home. She didn't know how she was going to get through all the chores she needed to do to get Destiny fed, bathed and into bed before she could rest. Plus, she was hungry, but afraid to eat anything for fear of how her stomach would react.

"I'll be back as soon as I can," he told her. "And let me have your door keys in case you're sleeping when I get back, so I won't have to disturb you."

She gave him the keys without a word. Thankfully, he took Destiny with him. *Sometimes being stubborn just wasn't the way to go,* she thought, as she ate some crackers and struggled up the stairs to the bedroom to lie down. That was the last thing she remembered until the wee hours when she woke up to use the bathroom. Destiny was sleeping peacefully in her bed, and the door to one of the bedrooms across from hers was closed but not all the way.

She hardly spoke to Ron the following two days except for things concerning Destiny. He left early each morning after getting the baby dressed and fed, to drop her off at daycare. The first day, she pretty much remained in bed, getting up only to answer bodily demands. He came back everyday with containers of soup and jell-o for her. By Thursday morning, she was feeling almost normal again, and duty was calling.

By the time Ron and Destiny arrived home, she had accomplished some things she had gotten behind on – homework, work on the Foundation. Her sons, C.J. and others, including Tyson, who had heard about the Foundation and had questions, had all been blowing her phone and e-mail up. But most importantly, she spent some time praying and getting her attitude toward Ron straight. She was ashamed of the way she had been treating him. He was right to call her the wicked witch of the west.

When Ron came in with a bowl of homemade vegetable soup sent by Jaci, and dinner for himself, she spoke pleasantly and smiled at him. They ate dinner, and while he was still feeding Destiny, she said with a satisfied smile, "Now all I need is a piece of cheesecake."

"Are you sure your stomach can handle that?" Ron asked, with a smile.

"Hey, ready or not, tomorrow I'm getting out of this house and getting the biggest steak I can hold, and some cheesecake. I'm tired of all this soup."

"Do you want me to go get you some now? There's a pie shop right up the street."

Despite the fact that she had been acting so hateful toward him, he continued to blow her away with his kindness. She knew he was extremely busy, but she would never have guessed it by the way he was taking care of her and Destiny.

"No, Ron. You've already done too much and I can't tell you how much I appreciate everything. And I apologize for being so mean. You didn't deserve that from me and I know it."

"I haven't minded doing anything and you know why." He looked at her with nothing but love shinning in his eyes.

It brought tears to her eyes. "I don't know how I can ever repay you."

"Repay? You can't repay what's freely given. But I do want us to talk, Babe. We need to get some things between us settled. Can we do that tonight because I have a feeling I've spent my last night here."

She grimaced. "Okay, we'll talk when Destiny goes down for the night."

It started out innocently enough. They rehashed a lot of what they had already discussed, and she was fine until Ron slid to his knees, proclaimed his love again and produced a ring with a large princess cut center diamond, surrounded by smaller accents diamonds.

"Will you wear this, Nita? You're already Destiny's mother, but will you be my wife? Will you let me take care of you all the time like I have this week? Will you let me come home to you everyday – see your smile, receive your hugs and even that wicked witch tongue. I'll gladly accept whatever you have as long as we're together. Will you marry me, Nita?"

She was in tears before he finished. "Ron, I don't want to do this now."

"One question, Nita. Do you love me? Do you have any feelings for me at all?"

"Yes, you know I do, Ron. But that's not the issue here. The big question is whether either one of us is ready for marriage. I don't want us to be a statistic."

"We'll go through pre-marital counseling, post-marriage counseling, anything, Sweetheart, and I promise that whatever the results, I'll accept them. But Nita, we could be at this same place two years from now without being any closer to a resolution. Or, we could be happily married at least part of that time. But the time is going to pass whatever the case. I want to be your husband and fulltime daddy for my baby. I'm tired of Destiny being transported between two houses. And I don't ever want to stand in fear on the other side of a door and not be able to get to you when you need me. I know we're both stretched to the limit, but maybe we can handle things better together. And Babe, I don't mind fighting other dudes over you, but I want to know I have that right."

She cried harder. "I'm scared, Ron," she confessed brokenly. "I can't live through again what I had to endure with Frank. I just can't do that, Ron. I know you say the womanizing is behind you, but how do you know – how can I know for sure?" She fell into his arms and sobbed.

"I know, Babe. Don't cry, okay. The best I can do is promise you I won't do that. But if the time ever comes that I feel tempted to do it, I won't sneak around, I'll be up front about it. And I've asked God to take away my ability to, uh, you know, if I even think about it." He chuckled and soon she was chuckling with him. He slid the ring on her finger and hugged her.

That's where things went awry. He kissed her, and things spiraled out of control. Although they stopped – just in the nick of time, her anguish over how close they had come made her put him out, and ban him from her presence. She wore his ring and communicated with him constantly, but wouldn't let him come near her. She dropped Destiny off at daycare herself the next day, and Ron picked her up for the weekend.

CHAPTER TWENTY-SIX

Sunday evening, Ron came in and lost no time in catching her in a tight hug. "I missed you, and so did Destiny." He unloaded Destiny's stuff before sitting down to talk about the pre-marital counseling. "Pastor Robinson and his wife have handed most of the marriage counseling responsibilities off to the marriage counselor on staff, but after I talked to Pastor on Friday, he checked, and the counselor's schedule was full. So they decided to take us on themselves." At her skeptical look, he said,

"Hey it helps that they've known me all my life and are really curious about who I'm so anxious to marry. They counsel as a team and have agreed to start in two-weeks. They've scheduled us on Thursdays at four. So what do you think? Will you be able to do it then? It's going to be about twelve weeks, with one or two weekends thrown in for us to attend marriage preparation boot camps. Well?"

Nita's heart pounded in her chest. Was this really happening? Should it? "I, uh, guess that's okay, Ron. I admit I'm nervous about this though."

"Yeah, I am too. But I really want to move forward, Babe, and this is the first step in doing that. I know you're busy and I am too, but when they told me they had rearranged their schedules to accommodate us, what could I say but thank you. Now Pastor Robinson may be out of town one or two of those weeks, but we'll deal with that as it comes up. Are you okay with this?"

"I suppose I am," she said with an unsure look.

Two weeks later, Nita, with a stomach full of butterflies, met Ron at the church for their first counseling session,. It was a roller coaster ride from then throughout the remaining sessions, filled with tears, laughter and requiring much prayer and self-examination on both their parts.

The first four sessions covered the elements of a Godly marriage, and the different types of love that must be expressed during marriage. Those sessions were difficult, but were a picnic compared to what would follow.

During the remaining sessions they delved into their personal relationship, and the Pastors pushed into light, some issues that could be detrimental to a marriage between them if not dealt with in an open and honest way. The big question they both had to continually answer was, did they believe their love for each other was strong enough to overcome them?

Grueling. That was the best word Ron could find to describe the pre-marital counseling. There were times when he questioned his desire to get married, and had to fight the urge to say forget it and return to his old life. But he knew that life held nothing for him anymore, and he also knew Nita experienced similar struggles.

After several counseling sessions, he started receiving calls from Frieda Goodwin. That was disturbing. He had finally gotten rid of Shayla and Velma – he hoped - and now another troublesome woman from his past had popped up. Frieda was the interior decorator he had hired to decorate his brother's house. During the course of the job, Frieda had gone after Jason in an aggressive way, which turned Jason off. She had then turned her sights on him. He had no interest in playing second fiddle to his brother and he told her so. After that, he had stopped using her on his jobs. Why, after several years, was she calling him now? And just when he didn't need the aggravation. He blocked her calls on his phone, and informed his secretary he was not taking her calls. The Pastor kept telling him to be prayerful because the harder he worked to turn his life around, the more Satan would work to keep him from doing so.

As the counseling sessions progressed, so did all other aspects of their already full schedules. His on-going projects had to move, and required several out of town trips. Thankfully, He was able to convince Nita to travel with him when she could.

Their house was close to completion. It had been a while since Nita had seen it, and then it was in a very rough condition, both inside and out. Now it looked totally different, and he was anxious for her to see it. Her reaction was one he would always cherish.

When he opened the door and she walked in, it was worth everything he had put into it. She gasped when she stepped onto marble floor of the large foyer. "Oh, goodness! It's absolutely beautiful. I'm overwhelmed, and I love everything you've done. I can't imagine what I'll see that will top this," Nita said.

Ron smiled. "You've only just begun. And remember, we need to pick out the paint, cabinets and countertops you want for the kitchen and bathrooms, as well as the plumbing fixtures and appliances. I went ahead with everything else because it's similar to what you have in the condo, and I know you like it. If you want, we can get a professional decorator to come in and give us some help with those decisions as well as window treatments. We need to do that as soon as possible too."

"I like that idea. I wouldn't know where to start, and this house deserves the best."

When they finished the tour and walked out the door, Ron asked, "Well, what do you think?"

"Wow! That's all I can say, Ron. You've really outdone yourself. I'm glad you waited until now to show it to me again. I'm blown away, Honey. It's beautiful."

He grinned. "It'll be ready for us soon. You ready?"

CHAPTER TWENTY-SEVEN

Joel was finally moving into his apartment at Prairie View University. Nita, Ron and Joel, with all their vehicles loaded, traveled the hour's drive to move him in.

In the meantime, Nita's Dad called and asked her to come to Riverwood to see Aunt Muriel, whose health was failing. In spite of her demanding schedule, she decided to go. Aunt Muriel's hatefulness toward Nita as a child didn't stir much compassion, but she had missed out on too many chances to rally around her family because of Frank's domineering control, and now she had no excuse. She also wanted her sons to get to know her family, so she called them to find out if they would be available to go, and surprisingly, they both agreed. Frankie would fly in from Atlanta, where he was in summer school, and it was no problem for Joel to drive in from Prairie View.

When she told Ron about her plans, he asked if he could go. "Yes, but you should talk to Jason. When he went up there with Jaci, she said he was so bored he didn't know what to do, because she was busy visiting with relatives and didn't have a lot of time for him."

"I still want to see where you grew up, and meet your relatives. And is that crazy dude, Tony, still there?"

She laughed. "Yes, as far as I know, but he won't be a problem. I heard he's found another woman willing to marry him."

"Oh, well, good for him."

So the weekend after their sixth counseling session, they headed to Riverwood, Arkansas.

Her dad had two other sisters, who had recently moved back from California. Nita hadn't seen them since she had married Frank. And Nita's much older sister, Madelyn, who she hadn't seen or heard from since Frank died, was also there with her family. It turned into a mini family reunion of sorts, in spite of the reason they were there. It was obvious Aunt Muriel wasn't doing well. When Nita went to visit her, Aunt Muriel caught her hand, and although she couldn't speak, her eyes begged for forgiveness, which Nita gave.

It was also great to visit with her other aunts and uncles – her mother's sisters and brothers – as well as cousins and other relatives. All in all, it was a good trip and Nita was glad they had gone.

After their seventh week into the counseling, Ron asked her to fly to Maryland with him to look in on her brother's projects. They left Thursday night after their session, with plans to return Monday night, which gave Ron two full workdays there and gave Nita some time to visit with her brother's family and look around for Mikey. According to the Investigator, her son could still be somewhere in the D.C. area. Nita boarded the return flight in tears. She had searched the face of every young man she saw, hoping and praying that by some miracle, one of them would be her son. The cloak of disappointment was heavy upon her when they left.

Their sessions were cancelled the next two weeks, since the Pastor was out of town. Nita and Destiny drove with Ron to Austin, Texas to check on a home he had designed that was being built up in the hills. While there, they toured the State Capitol, the Hill Country around

Austin, and ate at a fabulous restaurant situated on a hilltop with a view of Lake Travis.

C.J. and Jaci had been trying to schedule some cousin time with her, so the following Saturday, they finally had a girls day out together. The day was spent with a visit to a spa and salon, and a long lunch. Another refreshing day for Nita, who needed it badly.

Her cousins were full of questions about the counseling sessions, as well as wedding plans. "I don't know, girls. I haven't gotten that far in my mind yet - much to Ron's displeasure."

"Well, has the counseling produced any big, hidden revelations that would make you doubt if y'all are ready?" C.J. asked.

"No. As a matter of fact, they've been very enlightening. We've addressed some issues about ourselves and each other, and although it's been difficult, I think we've resolved most of them."

"Well, let's cut to the bottom line. Do you love the guy, and what have you discovered while y'all been traveling all over the place together?" C.J. asked, with a chuckle.

"Yes, I love him, and I love being with him. I don't think there's another man alive who would treat me as well as he does. And even though I know he's getting impatient, and wanting to set a wedding date, he's not pushing for us to sleep together, although I know he's very frustrated in that area. He's really trying to honor God and me."

"Well, the house is gorgeous," Jaci said. "Ron took us over to see it the other day, and I just love it. Not as much as I love mine, of course," she smiled.

"So, you're going to keep us all on pins and needles huh?" C.J. asked. "That is just not right, Nita. I'm ready to be planning a wedding."

"Me too," Jaci said. "Why don't we just start some preliminary plans?"

"Nope. I'm still praying and asking the Lord for guidance. In the meantime, I'm helping Ron get the house ready for him and Destiny. He's going to be moving into it whatever happens because he's already sold the building where he is."

"Oh Lord, please help her," C.J. groaned.

The next two counseling sessions were boot camps. In the first boot camp they were asked to explore and reveal how much they really knew – or not - about each other; and in the other, they were sent through physical, emotional and spiritual exercises designed to test and strengthen their trust in each other.

Finally, the big day - their twelfth and final session in which they were to hear the Pastors' conclusions and recommendations. Ron entered the church filled with nervousness.

Nita was waiting for him and after a brief hug, they entered the Pastor's study together, where the Pastor and First Lady were waiting.

The Pastor began immediately. "We've counseled couples we thought had a lot more going for them than you, and their marriages failed. On the other hand, we've counseled those who had less going for them who have made it. We've counseled those who just went through the counseling to get to their coveted destination – a big, grand wedding, with no thought to building a strong marriage. And we've counseled those who had the best of intentions, but not the fortitude to sustain. I'm just saying that as your Pastors, we can only offer recommendations based on what we've learned from our sessions."

Ron's nervousness increased. He knew the ultimate decision rested with him and Nita, but he really wanted a favorable report from the Pastors. He felt a little better when he noticed both Pastor Robinson and First Lady had smiles covering their faces. First Lady said, "You have already succeeded in some things that many haven't been able to cope with. For instance, you're already successfully parenting a child together in very unique circumstances."

Pastor Robinson added, "Ron, I'm really proud of the progress I've seen in you. But you have to continue to grow spiritually stronger so you'll be equipped for the role as head of the household." He gave Ron a long, stern look. "Understand what I'm saying to you?"

Ron nodded with a sincere and determined look on his face. "Yes, Sir."

Pastor continued. "Now, we've compiled a list of things you'll need to follow as though the survival of your marriage depends on it. Blow it up and tack it on your wall. Keep it on the bedside table – whatever you need to do to keep these things in your minds, prayers and actions. I call it your Focus -Twelve Plan, and you'll see why I call it that as we go through it." He read through the twelve Scriptural- based items.

After he finished, the Pastor looked over his glasses at them. "You both need to decide if you are willing to do these things. If so, your marriage has a chance to succeed. If not, you could end up as a statistic."

"Nita looked at Ron, worry written all over her face. "I don't know if I can do it, Ron."

Ron felt sick. "I don't either. There are some heavy things on that list."

The Pastors laughed, then First Lady said, "No, you can't do it, not in your own strength. It will require constant dependence on God, and considering how we like to handle things ourselves, that's easier said, than done. But God promised to never leave or forsake you."

Pastor Robinson said, "From our observations, we believe marriage between you can work, and will work, but it won't be easy, and will require consistent effort on both parts, with much prayer and trust in God. We'll be available to mentor you and do some regular check-ups, because marriage, like our bodies, cars or anything else, need to be checked, adjusted and tuned up on a regular basis for maximum efficiency. Of course, the final decision about entering this marriage rests totally with you. Any questions?"

"Yes, uh, Pastor Robinson, do we need to give you our decision today?" Ron asked.

"Yes, we're a little overwhelmed. We really would like to review everything we've been over and talk about it, pray about it and give it some serious thought," Nita added.

"That's a wise thing to do. Just take your time and let us know what you decide. It's been a pleasure working with both of you, and remember, whatever you decide, God has to be the One who'll get the glory, so be prayerful."

They left the office in silence. Ron's first words to her after they walked out were, "Well, I know we need to pray and talk about this, but will you marry me?"

CHAPTER TWENTY-EIGHT

The counseling had been one of the most difficult, but empowering and spiritually strengthening experiences Nita had ever gone through. But as she left the church, her mind swirled with confusion. Were they ready? She started praying as she was driving. "Lord, as we take steps toward this marriage, please guide us. And if we're not ready, please show us."

Ron didn't know whether to laugh, cry, or whoop with joy when, after a week on pins and needles, much prayer, and in-depth discussions on the Focus-Twelve Plan, Nita said, "Yes, I'll marry you."

They set a date just three months away, which was the maximum time he would agree to and the minimum time Nita said she needed to get her house packed up and plan the wedding, which would be a small affair.

"Okay, that'll give us time to get the house completed. We still have to decide on a decorator. Keep in mind that I'm going to be moving in, but since everything we do from this point will be cosmetic, that'll be okay."

Nita groaned. "I just dread this process. Besides hating to pack, I have to decide what's going from my house to the new house, and what's going into storage. I still have stuff in storage in Dallas. A lot of it I kept for my sons - things I thought they would like to keep of their dad's. But there's quite a bit of furniture there too."

"Well, the good thing is, we shouldn't have to buy any new furniture. The bad news is deciding what to do with the stuff we don't want. Maybe we can sell it."

"Oh!" She turned to him, green eyes shinning brightly. "I just had a thought. You know the mission of the Foundation is to help women get back on their feet and make a new start. Some of them have to leave their homes with little more than the clothes on their backs. Why don't we use that furniture to start a furniture center where women can go and get things that will help them set up housekeeping again. It can be a collection place where people can donate unwanted, but usable furniture and clothes and household items. What do you think?"

"I think it's a good idea, but how much more of your time will that take up? I'm telling you now that I'm going to be selfish when it comes to sharing you."

"Don't worry, I'll have this component added to the services the Foundation provides and the actual implementation will be the responsibility of the agency overseeing all the services."

"Okay, Sweetheart. When are we going to meet with the decorators? One of my assistants has three lined up to give us proposals. He said they're all tops in their profession."

"Let's see, this is Thursday, so why don't we set it up for next Thursday. That'll give us time to get you moved in, and maybe I can get started bringing some of my small things over."

He hugged her. "Sweetheart, I can't tell you how happy I am right now. "

He told Monique the good news when she finally showed up. She had been missing around the condo for weeks. He'd figured she was staying with a friend since she had decided she didn't want the apartment he had offered her. "Where have you been?" He asked.

Monique looked uncomfortable. "Oh, well, to tell the truth, I've been trying to stay out of your way as much as possible. You haven't been real good company lately. But listen, I want to ask you about Nita's condo. Do you know what she's going to do with it?"

"Yeah, she's got Jason looking for someone to lease it to. She doesn't want to sell it."

"How much is she leasing it for? And when could I move in?"

"I don't know how much she's leasing it for, or if she'll even lease it to someone in the family. If you got behind with your rent, she'd have a difficult time putting you out."

"What if I give her six months in advance, plus first and last month? Since I'll be starting my new job soon, I can do that. Do you think she'll consider it then?"

"I don't know, Monique. You'll have to talk to her."

"So when are you moving? And most importantly, when is Nita moving?"

"I'm calling a moving company tomorrow, and by this time next week, I'll be out. But you know Nita won't be moving until after we're married."

"Okay, I'll talk to her tomorrow then. I just don't like that place y'all found for me. Will I be able to stay here until Nita is out of the condo?"

"I think so, but you might have to get some furniture since I'm moving everything." He smiled. "You know, I was just thinking on the way home. It's the darnedest thing. I've noticed the difference in the way Destiny acts when she's here, and when she's at Nita's. Here, she basically gets in one spot and just sits there, like she's afraid to move. But at Nita's she's running all over the place playing, getting into things or in the kitchen begging for something. The first thing she wants to do when she gets home is pull her shoes off. Here, she screams when I try to take her shoes off."

"In other words, she feels like she's at home at Nita's. Understandable, since she is there more than she's here. But considering that you're her daddy, and Nita's not her mother, you have to know there's something wrong with that picture."

"I realize that, and so does Nita. In fact, one of the things we discussed during our counseling was that Destiny needs one place to call home."

Monique looked at him a long time, then asked, "Ron, remember when you were seriously considering giving Destiny up for adoption? What if you had done that? Where would that leave you and Nita?"

His head fell back against the cushions and he closed his eyes. "Heavy questions. I shudder to think what would have happened if Nita hadn't been in the picture because she's the reason I didn't follow through on that. But if I had, I don't think I could live with myself now. I love that little girl so much, and my head gets twice it's size every time she calls me 'DaDa'.

"Wow, Brother. Heavy answers. But are you really ready, Ron? I mean to come in off the street and settle down with a family? I would hate to see Nita and Destiny hurt."

Several seconds passed before he answered. "You know, I admit God is still working on me. The thought of failing to live up to being the man, the husband, the daddy, that I know I should be, makes me sick. Not only would I be failing God, myself, Nita, and Destiny, I know there would be consequences. I could be dead or dying, or in jail right now because I've been in situations where any of those things could have easily happened. All it would have taken was one AIDS infected woman, or a crazy woman or man who decided to do me in. God is merciful, and kept me from the worse that could have happened. Consequences can take us down a road we don't want to walk, and knowing that will keep me from doing something stupid."

CHAPTER TWENTY-NINE

Frieda Goodwin drove into the circular driveway and admired the elevated garden on the outer perimeter of the wide lawn which was filled with an assortment of trees, flowers and shrubs that partially shielded the house from the street. It would be gorgeous when the plants grew into maturity. She felt a jolt of exhilaration when she turned her attention to the absolutely fantastic house. The traditional redbrick was set off by white columns, dormer windows, a covered portico on the ground level, and a white framed balcony that ran across the front of the house. Ron Gilmore had created another masterpiece.

Frieda had no doubt it would be exquisite on the inside. Ron Gilmore was known for his innovative and beautiful designs. He was also one of Houston's most notorious womanizers, but she believed that like his brother, Jason Gilmore, Ron could be captured by the right woman.

Ron hadn't returned any of the calls she'd made to him over the last several weeks, but she was glad she hadn't given up. Apparently, they had helped her get an inside track with Ron for this job. She had blown things with him several years ago when he had hired her to decorate his brother's house. Like a fool, she had gone after the wealthy, older brother, who owned a computer software technology company and was a real estate developer. But he had sent her packing when his house was complete. However, there was no shame in her game. She merely re-set her cap for Ron.

But Ron, knowing the score, had ignored her. She'd watched him float from woman to woman, deciding to give him a little time before she went after him again. Then, he'd simply dropped out of circulation. She had been fearful she had lost him for good, but surely she would have heard something since they moved in the same industry circles. To be honest, she had missed the lucrative jobs that used to come through the pipeline from Ron. Needless to say, she had been over the moon with joy when his assistant had informed her that Ron was taking proposals for work on his own house. Finally another chance! And she wasn't blowing this one.

So it was with eager anticipation flowing through her at the thought of seeing Ron again that Frieda pushed the doorbell.

"Whoa!" Disappointment hit when the door opened to reveal a woman who reminded her of Halle Berry in spite of her grungy appearance. She was older, taller, heavier, than the actress, but beautiful, with unusual green eyes and smooth caramel colored skin. Although no slouch in the looks department herself, Frieda – who was bordering on desperation – for a job, and even more so, a wealthy husband – felt threatened.

Frieda had been entertaining fantasies of marriage – literally and career wise - to the famous architect, and envisioning the tremendous impact they could make as a team in the world of architecture and interior design. The fantasy was so strong that after the initial shock, even the beautiful woman's presence in Ron's house couldn't eradicate it. Frieda quickly dismissed her. No woman dressed like this could hold the interest of a man like Ron Gilmore. She reassured herself that both the house and Ron Gilmore were hers.

"You must be one of the designers. Please come in. I'm Anita Stanhope, Ron's . . . "

Frieda ignored the hand the woman extended and stepped through the door without acknowledging the greeting. Her eyes took in the woman's faded jeans and tee-shirt in a disparaging way. "I don't really care who you are, I'm here to see Ron Gilmore, not the hired help," she said dismissingly. "Just tell Ron I'm here."

A child's scream split the air startling Frieda. She hadn't noticed the baby standing behind the woman. The child looked at her and let out another scream as she held her arms up to the woman to be picked up.

A guarded look had entered the woman's face. "Sorry, she's nervous around strangers. Ron just called to say he's on the way, but said we could go ahead and get started."

"No thanks. I prefer to work with the homeowner," Frieda answered in a rude tone.

The woman gave her a look she couldn't interpret and led the way into the spacious house. "Have a seat," she said, before she put the child down, and told her to go find something that Frieda assumed was a toy. Then she went to the oven and opened it to check on whatever it was that was producing mouth watering aromas.

"So how long have you worked for Mr. Gilmore?" She asked.

"Not long," the woman answered, as she unpacked a box of dishes. She jumped in surprise when the volume on the TV suddenly increased. "Destiny! Didn't I tell you to leave that alone?" She ran to the child, took the remote control from her, and tapped her hand so softly it couldn't have hurt very much.

Frieda observed the interchange with disapproval. "I don't think Mr. Gilmore will appreciate having an uncontrollable child running through his house. If you want to continue to work here, you'd better find someplace to leave that child."

"I'll keep that in mind," the woman answered, before going back to her task.

Nita was weary. She had been working all day to make the house livable and comfortable for Ron and Destiny. She'd spent the morning shopping and stocking the refrigerator and pantry, then getting some of

Destiny's clothes and toys unpacked. Odessa, Ron's housekeeper, had cleaned the bathrooms, filled the linen closets and made the beds before she left. Nita was now busy in the kitchen, where she had put together a casserole and salad for dinner and was unpacking dishes. She didn't have a lot of patience for the snooty woman's attitude.

A few minutes later, a loud crash came from across the room. "Uh, oh!" Destiny yelled. Nita ran to see what the noise was and discovered the baby had knocked over a stack of CDs waiting to be placed in the large entertainment cabinet. She tapped Destiny's hand a little harder this time, before going back to the kitchen. Destiny followed, saying, "Duice, Mama. Duice," in a whining voice as she pointed to the refrigerator.

Nita filled a sippy cup with juice and handed it to Destiny.

"I'm afraid I'm going to have to strongly recommend to Mr. Gilmore that you not be allowed to bring that child back here," the snooty woman commented. "It's apparent she's destructive and out of control."

Nita looked at her without changing expressions, then went into the pantry and came out with a small bowl filled with cereal, which she placed on the high chair sitting in the corner. She lifted Destiny into the chair and left her happily munching on her snack.

"You do whatever makes you happy," Nita finally replied before going back to her unpacking. *Maybe I'm being mean not telling her who I am, but it'll teach her not to be so fast to make assumptions,* Nita thought.

"Umph! It's so hard to find good help these days. I suppose that's why Mr. Gilmore puts up with you and that heathen child."

Nita turned and gave the woman her full attention, her green eyes blazing dangerously. "Her name is Destiny. She is not a heathen and don't call her that again."

"Well, I doubt you and that brat will be coming back here anyway. I've known Mr. Gilmore a long time and he respects my opinion. When I tell him how destructive she is, and how rude you are, take my word for it, you won't be back."

"We shall see," Nita said, quietly. No sense getting too angry, she knew what the outcome would be.

"People who do the kind of work you do are a dime a dozen in this city. And those of culture and good breeding know they don't have to put up with bad attitudes and heathen children."

Nita slammed a dish down on the counter. "Okay, lady, that's it. Your services are not wanted or needed here. Please leave. Now!"

The woman gasped. "You can't put me out. I'm here to see Mr. Gilmore and I'm not leaving until I do."

"Oh yes, you are leaving, and I will throw you out if I have to. You've been rude and disrespectful of me and my baby from the moment you stepped through the door. I don't have to take that kind of treatment. Now get out of this house, and off this property."

"I . . . you have no right to tell me to leave!"

Nita stepped toward her, a fierce look on her face. "Yes, I do."

She almost ran toward the door. "You just wait until I tell Mr. Gilmore about this." She opened the door and ran out. But before she could get into her car, Ron pulled into the driveway.

He got out and walked toward the woman. "Frieda? What are you doing here?"

"Ron! Your assistant called me. I'm here about the decorating job. Didn't you know?"

He looked aggravated. "No, I didn't, but since you're here, we'll look at your proposal. Did you look around and discuss things with Nita?"

"No." She answered with a frown. "Ron, I so appreciate your letting me decorate your beautiful home, and I promise to make it a show place we can both be proud of, but I really need to talk to you," she said, urgently. "Sometimes men don't understand that inappropriate help can really hurt your image, if you know what I mean.

"Now, I hope I'm not being too pushy, but I'm only saying this to help you." She cut her eyes to Nita, who was standing in the doorway. "I don't know what your relationship is with that woman, but you're going to have to get rid of her or put her in her place. Also, she'll have to leave that heathen child someplace else. That child has been getting into everything, and once we get this place decorated, a child running loose through here, especially one as out of control as this one, cannot be tolerated. When I told her that," she pointed to Nita, "she rudely told me to get off the property. Really, Ron, what kind of people do you employ?"

Ron turned and looked to Nita with puzzlement. Before he could say anything, Frieda ran over to him and grabbed his arm.

"Why don't we talk while we tour the house," she said, as she hooked her arm through Ron's. "That way, we don't have to worry about being disturbed."

Ron disengaged his arm. "Didn't you and Nita introduce yourselves?"

"No, she wasn't particularly interested in meeting the help," Nita answered.

"What?"

"Well, I just assumed she was the housekeeper, and as such, shouldn't be allowed to bring her little heathen child here to tear up the place and eat your food. You have to nip things like that in the bud."

Ron finally caught the full gist of what was going on. "Well, let me enlighten you about something, because you have jumped to a lot of conclusions. This is my fiancee, Anita, and that child you keep referring to as a heathen is my daughter, Destiny."

Frieda gasped. "Your fiancee? Well, I hope you know what you're doing, getting involved with a woman of this caliber," Frieda huffed.

"Yes, I do know. And I'm very thankful."

A look of desperation flittered across Frieda's face. "Are you sure that is your child? Women like her know exactly how to pull the wool over the eyes of unsuspecting men."

Ron reacted with the same anger Nita had. "You need to leave, Frieda. Before I say something I may regret. You shouldn't have been called for this job anyway."

Frieda turned and glared at Nita. "You should have told me who you are, instead of trying to make a fool of me."

"Lady, you didn't need my help, you did a perfect job of making a fool out of yourself. And I certainly didn't want to spoil all the fun you were having from your superior perch? Thank you for coming, but as I said, your services won't be needed here."

"Aargh!" Frieda huffed in frustration as she turned and walked briskly toward her car. Before getting in the car, she turned to say something, but thought better of it, and instead, sent a malevolent look in Nita's direction.

When the door closed behind them after Frieda pulled away, Nita said, "I get evil vibes from that woman, Ron. I don't care if we hang sheets up to the windows, she is not welcome here. Do not, I repeat, do not, ever let her into this house again. She's a witch if I ever met one, and I've met a few. Why did you ask her to come over here?"

Ron smiled. "Hmmm, something smells delicious," he said, sniffing. "Okay, Sweetheart, she won't be back. And I didn't ask her to come. I left it up to my staff to line up some designers for me. I guess they figured that since Frieda was the designer for Jason's house, that I would like her to do mine " He lifted her left hand. "Where's your ring?"

"Oh! I've been cleaning and doing some heavy work and I didn't want to lose it, so I took it off. Why?"

"It might have helped if Frieda had seen the ring on your finger. Maybe she wouldn't have been so quick to assume you were the housekeeper."

"No, Honey. That woman walked through the door with plans for you and this house already made. My wearing a ring wouldn't have made any difference. I've met her kind before – they don't let anything deter them. Stay away from her, Honey. I'm telling you, she means us no good. She's on assignment from hell."

They chose the designer who was willing to comply with their desires, and who was capable of fulfilling them promptly.

Frieda tore into Ron's office the next day, fuming. "Ron, we've known each other a long time. We've worked together, and you know my work. You know I would do a good job on your house. How could you let that woman dismiss me like that?"

Ron gave her a hard look. "Frankly, you wouldn't have even been called on the project if I had thought to tell my staff to delete your name from the lists. Yes, you do good work, but the fact is, you don't know how to treat people, Frieda, and you always manage to provoke and alienate the wrong person. That's exactly what you did yesterday."

"Look, Ron, I believe we could be good together – in more ways than one. Don't let the fact that this woman had a baby for you stand between us and the success we could achieve together. From what I saw yesterday, she's tacky and without an ounce of class. I can do a lot more for you than she can."

Ron chuckled. "Let me be very clear here, Frieda. I'm the one doing the chasing, not her, and like I've told you before, I have no taste for women who preferred my brother first."

An indignant look covered her face. "You or your brother don't know the kind of woman you need to take you far in this world."

"Maybe not, but my brother is extremely happy with the woman he has, and I am too. And actually, we're doing okay in this world. Are you?"

"You will regret this." She stormed out with an angry twist to her neck.

Ron followed her out of his office and went to his secretary. "Please make sure Ms. Goodwin is deleted from all of the resource lists we use in this office."

Three weeks later, the house looked beautiful. Nita was pleased and Ron was happy. All he wanted now was for the next two months until the wedding to fly by.

He could only hope he wouldn't run into anymore crazy women, especially Frieda Goodwin. Like Nita, he also believed the woman had evil intentions. She had come on too strong for someone who hadn't seen him in years, and assumed more than she had a right to. Something was definitely not clicking right in her mind. He was happy Nita hadn't mentioned her again, but he knew what she had to be thinking, even though she didn't say it to him. "Lord, please don't let any more crazy women show up."

CHAPTER THIRTY

Was she actually getting married? And to another womanizer? Even in the midst of the whirlwind preparations, Nita still had moments of disbelief. Also, it was impossible to forget that one of her children was missing. She had managed to push worry about Mikey to the back of her mind by staying busy, but the Investigator, who, up to this point hadn't reported any progress, called her a few days before her wedding to tell her the cell phone company had finally reported there had been no activity on Mikey's phone for several months. She knew that from looking at the bills each month. But hearing the disturbed tone of his voice caused terror to jump to the forefront of her mind. She started sending several e-mails a day, begging Mikey to reply just to let her know he was okay. "Father, I trust You to take control over this situation with Mikey. There is no place he can be that You are not. Please keep him safe, and give him the strong desire to call or come home. In the meantime, Father, I thank You for peace that passes all understanding to keep my heart and mind concerning Mikey."

The wedding would be a small affair with just family and a few close friends, associates and church members. But who knew members of those groups would come out of the woodworks bringing others with them. Nita's biggest surprise, which brought tears to her eyes, was that her cousins, Buddy, Big Ben and Dusty, would be there.

What most surprised Ron was the fact that his grandparents, well into their eighties and experiencing recent serious illnesses, were determined to come.

The high noon ceremony would be held in the original church building, now called the chapel, and mostly used for meetings, classes and small weddings. They had thought it more than adequate, but were now questioning that decision.

Before she was sure she was ready, Nita was waking up to her wedding day. At this point she and Ron both wished they had just gone into the Pastor's study and gotten it over with.

The limousine arrived to pick her up and take her to the church early. She fought back tears as she was having her hair and makeup done. She thought about all the times she had feared Frank was going to kill her. She wished for the mother she could barely remember, her grandparents, and most of all for Mikey. She prayed God was indeed ordering her steps, and that He would bless their marriage and life together. And she prayed that somehow she would make it through the ceremony without crying. No such luck.

As a soloist sung an old school love song, Nita walked slowly down the aisle of the packed out Sanctuary, clutching her daddy's arm, but with eyes fixed on Ron. His eyes shone brightly and the smile on his face couldn't have gotten any bigger. When he winked at her and mouthed the words, "I love you," she felt her heart lift in joy.

Her sons, who walked in front of her, stood in the place of bridesmaids at the altar, while Jason stood beside Ron as best man. Just when she thought she might make it through dry eyed after all, her cousins walked into the choir stand and Jaci sat down at the piano, while Gina took a seat at the organ.

Dusty lifted the microphone and said, "We're going to sing a song that was one of our Grandmother's favorites, and is one of Nita's, as well. Some might not think it's exactly appropriate for a wedding, but those who know what today means for Nita and Ron, will understand."

When the music started, and Nita heard the melody to the song, she knew she was going to shout. Words from the chorus flowed out as though it hadn't been years since the cousins had sung together.

"Your grace and mercy, brought me through. I'm living this moment, because of You."

Buddy opened his mouth and in a strong voice, belted out the first verse. They went to the chorus again, and moved to the next verse, which sent things over the edge.

Before Nita could let loose with her own praise, Ron was lifting his hands in the air, saying "Thank You, Lord, thank You, for Your mercy."

As they went into the chorus again, Nita shouted, "Hallelujah!" and start jumping up and down, while Ron went to his knees, in praise and worship. Her aunts were out of their seats, shouting in the aisles, and Ron's grandmother, who had needed help to get to her seat, was trying to run, shouting, "Thank You, Jesus." Joel grabbed Destiny out of Cecelia's arms when she ran to the altar and knelt beside Ron. Soon the cousins couldn't continue singing, and Pastor Robinson began to preach as though it was Sunday morning worship.

CHAPTER THIRTY-ONE

Ron overruled Nita's suggestion that they forego a honeymoon so they could rest and get settled in the house. Yes, they were tired, but they also needed some time alone as husband and wife. He had booked them on a cruise, thinking that was really where things started with them.

It was the best thing they could have done. It was a relaxing and satisfying trip – much different from the last cruise when he left feeling frustrated with her.

After several weeks of marriage, Ron was still praising God for the exhilarating and spiritual outpouring during their wedding. They hadn't planned it that way, but God obviously had, and he wouldn't change a thing about it.

He couldn't stop thanking the Lord for using Destiny – the child he hadn't wanted - to bring them together and set them on the path of love and marriage. One of the first things they did after the wedding was see his attorney and start the process for Nita to adopt Destiny.

Now, he was waiting on Nita to return from a meeting in Dallas. If there was anything he would change, it would be all the things Nita was involved in that limited her time and attention for him. Selfish? Yes, he admitted, but at least he was honest.

He picked up the phone to call her again, and smiled when he heard her voice.

"Hey, you!"

"Hey, Babe. Where are you? Getting close yet?"

"Not as close as I had hoped. I'm caught in traffic because of this aggravating construction. I haven't seen one person working, but they have two lanes closed. I'm having to take deep breaths and tell myself to relax, grin and bear it."

"Maybe you should start flying up there for these meetings. I worry about you out there on that highway by yourself. And at least you wouldn't have to deal with traffic."

"Well, while I'm fighting traffic to get to the airport, then deal with getting through security, I can almost be where I'm going. The good thing is, I don't expect to have to make these trips as often once we are well established."

"Well, I hope that won't be too long."

"Did you pick Destiny up yet?"

"I have her. We're both waiting anxiously for you to get here. Oh, Frankie called looking for you a while ago. Did he get you on your cell?"

"Yes, I spoke to him. I'll have to tell you about our strange conversation. I'd better get off so I can concentrate on this traffic. I'll call you when I'm close, and I hope you have something for dinner because I really don't feel like cooking."

"Aw, heck! I was waiting for you to get here so you could cook something. Okay, I'll run and grab something." He was disappointed. He wanted some of his wife's cooking.

Nita took a long frustrated breath after she hung up with Ron. She knew he was dissatisfied with the amount of time she was spending on her various projects, but doggonit, he knew that before they got married. Overall, she was pleased with the response she'd gotten when she presented the furniture and household collection idea to the Dallas Pastors Alliance. They had all pledged support. It was what happened afterwards that bothered her.

Frank's sister and brother were waiting for her after the meeting. His sister, Christine, had asked to be a volunteer for the Foundation when they first started, but today they were demanding that both of them become paid staff. "Why should strangers benefit from our brother's hard earned money while we can't get nothing?" Christine demanded. "That ain't right and you know it."

Nita took a frustrating breath. "No one is receiving a salary. Besides that, most of the funds coming in now are from sources other than Frank's estate."

"But you started that Foundation with money our brother worked hard for. And if he was still alive, it wouldn't be going to no bunch of strangers," Frank's brother stated hotly.

"Yes, but the fact is, he's gone. And it's up to me and my sons to see that the money he left is used for good. Maybe later, we can pay people for their services, but not now."

Nita's denial so upset them that the resulting verbal attack was akin to those Frank had dumped on her for so many years. She shivered as she recalled the last words Christine had thrown at her. "I just wish my brother could come back long enough to beat your behind again."

As she inched along in the slow moving traffic, remembering Christine's hateful wish, tears came to her eyes. "Lord, why can't things just roll along in a peaceful way, like they're supposed to? But I guess the devil wouldn't be on his job if they did."

Frankie's call a little while ago was another source of unease. "Mom?" He stated, hesitantly.

"Hey, Son. What's up?"

"I, uh. I've been getting these calls, but whoever it is never says anything. They just hang up. I talked to Joel, and he's getting the same kinds of calls, and I was wondering if the same thing was happening to you."

"No, I don't recall getting any calls like that. Why?"

"Well, I, uh, we - me and Joel, were thinking that maybe it could be Mikey."

Her heart rate sped up and she thought she would have to pull over. It had been nearly a year and a half since Mikey had walked angrily away from her. "Oh God, Baby! Do you really think so?"

"Now, Mom don't go getting your hopes up. We just think it's weird that both of us are getting these calls all of a sudden from the same number. It could mean nothing, so don't read anything into it, okay. I just wanted to let you know."

Troubling thoughts rambled around in her head as she completed the drive home. When she drove into the garage, a long sigh of relief escaped her. Home. It was wonderful to see the door leading into the house open and Ron and Destiny running out to greet and hug her.

"I am tired, hungry and happy to see you guys," she said, in the midst of their hugs and kisses. "I feel like it's been days instead of hours since I last saw you. What did you get to eat?"

"I know you like the food from the restaurant in that strip mall down the street, so I got that, and I stopped at the pie shop and got a cheesecake."

"Oh, Baby, I love you, and I promise to cook your favorite meal soon. Not tomorrow though, because I have to work on some stuff with C.J."

Ron frowned. "I don't think I like being pushed to the back burner all the time," he grumbled. "We're going to have to talk, but come on, relax so we can eat."

Later, as they sat on the sofa cuddling, while Destiny ran around the room playing, she told him about the two disturbing conversations that had overshadowed the joy of her victory. "Christine's hateful words shocked me. I guess it was unrealistic to hope they had gotten past that. They actually wanted to take over Frank's estate right after he died, but my cousins jumped in and told them to back off. I don't know, it seems as though I'll never be rid of Frank."

"You are rid of him, Sweetheart. And you were his wife and rightfully, everything belongs to you. Don't let them send you on a guilt trip. I didn't know the guy – thank God – but I have a feeling if he were still alive they wouldn't be bugging him because he wouldn't hesitate to tell them where to go."

"You got that right. Frank hardly ever went around his family, and called them a bunch of lazy thugs."

"Well you should do the same thing, Babe." He hugged her close. "Isn't it about time to put that little girl to bed?"

"Yes, and this big girl, too," she said, with a huge yawn.

Nita heard a strange noise and raised her head slightly from Ron's shoulder to listen intently. Nothing. She snuggled closer to Ron and tried to get back to sleep. Then she heard footsteps creeping stealthily down the hallway toward their bedroom. "Ron!" She screamed. "Ron, wake up!" She yelled again, but he still didn't move. "God, help us," she prayed, as the bedroom door slowly opened. "Ron, you have to wake up! Someone's in the house!"

She tried to get out of bed to grab a lamp or something to protect them, but for some reason, she couldn't make her legs move fast enough. When she struggled to move her arms to shake Ron awake, they felt like heavy weights were attached to them. She screamed as the door opened further and the silhouette of a large man moved into the room. Her screams reverberated loudly in her head but didn't make it through her vocal cords with enough force for Ron to hear.

The man was standing over the bed now, looking down at her. Pure evil emanated from him and he let out a malevolent laugh as his hand closed around her throat.

"Nita," her name seemed to echo around the room, "Nita, you're going to die, and then I'm going to kill this family you went out and got," the menacing voice said.

She ceased struggling and froze in shock when the man's features and voice became recognizable. It was none other than Frank Stanhope – her dead husband.

"No! Please don't hurt my family," she tried to plead through her closed throat, "please don't hurt my family, Frank, please don't…"

"Nita! Nita, honey! Wake up!" a light came on in the room and Ron was shaking her. "It's just a dream, Babe, wakeup!"

She was finally able to open her eyes and look around frantically. The bedroom door was closed and the only other people in the room were Ron, and Destiny, who had been awakened and was standing in her bed across the room screaming. Her night gown was twisted around her and soaked with perspiration and Ron was leaning over her, concern written all over his face.

"It's okay, Honey. You're alright. You were just having a nightmare, okay?"

Nita burst into tears and grabbed him close. "Oh, God, Ron. Frank was here and he was going to kill us." She collapsed against him, shaking in fear.

"No, Sweetheart, look around. Nobody's here but us. It was just a bad dream."

Still shaking, Nita got up and eased into the bathroom and closed the door. She struggled to calm her nerves and shaking hands as she changed into a dry nightgown. She went back into the bedroom and drew on her robe, then crossed the room to the bedroom door, opened it cautiously, and eased into the hallway.

"Where are you going?" Ron asked, sleep still clouding his voice.

"I'm not going to get back to sleep, so I think I'll make a cup of tea, and talk to Lord awhile. Go on back to sleep, I'll be okay."

Still unnerved as she went into the kitchen, she kept looking over her shoulder. The dream had seemed so real. She made her tea and went into her office, grabbed her Bible and curled up on the loveseat. It had been a while since she'd had one of those dreams, and as she thought about it, she realized Christine's vile words must have given life to dormant fears. She'd thought they were buried deep enough to no longer torment her. Wrong.

CHAPTER THIRTY-TWO

Their lives continued like a roller-coaster, until things came to a head the following week when Ron came home with Destiny to find the house empty and Nita nowhere to be found. About ten minutes later, she came rushing in, apologizing for being late.

Ron said, "Babe, you need to slow down. I don't know where you are half the time – in town or out of town. And another thing, we have to chisel out some time to spend together. Why don't we plan on going somewhere in a couple of weeks?"

"Oh." Nita gave him an apologetic look. "I'm sorry, Honey, but I start a six week class next week. The best we'll be able to do is maybe a couple of nights somewhere."

"Class? Why are you starting a class now? You hardly have time for everything as it is. Couldn't you put it off until next semester when things have settled down a little?"

"I could, but that'll just put me that much more behind."

He blew out a frustrated breath. "What's the hurry? You've waited this long."

"That's why I'm not waiting any longer. And this particular class isn't offered every semester. Believe me, Honey, this six weeks will pass quickly, and then we can plan to go on a long trip somewhere."

Ron huffed in agitation. "By then, it'll be something else. I came home looking for my wife, a warm house and a good meal, and found nothing but a cold, dark house and no food. You fixed me more meals before we were married than I've had since then. I could tell you I was hungry and you'd have me something fixed by the time I got to your house. Now I live in the same house with you, and I'm lucky to even see you, not to mention get a good meal. I can almost count those on my fingers. That is not acceptable, Nita."

Nita was quiet for a moment, but he could tell she was getting upset. "You knew I was planning to take some courses. You said you were fine with it. So I know you're not trying to say you don't want me to do so at this point. I gave up my education for one man, and I will not, hear me, will not, give it up for another one." When he didn't answer immediately, she left him sitting there with his mouth open and went down the hallway and into her office.

Ron followed her into the office but didn't get a chance to say anything.

"Well, what else do you have to say?" Nita said in a hostile voice.

Ron was tempted to back slowly out of the room. The loving greeting his wife had given him a few minutes earlier when she walked through the door, had been replaced with someone he didn't want to deal with. Why had he even brought it up? Yes, he wanted her home more, instead of rushing around with all her projects. Yes, he was tired of coming home to an empty house. Maybe he was just thinking about his own needs, but it wasn't like she had to go to school, or to work either. And she did have a husband and a baby who needed her at home.

He tried to bring reason back into the conversation. "Wait a second, Babe. I just want to talk about this, that's all."

"You didn't start out wanting to talk. You started out saying you don't want me to take the class. That sounds like you've already decided what I should do. Uh, uh!"

"Okay, maybe I didn't approach it the right way," he said, "but you don't have to get so hostile about it. I do have a right to feel the way I do," Ron shot back.

"Yes, you do, and so do I. And I'm angry because you're trying to change things after the fact. Well, it's not going to happen, Ron. So why are you still in my office?"

"I'm still here because we need to talk about this rationally. You need to calm down."

"No, you need to understand that I'm not giving up my education for you like I did for Frank. We talked about this before…"

"Wait! Just hold up a minute," Ron interrupted. "We need to get something straight before you go any further. I am not Frank Stanhope. So don't compare me to him."

"Why? Because you realize you might have something in common?"

Ron held onto his temper with difficulty. "No, we don't, and that was uncalled for, Nita, and you know it. Yes, we did talk about this a little, but that was before you were my wife, and before I realized how much you were actually involved in."

"Okay, so now you know. So, what else do you have to say?"

Ron had a baffled look on his face. "I had no idea this was going to get so out of control this way," he said, shaking his head.

"No, you thought I was going to back down and say okay, I won't take any courses now. But that's not going to happen." She stepped around him and left the room.

Ron stood in the middle of the floor with a 'what the heck just happened' look on his face. He picked up a screaming Destiny and walked slowly into the kitchen.

Nita stormed through the bedroom and into the bathroom, slammed the door, and stood in the middle of the floor, taking deep breaths. She turned on the water to fill the jetted tub, stripped out of her clothes and stepped into the tub. She laid her head back against the headrest and closed her eyes. A few minutes later, her eyes popped open and she sat up in the tub as though something or someone had pushed her. "What's wrong with me, Lord? I know good and well that Ron is nothing like Frank." She let her mind visit just how that scene would have gone with Frank and knew she would still be on the floor unconscious, or worse.

"Ron is right. I have gone overboard with things. I should have told C.J. I couldn't go with her to look at that facility this evening. Instead, I put my family on the back burner and left the house without a second thought. And I should have talked it over with Ron before I enrolled in that class. I'm acting like a single woman instead of a married one. Help me fix this, Father."

Her eyes landed on the large framed poster hanging on the opposite wall. They had placed it there so they could sit in the tub together and review it. The poster listed the Pastor's Focus Twelve Plan, and now, some of them seemed to pop out: Feed each other - spirit, soul and body; Fix-it as you go - There'll be times when you'll get off-track. As soon as possible, pray, then do what is needed to get things right with each other; Fight through the storms together - trusting that God is with you, and will show you what is good and stable about your marriage; Forge ahead together - How can you reach the same destiny if you can't agree to walk the path together?

Nita felt tears slide down her face. "Father, I can't do this without you." She finished her bath, pulled on a comfortable lounging outfit and went in search of her husband. She found him in the kitchen, feeding Destiny. "I'm sorry, Sweetheart. If you don't want me to take the class, I won't," she said, quietly. "You're right, I have gotten out of balance."

He gave her a long look. "Where did the wicked witch go?"

She laughed. "God ran her behind out of here."

He chuckled. "Whew! Thank you, Lord. I was beginning to think me and Desi would have to leave." He fought with Destiny over the spoon, before he let her have it. She was at the stage where she wanted to feed herself. Then he said, "No, Babe, we'll work around it. But after this, no more classes or new projects for a while, okay?"

"You know what?" She walked over and rubbed her hand over his face. "I'm going to drop the class plans for now. You're not okay with it, and you're right, I have been running a hundred miles an hour lately, and neglecting you and Destiny."

He grabbed the spoon and bowl that Destiny was using to make a mess, and lifted her down from her highchair, then went back to Nita and hugged her. "I still think we need to get away from it all for a few days."

"Okay, Sweetheart." She hugged him again."

But it wasn't to be. As they were preparing for bed, Nita's cell phone rang. "Daddy, how are you? Is anything wrong?"

Ron stopped what he was doing and started listening to her end of the conversation. "What?" He whispered.

She held up her hand, telling him silently to wait. "When?" she asked, then listened a while. "Oh dear," she said, looking at Ron.

"What is it?" Ron asked again.

She covered the mouthpiece and whispered, "Aunt Muriel died today."

"Oh. That's too bad." Ron remembered what Jaci had told him about how badly that woman had treated Nita. He couldn't bring himself to feel any sorrow over her death.

"Daddy, will you let me know when the service will be? I'll see if I can come." She hung up and looked at Ron again. "Well, she wasn't my favorite aunt but I guess I should try to go. Daddy said the service probably won't be until next Friday or Saturday."

"I can't go. I have meetings on those days. Will you take Destiny with you?"

She shook her head. "I would really rather not, Sweetheart, since I don't know what all I'll have to deal with. See if your parents will help you with her for a couple of days."

"Alright. I'll call Mom in the morning. I sure wish I could go with you."

"Me too."

Nita left on Tuesday of the following week for her aunt's funeral. The service would be Friday morning, but her sister had called and asked that she come a couple of days early and help her with cleaning out her aunt's house and getting her papers in order.

"I'll leave immediately after the service is over on Friday," she promised Ron.

Ron had debated whether to tell Nita that Frieda had somehow wrangled her way onto the team for the new hotel project he was working on. He could have pulled some strings and had her removed, but it seemed like such a petty thing to do. And why rock the boat with Nita if he didn't have to? He would just have Frieda understand that he was a married man and not interested in her in any way.

He was about to learn the hard way that some women didn't care one iota about a man being married when he had something they wanted.

CHAPTER THIRTY-THREE

Frieda still burned with anger at the woman who was now Ron's wife, and had been watching for an opportunity to get revenge. The building contractor on one of Ron's projects pulled some strings and helped her get the job as interior designer. She was in the contractor's office when she overheard him on the phone joking with Ron about getting hooked into marriage. She listened closely, hoping to hear something that would help in her quest for revenge, and maybe, find out if all was lost where Ron was concerned.

She heard the contractor say, "So you're having to spend your first nights apart, huh? Yeah, that can be rough since you guys haven't been married that long. Some things you get used to very quickly, but that'll make Friday night that much better," he chuckled.

Jackpot! It sounded like Ron's wife was away and wouldn't be back until Friday. A plan started forming. She just needed to find a way to get into the newlyweds' house.

Ron woke up Friday morning with a sense of relief. *Nita would be home today, thank God,* he thought as he prepared for his meeting that morning, which was about an hour away in the next county,. He planned to leave early enough to stop and get some breakfast on the way. The telephone was an unwelcome interruption.

"Ron! This is Frieda. I really hate to bother you but I'm having car trouble. Do you think if I'm nice to your wife, I can catch a ride with you? My sister can drop me off at your house."

Ron had to hold back a groan. "Look, Frieda why don't you grab a cab? I'm sure you can get a ride back. I have to stop on the way and was just getting ready to leave."

"Please, Ron. It'll take a cab forever. My sister is already here and I can be there in ten minutes. I've already called at couple of other people and they've already left. Ron, you have to help a sister out."

He was in a difficult position. He could refuse and look like the biggest jerk in the world, or he could go ahead and give the woman a ride. Nita said she didn't want Frieda in the house. He would wait for her outside so technically he wouldn't be breaking his promise. He hurriedly loaded his truck, and went back to turn off lights and set the alarm. The doorbell rung. "I know that can't be Frieda. It hasn't been ten minutes," he grumbled.

But when he looked out the window, there she stood. He opened the door to tell her he was on the way out, but she was doing a little jig, as though ants were in her pants.

"Oh, Lord, Ron. I forgot to use the bathroom before I left home, and knowing how the traffic is, I know it's not wise to start a long drive in this condition. May I please use your bathroom? I promise I'll be nice to your wife."

Now what? He asked himself. But how could he refuse? "Okay, there's one right around the corner there. He didn't have a good feeling about letting her in, but hopefully, Nita would never have to know about it. Frieda took longer than he anticipated and he was getting ready to go look for her when she finally appeared.

"Sorry," she said, hurrying back to the door. "I just couldn't resist looking around a little. I could have done wonders with this place."

"Well, we like what we have, so I suppose that just wasn't in the plan. Let's go." He failed to see the smug look on Frieda's face, or the pleased gleam in her eyes. He was too busy trying to get her out of the house.

He talked to Nita right after his meeting and discovered she hadn't even left Riverwood yet. That left him disgruntled. He had been hoping she would be on the road. "Well be sure to call me when you get on the highway. The gang is getting together for a fish fry tonight. If you leave soon you can make it in time to eat."

Later that evening, Ron was at Jason and Jaci's house with their usual crowd, eating fish and playing cards. The last time he'd talked to Nita, she'd said, "Let me call you back," in a hurried tone. She hadn't called back. He couldn't help looking at his watch and checking his phone for messages every few minutes. When he tried to call her, he didn't get an answer. He knew there were dead zones along the road that made it impossible for her to use her cell, but he was getting worried.

He was relieved when his phone buzzed to indicate a call and he saw it was her. "Hey, Babe! Where the heck are you? I was hoping you'd be here by now." He was quiet a few minutes, then yelled, "What! Aw, Honey, how did you let yourself get roped into that?"

The people in the room started chuckling. He threw his cards down – his game was off anyway. "So when are you coming home? Next week!" He rubbed his hand over his head in frustration. "I wish you had called me before you made that decision." He was angry. "Look, I gotta go." He slammed the phone down and looked around, daring anyone to say a word.

His back was to the entrance into the room so he couldn't see who was behind him. Hands went over his eyes and a voice whispered in his ear, "So where do you have to go?"

A smile whipped across his face and he grabbed her and pulled her into his lap. "Woman, you are too wrong. You almost had me cussing." He hugged and kissed her, then pushed her up from his lap, grabbed her hand and led her into another room so he could kiss her the way he wanted to. "I'm so glad you're here, Babe. I missed you so much."

"I missed you too. Forgive me for doing that, but I wanted to surprise you."

Ron hugged her close again. "Well, you did that."

"I'm hungry. I'm going to get something to eat and then we can pick Desi up."

"Uh, uh. I've already told my parents she's spending the night. So hurry up, I'm ready to leave."

A little while later, he followed her home and into the house. She headed straight for the bedroom, then the bathroom. "I'm going to take a hot shower," she said over her shoulder, disrobing as she walked.

"Okay, Babe. Don't take too long."

Those were the last words they would exchange for days that were not uttered in anger.

CHAPTER THIRTY-FOUR

When Nita came out of the bathroom and turned back the bedding on her side of the bed, she found lacy black underwear between the sheets. She gasped, and tears filled her eyes. "Those are not mine, Ron. I can't believe you brought another woman into our house, and into our bed."

Ron jumped up from where he had been sitting on the side of the bed, a baffled look on his face. "Honey, you know I wouldn't do that." I don't know how those got . . ." The answer popped into his head. *Frieda!* But how could he tell Nita? "Oh God, help me," he mumbled.

He ran around the bed to where she stood with tears streaming down her face. "Honey, I know this looks bad, but I can explain. It won't be good, but it's the truth." He fumbled for words to tell her about Frieda's request for a ride, and how he'd been fool enough to believe her.

All Nita needed to hear was that he had let Frieda into the house. She turned and ran into her closet and threw on some clothes, then grabbed the suitcase she had just brought in and opened it. She went to her dresser and dumped more clothes into the bag, and snatched more clothes off hangers. "Yes, it does look bad, Ron. And one of the things I've promised myself since Frank died was that I'd never be a victim again. I begged you not to let that woman into this house. I told you she had evil intentions. Now whether you had her in our bed or not, she shouldn't have even been in this house. You broke your promise."

"Babe, you have to listen to me." His hands were stretched toward her beseechingly. "That woman tricked me. I don't know how she knew you weren't here, but somehow she did. Okay, I shouldn't have let her in, I concede to that, but that's all I'm guilty of."

"How very admirable of you," Nita said, sarcastically, as she continued packing. She picked up the bag and an armful of clothes and started toward the door to the garage.

Ron ran behind her. "Nita, you can't just walk out without giving us a chance to talk."

She turned to him with rivers of tears streaming down her face. "Watch me."

Nita could hardly see where she was going because her eyes, already tired from the long drive, were filled with tears. She had no idea where she would go. She needed to think, to pray, to rest. After three days of hard work, and hard to understand confessions of jealousy from the sister she hardly knew, she had looked forward to getting back to Ron, Destiny and her home.

Now, she felt like a ship floundering on stormy sea waters. She couldn't face anyone tonight, so the obvious places were out. Her only other option was a hotel room. She forced her mind to function enough to find a decent hotel. By the time she arrived and checked in, her phone had started ringing. Ignoring it, she undressed, and sent a text message to C.J. that merely said, "I'm okay, will be in touch later". She turned the phone off, and put it on charge, then slid to her knees beside the bed to pray.

Her phone's mailbox was full the next morning, mostly calls from Ron. There were also several from C.J. and Jaci, begging her to call them. Some were hilarious as her cousins described how they had put a contract out on Ron, after he told Jason what had happened.

After she got dressed, she called C.J. and asked if she could stay with her until she sorted out what she would do.

"Nita! Girl, we have been so worried about you." C.J. stated, when Nita made it to her house. "And Ron is running for his life. Come on in. We won't even talk about him right now. Tell me about the funeral. That old hag finally bit the dust, huh? I wonder if she took all that hate and meanness with her to the grave?"

"No, she didn't. She actually asked for forgiveness when I went to see her a while ago."

C.J.'s mouth fell open. "Uh, uh, uh. I guess that means I have to forgive her. I've been hating that old woman for years. So were the services nice?"

"As nice as could be expected. It was poorly attended because Aunt Muriel wasn't well liked. Some were there out of respect, and some came just to see who else would be there. Sad."

"And how's Uncle James, and the rest of the family?"

"Pretty good. His other sisters just moved back to Riverwood since their husbands are gone. They're both living in nice manufactured homes. I visited with your parents a little too.

"I guess the biggest shock came from my sister," Nita continued. "I spent years wondering why my own sister disliked me so much. Well, I finally found out. She was jealous of me. She's had a hard life, and believed I had it easy because Grammy and Gramps took care of me, and

I also had you guys. She married a sorry man who wouldn't work, and who took the money she made. Even when she found out Frank was abusing me, she had no sympathy because her feeling was that at least I was married to a doctor, lived in a big house and had plenty of money. You never know what's going on in a person's mind."

"Lord, have mercy, Nita. She was years older than you. You would think she would've had more understanding than that for you."

"Ten years older. I was only ten when our mother died. She was twenty, and already married. But her life was such a mess that she couldn't have done anything for me, even if she'd wanted to. Anyway, her husband finally got himself together and is working steady. So she's finally feeling guilty about the way she treated me."

"Whew! You came back with all that on your mind, and ran into an even bigger mess. Well, don't worry, you can stay here as long as you need to. Go on up to the guest room and get comfortable. I'll fix us something to eat, and we'll talk about the Riverwood folks some more."

Nita hesitated, then said, "C.J., you know Destiny will be here with me. Is that okay?"

"Girl, Destiny is your child, so you know that's okay. But who knows, maybe you and Ron will work things out before that even becomes an issue."

Ron was deep in misery and self recrimination. He played over and over in his mind, all the would've, should've, could've, scenarios. He should've told Nita about Frieda working on one of his projects. He could've had her thrown off the project. Still, none of this would've happened if he had given her a firm 'no' when she asked for a ride with him.

But the important thing now was how to get his wife back. He was curious about how Frieda knew his wife wouldn't be home. The only person he could think of who could have told her was the construction contractor. First thing Monday morning, he called him and asked if he'd told Frieda any of the conversation they'd had about his wife being out of town.

"No, but she was here looking at the plans when I was talking to you. She could have easily overheard and put two and two together. Why?"

Ron explained what Frieda had done, and the man cursed. "I'm sorry, Ron. I twisted arms and called in favors to get her the job, and now I'm going to do the same thing to get rid of her."

"I hope you'll do that, otherwise, I'll have to withdraw, and that would cause problems for everyone on the project. But I have to do everything I can to get my family back together."

Ron's next stop was Frieda.

When she opened her door and saw Ron, Frieda smiled victoriously and invited him in. "Would you like something to drink?" She asked sweetly.

"No, I won't be here that long," Ron answered.

"Oh come on, you just got here and you're not going to stay long?" She moved closer to him. "Come on, why don't we get more comfortable?"

Ron looked at her like she had lost her mind. "My wife left me because of that little stunt you pulled, Frieda. Why would you do that?

Have I ever indicated to you that I wanted anything more than a professional relationship with you?"

"Oh come on, Ron, you're not fooling me. You just married that woman because of that little bad tail girl. We could be good together."

Ron moved away, trying to put some distance between them. "That was a despicable thing to do. All I was trying to do was show you kindness. I love my wife, and I should knock you from here to the other end of town for hurting her like that."

Frieda looked at him smugly. "Well, I told you that you would regret how you treated me. I think I've gotten my revenge and showed you what I think of your little family."

Ron's fist went into a ball. Never had he wanted to hit a woman before, but he already had enough trouble because of this woman. "Fine. I hope you enjoy your revenge, because there is also this thing called consequences. You won't have to worry about transportation to meetings on any of my projects again, because you are banned from working on them. I'll also see to it that others in the industry know what you did, so basically, you'll be black balled. No one wants to work with someone capable of doing what you did. Now, ask yourself if it was worth it." He turned and walked out the door.

When he got to his car he removed the small voice activated tape recorder from his pocket and rewound it to make sure it had done its job. He believed it was against the law to record anyone without their knowledge, but radical actions called for extreme responses. His reputation was working against him, and almost everyone he knew wanted a piece of him. He had to have proof of his innocence and he hadn't been able to think of any other way to get it. Frieda wasn't about to voluntarily admit what she had done.

Nita was at C.J.'s house, and was still refusing to talk to him. However, his mother told him she had agreed to attend his dad's birthday celebration the next weekend. He arranged for Destiny to stay with his parents after the party, because whether she went kicking or screaming, his wife was going home with him, and she was going to listen to that recording.

Nita didn't attend church on Sunday because didn't want to run into Ron. She went to his parents house early Sunday morning and picked up Destiny, then went back to C.J.'s house. She decided to drive up to Prairie View to see Joel, and get a hotel room near there for a few days. That way, she and Destiny wouldn't be underfoot at C.J.'s house. There was a large outlet mall near the university and she needed to go shopping for birthday gifts for Ron's dad and his twin brother, even though she dreaded going to that party down to her very core.

Nita and Destiny spent the next few days shopping, exploring the small towns near Prairie View, and visiting with Joel whenever he was available. By Thursday, she was tired of that and missing her husband. She fought off the urge to go home and headed back to C.J.'s house. She knew Ron was missing Destiny, so she dropped her off with Cecelia so Ron could pick her up. Again, Cecelia made her promise she would be at the party.

Saturday afternoon, she begged C.J. to go with her, but she begged off, claiming she already had other plans. She would have backed out, but Cecelia had called her everyday to make sure she was coming. "You're still a member of this family," Cecelia told her.

Nita arrived praying for strength. Before she could get around to the back yard where everyone was, she heard Destiny screaming. "Oh Lord." She went to Cecelia to hug her and give her the gifts, then crossed the yard to where Ron stood, holding Destiny. "What is all that noise about, Baby Girl?" She took the baby, and reached for some napkins to clean her face up.

Destiny laid her head on Nita's shoulder, and the screams finally quieted.

Ron hugged Nita and whispered, "I love you, and we have to talk."

Nita didn't respond. She noticed Destiny's clothes had stains from several food groups, and she was probably in need of a new diaper. "Where's her bag? I need to change her."

"Come on, it's in the house."

He led the way up the stairs to the bedroom where Destiny's things were. She found a clean outfit to put on her, then went about stripping the soiled clothes and diaper off of her. Ron watched her, then said, quietly, "Babe, we have to talk."

Nita shook her head. "No, not here, not now." She pulled moistened baby wipes from the bag and wiped the baby all over before re-dressing her.

Ron frowned. "Then when and where? You left our home, and you won't answer my calls." His frustration came through in his voice. "You can't shut me out like this, Nita. You said yourself that Frieda is evil. At least give me a chance to explain what happened. I know I was wrong to let her in the house, but you owe that much to our marriage."

Nita closed her eyes. All the praying she'd done over the last week had brought her to the same conclusion – she did owe it to her marriage to hear him out. She knew he hadn't set out to do anything wrong, or to hurt her, but her wounded heart argued that he'd still done it. "Ron, you hurt me and damaged my trust in you when you let that woman come into our home to disrespect it and our marriage bed. Give me some time to get past that."

"Babe, I miss you and I just need you to come home and listen. I've already dealt with Frieda about what she did. Trust me, she'll be regretting it for a very long time. I know she hurt you, and I let her do it. I used poor judgment, but I did not break our marriage vows."

Nita went back to dressing Destiny. "Give me some time. Now just leave me alone."

He hesitated, then turned and walked slowly out the door, as though uncertain if he should leave. "I'll be downstairs," he stated before closing the door.

She finished making Destiny presentable then went back to the party. She found Jaci and Jason sitting at a table with the twins and made her way over to them. She put Destiny down to hug and kiss the babies and sat down at the table. "What?" She asked, when she noticed Jaci looking at her and smiling.

"Did Ron tell you how close he came to getting his behind whipped? He's on everybody's hit list. But after I heard how things happened, I felt sorry for him. The guy's just too nice for his own good. I can't tell you what to do, Nita, but I will ask you to at least hear him out. That dude truly loves you. And here he comes with a plate full of food for you."

Nita looked up and indeed, Ron was on the way with plates piled high with food. In spite of her hurt, she acknowledged that he was always looking out for her. And her growling stomach was letting her know it had been a while since she'd eaten a good meal.

"Here you go, Sweetheart," Ron said, placing a plate on the table in front of her. "I think I put everything you like on there. Want something to drink?"

"Thanks. And yes, I'd like some iced tea." Destiny was already trying to crawl into her lap to share the food, even though Nita knew she probably wasn't hungry.

Ron came back with glasses of tea and pulled a chair over to the table to sit close to her. "Feed her at your own risk. She's been eating all day," he told Nita, as he dug into his own food.

She put a spoon filled with mashed up beans and a little potato salad into Destiny's mouth, and gave her a piece of bread before she started eating herself. "Hmmm, this is good." She remembered – too late – that she'd only planned to show her face, get Destiny, and leave.

Big Pat made his way over to them and hugged her. "Thanks for the gift. And would you please cut this son of mine some slack? He's not guilty of anything but poor choices. If I thought he was, I'd be the first in line to beat him down, and there's a lot of people in that line." He kissed her cheek and walked to the next table.

Ron's pleading, along with his family's, convinced Nita to go home and hear what Ron had to say in his defense. She wanted to take

Destiny, who was already asleep, but Ron insisted they leave her there. They got home in time to catch C.J. and a couple of Ron's friends leaving the house. Nita frowned. "What in the world were they doing here?" She asked, after she followed him into the garage and got out of her truck.

Her mouth fell in amazement when she entered the house. There were candles and flowers everywhere. An ice bucket with a bottle of sparkling grape cocktail, and two of her gold rim wine glasses sat on a table in front of the sofa, and soft, romantic music came from the speakers around the room.

Ron took her by the hand and led her down the hallway to their bedroom. "I need to show you something." He pushed the door open to reveal a room full of new furniture. "I didn't want any reminders of the old bed."

It was similar in design to the other one, and had been made with all new bedding. "You didn't have to do this, Ron."

"I know I didn't have to do it, but I wanted to. The other stuff seemed to be tainted somehow by Frieda's touch. Do you like it?"

"Yes, I like it." She wiped at the tears running down her face.

Ron led her back into the family room, where he turned the music down and filled their glasses. "Babe, I want you to listen to something. Just listen, okay?" He produced a small recorder and pushed the play button.

Nita listened to the conversation between Ron and Frieda, and felt revulsion for the woman. She grabbed his hand when she heard him telling the other woman he loved his wife, and tears slid down her face.

When the recording ended, she turned and hugged him. "I'm sorry. I should have let you explain but I was so hurt that I simply reacted."

"I can't blame you for that, but maybe, hopefully, this will teach both of us something. I learned that if I want to keep my wife, I'd better listen to her, and I'm praying you learned to trust me a little more."

"I'm trying to get there. I think we should make an appointment with the Pastors for a marriage tune up. We haven't even made three months and just in the last couple of weeks we've had two major disagreements. And we definitely need to review the Focus-Twelve plan."

"Okay." Ron stated, looking at her with a big grin. "But are we good now?"

"Yeah, Honey, we're good," she said, with a smile.

CHAPTER THIRTY-FIVE

Ron scheduled an emergency meeting with Pastor Robinson. He was a little embarrassed that they had to go back so soon, but Nita said they needed it, and what Nita wanted, Nita got.

As they described the two recent disagreements, Ron hung his head and said, "I know it's crazy that I fell for Frieda's trick. Why would she need to use the bathroom so soon after leaving her own house? And why couldn't she wait until we got where we were going? It's not like she's a child with no control. I'm just disgusted with myself for letting her play me like that."

Nita said, "I'm disgusted that I let my past rear it's ugly head and cause me first to get so out of balance with everything, and then to jump to conclusions about the Frieda situation without giving him a chance to explain."

Pastor Robinson listened, then said, "It's all for good if you gained some wisdom and spiritual insight from it. Remember that what God has joined together, no power in earth or hell should be able to tear apart. I believe you are together by divine destiny, and the devil knows it too. That's why he's hit you so hard this soon in your marriage. He wants to tear you apart.

"It's normal to go through a period of adjustment. You're still learning how to live together. But in this other situation, this woman was just the devil's instrument, being used to carry out his evil purposes. I know – it's hard to separate the person from the deed, but Satan loves to throw a rock and hide his hand behind the person he's using. So, don't be ignorant of his tricks. He'll use anything or anyone to steal, kill or destroy. He hates God, His children and marriage, which is why he works so hard to destroy marriages and families. My advice is to do exactly what you're doing – stay close to God, each other, and those who will pray you through. If you do, you'll be okay. But I can't stress enough – be wise, be vigilant and prayerful. You've already found out your marriage is on Satan's hit list. Consider yourself in a battle. But remember it's God's battle, trust Him to fight it. Now let's pray."

Ron and Nita left with a greater understanding of Satan's strategies.

"Did you know all that?" Ron asked Nita.

She nodded. "Some of it. I saw Satan work in my marriage to Frank in so many ways. Crazy things that shouldn't have happened, did, and since Frank didn't even acknowledge God most of the time, it was easy for him to get in. I never stopped praying, but I admit, I let him win much too often. I'm not doing that again."

"And I'm not doing it this time," Ron declared. "But I'm going to need your help."

"No, Honey, we're going to need each other," Nita replied, solemnly.

A month later, Nita was standing in the church foyer talking to some people while she waited for Ron. She shifted Destiny from one arm to the other when her arm grew numb from the baby's heavy weight. She could have kicked herself for not driving her own truck. Now she was forced to wait for Ron to finish his duties in the media room.

She finally gave in and put the wriggling toddler down to explore, then had to chase after her to keep her from getting too far from her. She noticed a woman watching from across the room and tried to convince herself that it wasn't her and Destiny the woman was so intently studying.

Ron finally came rushing up to them. "Ready?" He asked as he picked Destiny up.

Nita turned to bid her friends a blessed week and when she turned back, the woman who had been watching them had made her way across the foyer.

"What a gorgeous little girl!" The woman gushed. "She is absolutely beautiful, like a little doll." She gently pinched one of Destiny's plumb cheeks. Destiny shrunk away.

The woman turned to Ron. "Aren't you Ronald Gilmore, the architect?"

"Yes," Ron answered, cautiously.

"What is your little girl's name, Mr. Gilmore."

"Destiny," Ron said, "and this is my wife, Anita," he added.

"Uh, huh." Her eyes returned to Destiny. "Well I want to take this little sweetheart home with me," she said in her gushing voice.

"Excuse us, but we have to go," Ron told the woman, and with a hand on her back, guided Nita to the door. "I don't know who that lady is but she reminds me of someone, and she gives me the creeps for some reason."

They didn't notice the cell phone in the woman's hand, or the sly speculation in her eyes as she punched in a number. "Chantal," she said, excitedly. "Guess what? I just saw that Gilmore guy and his wife with your baby, and the baby is calling her 'Mama'. Ummm - hmmm, now how did you let that happen? Anyway, I took some pictures."

CHAPTER THIRTY-SIX

The week of Thanksgiving Nita was busy getting her house ready, and coordinating the menu with everyone. T.C. was preparing all the meats, and Nita was responsible for only a few side dishes, although she decided to make a couple of deserts. Her sons were out of school the entire week, and arrived the Friday before the week of Thanksgiving. They tagged along with Ron on some of his jobs, and hung out with Patrick. The rest of their time was spent eating Nita out of house and home. It brought back memories of when they were growing up, and along with those memories, came worry over Mikey.

Her family from Arkansas arrived Wednesday afternoon. She fixed dinner and after eating, they were anxious to relax and tell her about everything happening in Riverwood.

The Gilmores started arriving early Thursday, loaded down with every imaginable side dish and dessert. Jaci had warned Nita that relatives and friends of the Gilmores would be dropping in throughout the day to eat and visit, so they had set up tables and chairs in every available space.

While the women scurried around getting the food ready, and the men watched television, she noticed her sons were missing. When she got close to Ron she asked, "Where are Joel and Frankie?"

"Oh, they said something about running an errand. I think they may be a little overwhelmed with all these people here."

"Well I hope they get back soon. We'll be ready to eat in a little while."

Her sons were still not back when the food was ready. Everyone eagerly dug in, piling plates high. Nita was busy putting another pan of rolls into the oven when she caught a glimpse of them coming in the side door. She gave them a reprimanding look. "I thought I was going to have to come looking for you guys. Where have y'all been?"

Joel said, "Uh, Mom, can you come into the foyer for a minute?"

"Come into the foyer? For wh . . .?"

The doorbell pealed, interrupting her. "Oh well, let me see who this is," she said, rushing to the front door, with them following her.

She opened the door, and stood there a minute, starring at the scraggly looking, extremely skinny young man who stood there smiling down at her.

"Hi, Mom."

Nita screamed. "Mikey? Oh, God, Mikey! My baby!" Then she grabbed him in a tight hug. "My baby! I can't believe it, my baby is home. Thank You, Lord! Thank You!" Joel joined the hug, but Frankie stood back with a frown and said, "Ima still kick your behind, Squeak."

Everyone crowded around to hug and welcome Mikey home before returning to their food. She found out later that Mikey had finally made contact with his brothers and they had decided to surprise her and had disappeared to go pick him up at the bus station.

Surprise? She'd almost had a heart attack, but what a joy to have her baby home, no matter now pitiful he looked.

Nita kept hugging Mikey, feeding him and then repeating the actions. After most of the company left, and the others took naps, she and Ron took him into her office to talk.

Mikey hung his head as he spoke. "Mom, you were right. Those dudes in the band just wanted me to finance the tour and when I couldn't they didn't have much use for me. I hung around with them until one of my buddies overdosed and died. I had started messing around with the stuff too. I . . . I just did it because everybody around me was doing it. But when that happened, it scared me so bad I knew I had to let it go."

"But son, why didn't you call me, or just come home?" Nita asked, with tears in her eyes.

"I was ashamed, Mom. Seem like the worse my life got, the more ashamed I was. I just knew I had to get myself together before I could face you."

"So how have you been getting along? What about the drugs?"

"I sold all my stuff, including most of my clothes and my computer, just to eat and get a room. Then when that was gone, I started going to a shelter where I could stay and get some food. One of the dudes who run it kind of took an interest in me, and he helped me get clean, let me work for food and a bed, and later on, he got me a job. Every once in a while, I get to play at this church I've been going to, and they pay me a little."

Nita was crying hard again. "Oh God, I hate to hear about you going through that by yourself, Son. It was all so unnecessary."

"I got into a fight and the dude grabbed my phone and threw it in the lake, so I don't have a phone. I go to the library and check my e-mail, and Mom, every time I read your reminders about remembering who I am and whose I am, I'm more determined to make it. You don't know how much it means to know that you love me, pray for me, and that God loves me.

"Then, people started telling me some guy was asking around about me. I saw a flyer with my picture on it, asking for information, and I was getting more e-mails from you, begging me to contact you. I knew then that I had to let you know I was okay. But I was so ashamed for getting myself into all that mess that I . . . it was hard."

"Well, you're home now, and all of that is behind you," Nita said.

"But I have to prove that I can make it. I don't want to touch anymore of Dad's money until I can get back to the place I was before I messed up."

"We can help get you back in school and back on the path you're supposed to be on."

"I am in school, Mom. I'm just taking a course a semester, which is all I can afford, but I plan to continue until I can get back to where I should be. Then, I'll use the money in my fund."

"But Son, you don't have to do that! Let us help you. You can go to Prairie View with Joel, or even to Morehouse with Frankie."

He shook his head. "I just have to do it this way, Mom."

Nita shook her head. "We'll talk about it."

"Mike, your mother has worried herself sick over you, and I don't particularly like the way you've gone about it, but I have to commend you for wanting to get yourself back on the right road," Ron, who had been quietly listening, said. "How did you get here from D.C.?"

"I managed to work some extra hours and save enough for a bus ticket. I had a little extra for food, but not much, and I was afraid to sleep because I didn't want to get robbed. That's why I was so hungry and tired when I got here. One of my buddies let me use his phone to call my brothers, but it took a while for me to get up enough courage to talk to them. But when I knew I was coming, I finally let them know it was me. I'm glad I did too, because I wouldn't have known where to go."

Nita wiped at the tears that continued streaming down her face. "I've been in D.C. looking for you several times. I would look into the face of every young man I saw, hoping it would be you."

"I'm sorry, Mom. I know I hurt you, and I'm so ashamed of myself. And my brothers already told me I've got a butt kicking coming. Now, I just want to show you that you raised me right, and that all that hell you went through with Dad to make me who I am wasn't for nothing. I'm not going to let you down again, Mom."

Nita boo-hooed again. "You've already made me happy just by coming home to me. You don't have to do anything else."

"Yeah, I do," he sighed. "Hey, I'm hungry again, and I really need to crash."

"Okay, Baby. Come on, I'll fix you a plate and then find somewhere for you to sleep." She got up to leave and heard Destiny crying over the baby monitor. The baby had gone down for a nap a while ago. Ron went to get her and when he walked back into the room with her, Destiny reached for Mikey and said, "JoJo!" Then realized it wasn't Joel and shrunk back.

"Who is that?" Mikey asked.

"This is Destiny, your little sister," Nita told him.

"Wow, Mom. You've got a whole new family, huh?"

"No, Son, I have an expanded family – all the more to love."

Frankie and Joel took charge of Mikey after he finished eating. They went upstairs to the media room and Nita could only imagine what was going on. She entertained her family for a while, then excused herself and went into her bedroom. She dropped to her knees, grabbed a pillow to cover her mouth, and let out a wail of praise and thanksgiving to the Lord. An hour later, she was still on her knees, worshiping and praising God for bringing Mikey home, as well as all the other good things He had done. That's where Ron found her and he too, dropped to his knees beside her and wrapped an arm around her.

CHAPTER THIRTY-SEVEN

Saturday morning, Nita's dad rushed his two sisters, and Nita's sister and her husband through breakfast. "I'm ready to get home. We had a great time, but it's time to get back to Riverwood."

When they pulled away an hour later, Nita collapsed on the sofa. Admittedly, it had been the best holiday she had ever had. Having her husband, all her children, family and extended family and friends in her home had been a wonderful experience. Two years ago, with Frank still alive, she wouldn't have been able to even dream it could happen, and she could be this happy.

"I can't wait to get to church with my family tomorrow to worship and praise God," she told Ron. Then a thought hit. "I just realized something. I don't think Mikey has any decent clothes. In fact, he probably needs a whole wardrobe. I have to take him shopping."

Ron nodded. "And he needs a better coat if the one he's wearing is the only one he has. Do you want me to go with you?"

"No, Frankie and Joel will probably tag along, so that means you and Destiny will be hanging out together."

"Oh, no, that means she's going to Granny's house. I think I'll go hang out with Jason and the fellas awhile. You need any money?"

"No, Honey, I got this, but thanks for asking," she said hugging him.

CHAPTER THIRTY-EIGHT

A week later, the house was back to normal. Mikey was back in D.C. – traveling by air at Nita's insistence. He had a place to live, thanks to her brother's help in securing an apartment for him. Nita pre-paid the rent and utilities and bought him another phone. He would complete the semester, then transfer to Prairie View University. Frankie tried to talk him into coming to Morehouse, but Mikey shook his head. "Naw, I need to be close to Mom and home."

They were hoping for a period of calm, but that was not to be. Ron had two disturbing e-mails when he returned to work. One was from Samuel Morris, who had stayed in touch with him after Chantal went to jail. Sam had a contact in the prison system who kept tabs on Chantal for him. His e-mail said she had been paroled and was back in Houston. A few e-mails later, there was an e-mail from Chantal, and attached to it was a picture of Destiny.

"This is my baby and I want her! My aunt took pictures of her and told me she was running around calling another woman, 'Mama'. You and that woman can get ready to give her up, along with lots of money. I have filed petitions for back child support and to regain my parental right. So get ready to pay me some big bucks! My attorney will be in touch."

Ron's heart plummeted, as flashbacks of Destiny's condition the first time he saw her in that home for neglected children jumped to the forefront of his mind. He made two quick calls – one to Samuel, letting him know Chantal was up to her old tricks, and one to his own attorney. Then he rushed home to tell Nita what was going on. But when he ran into the house, the same look of panic he felt, was reflected on his wife's face, and a letter from an attorney lay on the floor where she had dropped it.

Tears streamed down Nita's face, as she ran to him. "How can she do this?" She cried.

"I don't think she can, Babe. The law is on our side, and her criminal record stands against her. God gave Destiny to us through His mercy, wisdom and power. Surely, He didn't do that just to leave us open to this evil woman's desires." They started praying.

"Father God, we trust You. We trust Your love, Your grace and mercy, Your faithfulness and Your delivering power. We commit our way to You, and trust that You are guiding us along the path and the destiny You would have us walk together. And Lord, we thank You for protecting us from the evil strategies of Satan. Thank You that Your plans for this family are for good and not evil. Thank you for hope and a future together as a family."

They, and many others, continued to pray over the next several weeks, as more harassing e-mails and letters arrived from Chantal and her attorney

CHAPTER THIRTY-NINE

E-mails, text messages and phone calls started hitting one after the other – Ron's attorney, then Samuel Morris, Walt – his Criminal

Judge friend, C.J., Jason, and others – all informing them of a breaking news story . . .

"An ATF Officer has been shot and killed during a raid on a black-market drug ring responsible for bilking the Medicaid system of millions of dollars. At least ten members of the ring were involved in the shot-out with officers. In addition to the Officer who was killed, two members of the ring were also killed in the raid. Others were critically wounded and taken to area hospitals. Among those wounded, was recently paroled, Chantal Smith, (picture flashing) who, according to hospital personnel, is not expected to survive. Other wounded members of the ring include . . . "

"You shall not need to fight in this battle: set yourselves, stand ye still, and see the salvation of the Lord with you." 2 Chronicles 20:17

17594041R00186

Made in the USA
Charleston, SC
18 February 2013